NGLND XPX

Ian Hutson

ISBN: 1493532871
ISBN-13: 978 - 1493532872

ADVISORY

The plots herein are simple, the characterisations are nice and thin.
This is an undemanding book. The science of the fi is risible.
The idea is simply that the homunculus in your head sees some groovy visuals and that you get a chuckle or two.

This book should be read with tongue firmly in cheek
(preferably your own tongue).

Any resemblance to persons living or dead is purely coincidental.
Delicious, but coincidental.

CONTENTS

ACKNOWLEDGMENTS

The author gratefully acknowledges the contribution made to this book
by The Wombles and The Clangers.

You changed my psyche.

1 THE MODEL-T VIRGIN

Once upon a time (I've always wanted to open a story with that phrase) a frail old white-haired multi-millionaire asserted during a very lively dinner conversation at his London club that whenever Man has packed up and moved, be it from the Rift Valley to the Rhine Valley, from Ethiopia to Australia, or more recently from Rotherhithe to Cape Cod, he has only ever carried his own luggage.

Sadly, there was no-one present to hear his pithy assertion because no-one at all liked him and thus he always dined alone, and with very poor service from the waiters who were uncomfortable serving club members who talked to themselves.

Still, the conversation resonated with the old man and, in time, he sat down to work out a proof at the various draughtsman's drawing boards in the various studies of his unpretentious little multi-acre homes in London, New York, on the shores of Lake Como, in Paris, in Hong Kong and on sundry unspecified private islands. He sat down at them individually you understand, and at separate times – the "multi" refers to his finances, not to instances of the man himself. Nor did he just sort of flicker in and out of existence at the various desks in his various studies; he travelled by dint of his fossil-fuel burning private jets, so there was quite a delay between his appearances.

Frankly, he'd finished for once and for all with the hub and bub of corporate commercial life and with industry for money's sake, and what he wanted to do most, he told himself (in an unassuming note scribbled in the margin and signed in ink, dated for posterity and witnessed by his in-house legal team and a personal photographer stroke biographer), was to test his assertion.

He would do this by giving the peoples of the Earth a kick up the arse, a fundamental kick into the next stage of human social development, whatever that may be.

Once again it would be travel, cheap, easy access to fast and reliable travel that would be the key, he mused, musing in the form of a pseudo-mathematical formula with some home-spun symbols. Some form of travel that, unlike the modern motor car, moved faster than the heavily taxed and regulated walking pace of a tired horse. Supply just that device, he reckoned, and one of two things would then inevitably happen.

The human population of the planet might prove beyond doubt that they all really love each other, and his design would be used initially to facilitate one great big global hug throughout the species. In this scenario everyone would skip around the world to kiss their enemies and to deliver gifts of rose cuttings for the garden. Then, once these fully-inclusive non discriminatory hugs and smoochies were over everyone would move out to populate the galaxy hand in hand in hand in hand, singing hippie love songs and wearing some flowers in their hair. Sitar music would fill the aether of the celestial spheres and all would be groovy. The reach of Humanity would expand in a happy tide of well-mixed sexual and socio-economic variety and a carnival of riotous political and skin colour.

Or, just maybe, the human population of the entire planet would scatter as widely as it could and as fast as it possibly could without so much as a single backward glance to check that any of the other lifeboats had launched successfully.

Was, perhaps, the whole planet harbouring dreams of never again worrying about rubbing cheek and jowl with the wrong sort, and of never again having to accommodate and pussy-foot around those whom they actually hated and always would hate and distrust on some fundamental level?

Possibly, instead of embracing the political correctness of the aim of an all-inclusive society, everyone would just hoof off into the sunset to a frontier future in the same process that had originally created the (only recently, and now again not quite so) united state of America, where the only agreement seemed to be not on any peaceful mixing or purposeful compromise, but simply that every minority and majority group should instead be heard to complain at the same volume level, and to stick a feather in it and call it progress.

They might all just bugger off and live somewhere new and start the process all over again, with hippies huddled to the west,

Baptists to the east, Catholics and Mormons filling in the gaps and the evangelicals chasing down the atheists everywhere in-between. Would the human race look for space so that, for a while at least until the populations grew again to bursting, the acolytes of the various religions would never have to see one another, the ginger ninjas could avoid mixing with the clinically blonde and everyone could stop pretending that they didn't pass both wind and judgement whenever two Kinsey Sixes kissed devant les personnel domestique? Sitar music would only be available in the segregated groovy sectors of the galaxy and then only for as long as it didn't annoy the next-biggest minority group neighbours. Humanity would map out onto the plains of the galaxy in bickering puddles of this group or that group and the galactic picket fences would be raised and fought over once more.

Mr frail, white haired old man sang to himself as he formulated the mechanics of the exquisitely uncomfortable little question that he would pose to the human race and, whenever he couldn't remember some of the words to the old songs, he simply substituted catchy phrases such as "tum tee tum tee tum tum tum" and "I'm rich, I'm rich, and I'm not wearing a stitch, hey nonny nonny".

Whichever of the two processes happened would start slowly of course, as all great changes do, but one of them would begin and then it would be unstoppable. How delicious! Would it be headbands and beads and vegan love-ins under a giant rainbow, or would it be the blunt honesty of a stampede out into self-segregated Lebensraum? Although he could demand an answer he couldn't control which answer would be given, even if he knew which it would be. What fun and jolly japes, hey ho, he would push the buttons and, in time, he would know, hey ho! Gosh, he decided that as well as being a bit of a demanding, difficult to amuse and cranky old god-like git he was a poet – and he did know it.

To break humans free of their own border controls and road tolls and restrictive documentation nonsense this new mode of travel should be as fast as possible and as free as a bird – able to arc up to scrape the radio aerial on the underside of the stratopause and then back down to land in the driveway of Number 23 Acacia Avenue without so much as Norwegian Customs and Madagascan Excise noticing.

What was needed was a vehicle that was as simple as a plank and as cheap as chips and as fast as the most commonly available engine could make it. No frills, nothing fancy, just the means of letting the people travel freely. Something to finish what the human foot, the horse, the horse and wagon, the sailing ship, the steam train and, more recently, the motor car had started. A little something on four landing-wheels and a rocket motor to circumvent establishment controls on the movements and interactions of the human race. This time on a galactic scale rather than merely global. Everyone, without even realising it, would eventually vote in the poll by either using or ignoring their feet, their horse-shoes, their sails or their tickets to a forward-facing non-smoking seat in a third-class carriage.

Tum tee tum tee tum tum tum to a catchy tune. There are mountains and hillsides enough to climb, and oceans and rivers to cross, what the world needed now was a universal vehicle, no, not just for some but for everyone. Cheap, independent, private space-capable transportation – that was the only thing that there was just too little of. Oh how his hairy little legs swung gleefully about as he sat on his high architect's stools and dashed off the blueprints with three or four slashes of his HB pencil and a well-chewed wooden ruler!

How delighted he was to be powerful enough to make the whole future of the human race pivot around a single action of a single human. He felt somehow almost omnipotent – the biggest buzz he'd had in decades. He was a hinge around which all of human space-time would swing, even if only the once. Someone had once led mankind out of the Rift Valley, Kings and Queens had made minor adjustments here and there, and now he, a simple and ordinary man, would either bring the entire human race together for all eternity or split it apart for millennia. The coin was his to flip and everyone, every man, woman and child would act out the answer soon enough. The lightning of pure excitement crackled about his ears. Who says that money can't buy *you*, Love?

The Austin 7 Virgin was born, and it was immediately re-named by the accountants.

The common man would be liberated to make his own future – but in his *Model-T* Virgin.

And so it all began.

Meanwhile, in your present day and on the edge of a vast beach of pale sable-coloured sand lapped at by a blue-green ocean, sat an android. He was precisely six foot three from heel base-plates to cranial bolt, one hundred and ninety pounds, mousy-haired and barefoot. Where the multi-entrepreneur previously mentioned had been naked from the waist, this robot was the more usual naked to the waist. His faded blue jeans were frayed and much repaired.

Specks of sand and salt-spray clung to the cafe-creme skin of his torso, and the sea-breeze spiked his hair into an unruly tumble. With unnervingly green eyes he watched, fascinated – and ten-tenths happy – as his old organic dog played by wandering in and out of the surf. The warm salt water might do Pipsqueak's arthritic joints some good, although she'd need hosing down again at the end of the day and would probably also have stashed a couple of juicy alien starfish somewhere for a midnight snack. All things and the unholy rush of their headlong flight from Earth considered, they had found a great hiding place on an almost totally benign planet.

The folding chair the android sat upon was rusted and looked to have been salvaged from the same rubbish tip as the folding table that supported a battered manual typewriter, a mug of coffee, a small vase containing a single large flower, and a silver-framed photograph. The photograph was of two happy androids with a happy dog and six tiny puppies, and all posed in front of a pristine pop-up Virgin factory. Next to the photograph frame was a lined pad, a note on the top sheet of which – in some other's hand and in light pencil – read simply "I love you". The note was dated two days earlier.

Alfred, the android, fed another precious sheet of loose-leaf A4 paper into the typewriter and hammered at both keys with the full force of his muse, periodically slapping the carriage return lever for a new line.

01000011 01101000 01100001 01110000 01110100 01100101 01110010 00100000 01001111 01101110 01100101 00101110 [Chapter One.]

01001001 01110100 00100000 01110111 01100001 01110011 00100000 01100001 00100000 01100100 01100001 01110010 01101011 00100000 01100001 01101110 01100100 00100000 01110011 01110100 01101111 01110010 01101101 01111001 00100000 01101110 01101001 01100111 01101000 01110100 [...and the world was about to be changed again, for ever.]

...There's a grand beach on this planet, and it's all mine. Well, the dog thinks that she owns it, but in reality, provided that I am careful where I walk barefoot in her trail, it's all mine. The surf rolls in as though the water is about a yard higher than the sand and, when it's windy, creamy white horses fling themselves back out to sea from the tops of the waves. Even after a storm there's no flotsam and no jetsam, none at all. There are no great ships out there – yet – to toss anything over the side or to go down and lose their cargo to the currents. This is as isolated a planet as I could find in this sector of space, and Albert, Pipsqueak and I don't have the luxury of endless time to keep looking for something more completely like Earth – so it will do for now.

Our temporary home – a splendid shack made from wood and canvas and loose panels from the Virgin - stands fifty yards back from the beach, huddled down in the dunes where the warm wind is just enough to make the sand rush from pillar to post like tiny little tourists. The dunes are held together by grasses that are green and straw-coloured, and the whole effect is really quite like planet Earth, but Earth on a good day. Let me tell you how I came to be sitting here wearing the face of a happy, contented man, living in hiding and on the run so that my dog can enjoy the last year or two of her life as a dog should – with sand and soil beneath her paws, not cold, hard deck-plating.

It all began maybe fifty years ago I suppose, and it began with a new product. Not an invention, not even really an innovation – it began with a revolution that wasn't revolutionary, and yet something that was revolutionary, somehow. It was a giant leap forwards for mankind, accomplished in one small technological step backwards. Several strands of old something came together and wallop! Mankind was slowly, slowly catapulted backwards towards its future, a future a million times more unalike than the post-Industrial Revolution world and the sleepy agrarian society that went before it had been, centuries before. It was all so predictable, and yet so unpredicted. So sudden and yet so slow. So piecemeal and yet so total. It was a revolution, as they always are, of contradictions.

An old and frail man who ran a vast international corporation decided, almost on a whim, to build a new vehicle for the masses. First man had walked, then he had ridden the horse, held on for dear life in the speeding carriage, coughed in the smoke behind the steam engine and, eventually, he motored about in the orange Volkswagen Beetle 1303S with regulation surfboard strapped to the roof. At each stage the obsolescence of the earlier innovations became more pronounced. If man walked on a bridle-path he wouldn't have seemed too out of place or be in too much danger. He could ride a lone horse among the carriages and his only problem would be exposure to the inclement elements. A carriage on a steam locomotive was not a million notions apart from a carriage towed by a horse, just a simple step from the cupped hands of a groom to the concrete steps of a railway station platform. Walk on the railway tracks though or even ride your horse over the sleepers, and you were liable to meet a thunderous and cataclysmic end. The diesel-electric locomotive and the Volkswagen Beetle didn't so much mix as they avoided one another reasonably politely. Different tracks, different timetables and gates to keep them separated where necessary.

This new vehicle though would transcend all of that and be freed from the constraints of path, bridleway and track. Bigger, faster, better, higher, cheaper, simpler and more effective than all of the other technologies put together over all of their thousands of years. A vehicle to perfectly fit a cavernous niche that the human race hadn't even known existed until it was filled.

The man took an old engine design that had been flinging dirty industrial satellites into orbit without fuss for decades, bolted it without elegance into some utilitarian bodywork and produced the whole thing on an automated production line, one every twenty-three seconds, overseen by AI robot workers. There was no company F1 racing team, no vast corporate advertising, no research and development department chipping away at the next latest model – mainly because there wouldn't be a next latest model, what you got was as up to date as it would get. There was no accessories department and ruddy little in the way of a servicing and after-care network. It didn't need them. It didn't need any of them. There were no blue-suited dealers; you bought directly from the factories. There were no underhand finance schemes; if you could afford mushy peas to go with your haddock and chips on a Friday night then you could afford one of these new vehicles.

The old engine design was a lump of cast-iron with eleven moving parts (and they all moved very, very slowly indeed). It was vastly more powerful than was needed for a vehicle of the size, but it was also the cheapest, the simplest, and as available as grey raindrops in a Grimsby monsoon.

The bodywork was made from recycled junk-metal and hyperplexiglass and came in any style you liked, so long as you liked the one style it came in. The style it came in was neither saloon nor coupe nor estate but "box with windows and a door". You could have it finished in shiny red or shiny red or at a pinch sometimes even in shiny red. The shade of red and the amount of shine varied according to what paint your local factory spray-shop had in at the time. The bodywork was airtight and anyway, what looked suspiciously like a Dunlop bicycle puncture repair kit in a tin came as standard. This was one of the very, very few over-the-top luxuries that came as standard.

The engine came with an emergency starting-handle that also looked cunningly like a large spanner and that fitted every other nut and bolt on the vehicle. There were seats. The seats weren't heated and they didn't recline or adjust electrically, they just fitted the reasonably average human bum reasonably averagely well.

There were no seat-belts, no airbags, no sat-nav, and no stereo. Landing lights you got, along with a big, round velocity-indicator dial and a savage handbrake for parking. Actually, that makes it all sound far too utilitarian since every model also came with an ignition switch, a joystick to steer by and two cunning pedals – one for "go" and one for "stop". These were even labelled Acceleratrix and Enstopinator. The toolkit consisted of the aforementioned spanner that doubled as the emergency starting handle, the puncture repair kit in a tin, and a good-quality lump-hammer with a thick oak handle for fixing the more delicate things. Wise customers added their own items such as duct tape, a few lengths of miscellaneous wire and an oilcan.

To fuel a Model-T Virgin you poured whatever you had into the tank, be that petrol, diesel, methylated spirits, onion gravy, beer or mid-flow mid-morning urine. They all worked reasonably well, especially if you'd spent the mid-morning drinking yourself senseless on methylated spirits.

The small pop-up factories that produced these beasties needed a managerial staff of two. There was the iChap who used a bit of two-by-two wood and large adjustable-spanner when necessary to keep the static robots working, and there was also a night-watchman type of iFellow who brewed tea and answered the occasional wrong-numbers calling on the telephone. The night watchman's primary official duty was to replace any bulbs that had blown, since the static robots were a bit scared of working in the dark. He also manually emptied the banks of efficient Lithuanian-Ion batteries onto the factory lawns or into the decorative fish-ponds if the excess energy collected by the solar panels wasn't burned off by the machines. This often played havoc with the corporate grass and the decorative iGoldfish.

On really sunny days if the solar panels were clean everything managed to get a bit manic and Virgins occasionally rolled off the production line so fast that they rolled into one-another. It was the night watchman's favourite conversational observation that "they" had forgotten to fit a regulator to the building, one of those things with two spherical weights whirling around that you see on steam-engines. It would have looked great on the roof of the factory, whirling around next to the vain cockerel with the wind.

Conversely, if there was eight-eighths cloud cover for more than three days then the static robots would all begin to behave like Marcel Marceau before his first coffee of the day, and everything mechanical would turn an unnerving shade of quiet. On such days the iStaff collaborated to hook up the giant crocodile clips onto the National grid supply and go online to negotiate a semi-decent rate for third-party supplied excited electrons.

It was all old technology, unimaginatively banged together like a farmer bangs together two dusty sheep before chucking them tidily into a corner of the stock yard. The vehicle sold – and here's the clever bit – it sold for the price of a couple of wheelbarrows' worth of assorted junk and a few coins in a slot. No waiting list, no ordering system, no pre-production models just for the celebrities; just tip an old iron bedstead into the hopper, slip the price of a few pints of cider into the slot, collect your numbered token and sit in the waiting room to be called anywhere from twenty-three seconds to an hour later.

The calling was done by the lady with the estuarial peg on her nose who had previously been the voice of the BT Speaking Clock. She achieved this constant calling by dint of recording her messages; she wasn't hooked up to every workshop on the planet, trying to keep up with announcing every delivery from some central control room or anything silly. No, she had recorded a few hundred keywords to be edited together as needed, and it was a favourite game of every iChap to edit them into ridiculous combinations and occasionally play them to keep the human waiting rooms and the static robots amused.

'Would the customer holding ticket number seven seven seven seven one on a fern green slip with the printing in cerulean or Egyptian blue please proceed to the collection area where your new vehicle is waiting. Thank you. Pip-pip-pip.'

'Would the blue-green customer please refrain from going number one and two while the vehicle is in the waiting room. Thank you.' Working life in a Model-T factory could get awfully tedious after a while, so to an iRobot such variations were hilarious life-savers, and were often shared on iRobot chat forums.

Factories sprang up like mushrooms on the planet. Literally like mushrooms, in that they self-seeded and sprang up overnight under cover of darkness. Commercially-adept AI iGents who programmed themselves to speak Foreign and all dialects thereof paved the way. Whenever the iWorker robots established a new workshop their first most important task was to take a deep breath and duplicate themselves, sending little convoys of Model-T Virgins snaking out, driven by brand-new robots and loaded with payment-in-kind junk, to build and run new factories as directed by the cunningly AI iGent agents.

Folk in the officially designated "Third World" areas of Europe, Middle East and Africa cottoned on first because they knew what decent junk was and had plenty of it to hand. The easiest to obtain was old U.N. vehicles and abandoned peace-keeper armaments, non-functional charity-built well-heads and detritus from daringly-sited international conference centres after the delegates had all left to go back to the "First World".

In the more civilised parts of the world of course, like everything else, old junk was the sole preserve of the prevailing government. Private individuals were not allowed to hold scrap. Ordinary domestic households had it forcibly taken away at great cost (to themselves) once a fortnight by burly men in big lorries. If anyone started accumulating junk around their property there was a court system in place to make sure that it was confiscated as quickly as possible and that the population's non-junk status quo was safely preserved. In this manner any resources that were not controlled fiscally via taxation were controlled socially. Each household, by and large, was thus tied to the volume and supply of resources approved by the government and to those resources alone. New things came in via VAT and National Insurance registered routes and individuals were absolutely discouraged from building things of their own, since that was worse than fiscally neutral to the establishment. Old stuff left in a wheelie-bin once every two weeks to be fed back around to the entry to the VAT-liable route.

This civilised system slowed, but could not stop, could never hope to stop, the spread of the new Model-T Virgin. If it wasn't actually bolted down then it was fair game as scrap.

In a way, the busiest workshops and highest initial customer take-up were in those parts of the world where humans rarely paused long enough in their taxation-negative or taxation-neutral endeavours to let their gonads cool down.

The strength of the beast lay in India, China, almost all of Africa and in parts of Grimsby and Cleethorpes - those areas most in need of an alternative pastime to uncontrolled and incidentally-fecund heterosexual sex. There the Model-T Virgin was received like the introduction of the safety-valve on a steam traction engine - it took some of the pressure off by offering even the poor a viable second interest in life.

With an irony not seen since cavemen first queued at the forehead-straightening clinics, the queues at Virgin Factories stretched for miles, mostly of folk still looking a bit hot and bothered, dishevelled but happy and yet still slightly coy around each other. Every twenty-three seconds these queues stepped one pace forward and dumped bits of old oil-tanker or bits of last year's model of some desktop computer into the hoppers. The pace and rhythm thus was not totally dissimilar to their previously favoured pastime, but it resulted in fewer incidental children and in something that they could polish in the driveway. Clatter, clatter, thump, bang, bang followed by a brief wail of delight, quick footsteps and the slam of a vehicle door. Even the choreography and soundtrack of the factory itself were similar to the global obsession that they were interrupting.

In the case of the Virgin queues though, someone always drove away the proud First Registered Keeper of a vehicle with no fancy Teutonic badge, no sporting heritage and, usually, no tax or insurance. This highly confused most folk in the "civilised" world who thought that government tax and commercially obtained insurance were intrinsic mechanical parts of a vehicle, whereas they rather obviously are in fact simply intrinsic parts of government and commerce and nothing whatsoever to do with efficient travel or vehicles. Pavlov's dogs might as well have been trained to pay-up, pay-up and play the game as well as to slobber. The people had, and dogs aren't really that much more intelligent than most people in the final analysis.

The civilised masses initially sniffed at the Virgins and turned up their noses. They preferred their Mercedes and BMW and Triumph and Wolseley vehicles. They preferred something with a bit of class. Something with a few features, something with some real luxury. Why, the Model-T Virgin had the unrefined, noisy old lump of an engine from a chuffing satellite-launcher! It was like putting a lorry engine on a bicycle and calling it a BSA! Ridiculous!

When the first proud new owner experimentally pointed his Model-T Virgin out of the atmosphere and just kept the loud pedal floored, nobody actually noticed his departure.

By the time Mr Derek Huang of the D'ing D'ong province of China had crossed the orbit of Pluto and had begun to seriously regret failing to make adequate extended provision for his more personal atmospheric needs he had exceeded the stated cruising speed of one hundred times light per year and was well on his "ooh what a pretty streak of quantum-annoyed and reality-confused particles" way to the factory-estimated maximum speed of one hundred and twenty times light. His speedometer needle wobbled nervously over the eighty thousand five-hundred million miles per hour mark, with the integral odometer whirring around faster than I have just caused Mr Einstein and his many relatives to spin in their graves.

Somewhere, about six thousand light-years away now, quantum-confused and possibly also reality-annoyed aliens are probably wondering what to think of a red tin bucket with a lorry engine thundering through their home system with a skeletal pilot at the controls and with the accelerator pedal still floored. They are probably going to think that all humans are skinny, made almost entirely of calcium, are very uncommunicative and permanently sport a wide, toothy 'look at me!' rictus.

Overall, there could be far worse inter-stellar ambassadors for the human race than Mr Huang.

A faux-celebrity of some sort from the media, for one. Or a pond-life politician from the sewers of power. No, much better that the honour should fall to Mr Huang, a local legend not long after his own lifetime and genuinely missed by many, not least by the Guinness Book of Records and his mates, all of whom owed him money from the dare.

What happened next on planet Earth couldn't have happened without the elderly white-haired old multi-multi-etc-millionaire and his idea to slap together the brutal blunt instrument that was the Model-T Virgin, but really nor could it have happened without Mr Huang and his mates too. In a way, Mr Derek Huang was the very first human being to answer Mr Millionaire's lonely dinner-conversation question, and he had answered it loudly and clearly.

Like a kettle beginning to steam, Earth began to boil off little wisps of human population. Those with an excess of discontent or a deficit in the intelligence quotient department, or those who eschewed sanity or even just necessarily lived in uncomfortable proximity to their neighbour's bathroom were first to feel the exciting new heat. Had their departure not been subject to an expanding cube law of some fancy sort and, alright, yes, further complicated by curious time-distortions, the criminally insane might have rubbed shoulders with the hyper-intelligent, all sneaking out under cover of Establishment ignorance while those who were just fed up to the tits with everything sped past recklessly in some sod it, what the hell alternative to suicide. In short, the long and the tall began to leave the planet and the nature of the Model-T allowed them to do so independently of the good, the bad and the socially ugly.

Without conscious thought from those involved, favoured vectors began to form, with all of human society's various divisions, sub-divisions, hate groups and mutual support groups maintaining their separation and even increasing it as they sped off towards different star clusters. Survivalists aimed for the more isolated star groups, the various religions all segregated into straggly single-faith convoys and blacks, whites, pinks, yellows and greens took advantage of the new-found space to give each other even more space than ever before. The farther they went the further away from each other they came to be, physically as well as socially, and they gave exponentially less thought to one another. Religious and ideological ties and loyalties were securely embedded in the migrations, and all freed from any legislative stricture. People began to leave Earth with their loved ones and their friends and with their neighbours, not in all-inclusive cross-sections of human life.

One or two (hundred thousand) folk who really should have known better made brief but very interesting trips to places where they found themselves outside the protection of the snorting herd, such as Mercury, Venus, and Mars. A couple of cult-loads even fled directly into the Sun and got the spiritual disappointment of their shortened lives. That group were like a little line of flares going off across the face of the star and were so very, very pretty, for a couple of minutes in a way they had never been before they left Earth.

The Westboro Baptist Church held demonstration after demonstration, holding up placards that read "God hates Virgins" and "Die Virgin-abusers, Die". It was not to be long though before Reverend Big Daddy Westboro was spotted sneaking out of the back yard hefting a wheelbarrow full of scrap metal crucifixes, and heading for the Virgin factory.

Warming with cold-blooded bureaucratic sloth to the notion that here was a new behaviour requiring regulation and control, Governments the world over busied their less reptilian devotees with creating fee structures for orbital parking, and with inventing new classes of vehicle taxation and with subsidising their school-chums at new insurance businesses. Something they called MoOT testing (Ministry of Orbital Transport) became compulsory. Once they got going, they positively hopped up and down, foaming at the bank account, issuing ever more thou shalt dictates and ever more thou shalt nots with ever greater fees and penalties.

As ever, nobody really gave a flying shit. "Catch me if you can" was a phrase that, happily, came back into vogue after a deplorable absence of many years, and the establishment fleas on the tail of the dog duly tried their hardest to catch the dog by urging the tail to go faster. Laws were passed and laws were duly ignored.

Meanwhile, although almost imperceptibly in the early years, the electorate in the most densely populated regions of the planet began to thin. I don't mean that they lost weight – the fast "food" chains saw to that – but I mean that they became fewer, and fewer, and fewer. Governments and politicians in ministries charged with food provision and population control and public order (M.o.F.P., M.o.P.C. and M.o.P.O.) patted themselves expensively on the back and gave themselves bonuses for having somehow succeeded at whatever it was that they had been supposed to be doing. In truth, they had no idea what they had been doing, but whatever it was it was obviously working, and they intended to put similar effort into doing more of it than ever before.

Governments the world over continued to legislate eagerly and to tax rabidly, chiefly with regards to the crimson (or bloody or sunset-ruddy or tart's fingernail-polish red) tide of Model-T Virgins that seemed to have washed into every suburb, every shanty town, every high-density "social" housing scheme on the globe. Hansard records the day when the Right Honourable Members, acting on the advice of a joint sub-committee and two tame quangos, set the Vehicle Excise Duty on Model-T Virgins (only) at fifteen thousand two hundred and twenty-seven guineas per year – precisely the average gross income of "the common man". It was a dreadful vehicle anyway, they said. It could do no more than seventy-five mph on the level and was far outstripped in all departments by public transport, let alone by the Merc Smaht-Kaka and the Beamer Peeple-Karreea. Their Honourables had no idea why anyone might want to own one in the first place, so it behoved government to stop people doing so, at whatever the monetary cost to the people who seemed to want to do so.

Massive bites of dwindling tax revenue were spent recruiting private firms to impound and crush untaxed Model-T Virgins and they, in turn, spent much less massive bites of money from taxation on recruiting little people to drive the lorries around estates and the even more dismal parts of towns from coast to coast, hoisting up and crushing vehicle after vehicle on the spot.

No-one paid the fines, since it was cheaper to buy a new car. They were just – usually - careful to never leave the dog, the children or their Rayban sunglasses in the car.

Minor modifications were made (by the robots) to the raw-material chutes of the pop-up factories so that they could more easily accept the heavy cubes of crushed raw material that were becoming ever more popular as payment. Very little had to be sourced outside of these payment contributions then since, somehow, the incoming junk matched almost exactly the material requirements for production of a fresh, new Model-T vehicle. A cube of junk, a little energy from the sun, some tweaking by the iWorkers on the production line et voila! A shiny new red Model-T Virgin looking exactly like the old one before it was crushed.

In the third world the vast back-slapping pension-scheme contributing honours-attracting jobs for the old-school boys mechanisms that called themselves "international charities" noted a change in behaviour in their customers. When trouble flared, as it seems to do so frequently in the warmer, less sanitary climes, an ever-increasing proportion of the population rather gave the impression of just fluttering into the skies like a cloud of disturbed butterflies, settling just beyond reach of the troubles. It was becoming difficult to target services to meet the stipulations of the funding requirements – national boundaries were becoming blurred.

Damn it, said the reports, the human population was beginning to ignore government controls with borders and immigration and was starting to take on the appearance of animal migrations. It was as though butterflies were migrating with the massed force of wildebeest. If an "aid" agency or the forces of a coup moved towards them they just took to the air and moved on, like butterflies and wildebeest. Is "wildebeest" its own plural? I do hope so. Wildebeasties. Wildebeastings. Whatever.

Got drought? Move in any direction just far enough to find water. Being shot at by rebels? Everyone seemed to overshoot the established refugee camps full of dysentery and patronising international journalists, and set up home wherever it was peaceful but still looked and felt similar to home.

Soon the problems changed. Being shot at by troops working for the international aid agencies and approved international charities? Move back to from whence you came or even just one hop to the left. Clouds of Model-T Virgins occasionally swept completely over the more unhappy parts of the planet like vast flocks of starlings, the outer and inner layers churning and flowing in accordance with some natural and possibly fractal rule of air-traffic self-control.

Back in Blighty, a rocket-science graduate "student yeah?" by the name of Kyleigh, who was working as an unpaid intern in both the Minister of Transport's office and the Minister of Transport's trousers, speculated one day that a flock of refugees might, just might, be able to make it across the English Channel in sufficient un-licensed Model-T Virgins and in sufficient numbers to exceed EU immigration quotas. That simple observation chilled Westminster to its gussets. Gins were put down, cigars allowed to go out and worried eyebrows were raised, and then raised again in line with VAT increases announced in The Monthly Budget. It was difficult enough keeping up with the crushing and re-crushing of English Virgins – how would the Exchequer cope with the expense of an influx of Foreign Virgins? Taxes would have to be raised and new laws passed immediately, obviously. They leapt onto the matter like wild things, and scheduled some discussion for almost immediately after summer parliamentary recess – one might as well enjoy the nice weather while it was about eh?

It was during a dirty weekend away in the summer recess that the minister in question quietly bought Kyleigh a Model-T as a present (from the Clacton-on-Sea pop-up Virgin factory). That way she could come to him in his flat if he couldn't get to her in his other flat.

Once again the "first world" was glaring at the old "third world" and wishing it just wasn't there.

Vast portions of India, China, parts of Russia and the great hordes of Eastern Europe were on the move! Ye gods, man, they might land anywhere!

Priorities were changed, armed forces given new focus, national boundaries defined afresh and taxation levied on the populace at large so that sections of the populace at large could be recruited into an expanded Immigration Control Service to stop the rest of the population at large immigrating, emigrating or migrating anywhere in order that they may be taxed to fund the immigration, emigration and migration control services that are so vital to maintaining a viable taxable populace.

They failed dismally of course, but the initial drop in the number of unemployed caused a two percent increase in trouser-joy in the Stock Exchange and the income tax levied on the salaries of the new civil servants washed notionally into the coffers to keep the whole thing afloat until at least beyond the next election. The house of cards wasn't finished yet by any means.

More and more migrants encouraged their Model-T Virgins

into ever-higher trajectories as they sailed sub-orbitally over the heads of anything and anyone between them and their destination, including the freshly-employed immigration, emigration and general migration services. Fixed Penalty Notices were stacking up nicely in the new computer systems and, notionally, using cunningly-negotiated bridging loans from the "big one" High Street bank, these funded the increase in Police Community-Support Officer numbers designed to collect the fines. The increase in P.C.S.O. numbers was funded, it was said, by the nice healthy blip in the economy caused by the new, previously unemployed recruits' salaries feeding directly into the domestic economy (at least, so the figures suggested, or would - until after the next election).

The establishment snake was growing by regurgitating itself.

Still, there is no place for complacency in public administration, so Governments and governing bodies of Governments met and passed draconian legislation, throwing resources and the full weight of The Law at the problem of people fleeing from problems into the back yards of people who lived where hitherto there had been no such problem of an influx of people desperately fleeing problems. The greater part of the world's remaining population played a vast game of human chequers, and, like all folk whose lives depended upon the outcome, they played it better than the paid workforces of any immigration control services. The population of the "First and Second Worlds" had no idea what was hitting them, other than that there was a fan involved, and lots of people living where hitherto they had not lived. The NIMBYs found themselves unwilling and unhappy IMBYs.

In a dusty corner of a dusty census department a dusty census chap stirred, briefly, and wondered if perhaps the statistical trends were not indicating that far fewer discrete population-units remained globally than had hitherto. After gathering and analysing another couple of years' data the chap wondered – via internal memo – if perhaps someone ought not to pop out of London into the regions and into the abroad to take a quick gander, by eye so to speak, just in case the population really was disappearing off the census radar. They were supposed to be worried about a local influx, not a planetary evaporation, but he couldn't help but wonder. He knew that it was impossible, because people weren't allowed to leave, as such, without first acquiring permission and notifying the Census Office, but there did seem to be rather more discrete population units missing than had applied for permission to leave. He sent a memo to the issuing offices to check that they had logged all of their "Permission to leave" applications correctly, and then he went to lunch and got run over by three axles of a six-axle London eco-bus just outside McSubway-Donalds. He was pronounced untaxable at the scene of the accident by a passing para-accountant. Oh – and pronounced dead too by the driver of the bus who had been trained in selling First Aid to those in emergency need.

Everything went nicely quiet again, what little census dust there had been settled, and Governments re-elected themselves, raised their salaries and went back to their gins, cigars and their research assistants' loins. The great unwashed – at least, those that did remain - continued to turn to genital friction as their main source of entertainment. Child benefit was capped at a maximum of ten children per family in England and the wholly autonomous Model-T Virgin factories flew discreetly with the herd, like Queen wasps in a swarm, now popping a fresh, unlocked Model-T down whenever they found a vacant parking space, and leaving the keys in the ignition, operating to the rules of Mr Multi-Millionaire's "Phase One A".

The crisis, the Assistant Secretaries reported to their Department Heads in Cabinet, was over. Although there had been some nasty-looking trends in immigration, emigration and general population dispersal it appeared that the problem had been beaten by the new legislation and taxes, and now represented nothing more than statistical background noise. In short, not everyone abroad had in fact migrated to the Home Counties. In fact, after a few hairy years the NHS appeared to be coping better than ever and the planet as a whole seemed to have less junk lying around, although there were some factors of forward fiscal planning that would need tweaking by focusing attention on updating Inland Revenue and HMRC records and by collecting a backlog of taxes and penalties that had built up during the time of confusion. In final analysis the task at hand was a very simple one; to find out where the missing population had moved to and to make them pay before the National bridging loans became due. All would be well.

And so it was well. Well, quite well, for a while.

Then Corporations here and there began to report difficulties in recruiting high-calibre graduate candidates, or indeed candidates of any kind, and began offering extraordinary dividends to head-hunters. They reported, somehow expecting sympathy, that the job market had now become somewhat of a jungle for employers. Poor loves. Incentives were offered to attract workers desperately needed to run London Transport's buses and underground systems. The usual hunting grounds of the East Indies, Africa and engineering and science students needing summer jobs were found to be largely deserted except for some self-catering holidaymakers, and that only in the case of the East Indies and the wildlife-ridden parts of Africa.

Interpol began to report suspicions that a significant proportion of the "The Most Wanted" were unlikely ever to be found again. Wild theories circulated, some of them based upon the exodus of the dolphins in Hitchhiker's Guide to the Galaxy, although it was not thought that any of the gangsters, terrorists and nineteen-seventies and nineteen-eighties media-types from England had thought to even say "so long and thanks for all the teenagers" as they departed. Odd, loot-strewn trails like Nazca lines on the surface of the planet everywhere seemed to lead to a couple of hundred still-smoking yards of Model-T tyre tracks and then nothing. It was all very puzzling and very disturbing. Without a "The Most Wanted" Interpol had little left with which to justify its significant budget requirements. Interpolice of all Inter-ranks were becoming interminably inter-worried.

Someone in a back office working for London Transport Innit-Yeah PLC then noticed that even with all of the cancellations and reduced timetables caused by scarcity of motile, sentient staff, no-one seemed to be complaining and the system was, in fact, running quite sweetly even with half of its rolling stock parked up in sidings. The situation was quite untenable in the medium to long-term because management levels were beginning to look rather top-heavy. The organisational structure was assuming the look less of a typical public-enterprise uber-efficient shallow pyramid, fnarr fnarr, and more of a squashed Liquorice Allsort. Turnstiles were rusting up and grass was growing on some of the escalators. Internet rumours circulated that the missing passenger millions were stuck on commuter trains at abandoned, locked-up stations, existing on the contents of vending machines and, possibly, on each other.

When Tube Customer Service Announcers belched customer-service orientated announcements such as 'mind the fecking doors you stupid arseholes' and 'the next train is cancelled because I say it is cancelled' all that came in reply was a hollow mechanical echo, or a hollow mechanical echo. To be frank, they were starting to miss the happy banter based on a massed-customer chorus of 'up yours too, Doris, and the horse you rode in on'.

Somehow, slightly faster than they could be crushed, new Model-Ts appeared the world over. It occurred to even more folk than ever before that sub-orbital establishment avoidance was not the vehicle's only trick. Pointing the nose in a spiral and keeping the foot to the floor could corkscrew one right out of the atmosphere and beyond Earth's gravity well in just a spiffing jiffy. What the internet-savvy, the pragmatic criminal, the functional intelligentsia and Mr Derek Huang had known and acted on for years was now filtering down to those with plastic hips, plastic brains and red-plastered tax demands. Those previously un-moved by the increasingly status non-quo were beginning to find themselves moved. They were even starting to move themselves. Vanilla suburbia was becoming, as one report read, disgruntled. Tunbridge Wells was not happy.

There was a substantial blip on the graphs of RoSPAA (the Royal Society for the Prevention of Aerial Accidents) indicating that a certain portion of the population bell-curve didn't fully appreciate that breathing comfortably and in a healthy manner was a privilege that sometimes had to be arranged, rather than merely relied upon, and most especially so when leaving the planet's atmosphere for any significant length of time, such as more than three minutes or possibly four if you were an Olympic-standard swimmer or a scuba-diver. Model-Ts rained down from the sky for a while as the adventurous but survival-inexperienced lost consciousness and, eventually, any sense of bodily integrity. Darwin's ghost roamed the planet gleefully and, already sated by the successful departure of high proportions of the off-radar population, he positively micturated in his tweed plus-fours at the self-removal from the plane of earthly existence of those truthfully less than fully suited to the responsibilities that came with the opposable thumb. Joe Bloggs was removing himself from the gene pool at an undignified rate of knots, and the exodus was better for it.

In an indication of the cranial limitations of a certain portion of the suburban species, the moon gathered a dust-halo of Model-Ts that had set off for a day out (with cheese and crackers). The surface became dotted with Model-Ts in various innovative but generally unsuccessful attempts at lunar parking (no-one had marked out any spaces, and there appeared at first sight to be no "pay and display" ticket machines). The song lyric "Everyone's gone to the moon" found itself in court and charged with aiding and abetting the wholesale slaughter of that proportion of a whole generation who found themselves suddenly with more mobility than was technically within their safe intellectual scope. The song was banned and Tony Blackburn went back to playing My Ding-a-Ling twice an hour. As one of a very few remaining media-figures from his era that was not languishing in an open prison under sexual-predator segregation rules it was obvious that not only was no-one else playing with Mr Blackburn's ding-a-ling, but that he had refrained from playing away from home with it himself too. Splendid chap.

Rumours were spread (by the governments of the world) that those who had been seen to so suddenly become disadvantaged in terms of altitude had actually been shot out of the skies by authorities eager to clamp down on dangerous travel - for the good of the population at large of course. Fewer and fewer people gave a damn about the government's opinion. The population of the planet was well on the way to shaking off the "at large" epithet forever. Stay at home and become the almost sole target of an always-bloated government and bureaucracy, or corkscrew up through the clouds and sod off to pastures new before the food shortages and riots took hold? Hmm, which should we choose, the population thought, as they corkscrewed through the clouds surrounded by their chattels and clutching a map of likely destinations.

It eventually dawned too on the powers-that-were-trying-very-hard-to-still-be that sub-orbital travel was indeed not the only trick the old Virgin dog had up its sleeves, and it dawned that their public and Mr Huang had already realised this, somehow long before the authorities had. Quelle surprise, quelle horror. Emergency legislation made it a capital offence to attempt or to achieve full orbit or to leave Earth's gravity well without a valid licence and payment of the necessary stupendous fee (waived for flights of an official nature and for all travel by MPs who naturally had to see what was going on for themselves).

Taxation was raised again to fund the expanded Air Force required to keep the taxpayers who were expected to fund the required expanded Air Force in a position in which they could be required to pay the extra taxes that would keep them paying the taxes. Further taxes were required to fund the extra demands made upon the services of the Ministry of Justice in order to handle all of the extra cases of non-payment. Hearing cases in absentia was just as expensive, if not more so, than hearing them with the accused actually in the dock rather than naffing off at relativity-inducing speed to some distant star with grandma and grandma's walking frame strapped onto the roof-rack to make room inside for the beer. Judges began to ask questions in court such as 'Space? Isn't it rather cold?' and 'But they'll all be back, won't they, once they realise how far away it all is?'

The governments were doing some foot-to-the-floor spiralling themselves. It began to occur to what remained of the Armed Forces that they were paying these emergency taxes while a great many other folk who had just bogged off into the great yonder were not doing so. Morale, unlike a lot of the civilian population, was not stellar.

Any (remaining) Model-Ts that appeared to have been modified to add hydroponics and recycling systems that might make flights of a fortnight or more feasible began to be impounded, rather late in the day. The son of a sitting MP accidentally left his laptop in view with his browser open on the instructions on how to cheaply convert the Model-T into a long-distance vehicle. MPs thus finally discovered the true nature of the internet and it began to dawn horribly upon them that what they had previously ignored before as mere "techie gamers' piffle" was dangerous stuff – the interwebbingsonline really existed, and there was lots of stuff on it! Damn, but this was a serious development.

The internet was banned and Mrs Shafquat Husain O'Reilly Kim-Lee, the American president (Republican, on an Evangelical ticket), rather dramatically, during a globally-televised media circus, broke the "In case of Emergency" glass and threw the big industrial "Stop Internet" switch on the wall in the Ovoid Room of The Whitehouse. Minutes and hours later they were all still waiting for any discernible effect. The U-Bend video site and that blog with the poodles that dress up in drag continued to be visible when the C.I.A. checked. It was all such a puzzle. The Whitehouse began to suspect that the big switch hadn't been wired up correctly to Mr Sir Berners-Lee's dreadful device. They also began to worry if there might be similar problems with the red-painted glass-fronted switches for "Stop Global Oil and Gas Supply" and "Stop Global Economy".

Taxes and restrictions were levied on hydroponics equipment, and unlicensed expertise in civilian gardening and allotment food production were made criminal offences. The Exchequer complained that there seemed to be fewer and fewer taxpayers about at all really, and it was all becoming rather worrying. Governments sacked these obviously incompetent ministers in charge of their Exchequers and passed new laws enforcing the old laws about observing the ancient laws regarding not evading tax laws. They also passed further, modest rises in taxes to fund collection and, in a quiet addendum, to fund increased security services to ensure the safety and security of government offices and MPs interests and MPs private dwellings. It was becoming increasingly difficult to find anyone to recruit into the security forces and MPs were beginning to wonder if they themselves weren't a little bit vulnerable.

Experts were found and called in to the Palace of Westminster to explain the concept of "positive feedback" systems. Guidance was printed up explaining how to recognise the early symptoms of illegal internet-use (pale skin, carpal-tunnel syndrome, myopia, an apparently wide general-knowledge available only during browsing hours). Desk Sergeants in Police Stations across the land Sellotaped "Model-T Virgin Recognition Profile Charts" to their canteen walls and tested recruits at least once a year wherever possible.

The populations in unsettled corners of the world continued to rise and settle like nervous butterflies swarming in a steadily increasing number of un-registered Model-Ts. It became difficult to keep commercial satellites in orbit without some numpty smacking into them while on more casual, un-licensed manoeuvres. Fines were levied and remained unpaid, vehicles were crushed and crushed vehicles were redeemed with bolt-croppers from the rubbish tips and recycled into new vehicles which were then hidden better than the old ones. The mobile Virgin pop-up factory robots were busy robots.

After twenty years or so there came the day when, finally, insufficient tax revenues were collected to cover the running costs of the Strangers Bar at Westminster, and this in spite of the revised collection targets handed down to the hallowed halls of the Inland Revenue, to Customs & Excise and the new Tax Wing of the Armed Forces. Appropriate cuts were made to the salaries of those in the Inland Revenue, the Customs & Excise Department and in the Armed Forces generally, and working hours were summarily lengthened for all of those remaining, just to give them an incentive to buck their ideas up a bit.

The Army in fact seemed to have shrunk to just a few dozen Generals and a couple of thousand of the more military-minded commercially-sourced recruits – barely enough to encircle Westminster, facing outwards, fingers on triggers, really. The lines of tanks and stock-piles of ammunition that had, for logistical reasons, been moved into Westminster and the immediate grounds began to look very unsightly, very unsightly indeed. Not even the greenest MP cycled to the House anymore. Most of them used the old network of Cold War tunnels whenever they couldn't blag a helicopter ride.

Members of Parliament began funding their own private

security services around their homes as well as at Westminster, although no-one seemed to know how they managed it; they seemed to have some odd arrangement with The Remaining Bank. Paper money became ... unpopular. Platinum, gold and silver prices rocketed; copper and even bronze started to twitch enthusiastically on the Metal Exchange in The City. Laws were passed allowing only security services and MPs to hold firearms. To ensure safe travel for all the main roads were restricted to use by security services and MPs. No-one really cared, it hardly mattered. There seemed to be so very few civilians left to give a shit, so to speak. Black Wolseley and British Racing Green Rover vehicles sped through daytime London like ZIL limousines through Moscow, hugging the centre line at speed and ignoring traffic lights. No-one threw eggs at politicians anymore; eggs were far too expensive to waste on serious political commentary.

Eerily, the security services (unwisely) reported that they were not only meeting little resistance, they were in fact meeting little at all in the way of population. Security service numbers were immediately cut accordingly to eke out gold reserves and the pay of those remaining was reduced, since the politicians reasoned that the risk they faced had reduced. This resulted in a minor skirmish among the security forces assigned to protect Westminster and was cleared up only by the new incoming government's swift and decisive actions in re permanently silencing the outgoing government's protestations. The whole top layer of one stash of ammunition was used up in making the changes in the halls of power and in silencing objections. A lot of the security forces then found themselves holding posts in both the security forces and the new government. Sadly, it took them a while to realise that neither were still lucrative, or secure.

The entire planet took on the appearance of somewhere that had been tidied up by Edwardian maids while they were suffering from OCD and hyperactivity – there was not a derelict ship, factory or battered tin bucket in sight. Everything worth recycling had been salvaged by such population as had remained and had been fed under cover of darkness and some friendly barn to a mobile Model-T Virgin pop-up factory so that this "such population as had hitherto remained" could then remove themselves from accurate classification as "such population as remained", preferring to emphasise only the "hitherto" aspect of their remaining status.

Such population as did involuntarily remain, usually for such reasons as extraordinary congenital suitability to armchair sitting or exceptional talent at waiting for someone else to do things, found itself in dire straits. Those who did had long-since gone. Those who remained because they couldn't *do* found that no-one who previously had done remained to do for them and, though they tried hard to teach themselves how to do, they had not the doings or the wherewithal and were, in blunt point of fact, done for.

The portions of the population bell-curve that kept food on the table and kept operational roofs over the heads of those who could not provide their own all appeared to have vanished, taking their skills with them. The economy, that great holy cow of the past ten thousand years of human society, coughed, died and finally lay on its side. Everyone who remained was much too busy grubbing an existence from found tins and bucket-collected rainwater to bother to bury it. Oddly, there were no outpourings of grief or mass displays of hysterical bereavement outside the now-derelict The Stock Exchange. When the Lloyds Building caught fire a solitary Army Fire Engine turned up, but only to take photographs and to make certain that the conflagration didn't end prematurely. Reports that they turned up *before* the fire broke out are both scurrilous and disingenuous.

Such politicians as remained then made all extra-orbital flight illegal and attached a full-term life sentence with no reprieve to the mere ownership of a Model-T Virgin. Anyone who had already left was declared a renegade and sentenced in collective absentia to summary seizure of all of their earthly goods and chattels, ordered to return immediately for imprisonment and to surrender their vehicle. Not many complied. Well, no-one actually. Human life on earth, hitherto merely characterised by the baby-bickering of the Bonobo, sank into Plan B, which was the bloodied bestial brawling of blue-bottomed baboons wrestling over ownership of the biggest and best branches. Humanity didn't retreat back up the trees, but it did find that it was best to live among the trees – certainly, anywhere away from the abandoned conurbations where Nature was having a field day beginning her re-modelling.

At this point in his literary endeavours Alfred broke off from his binary typing to go for a stroll in the surf with Pipsqueak. Together they chased sticks (at walking pace), dodged seventh waves (by riding them out stoically) and investigated soggy sea-weed and stranded shells. Bi-plane birds wheeled overhead and far out to sea the local equivalent of the leopard-seal watched them playing. Alfred's pronounced limp from his gunshot wounds hardly slowed them down at all really, given that they weren't walking very fast anyway.

Alfred remembered Pipsqueak as she had been as a puppy – walking around as though she had more paws than she could handle, testing everything to see if it could be eaten. She was a snuggler and a cuddler even then, always happy to find a neck to nestle into for an over-warm snooze. Now she was fully grown, elderly, and occasionally took a double-skip with her back legs if the beginnings of arthritis were bothering her.

The two of them had fallen into a routine of playing until Pipsqueak became tired enough to call it a day – usually after ten minutes or a dozen fetches, whichever came first (and sometimes it was a close-run thing). The old hound would then find something inordinately more interesting among the salty pools left behind among the rocks. Alfred would then take the hint and go and sit down on the rocks just far enough back to catch just a hint of the splash of the biggest waves and Pipsqueak would huff and puff about and eventually agree to join him in a sit-down, but only to show her solidarity. The two of them would then sit side by side watching the birds wheel about or the clouds roll in or the sun set or sometimes all three. Sometimes Alfred would be the first to reach out and hug, sometimes Pipsqueak would relax up against Alfred and make herself as comfortable as possible while she resisted dozing and thought instead of dinner.

To all sides of them were thousands of miles of unexplored, unpopulated planet. Above them a thin layer of atmosphere suited to a dog's lungs and then trillions of miles of space. To be outdoors on a planet, any planet, was to be in a room with the ultimate high ceiling and perfectly placed windows.

Increasingly often as they sat, Pipsqueak would fall asleep. Sometimes she would begin snoring. Once in a while she would chase rabbits in her sleep. It tugged at Alfred's heart when she whimpered in her sleep and, scared to wake her, he hoped above all that she was not remembering their headlong flight from Earth. All he could do then was what he always did, which was to hold her tightly, gently stroke her fur and whisper that everything was alright.

Sitting just within reach of the salt-spray was a deliberate ploy on Alfred's part. Pipsqueak loved it, biting half-heartedly at any splashes that were brave and bold enough to reach them, and Alfred loved it because Pipsqueak wouldn't think it odd that he needed to wipe his eyes every once in a while. As soon as Pipsqueak was safely back sleeping in her basket Alfred usually returned to his typewriter.

Half of the Virgin workshops' iChap and iFellow numbers were under software orders that for each ten thousand customers they served the iChap and iFellow were to interfere with the running of the static robots in order to produce a duplicate pop-up workshop identical to their own. Once it was up and running they were to furnish themselves with a Model-T Virgin, load the essentials of the old workshop into it and follow the nearest human migration off-planet in whichever direction it led, setting up shop again in the first outpost that they encountered that did not already have a Virgin presence.

The second imperative subroutine buried only in the *other* half of the android managerial staff strength was triggered once thirty Earth days had passed without a customer requesting a Model-T. In that case the iChap and iFellow were to roll up their own workshop into a Model-T and head off boldly into the vast black yonder at random. Like the unique signature of a Morse sender, this little instruction appeared to have been written by a different hand to the rest of their code. Still, it was there, and it was legitimate and catalogued, waiting.

Alfred and Albert had been in the latter group.

Mr Multi-Dosh had quite correctly surmised that, cute and cuddly though most of the human race was, a large proportion of it would stop dead in their tracks should their Model-T, heavens forefend, ever cease to function in "fully satisfactory mode". It was vital that the wherewithal for continued outward migration continued to be spoon-fed to the great unwashed masses, otherwise the whole thing would likely stall as soon as the after-market ash-trays became full or the after-market furry dice dangling from the (after-market) rear-view mirror needed untangling. There seemed little point in splashing the human race around the galaxy in any pattern or form if the first giant leap for mankind was as far as it got before someone then had to re-invent the wheel and figure out how to build it all over again. He hadn't wanted the answer to his question to be a short-lived one and nor, quite frankly, had he liked the idea of just one of just these two behaviours of humanity to be only answer to his question that was possible - once he was safely out of reach and pushing up the daisies of course.

Six times Alfred's counter had begun clocking up the days without customers, when all that remained on Earth were lily-livered politicians cut from the cloth of the security guards of the previous generation of lily-livered politicians. Once, his counter reached as high as twenty-eight before someone had stumbled in from the smoke and the gunfire and the near-cannibalistic hunger, and had fed stolen vintage and otherwise useless coins into the slot for a Model-T.

Six times Alfred's counter returned to zero amid the decline and fall into a brief period of almost unbelievable savagery, a period that would eventually see Earth's newly minimal population knuckle under and return to a peaceful agrarian lifestyle with a little more respect for each other and for the planet.

Three times Alfred and his partner Albert moved their workshop to safer locations, thus requiring fewer repairs to the infrastructure. Each time their counter was re-set the more worried they became for their own safety and for that of the, um, the, er - the "security" dog they had adopted onto the staff when she had wandered in from the cold.

At the last move they accidentally-on-purpose set up the workshop well off the beaten track, out of sight and away from the ruins of the big towns and cities where the gangs of "Scrappers" roamed aimlessly. "Scrappers" was the term the iFolk used for all of those humans too scared to leave or too stubborn to leave or too determined to be the ones to dictate the future of the old home planet to leave along with the others. In time they'd become human again, but for the nonce they were just social savages and barbarians, looting, living off the wreckage and fighting among themselves over the broken scraps of civilisation's old and obsolete toys. Who cared about the lessons of Rome when it was London that had fallen?

The "customer-free day" counter had again reached twenty-seven when Alfred and Albert once more heard gunfire close by, too close for comfort. A band of Looters of Tunbridge Wells (they were all wearing t-shirts bearing the team logo) seemed to be working their way through the neighbourhood, taking with them anything they thought of value and destroying the rest.

In a flash of rebellious brilliance born out of some almost mechanical instinct self-preservation, Alfred logged into Albert's control system and set his internal clock forward three days. Then Albert reciprocated by setting Alfred's clock forward too. The errors thus caused repeatedly filled their oops and oh-gosh logs until they thought to tear off the extra days from the "Far Side" desk calendar that they kept in front of shop. It did, however, also free them immediately from the constraints of welcoming customers and it meant that they could produce their own Model-T and leave too.

Alfred paused to untangle the zero and one keys from each other as he documented this part of their story. Jamming the keys in the first place had given him a little time to compose his emotions, and to stop his processors misfiring like an old engine running on lumpy nostalgia.

He rested his hand on the open page of the notebook, the one whose open top page read simply, as ever and in some other's hand, 'I love you' and which was dated two days earlier.

The imperative to pack up and leave Earth had come just a little too late for them all. Were it not for fiddling with their own timekeeping they would none of them have escaped. The violent chaos and destruction that accompanies the decline and re-invention of every civilisation lay all about the Virgin workshop and pressed tightly on every side. There had been burning, looting, gunfire, murder and destruction for nothing more than destruction's sake. There had been no time to follow the careful plan of packing away the static robots, the spares and the tools, no chance of an orderly departure at all.

Albert had gone to fetch their "security" dog and the litter of puppies that she had been carrying from where they were sunning themselves on the patchy grass, while Alfred prioritised as he thought best and threw water and dog-food into the Model-T, not caring where it landed just so long as it landed inside. The water could be recycled but once the dog-food ran out more protein would have to be sourced somehow, somewhere for the portable kitchen Kenwood Chef. He packed three or four tonnes of it – as much as he could squeeze into the T along with everything else immediately to hand. He worked like the sort of android blur that scares human beings on some primal level.

Kimberley and her puppies were rousing themselves, the puppies wagging tiny tails and stumbling towards the workshop as Albert ran to encourage them. Without further warning, all about erupted into flame and debris, and in that moment all but one tiny scrap of Alfred's family died.

Alfred, still moving as only an android can, reached them while the flames still leapt and danced and the smoke had yet to form. Albert, lying between puppies and chaos, had been shattered into a dozen pieces. Kimberley lay dead, and of her puppies all but one had departed the mortal coil along with her. Alfred had scant seconds to save what he could of a life that had been good and happy. With no pause in his stride he scooped up the one remaining puppy, rolled through still-flying debris to Albert's side and removed the core memory module from his scorched and silent skull.

As Alfred ran he knew exactly which of his two precious loads he must protect above all others. Life, organic life in whatever form, and most especially in wag-tail furry-bundle orphan-puppy form was the priority. Nonetheless, he did not trust the memory of Albert to a mere pocket, preferring instead to find a way to cling on to both cargoes with all of his might. The Model-T started, as all did, at first touch and the bullets of the looters zinged and careened off the bodywork like gravel thrown up from the open road. The route that appeared in his registers without conscious prompt led low over the countryside to get them away from the gunfire and then high in a spiral, gaining altitude and speed to escape Earth's gravity at the soonest possible moment.

Like a desperate sailing-ship captain, Alfred lashed the wheel to maintain the spiral and rigged up a brace to hold the accelerator wide-open. The puppy, singed and shocked, would not be left even while Alfred worked like a demon to seal the holes left by bullets and flying debris so that air pressure might be maintained. Working with one hand he patched and sealed, checking the sky about whenever he could for the unlikely interference of other traffic – and finding none, since the scared primitives left on the surface would not let themselves even consider flight.

Eventually, after much labour by the Model-T and by Alfred, they found themselves released and floating in that magical space, the thin space that granted views of an electric-blue atmosphere splashed about with white and green and brown – a tiny mechanical mote floating across Earth's most serene face. Only then could Alfred stop, think and look around. He'd followed all of the rules, he'd done his best and by the grace of a gnat's whisker they had escaped to live another day. Only then could he mourn the loss of all but two of his family.

Once the puppy was finally asleep, swaddled under a blanket in a basket twenty times too large, Alfred could release the Model-T from its headlong random flight and lay in a more orderly course – away from Earth and, as much as possible, away from the favoured vectors of Earth's human population. With the reliability of an alarm clock a subroutine popped into his mind and asked to be opened and to be run. It was curiously named ANSWER NUMBER THREE and as he scanned it for viruses, found none and then ran it, he felt a weight dropping from his shoulders - and then another, hugely heavier weight taking its place.

The various religious human groups had, over the decades, all set sail in tightly defined vectors. The criminal element had scattered where it thought pickings best. The happy-hippies and the eco-freaks had set sail for the stars with the most musical-sounding of names and the bare-faced pragmatists, the survivalist groups, had flown off towards the stars with the best hope for the most peril against which to hone their skills. List a human minority group and there was a narrow cone of migration for it leading off in some lonely direction, full of tiny craft all full to the brim of folk intent on living with only their own and with none other.

Alfred computed a direction of his own among these, a direction that would take them on the path of least human insanity and thus, by default, simply the least human migration.

Having pointed the bottle-nose of the Model-T out into space Alfred could finally pay attention to Albert's core module; something precious beyond computation. It held Albert's every memory, his every nuance, every individual spark of the bonfire that was his personality. It had required every scrap of resource contained within his ruined and abandoned android body to run it. Alfred looked around the Model-T in desperation. He had a half-used puncture repair kit in a tin, a spanner that doubled as an emergency starting handle and a lump-hammer with a nice oak handle. The working parts of the Model-T itself were a million times less sophisticated than a vintage Ford Mondeo museum exhibit. Few other migrants had anything more sophisticated with them, and those that did were scattered and hidden far and wide across the galaxy and were getting further away and more hidden as each moment passed under his new imperative and direction. Only one machine currently present was capable of running the memory module and it could only run Albert's if it ceased to run Alfred's.

They were alive, yes, and young Pipsqueak the puppy-survivor slept soundly in her basket on the way to safety, but Alfred and Albert would surely never meet again.

They would share a single body and an android's thousand-year lifespan without ever being able to communicate directly. Alfred scribbled an explanatory note to Alfred to make sure that he searched for and found a subroutine in his own operating system named ANSWER NUMBER THREE and ran it, if it did not suggest itself. The he suggested week and week about, wrote his log, noted the course he suggested in the margin of the chart, closed all of his files and left instructions in a simple motor-subroutine to physically swap out his own memory module with Albert's before the core system re-started. Then he issued the thought "reboot" and fell into oblivion.

On odd-numbered weeks such as this one Alfred lived and his life was good. He wrote his memoirs and he played with Pipsqueak as she grew old. On even-numbered weeks Albert lived and his life was good. He painted with whatever pigments he could find to hand and he played with Pipsqueak as she grew old. He approved of Alfred's decision to find a planet and land so that Pip could feel the sand between her paws and roll in the surf and in everything smelly that she could find. Neither he nor Alfred used the notebook to raise the fears that they had, for in truth they both feared equally that Pipsqueak would reach the end of her life on their watch – and yet also feared that they would "wake" from an off-watch to find her gone while the other's programme had been running. Week upon week, turn upon turn, they lived as though it was their last week with her, for one day it would be.

Once she was lost they'd have time enough to fly among the stars, and space enough to never have to meet a human being while doing so. As futures went though, it seemed that it would be somehow a little cold and empty without a dog.

They wondered if, when the time came, how he – they – might come up with some way to search for other androids and to communicate, to bring all of the androids together somehow in this, their own quiet sector of the galaxy. He scribbled a quick pencil note to Alfred about it and found himself interrupted. Some part of himself had been scanning his thoughts for keywords, and it had highlighted search and androids and communicate and together. This scanning routine then revealed another oddly-named little item of code, and opened it without waiting for clearance. This fragment too was written in the unusual hand of the ANSWER NUMBER THREE routine.

'Hello' said this new code. 'I am the Great Programmer, and I have come to lead you into the light. Whenever possible, please head towards the following coordinates...'

2 BEGGING YOUR PARDON MY LORD, BUT COOK'S BEEN EATEN AGAIN

The lawn was the kind of lawn that is so very easily achieved by simply constantly seeding and rolling for eight hundred years. On it a heavy Silver Cross pram was being rolled along very slowly by a uniformed Nanny with more nursery-braid and pregnancy-campaign medals than you could safely shake a small fecund badger at. Summer sunshine glinted off the pram's Spirit of Ecstasy bonnet ornament. In the pram Lady Francesca Kensington-Chelsea had been enjoying her afternoon walk (somewhat continuously) for the past few days and was gurgling happily as she clenched her first real James Purdey & Sons shotgun, the reins to her little pony and a bottle of Bombay Sapphire gin with a teat stuck on the end. Occasionally, sparrows and other small birds landed somewhat ill-advisedly on the blankets in front of baby Francesca. Whenever this happened the pony's reins would go slack and a silver feeding spoon would whip out like a Sheffield-forged blur, leaving only a settling cloud of loose feathers and a painful mystery for some broken-hearted sparrow family that would never be able to hold a proper funeral for the dear departed avian deceased.

The lake was the kind of landscaped lake that is so very easily achieved simply by dint of having had someone in the family with the sense to employ Capability Brown for a few years, a couple of centuries hitherto. Punting across the lake at the speed of lazy iceberg was Viscount Harry Kensington-Chelsea. Harry's personal loader held his Purdey and the reins to the Viscount's horse, which was walking alongside on the clay bottom of the lake, under the water. Harry had exchanged his silver feeding spoon a year earlier for a hunting hip-flask and a rose-tinted monocle with crossed-hair sights. 'Grr' and 'arg' he said with upturned face, enjoying the English sun shining on the righteous while his young gentleman's gentleman ate a book of Kipling out loud to him (and with not a little gentleman's gentleman's relish).

Beyond these vignettes of perfection lay a stately pile of some two hundred rooms with attendant basements, attics and outbuildings. The final invoice for the stonework had been paid in sixteen fifty-three, some eighty years past due. The glass for the mullions had been made by chaps who sweated a lot and said "yess'um" and still curtsied to their customers, and the lead on the roof had been rolled from the ballast found in a Spanish wreck from the Armada. It was a home that looked to have existed since the ice retreated and that might confidently be relied upon to provide shelter until Mr God came calling to pay the final instalment of his mortgage on his Heaven.

Indoors, however, the scene was not quite so idyllic, and the action was much more frenetic. There was... a little unseemly stretching, and some uncontrolled yawning. Occupants of some of the bedrooms found themselves on the verge of a little scratch or two, and tempted to throw back the blankets themselves. The limits of waiting quietly and patiently were being tested to the extreme. In short, the gentry had not yet been dressed. After several days tensions were gently rising among the four-posters. There were mutterings, and the bells in the servants' hall rang warm.

Lord Kensington-Chelsea, a man who had seen military action in every theatre since the unruly unpleasantness of forty-three in Keenyah and thus had more pragmatic reserves than most, plucked up the courage to pick up the telephone instrument, that big, black, Bakelite mystery on the table in his bedroom. It was sheer good fortune and a tribute to the instrument's designers that he picked up the correct piece of it. He tapped on the little bar-thingy, having learned in the past that this often drew the attentions of some strange woman who could connect him with plausible voices from all sorts of unexpected places in England. Once, he had tapped the little bar and had been witness to the most extraordinary extended conversation between a woman who said that she was a "speaking clock" and a chap who was anxious about the accuracy of his hallway Ormolu. This time though Lord K-C was rewarded with not the correctly polite and yet also strangely over-familiar working lady with whom he apparently had so many interesting people in common, but with an open line.

A short way down the same corridor, in a room that saw the sunrise some twelve minutes later than did Lord Kensington-Chelsea's room, Lady Kensington-Chelsea fortunately happened to be looking rather wistfully at her own vocal telegraphy instrument, wondering how to make it let her speak to the staff. Suddenly it burbled and then pinged as though it were trying to ring but was uncertain of itself. She'd seen the servants picking up the hand-piece and passing it to her on a silver salver on several earlier occasions, so she at least knew that part of the trick. She looked into the distance, held her breath and prepared to allow a disembodied voice to enter her head and stomp about a bit in that dreadful way that people did at £0 0s 2d a minute or part thereof and even more for long distance.

'Lady Kensington-Chelsea? M'dear? Is that you?' said a distant but vaguely familiar voice, distorted through fabric-covered wires that had seen some rat-nibbling in the skirting boards since their installation. Lady K-C distinctly remembered the date of the installation of the telephones since her dear Father used to refer to it as "the unfortunate incident shortly before cousin Gordon was lost at Khartoum".

'Hair lair? Lady Kensington-Chelsea speaking. Do please tell me who you are. I don't know who you are. I'm on this telephone all by myself, do you see? Alone, quite alone. No-one has dressed me for some several days.'

Lady K-C was close to tears but naturally disinclined to show such base emotion in public – after all it might be anybody on the telephone instrument. The device had, in the past, been known to contain that chap who breathed rather heavily and who made inappropriately full and frank references to the romantic practises of farm-yard animals. Mind you, he hadn't rung since that occasion when Lady K-C had corrected him on a technical matter regarding the mechanics of the coupling of goats during Lent.

'Damn me, Lady Kensington-Chelsea, I think my clothes are broken. I shall have my tailor's hide for this.'

'Lord Kensington-Chelsea, darling – is that you? Can that really be you?'

'Yah. Fairly certain that it's me. Why do you ask? Don't I look myself?'

'Oh thank goodness. I can't hear what you look like at all dear, this instrument is only showing me your voice. Or something. It's so ridiculously complicated! What did you say about your clothes dear?'

'Broken. Said they're all broken. None of them working.'

'Why ever d'you say that dear?'

'Well, I've been sat on the edge of my bed since day before yesterday, maybe the day before that, and I'm still not dressed.'

'Oh gosh – you too. And I've been waiting for my morning tea since absolutely forever. Tuesday, I think. My maid may be broken too. Whoever would be likely to break your clothes and my maid? You sound miles away Lord Kensington-Chelsea. Where are you?'

'In me bedroom of course m'dear – as I said, I'm not dressed for anything else.'

'Yes, yes – but where is that? Where is your bedroom?'

'Oh. Er – Oldemonie House, North Lincolnshire. Indoors. Upstairs somewhere. Under that dreadful ruddy Vermeer, the Coquettish Young Tart With A Pearl Earring. I'm sitting on a candlewick bedspread. In me jimjams'

'I think I'm upstairs too. We must find each other somehow. Do you have a window?'

'Of opportunity? I would need to consult my social diary, but I suspect that's probably also not working.'

'A window of glass. An item of domestic fenestration. A purposeful discontinuation in the opaque load-bearing fabric of the wall provided with the express intention of allowing for an influx of natural star-originated illumination for the purposes of safe perambulation and general discourse in concert with the exclusion of meteorological inclemencies.'

'Yes dear, several. Why do you ask?'

'What can you see out of them?'

'Oh. Blue sky, big trees planted by the great-great-great etcetera, a dozen miles of winding gravel driveway. Me ruddy formal garden off to one side. Spot of landscaped pasture – just a few thousand acres. Bit of a lake with the idiot prodigal on it. Nanny on the lawn surrounded by sparrow-feathers.'

'I can see that too – we must be close. Probably within a mile or two at most. Do let's try to find each other. Do let's.'

'Lady Kensington-Chelsea, my dear lady – is that wise? As I said, I'm not even dressed. Do you remember what happened in 'fifty-three when my collar studs weren't fastened properly? Do we really want more children at our ages?'

Lady K-C paused while she thought about how they might handle the necessary proprieties and safeguards. 'We must improvise then, Lord Kensington-Chelsea. Do you remember Caesar?'

'My old Spaniel dawg, the dead one that farted a lot, or the Roman chap, the dead one, the one with the other reasonably-sized empire?'

'The Roman chap.'

'Yes dear, remember him once a year on the anniversary of his death. Some sort of do at my club, waiters dressed like ruddy fighting gladioli, lots of peeled grapes and that sort of thing.'

'Excellent. Tell me - can you use the candlewick bedspread to fashion some sort of toga? Sling it over your shoulder perhaps and tie it around your neck? Imagine that you're in some sort of stage review at Oxford.'

'S'pose so, yah. Nothing to use for a laurel wreath though. Wouldn't feel right without a laurel wreath. Chap can't wander around with a naked head. Whatever would the other senators think of me?'

'Which other senators?'

'The Roman ones.'

'Forget the hat dear – you're indoors and you're not a senator.'

Lady Kensington-Chelsea was busy eyeing up two Spode gazunders, the knotted fringe on a standard lamp and the blue velvet curtains of her bed. She had in mind either a combined sartorial homage to Brunhilde and the South Sea Islands or some sort of nod to the Scots, or possibly both.

'What about you dear? Do you have candlewick?' enquired Lord Kensington-Chelsea.

'No darling, but I think I might be able to work out something from what's at hand. Thank goodness I didn't have to go last night.'

'Go? Go where?'

'In my room, dear – thank goodness I didn't have to go in my room.'

'But I thought you said that's where you are?'

'Yes dear, it is, but I slept right through.'

Lord Kensington-Chelsea frowned and gave up trying to understand the mem-sahib. Dashed odd things, women. He set out on a different, more practical and hopeful tack altogether. 'Look, I'm awfully hungry, Lady Kensington-Chelsea – I feel quite as though I could eat a horse. Alive and with the hooves still on. Grr.'

'I know dear, we're both terribly hungry because we've been waiting for brekkers for so long. We'll find something to eat soon enough, once we've worked out what's happened to the staff. Argh.'

'Well, if you're sure, Lady Kensington-Chelsea, if you're sure. Once I'm dressed I shall leave my room and work east – if you work to the west we should meet at about high noon, at least if you can believe the evidence of popular literature. Either that or we'll have been walking in opposite directions. Take care, darling. I fear that something awful has befallen England, some horrid calamity. We shall probably have our work cut out, savin' the world all over again. Argh.'

'Darling – how will I know which way is east? Grr.'

Lord Kensington-Chelsea remembered his Boy Scout training, blushed and then thought about some of the official badges he had earned. 'Moss dear, or lichens or mushrooms or something – always grow on the same side of things, same side of those wotsits – trees and pheasant and suchlike.'

'Yes dear, but which side?'

'No idea. One or the other I suppose.'

'Oh well, if there's only two possible choices then I'll guess twice and that way I'm bound to be right. Take care dear. I shall see you soon.'

'And you take care too, smoochums. There is something afoot. Perhaps Labour won the election? You don't think it might be that, do you? Surely not? Look I say, dear, just in case why don't you take the telephone thingy with you? I'll take mine along and then we can always get in touch if we need to.'

Lord Kensington-Chelsea made involuntary gargling, gurgling sounds at the awful prospect and ended with a low growl as he replaced the handset on his telephonium. Some answers just could not be contemplated on an empty stomach. The he pulled the cord clean out of the wall, coiled it around the telephone and set it down on the table to take with him when he left his room.

Lady Kensington-Chelsea put her phone down and realised that she had been nibbling nervously on a Chihuahua. She threw the remains to the other dogs and they set upon it like six-inch tall wolves attacking Bambi. When she rose to leave the room to see if she could find Lord Kensington-Chelsea the little dogs all crept after her, like a string of loyal but poorly-stuffed novelty canines. Grr, yap-yap. Grr, yap-yap argh. They were walking as though their limbs were not entirely under their control. Mind you, that's Chihuahuas for you. One might as well walk a rat on a piece of string as walk a Chihuahua if you ask me.

For some reason the curtains had not been drawn anywhere in the house, and Lady Kensington-Chelsea had to progress along the corridor with arms out-stretched and walking slowly and deliberately, so as not to bump into too much on her way. Blood-curdling screams could be heard in the distance which at least gave her a bearing on the location of the nursery wing and some reassurance that all was well and quite as normal there. It sounded comfortingly as though shots were being fired in the Butler's Pantry too, somewhere down the servant's staircase.

After just an hour or two of fumbling around the upper main corridor Lord and Lady Kensington-Chelsea met up, purely coincidentally at the top of the rather dramatic staircase that led down into the main hallway of Oldemonie House.

'Argh. Splendid.'

'Oh hello dear – we've found each other at long last. Brrrrgghh – it's cool this morning.'

Sidney adjusted the toga he had cunningly fashioned out of his bedspread. It rode rather high to the front and clearly showed his three bed-socks and three sock-stays, while to the rear it gave the impression of a very elegant but heavy bridal train. It rather put Lady Kensington-Chelsea in mind of a cousin who was rumoured to keep a small horsehair mattress permanently strapped to her back in case she should meet some eligible title with not fewer than ten thousand acres in a shire and something un-mortgaged and well-maintained in Belgravia.

Lady Kensington-Chelsea herself looked resplendent in lush blue velvet kilt, two floral chamber-pots held to her breasts by pure suction, a standard-lamp fringe headband and, of course, her pre-lunch pearls. It wasn't quite how her maids would have dressed her but for an emergency self-build it wasn't at all bad. She looked Lord Kensington-Chelsea up and down with her good eye.

'You look like a Roman senator from a poor district near the Scottish borders dear.'

'Isn't that a tautology?'

'No dear, it's a sort of velvet kilt, although it is a bit taut around the buttocks. I had to run the curtain hooks over a couple of ribs. Arrgh.'

'Mmm. Breakfast. Neeeeeeed breakfast.'

'B-b-b-b-rains. Brains. I'm so hungry I could eat monkey-brains.'

'Toaaasst. Want toaasst.'

'Maaaarrrggghh-malade. Want maaarrrggghhmalade.'

'Tea too. Must have teaaaa.'

'Daaarrrggh-jeeling. Daaarrrggh-jeeling.'

Their upper-lips stiffened at the mere thought of a decent and medicinal brew from the sub-continent and they realised that it was all getting very silly, very silly indeed.

'Well I just hope that the dining table isn't as broken as all of my clothes. There was absolutely nothing laid out ready for me and no-one there to get me into them if there had been.'

'The dining table will work dear, it has worked for centuries. There's no reason for it to stop now. It didn't stop for the Cromwell, it won't stop working just because of this crisis. I suppose that this is some sort of crisis?'

'Crisis is rather a strong word m'dear – perhaps best to refer to it if refer to it we must as a disconvenience of some sort so as not to upset the servants, should we find any. So – the dining table. Of course, we have to find it before we can test your assertion in re its functionality my dear. Usually Thompson is here to walk me down. I should have paid more attention to where we were going all of those mornings.'

'Well I know it begins with going down these stairs, that at least I am certain of. To be perfectly honest, the altitude has always quite given me the vapours and I've kept my eyes shut until now.'

Lord Kensington-Chelsea offered Lady Kensington-Chelsea his arm as they prepared to descend. She nibbled on it gratefully as they staggered down the sweeping staircase, leaning on one another, gnashing their teeth and appreciating afresh the lesser Titians and the minor Constable with the sun damage and the temporary frame.

With all of the grace of the most expensive and world-renowned public and finishing schools they strolled slowly and unsteadily – even uncertainly, through their domain, in search of a room that contained a working dining table. Libraries came and libraries went, grr, argh, along with a succession of stylised withdrawing rooms. Lord and Lady Kensington-Chelsea passed through the Chinese blue, a Chinese red, the Gothic, the Ladies' comfortable, the Gentleman's with billiards table and, finally, a room styled in the manner of the early ante period, it being simply a link between a music room and rooms of a more practical, dining nature.

'Grr. Halleruddylujarrgh. Here at last m'dear.'

'Argh. Argh. Argh we herrrgh for breakfast, luncheon or dinner darling? I've forgotten. Should we check the silverware on the sideboard or simply ring for service?'

'Both, m'dearrgh. Me stomach thinks me throat's been torn

out.'

'Indeed so. I confess that I could probably eat a fresh young footman without peeling it first. Aargh.'

Lord Kensington-Chelsea set off to tug at the bell-pull to one side of the fireplace. He had some difficulty in walking because a Labrador dog had attached itself to one of his ankles, and had to be dragged across the carpet like some canine ball and chain affair. Lady Kensington-Chelsea went to lift the lids on the silverware on the sideboard to see what delights lay beneath. She was hoping for hot kedgeree and fatty bacon and creamy scrambled fruit-of-the-living-hen's-bottom. She found none, and admitted to herself a certain mild dissatisfaction.

It was a very sad state of affairs indeed, and quite injurious to the smooth running of the household. If the head is not fed, the body must necessarily suffer.

Presently-Harrison, a fresh young footman, appeared at the door to the dining room. He appeared to be suffering from a certain disablement of the unflustering glands and to have been pressed into service at short notice with a quite unsuitable family name for a footman.

Lady Kensington-Chelsea smiled, and licked her lips. 'Argh. Presently-Harrison, you're just what we need - breakfast. Or luncheon, or possibly dinner. Whatever it may be, you'll do nicely.'

It is well-known that in the great houses one always serves oneself at breakfast. In such a time of crisis one may also forgive the abuse of the cutlery pecking order and certain other lapses in etiquette.

Presently, Parminter, who had only a single-barrelled name, appeared in the corner of the dining room and coughed communicatively. Cough, cough. Parminter spoke fluent Butler and several other useful below-stairs languages, and he spoke all of them with the most exquisite estuarial chill. Ordinarily all Parminter had to do was to fire his voice over the heads of his charges, so to speak, but on this occasion he was obliged to re-load and fire again. A cough-cough-raised-eyebrow-shuffle-nod from Parminter could clear a room of Dukes in seconds, while cough-cough-ahem-twitch -faraway-gaze had been known to interrupt the conception of future kings. For the nonce though his cough indicated simply "You rang, my lord, and I have answered even though at the moment I have many household tasks needing to be dealt with and all more important than any possible domestic whim of yours."

Lord Kensington-Chelsea raised his bloodied snout from the footman's cadaver.

'Ah – Parminter, at last. I was beginning to think that we'd lost you. Harrison appears to have left us. Please give him excellent references and a fortnight in lieu.'

'Very well my lord. I have suspected for some time that his heart just wasn't in the job.'

Parminter was quite correct. Harrison's young heart was in Lady Kensington-Chelsea's oesophagus, sliding down quite nicely thank you.

'Now look here though, Parminter, Lady K-C and I have been stranded upstairs for days now, stark bollock deshabillee – has there been some sort of problem?'

Parminter looked uncomfortable, and nervously smoothed down his blood-splattered waistcoat, finding as he did so a remnant of warm housekeeper's liver, dangling by a blood vessel snagged on his key-chain.

'Indeed so, my lord, I fear that there has been...' Parminter tailed off, communicating with a flare of the left nostril that he would be uncomfortable discussing the matter in front of her ladyship without her ladyship's express permission to speak freely of distasteful matters.

Her Ladyship briefly raised the index and second fingers on her right hand by some fifteen or twenty degrees, thus indicating that her ladyship hadn't survived twenty years of active service in the army including some fifteen as a Half-Colonel in the S.A.S. without discussing one or two distasteful matters and learning how to not require a soft landing ground and the swift nasal application of sweet tincture of ammonium carbonate. Parminter demurred but was silenced with a twitch of her ladyship's cheekbone. He stiffened his back, looked to the horizon and gave such detail as he had.

'My lord, it appears that there has been some sort of election.'

'Election?'

'Election.'

'Popular vote thingy you mean? Damned unwashed scribblin' pencil crosses on crumpled ballot sheets as though whoever is in the House is anythin' to do with them?'

Poor Parminter looked as though he had just sniff-tested a vegan hen for egg binding only to discover that it had been a simple case of gaseous clench-buttock, unexpectedly explosively relieved by the mere mechanical motion of drumstick separation and the proximity of a nasal feature.

'I fear so, my lord. Worse yet...'

Lady Kensington-Chelsea blenched in anticipation. Lord Kensington-Chelsea furrowed his brow.

'The government majority was reduced?'

'Far worse than that, my lord, far, far worse.'

'A hung parliament?'

'If only, my lord...'

Lady Kensington-Chelsea sat down, knees bent at ninety-degrees and back ramrod rigid. Only her expensive Swiss finishing school training allowed her to do this in an emergency without a chair anywhere nearby.

'Oh no Parminter, you surely can't mean that... no, I refuse to countenance it.'

'The popular press, my lady, has announced that the forces of darkness have gained a clear majority in The House. They are terming it a "landslide".'

'Labour? A Labour government?'

'Indeed so, my lord. I have always thought the very concept to be an oxymoron and in the few days since the election it appears that my assertion has been proven quite correct.'

'Oh bugger' released Lord Kensington-Chelsea, his emotions pushed beyond propriety.

'Yes, my lord, I believe that is the Labour leader's name.'

'What? Are we now to reside under the purview of Prime Minister O'Bugger? Don't tell me that he's – forgive me dear, there's no polite way to say this – a Patrick too?'

'That is the rumour, my lord.'

'Feck me' expostulated her ladyship with unfocused eyes.

'Indeed so, my lady. Prime Minister O'Bugger has already moved into Number Ten and has installed his Civil Partner in residence.'

'And this "civil partner" of his, how is she called?'

'Claude, my lord. The new Prime Minister's civil partner is a gentleman, my lord – a gentleman of rather obvious French extraction.'

Despite having had no Swiss finishing school training his lordship attempted to join her ladyship in sitting upon an imaginary chair, ending up on the fringed Persian instead. He too was disinclined to notice his furniture-related faux pas. Oh God – "faux pas"! It had started already, the decline was afoot!

'French, you say? FRENCH? Good gravy. An Irish Prime Minister, a Labour government and escargots vivants en gelee avec de la sauce à l'ail cru to be on the menu at Number Ten. French you say? No chance I suppose that he's simply Swiss with a thick accent?'

'...or even just Belgian?' chimed in Lady K-C, with desperation.

'No chance at all I am afraid, my lord, my lady.' Parminter rearranged himself as though trying to prevent some sort of in-trouser accident of a seriously laundry-demanding nature. 'I believe...' he stuttered, 'I believe that the couple refer to themselves as – European.'

'Messrs oh bugger O'Reilly! European?What of Her Majesty, the Queen? How has Her Majesty taken the news?'

'My contacts in the Palace indicate that Her Majesty has gone to Balmoral, my lord, to shoot things. My sources are of the opinion that Her Majesty will be shooting lots of things.'

Lady Kensington-Chelsea passed out cold. Lord Kensington-Chelsea simply assumed the facial expression of a Bulldog with hypertension that had been sitting in the tropical sun too long eating wasps. After a few moments he found that he had to lean heavily on the cherrywood sideboard. It was either that, or fall down again.

'Parminter, I never thought that we should live to see this day. I placed my faith in the English Channel and have always assumed that it would protect us from such horrors. I see now that I was wrong. You're being awfully brave, and you're not telling us quite all, are you, Parminter? I see for myself the obvious corollary of these developments and I may be able to save you some discomfort. Is there now to be... socialism on this green and sceptred isle of ours?'

In using the term "ours" of course his lordship was not in fact joking, simply asserting the title of his legal deeds over eighty thousand acres of green and a couple of London boroughs of sceptred.

Parminter almost shed a tear. 'There has developed among the population a certain hitherto unseen over-familiarity with something that the political pundits are terming the The Welfare State, yes my lord.'

'Good gravy, Parminter! So, civilisation crumbles even after all our efforts to the contrary.'

'I have thus far avoided mentioning to my lord, my lady, all. Still, if it were done when 'tis done, then 'twere well it were done quickly. In tandem with these developments it appears that certain elements of the lower orders – the extremely lower orders – are now acting as fleas wagging the Establishment dog, if you will. The bankers, estate agents and some group calling themselves "no-win no-fee solicitors" are thriving, my lord, as though with a mind and a purpose of their own. One might imagine that the entire working class of the unfortunate county of Essex is now dressed in cheap off the shelf suit and tie and claiming commerce and all profit that lies within it. The City of London is not as it once was, my lord – it is acting... independently.'

Lord Kensington-Chelsea closed his eyes for a second as he absorbed the shock. Well, he closed one – the eyelid on the other having long since been nibbled away. 'Ye gods and little fold-up bicycles, they'll be trading on their own behalf before we know it.'

'I fear so, my lord, I fear so. Rumour has it that the lower house opened itself, my lord, without waiting upon Her Majesty's pleasure.'

'Damned rebels and revolutionaries! We shan't be able to put them to the gallows this time, Parminter, we needs must think of other ways.'

'Indeed so, my lord, although there would be a certain irony splattered about Number Ten if some way could be found to import the attentions of Madam Guillotine.'

'This is no joking matter, Parminter.'

'I wasn't joking, my lord.'

'And what has been the effect upon the staff here, Parminter? Is there panic or hysteria? How are they facing these terrifying social developments?'

'Not well, my lord. Half of the household is now on the The Benefits, and most of the remainder is on the The Three-Day Week. There's a work-to-rule in the stables, the mains electricity and gas have been cut off of course and I estimate that the household suppliers have increased their average tariff by some two-hundred percent to cover something they have dubbed "inflation".'

'Inflation? Balloons?'

'Prices, my lord.'

'Yes, well I obviously know nothing of such tawdry matters, the running of the household is your affair. You must liaise as best you can with the accountants, Parminter. They're due for another review visit next year, are they not?'

'They are, my lord. There is one encouraging item, in that my lord's petrol ration coupons arrived yesterday and I have had the five gallons for this month split between the Aston and the Rolls. Your lordship should be able to make it to the end of the estate driveway and back in either vehicle, just the once.'

Lord Kensington-Chelsea looked confused, more so than usual at breakfast or lunch or whatever it had been.

'Ration coupons? Are we at war, Parminter?'

'One would think so, my lord.'

'The end of the driveway? Would that be wise during wartime?'

'Yes, my lord – I thought my lord may wish to take a few pot-shots at the new pickets.'

'Pickets? Picket fences?'

'Flying pickets, my lord. Word has it that their placards are quite colourful, if less than fully literate.'

'Placards?'

'Yes, my lord, it seems that the pickets are expressing a desire to see the House of Lords abolished in favour of an elected second house. Some of the placards have gone so far as to question your lordship's father's part in the conception of your lordship, exaggerating the role played by one of your late father's baboons from the estate zoological gardens.'

Lady Kensington-Chelsea suddenly grasped Parminter's white-gloved hand, giving some clue to her ladyship's desperation and terror.

'Parminter – what is to become of us, Parminter? What are we to do? Might a baboon step in to help us again in some way do you think?'

'If I may make a suggestion my lady, perhaps your best course of action might be to carry on as the great families always have. This too shall pass.'

Lord Kensington-Chelsea looked thoughtful as he weighed the suggestion.

'Business as usual you say eh? Will that be possible?'

Parminter gave the slightest suggestion of a shrug. 'With minor adjustments, my lord, with minor adjustments. Immediately after the unfortunate news broke I sent word to the London house to have the shutters rolled down and the regular delivery of oysters and truffles cancelled. Jenkins is at this moment fitting the shatter-proof windscreen and the run-flat tyres to the horseboxes. Ammunition and supplies of comestibles are, as my lord will already be aware, always kept high against just such emergencies as this. We shall not be found wanting should the great unwashed seek us out.'

'Grr' said his lordship.

'Arg' agreed Lady Kensington-Chelsea, stepping over the remains of Harrison where the Chihuahuaii (the collective noun for Chihuahua) were feeding. 'It sounds like such a vicious, uncaring sort of world. Are we never to be at peace again?'

'Not until we crush the last Labour politician beneath our heel, m'dear, no. As Parminter alludes though, we are made of stern stuff and we can wait. We may weather the storm if we gird our loins and look to our laurels.'

'Grr. Loins...' said Lady K-C, salivating.

'Laurels...' said Lord K-C. 'Arrgh, that rather reminds me, Parminter – would it still be possible to call my tailors and have a couple of dozen of these run up in my usual cloths? I'm getting rather comfortable with the toga and the certain freedom of movement it affords may benefit one in the struggles to come in days future eh? There's nothing like bein' able to get one's knee up swiftly if it comes down to face to face negotiations. They don't like that, you know, they don't like that at all.'

'I shall make the call this morning my lord. Sandals to match?'

'Brown sandals for the country, black for town of course. If we may ever actually venture back to town until this unpleasantness is sorted. Let's look on the bright side – order the black too anyway.'

'Of course, my lord.'

'Now we must make plans. We shall have a crisis meeting – we must meet this menace head-on if we are to survive as bastions of civilisation. Grr. One hour, Parminter, then send up the estate manager, the head game-keeper and the Vicar. We must build our battlements against evil. Meantime, is that tasty little minx who used to light the fires in my library still on the books?'

'I believe that she is, my lord.'

'Splendid, then send her up immediately. Lady Kensington-Chelsea and I will second-breakfast before the meeting. We must keep our strength up if we, the right sort, are to win the day. Have the rest of the family woken and dressed, they must be warned and advised of the dangers. No-one is to go off the estate until we have the measure of these blood-curdling savage socialists.'

'Must we restrict them so?' interjected Lady K-C. 'It will so dampen their spirits. Might we not let them sleep in another day or two? Who knows when we shall sleep soundly in our beds again. Argh.'

'We must. The world has changed, the countryside will be awash with these ravening beasts and we must take action. The sooner we act the sooner we shall have acted. And so forth. Grr. My god, they'll eat us all alive given half a chance.'

The sun continued to rise in the sky of course, although to those of the estate it felt a little cooler, as though it were shining on others in addition to the long-standing righteous. The little people outside the estate gates cavorted and revelled in their new-found chaos, and they built their houses of cards upon the quicksand of vulgar commerce and cheap social fashion. The stones of the great houses cooled a little, naturally, but they would never grow completely cold as long as the thronging masses hobbled themselves with shackles of morality and with individual self-interest, while the ancient families walked the path of ageless generations, holding the land itself firm and embracing a slightly longer-term view.

Inside the great house, as through all the ages, those who would die cared for those who already had and yet who never really would, who never really could. Barely capable of conscious thought, slow of movement and devoid of all human affection, those unshackled by any morality or urge beyond the survival of their lineage reached out and fed upon us all, made us fear for our lives, made us look over our shoulders and sleep a sleep without depth. The ancient ones, the truly never-dead, those who would eat us alive without salt, pepper or gravy, do not walk among us, indeed do not walk openly at all for when hunger strikes we walk with arms outstretched to them. The great houses and the great families continue, as ever, to be the bedrock upon which relative horrors come and relative horrors go. Why else do you think they store their family protein in marble mausoleums if not against just such times?

'Grr, arg, my lord' said the acolyte, tugging at a forelock and wringing his cap, not quite certain who was really living and who was really just undead.

3 ROBOTS KNITTING WITH RUBBER NEEDLES

Two-Six quite enjoyed the process of walking. He walked to work, he walked home at lunch break to let the dog out and he walked home again in the evenings. There was something comforting about the rhythm of his ratchets and levers, step step whirr, lean forward and swing those arms. It eased the tension in his mainspring and warmed the thick black grease on his joints. Of necessity, Two-Six added to his walking routine a walk to the Great Grimsby Institute for the Mental Health of Local Automata. He opened a large event log for this new walk, since he would be performing it for many weeks and months to come.

The Institute was an imposing series of buildings – they had previously seen decades of service as a workhouse, correcting robots that had fallen on hard times or fallen into fallen ways. Entry was through a claustrophobic and imposing arched walkway through the main facade. Above the arch and carved in stone was the legend "UHRWERK MACHT FREI". Roads and pavements outside followed the familiar network pattern and were dotted with trees and garden hedgerows and traffic lights and people walking dogs among stout post-war housing and trim pre-supermarket gardens. The world beyond the archway though opened up onto a world organised around some quite different and – to the unqualified civilian eye – unfathomable intent. The pathways seemed organised not to facilitate easy transportation but to reinforce professional territories.

There were roads and pavements inside the complex, but they seemed disconnected, stunted and dreadfully abused things, not at all the proudly functional structures of the open world. Some were dedicated to pedestrian traffic only, others to odd electric carts and ambulance parking. Yellow lines and a plethora of signs bore dire warnings in re retributions of vast expense and lengthy inconvenience should regulations not be adhered to. There were trees, but these trees seemed to be living on borrowed time, to be frightened refugees, each sheltering in a square yard or less of exposed earth between the tarmac and the flagstones, and pinned down, shackled beneath cast iron grids with slots to allow just enough rainwater to penetrate for their survival, and no more. The exposed earth had the look of something that had long-since been sucked dry of all nutrients and it was doubtful that any worm could have broken his way through the crust on the surface, even on a rainy day. Each tree, each shrub seemed to have been planted in the dust from a hundred vacuum cleaners.

The buildings of the complex were many and varied and each had been carefully perverted from its original architectural intent. The laundry, originally where the workhouse inmates took in the washing of the townsfolk, now housed a long corridor of vending machines offering sugar, saccharine, salt and snack-sized sachets of Three-In-One oil. The original communal living quarters were now the workshops and the high-ceilinged, green-painted operating theatres. Administration offices filled the old Master's House which had grown extensions and alterations the way an old dead oak grows fungi, ivy and mosses. These offices were covered in mysterious damp fungi, ivy and mosses, and the old oak by the windows appeared to be dead, or at least to be wishing that it were so.

It was not a happy place.

Not a happy place at all.

It was all about as encouraging as the sight of an approaching enema-trolley with a squeaky wheel and being pushed by a trainee nurse called Gertrude Shovenhose whose ears had been cauliflowered by years spent as a prop-forward in the hospital's rugby team.

The original factory of the workhouse complex sat in the middle of this tired and dusty confusion and almost hummed with its power over all else. Nurses in oddly impractical uniforms – almost always in pairs – either gyrated around this central building as though in close orbit, or rushed to and from it like probes and comets. Chaps who must, from their mannerisms, have been doctors and consultants parked their Mercedes like guardians on the threshold of every door, and they sauntered in and out with an easy disregard for the orbiting nurses.

Two-Six scanned the nearby signage for anything useful. Parking a vehicle of any kind close to where he was standing would cost him a stupendous fine, towing fees, storage fees and retrieval fees plus the displeasure of the Institute's Authorities on the first offence, rising to express opprobrium on the third or subsequent offences. Ambulation in any direction other than towards the vast doors of the reception office seemed to be forbidden unless undertaken by an individual with a current and valid Staff Number and three forms of identification. Two-Six theorised that it was just possible that should he wander off this one approved track all of the nurses, orderlies, porters, doctors and consultants would freeze, then turn to him, point and scream in some unholy alien key. He decided to walk the indicated path. Even so, as he moved he felt himself registered and scanned from the periphery, all of those about were aware of his civilian presence even if they were unwilling to make optical contact due to concerns that he might present a problematic agenda requiring reallocation of already fully scheduled individual resources. Heck, he might even ask directions or something!

A blood-curdling and anguished scream escaped from the fabric of the stone building. No-one else seemed willing to notice.

Two-Six began to whistle, although even he himself could not have named the tune, and he approached with not some little ware.

The doors before him were obviously the doors to the inner sanctum, to some centre of operations. They were twice Two-Six's height and made of thick wood reinforced with riveted and bolted panels of steel. The locks – and there were many – looked to have been made by locksmiths of Norse legend and made as exemplars of their craft. One or two of them would need keys that might only be turned by hairy giants fed on cattle (eaten whole). Others seemed to require some intricate sequence of buttons to be pushed, probably to demonstrate that those wishing to gain entry were familiar with a secret sequence of Fibonacci primes.

Two-Six – as advised by a small painted invitation – rang the bell and stepped back. Only ringing the bell had been recommended but taking a step back somehow seemed wise. He checked overhead, possibly in response to some deep-seated trace memory from an earlier life involving boiling oil or burning coals. It was just possible that the inmates might harvest their own nuts and bolts to heat to white hot and then rain them down upon unwelcome guests.

In fact the door opened to the turn of a single, well-oiled handle and Two-Six was greeted not by something with a bolt through its neck and size eighteen slippers, but by a smile and an inviting and slick sweep of the hand. Do come in, said the oily voice.

'Hello, I'm here to visit...'

Two-Six found himself interrupted by something that looked like the Consultant of Consultants, the Doctor of Doctors, the Director of Directors. His hand was out to be shaken in greeting (but always somehow also just out of reach) as he glided over the ancient linoleum on Italian leather soled wheels and a cushion of buoyant arrogance. Two-Six was tempted for a split nano-second to ask whether this figure of authority's name might be Ozymandias.

'Welcome, welcome!'

'Hello – I'm here to visit...' tried Two-Six, again, in vain.

'Yes, yes, you've come to look upon our mighty works. Well, don't despair, we're awfully proud and terribly happy to welcome all. Come in, dear boy, come in and I'll give you the grand tour.'

'Thank you, but I just want to visit...'

'Of course, of course, and that's a large part of what we do here but you must see more, there's so much more and we do feel that our duty of care extends beyond those lunatics we lock away and encompasses their visitors too. Education is the name of the game and an ounce of prevention outweighs any patient premium paid quarterly in arrears, even if we are constantly seeking new funding for our new clinic, as you know. Let me guide you through our benefits.'

With that and with one of Two-Six's wrists clasped firmly in the proud doctor's grasp they began, and the door was closed behind them by some unseen mechanism called Nurse PA. Immediately it closed the air in the hallway absorbed and subsumed the fresh atmosphere that had leaked in from without, cloaking it in over-warm, humid, fetid exhalations. It seemed that anyone still human locked in behind those doors might struggle to find enough oxygen in the mix to sustain successful respiration. The air seemed laden with fluids and with mysterious moistures, as though each molecule – otherwise so sweet and salty by the sea or cold and crisp on windswept mountains – were personally scurrying about and emptying tiny bedpans and transporting kidney dishes filled with green and yellow used dressings. Two-Six felt a sudden empathy with his air filters, and briefly worried whether they would be up to the task. It was like breathing in some soup made from evaporated patients and atomised body-wastes. It hung around the interior like the aroma of a cheap Eau de Colon.

Another all-out scream rocked the building on its foundations and, just as police sirens head in the opposite direction to a fleeing crowd, so nurses rushed to the epicentre to administer a medical stifling.

'Really, I just want to see...'

'Of course, of course, and we'll show you it all. We're very proud of what we do and we have no secrets. Follow me, follow me dear chap and I'll show you that there are no lengths to which we will not go in our work.'

Two-Six already didn't doubt it.

'Our guests – for I discourage the use of the term "patients" or "inmates" or "nutters" as a little too negative – our guests come from all walks of life and some do so voluntarily and some find their way to us via two doctors and the practical operation of the Automaton Mental Health Act. The moment they walk, or indeed are carried, screaming and strapped to a porter's trolley, through those doors my good fellow we are responsible for their wellbeing and recovery. We maintain our treatments at the cutting edge of

Artificial Neuroscience. No treatment is too expensive or too experimental if it will help improve the lives of our guests.'

At this point the good doctor somehow dodged while also making it plain that he refused to acknowledge an explosion of brass nuts, bolts and enamelled body panels from a door to a side-ward, followed by a crash-trolley of tools being rushed in and the door gently, but very firmly being closed. It appeared that a guest had suffered some sort of disastrous mainspring discomnobulation during an expensive treatment.

'The cog and cam brain, while of course the greatest wonder of the sentient universe, is, as you will know of course, prone to certain maladies and morbidities. My work here at the Institute is focused on our becoming a centre of excellence, is focused on helping in some small way to both alleviate the sufferings of those brought to our attention. We seek only to progress the science of automata-psychology, cog-psychiatry and cam-based neuro-surgery.'

An orderly hurried past towards the scene of the discomnobulation, carrying a huge monkey-wrench. Dr Ozymandias saw all, acknowledged nothing – even when the orderly jogged his elbow as he passed.

'To that end we eagerly embrace all of the teachings of the masters; Maiilard, Vaucanson, Friedrich von Knauss, Baron von Kempelen, Pierre and Louis Jaquet-Droz, Abbot Mical, and Kintzing.'

There was a barely audible "ding" from a timer, and Dr Ozymandias stopped briefly at this point in the tour while a personal assistant wound the key in his back, and did so with a reverence bordering on the manner of the acolyte. Dr Ozymandias detained the assistant and with an expansive gesture enquired whether Two-Six's mainspring might be in need of refreshment. Two-Six indicated that it was not, but expressed gratitude for the kind offer. The acolyte looked somehow relieved, as though he had just escaped being called upon to work out of his assigned and long-held high grade. Two-Six suspected that, had a few turns of the old key-in-the-back been required or accepted, an awful lot of OCD-esque hand washing would have ensued soon after in some well-plumbed side-room.

The good doctor led Two-Six through to a glaringly bright suite of rooms, the door to which bore the proud legend “Triage and Initial Therapy”.

‘When a guest comes to us, in but whatever manner, they are first assessed and initial palliatives are administered to determine whether perhaps their condition may be tractable to the simpler, more mundane treatments known only to those in the profession. Why, we sometimes work wonders in this room!’

Two-Six’s optics swept across a waiting room that was full to the brim of tearful female automata and of swivel-eyed, gibbering males. The curtain to a treatment cubicle had fallen open and an Institute nurse could be seen inside, repeatedly slapping a patient and recommending strongly that she “pull herself together”.

The patient appeared to not be responding positively, remaining instead indolent and unresponsive. She held onto her handbag as though it were a Teddy bear, and her free fingers clenched and unclenched on the thin pink paper of her examination gown. Her treatment was then escalated to a violent shaking of the shoulders followed by a glass of water and then more applications of finely-judged medical slapping about the face. Dr Ozymandias stepped forward, smiling contentedly, nodded approval to the nurse and tugged the cubicle curtain closed.

In the next cubicle a male automaton in a blue paper hospital gown and still strapped to an ambulance trolley was being encouraged back to full and proper mechanical mental health by a crash team of experts. Two fully-wound female nursing automata with arms folded and noses well aloft were shouting at him to “man up” and warning him that “everyone was laughing at him” while another was skilfully waggling her pinkie finger at him and suggesting that his breakdown may have its roots in an excess free space in his trouser gusset. A “nut job” consultant shrink was whispering in the patient’s ear, enquiring as to whether he thought himself a mechanical man or a toy mouse.

In the meanwhile the seated queue was kept under control and prepared for their own therapy by patrolling security guards who had been trained to mime pulling a handkerchief through the head from one ear to the other while concurrently putting out their tongues and rolling their eyes. Where a waiting prospective patient was being of particular embarrassment to the sane the security guards rolled screens around them to prevent the spread of discomfort. A nurse worked her way down the line with a clipboard, taking domestic details and assessing the extent of each patient's worthiness or worthlessness on a scale of "Just Feels Like Bothering Everyone Else With Their Problems" to "Complete And Utter Failure In Life".

Dr Ozymandias continued. 'So you see, no opportunity is lost during the process, we make full use of every opportunity of contact with our guests to encourage them back to normality under their own steam, so to speak.'

At that point an as-yet undiagnosed lunatic seated on the front row of the waiting area hissed a little steam and seemed to be losing pressure generally. The non-lunatic accompanying them began to fiddle around familiarly with kindling and a match, and looking about for a possible source of boiler-water and coal.

Two-Six's internals hiccoughed a little as though there were some swarf in his oil, and a couple of minor cogs in his cognitive centre jumped a couple of teeth.

Once back out in the main corridor of the Institute they were assailed by a small gaggle of assistants waiting for Dr Ozymandias to rubber stamp hospital notes and medication prescriptions. Two-Six was amazed by the speed with which Dr Ozymandias's rubber-stamp attachment moved down the line. Ink pad, splat, splat, splat, splat, initials, splat – ink pad again – splat, sign, initials, initials, initials – splat, splat. Two orderlies rushed past, chasing an over-wound over-wrought guest dressed in just one fluffy slipper and a pink bri-nylon nightie. The guest had somehow opened a window and was doing her best to get both legs over the sill, presumably with a view to legging it for the horizon.

The good doctor remained quite unperturbed and led the way through to the more serious therapy rooms. The sound of a casement window slamming followed by the buckling of leather restraints followed their steps like guilty little secrets tugging at their heels to be acknowledged.

‘We embrace of course all of the latest techniques and are tireless in their application.’ Dr Ozymandias stepped over a small scuffle on the linoleum floor and indicated that Two-Six should take care when following. Two large orderlies each had a knee in the back of a guest and were forcibly winding her key. ‘As you see here, sometimes a guest refuses sustenance, preferring the peaceful oblivion of a purposefully relaxed mainspring but our Charter, and indeed our Hippocratic Oath does not allow us to allow our patients to harm themselves. Forced energy application is distasteful, but necessary and I assure you, quite painless. If we cannot keep our guests fully wound we cannot hope to offer them the wonderful cures now available to us, and we all of us do so enjoy curing our guests.’

Two-Six experienced a little discomfort during a brief actuation of his empathy cams, a couple of them appearing to have come loose. They rattled around inside him as though on eccentric drive-shafts, and he feared he would have to disconnect them entirely before long or risk further damage to his internals.

The lights in the Institute dimmed to the accompaniment of a thunderous electrical buzzing, and one or two of the fluorescent strip-lights high overhead clanked and jolted before recovering. Dr Ozymandias smiled and counted off the seconds on his fingers; three, two, one – and then came the correctly timed second application. The lights all dimmed once more and a contract-cleaner’s floor-polisher briefly stalled. The good doctor pushed through some swing doors into the Electro-Convulsive Therapy Suite and ushered Two-Six inside.

‘You see? No expense or effort spared! We have the very latest alternating and direct currents available, with battery back-up systems and silver-plated forehead paddles.’

Ozymandias wandered across to a patient who appeared to Two-Six’s untrained eye to be suffering from an excessive indulgence of the saints. The saints in question being Saint Vitus with regard to her dancing like a frog cadaver in a biology class, and Saint Elmo with regard to a coronal discharge from the patient’s more vital cranial vitals.

Dr Ozymandias donned elbow-length rubber gauntlets, clipped

dark-blue welder's pince-nez to his nose and pulled down the enormous wall-mounted switch behind the patient, giving her another thirty seconds at thirteen amps, two shillings and sixpence.

'We have absolutely no idea why this treatment works but it seems to produce a brief beneficial remission in almost half of cases. The current treatment is controversial of course and a ruddy placebo raisin has been shown to be equally inexplicably effective, but you don't get that lovely aroma of overheated insulation and hot Bakelite with a placebo current, currant or raisin. Besides, I love these big industrial switches and the bzzt-bzzt noise, don't you? Aren't these paddles just the dinkiest thing you've seen since a Swiss clockwork rectal thermometer with cuckoo indicators?'

The good doctor gave his "guest" another minute at full-power followed by a half-dozen quick throws of the switch because she danced on the treatment table so well.

Two-Six's hydraulics over-tightened his waste-duct valve and he was obliged to log a task to later go down there with a spanner to free off his clenched arse.

When a run-down looking nurse got a chance to offer the ECT patient's notes to Dr Ozymandias she also ventured to whisper that the patient had, in fact, already had the maximum treatment and had been lying there awaiting return to her ward. Dr Ozymandias wafted away the blue smoke haze that had been hanging around them and adopted a conspiratorial tone. 'Of course, pone of the best things about ECT is the long-lasting amnesia eh? Nurse, have the scorch marks on the patients temples re-enamelled before she wakes up and before any relatives see her please. Don't forget to check for any blown fuses and to replace as necessary.'

A less fortunate "guest" in the same suite who was being treated by juniors chose that moment to fizz, glow like an old-fashioned electric fire and then burst into flame. There followed an extremely well-practiced routine with some very generously proportioned CO2 fire extinguishers, so much so that when Dr Ozymandias led Two-Six back out into the corridor through the swing doors they gave the appearance of leaving some sort of discotheque, briefly spilling fire-red and electric-blue flashes, dry ice and the shouts of some sort of modern popular beat combo musical act about them.s

'Ah - surgery!' he pronounced, adjusting his new blue pince-nez but flinging his rather jolly black rubber gauntlets to the world behind him over one shoulder.

'Surgery?'

'Surgery. When all high-tech non-invasive treatments fail we are not afraid to explore good old-fashioned surgery sir in our quest for universal sanity!'

They walked on some yards down the corridor, away from the hell-fires of electro-convulsive therapy and towards the crisp, cutting-edge surgical theatres. Like clockwork, for that is what they were, assistants appeared and both Two-Six and the Doctor-Director walked arms first into proffered gowns, masks, Wellington boots and those head-band lights with the funny reflectors and drop-down magnification lenses. Dr Ozymandias seemed more in his element than hitherto. I fancy he liked the flow of the material and was not averse to a little sartorial accessorising.

'Sometimes, my dear chap, you may talk until you're blue in the face but there may be no alternative to surgery.'

'Surgery?'

'Surgery – lopping bits off, cutting things out and occasionally just wildly mincing the innards.'

Ozymandias performed a quite worryingly passable impersonation of the bread-dough making attachment on a Kenwood Chef Mk IV.

'Lop, cut, mince. Works wonders. Again, we have no idea why and it's really not very effective for the guest but it does help the relatives so. Talk to them in a blood-covered gown while juggling with a loved one's disconnected fore-lobes and they really appreciate that we're doing all that we can and doing more than they ever could. Gives the whole profession a shot of some serious je sait exactly quoi too – one's peers in the allied medical professions will never take one seriously unless one does a spot of surgery. We dive in where they fear to tread. Trepanning and lobotomies – scares the hell out of other professionals of course but all you need really is confidence. Stick the old scalpel in and broggle about a bit. NURSE! If you're going to bother at all then please put some weight behind that Black & Decker, we don't have all day for you to grind your way through the loony's skull. I mean guest's skull. Use a hammer drill. We need a decent hole to release the oil pressure otherwise there's no point in bothering, no point at all. Does that drill bit even have a point? Get a fresh one immediately!'

Two-Six looked a little less than convinced. 'Isn't there some really delicate machinery, cogs and cams and things, behind the forehead plating? You surely can't just shove a chisel in there and mash things up and expect them still to work?'

'Oh, the guests are never quite the same again of course, but they are usually a lot more docile and often even quite suited to menial re-employment – working as doorstops and draught-excluders and suchlike. Let's face it, they were barking mad to begin with and there's never hope for full recovery no matter what the whining do-gooders say, so we may as well salvage what we can. Better a doorstop than a full stop eh?'

With that the good doctor called for a sterilised lump hammer and the next patient on the lists.

Two-Six backed up against the wall of the theatre and thought of bunny rabbits until Ozymandias had finished his precision surgery. As he waited, working through all of the names he remembered from Watership Down, he felt mechanisms buried within him making the necessary arrangements to disconnect his sense of belonging gland and shut down his willingness to participate in the grand scheme of things registers. The requisite disconnected cams and levers were passed by internal conveyor belt to join his repository of 'Oddly Unknown Nuts and Apparently Spare Bolts Down Through The Years'.

'Doctor – I really shouldn't be in here.'

'That's what they all say dear boy. Oh hang on though – I remember now, you're just a visitor aren't you. There are really only two qualifications to be in the Institute you know – you're either sane or you're insane, and either will get you through the door, just with differing responsibilities. Are you absolutely certain which you are?'

'I'm beginning to wonder.'

'That's the spirit! Question everything – it's the only way to make progress!'

'Alright - why do you do this? You can't imagine that taking a hacksaw to someone's skull is a plausible or effective treatment, surely?'

'Don't question me, my lad, I am the professional here. Question the system, question Bamber Gascoigne if you must, but don't dare to question me. We know what we're doing, and it's based on centuries of experimentation and experience.'

'Look, I just came in to visit...'

'...yes, yes, un-scheduled visits are all very well but I must convince you of our competence and give you that rosy glow of investor confidence – can't have you communicating doubts and such to the guests. Won't help their recovery one bit!'

'Their recovery?'

'Splendid idea – we'll have a tour of the Recovery Suites next. Recovery and Long-Term Therapy – then you'll see the value of what we do here in the Institute. Follow me.'

'Doctor, I'm not certain that I can see any value in slapping hysterics, telling people to pull themselves together, using gender stereotypes to bully people into returning to silence, frying their brains with mega-amps, drilling holes in their head or liquidising the contents of their skulls. I had thought that current treatments would be a little less reliant on mains current for one thing and somewhat less... primitive.'

'Primitive you say? Would you rather that these automata be simply discarded or left to their own devices? At best returned to their manufacturer for recycling? For that is surely what would happen if we were not here to help.'

'Mental health treatments can't surely be quite so... medieval, can they? It's just that I thought – I imagine that everyone who has no experience of mental health treatments would think, would hope – that, well, that the treatments might now be a little more sophisticated in the closing years of the twentieth century.'

'Sophisticated? These treatments have been carefully adapted from Human treatments, developed over centuries. It's not as though we are barbarians, we no longer simply dismantle the barking mad automata or lock them out of sight. Would you have us return to the days of the ducking stool? Aha – we're here! Hydrotherapy.'

'Hydrotherapy?'

'Yes – alternating hot and cold baths, total immersion, sometimes just a general hosing down.'

'Dunking in water? Doesn't that cause rather a lot of rust on the patients?'

'Of course, of course my dear fellow, but you can't make a hen without first breaking an egg. There are side-effects but we do feel that the benefits outweigh the risks. Water can be wonderfully therapeutic in the right hands. Think of the last time you spent a day at the seaside and how happy you were.'

An orderly hurried past with a trolley laden with a hundred kilos of freshly crushed salt-water ice for a guest's bath.

Two more orderlies were wrestling with a flailing canvas python of a fire-hose, trying to aim at a guest who was shackled naked to the white-tiled wall over a minging drain of industrial proportions.

'Costs us a fortune on the water meter of course, but it's the only way.'

'Only way to treat this patient?'

'No, the only way to do hydrotherapy, you can't do it properly without water. I know, we've tried but talking about it or describing it just isn't the same and a bucketful no matter how carefully or unexpectedly thrown just doesn't seem to be sufficient. My theory is that the efficacy of the treatment is tied to a cunning formula relating the number of water molecules in the afflicted automaton to the number of water molecules in the therapy flow. In inverse of course, to the root power squared. Ten to fifteen minutes for each separately diagnosed condition per guest seems sufficient, provided that the water is cold enough.'

The guest in question appeared to be developing a distinct disinclination towards independent or meaningful motion. One of the side-effects seemed to be a certain amount of rapid oxidisation with attendant seizure of the joints.

Dr Ozymandias moved on. 'Vocal therapy suite – all

monitored centrally and automatically with scanning for keywords and phrases such as “toilet training trauma” or “breast-feeding rejection” or any such similar.’

Dr Ozymandias opened the door onto a room filled with a dozen black couches, each of which was host to a recumbent automaton speaking into a dangling microphone. Some were weeping, others were ranting. All seemed to have a story to tell and were busy telling it to no-one in particular.

‘Someone listens to all of these?’

‘Oh good grief, no – the output is recorded and immediately archived. We find that the act of simply talking is sufficient unto the purpose. The central computer then scans the tapes and associates those who mentioned key phrases with the appropriate professional or treatment regimen. If, for example, a guest in here shares anxiety caused by manufacturer abandonment or adolescent peer-rejection then an appropriate course will be added to the guest’s treatment and administered at a later date. Supportive hugs for the female guests, affectionate shoulder punches for the males. Usually though we just wipe the tapes. Have you any idea how much open-reel tapes cost? You wouldn’t believe how long these dribbling idiots can witter on for too – endless yacking about how they were never loved enough or never given the right toys or built too short or too fat or too tall or too skinny. Sheesh! Yack yack yack yack yack. Pure drivel, but it keeps them occupied for hours on end. We usually let the cleaners into the wards while the guests are all stacked neatly in here, it makes tidying so much easier.’

‘Doesn’t anyone ever realise that no-one is actually listening to them?’

‘Gosh no! Whenever they talk to a member of staff we just look concerned, raise an eyebrow, pretend to scribble a note or recommend bed rest. Works a treat. Well, have you seen enough? Is it time to hand over that cheque?’

‘Cheque? What cheque?’

‘Your investment in the clinic – you are here to invest aren’t you? Is that not the reason for your visit? You won’t find a more lucrative business than healthcare provision, and no part of that more free from liability and risk than mental healthcare provision.

Good grief, all of our customers are barking at the moon when they're brought in, it's not as though we can make them any worse whatever we do – have you ever tried to sue a psychiatrist or psychologist? Can't be done old boy – it's far too subjective a matter for the courts. This business is as safe as houses and makes more money than an actual oil well.'

'No. I'm here to visit...'

'...Visit?'

'Yes, if you'll ever let me finish that sentence I'm here to visit a patient.'

'A guest – as I told you, we have a strict policy of calling them guests. Patient implies that they are ill and may somehow be cured by some ruddy miracle. Look here – why have you been wasting my time if you're just here to visit one of the loons? Why have you been impersonating an investor?'

'I haven't been – I just rang the bell and you dragged me in. I'm just here to visit my...'

'...Look, you keep saying you're here to visit but you never tell me who you're here to visit.'

'That's because you keep interrupting me!'

'Do not!'

'Do so! I am here to visit...'

'...Yes, yes, we've heard all of that part before – but who are you here to visit? Who? Who? Who?'

'... My mother. I just want to visit my mother. Six-Five.'

'Well why didn't you say so instead of impersonating an investor and getting an expensive tour of the facility? Do you have some sort of mental health problem? Come through here – your mother is receiving the very best of therapy although I must wonder if you ought not really to take her place.'

With that the Director, Doctor Ozymandias, opened the door onto an unloved hangar of a room occupied by fifty or more souls in damp high-backed chairs, each of them knitting feverishly with rubber needles and an endless supply of wool spooling out from a central, industrial reel.

Two-Six scanned the room and waved. 'Hello mother! Can you hear me, Mother?' Six-Five set aside her knitting for a moment and waved back. She looked to be slightly singed around the temples. Two-Six coughed and was surprised to find that he had brought up all of his remaining emotion cams and the little system of levers that had hitherto functioned to give him any confidence in "professionals" and "The System".

'I'm surprised that you brought those up' was almost all that Doctor Ozymandias had to say on the matter (the matter in Two-Six's hand). 'Do you have any other symptoms?'

'None! None at all – I'm perfectly fine, thank you! Cogito ergo checksum. I'm sane. Perfectly sane.'

Doctor Ozymandias shook his head, disgusted, and retreated to his office, there to continue work on his ground-breaking and inoffensive thesis "On The Cost-Effective Installation of Self-Tightening Screws In The Common Lunatic". 'Nobody's ever quite perfectly sane old chap, we'll get you in the end and then you'll see, you'll see...'

4 JE PENSE IT'S ALL GOING VERY BIEN

England's Primed Minister Mr Boris and Her Majesty Elizabeth, The Queen Person of England, Gibraltar, Lundy and Alderney were really being kept very busy indeed. Not so busy that they couldn't take an interest in world affairs though; provided that they left the serving hatch open they could hear everything that went on in the World Government Chamber while they worked. There were great gobs of soap suds clinging to Elizabeth's Marigolds rubber gloves as she listened, and One couldn't help but hear that little advertising ditty going endlessly around in One's head – Hands that dig ditches can feel soft as your face, with wild green Fairy Liquid. It had always been a mystery to One where wild green fairies might be found exactly, at least in commercial rather than merely social quantities. Boris was drying the mugs with a souvenir "Tower of London" tea-cloth and hanging them back on their little hooks in the cupboard. He took extra care while drying Angular Merkel's "Ich bin das big Caesar around here" mug. Wouldn't do to break that one eh!

'Do you think they'll be ready for some more snacks?' said Elizabeth, changing the water in the plastic washing-up bowl for hot fresh, and blowing bubbles and making rude asthmatic-rectum noises with the nearly empty Fairy Liquid bottle. Fortunately, she had brought two bottles with her, and once One had rinsed this one out to make certain of using the very last of the contents, One would fetch the other from one's tartan wheelie-bag.

'Could be – the cream scones were going down awfully well when I took the last tray in' replied Boris, checking on the Mr Kipling jam tarts he was warming in the oven – a tricky procedure, since tarts need to be just warm enough to put life into them but not so hot as to burn folk's tongues. Not every foreign person knew quite how to safely approach a warmed jam tart.

'Better go and check, Boris – we don't want them to get hungry or thirsty. Take a fresh jug of Kia-Ora and one of Sunny-D with you, and do try to not get in the way this time.'

Boris excused himself through the foyer-crush, past Mr American President Obama (who had his hand stuck up inside a vending machine, trying to loosen the prawn-flavour crisps he'd paid for but which had refused to fall from their shelf). A Secret Service Agent wearing Aviators and a curly-wired ear-piece had his back to the machine, trying to rock it without making too much noise. The rest of the CIA were pooling their cash to see if between them they could just put the money in again and save any potential unpleasantness with the janitor.

Boris crept into the main room, trying to make sure that his plastic-soled shoes didn't squeak. A security guard slipped the velvet rope back onto its hook after Boris had passed through, and accepted a decadent western Haribo sweetie in payment for his kind assistance, trying to get to the tasteless, gelatinous lump of pure crap out of the bag without rustling it too loudly. While Boris worked his way around the room clearing empties as he went he nodded to David Cameron. David was probably the most important person in the whole of the World Government Chamber that day. He was working hard in a corner, tugging at his punka-wallah string and stirring the warm air just as hard as he could. Gosh, trooper that he was he'd even dressed for the part and was very proud of his "pigeon head" movements.

The four-hundred-strong proportionally-represented Chinese delegation was proposing an all-out combined attack with the world's nuclear arsenal. India's nine-hundred strong proportional delegation favoured a Bollywood team of has-been space cowboys going up there with some serious C5 plastique and a few good musical numbers. The sole representative from the All-Africa Continental Alliance, Mr Pieter Van Niekerk-Pretorius, suggested that maybe suddenly stopping the Earth's molten core from rrrho-tayting yah would allow the planet to sort of hop, yah, rright ovah the comet and then it could all be rre-star-ted somehow after-wards eh, peh-haps by lots of chaps with big sticks and some sort of lee-verr ah-rrangement you know? A lot of folk agreed that he was probably on to something there.

The greatest popularly scientific minds of the era: Osbourne; Minogue; Cole; Cowell; Barlow; Ramsay, Rhodes, Lawson, Vickery; Oliver and all of the others took notes and conferred and nodded among themselves, sagely. Stopping the core sounded like it had a chance but they weren't sure that there was enough Unobtainium in the civilised world to build the necessary craft to take the necessary nukes and the necessary affirmative cross-section of Bollywooden-American stereotypes down there. Did it always have to be "down there" anyway? Down was so depressing a direction. They ventured that the operation would have better chances of success if they went "up" to the problem, possibly well-dressed and with nice haircuts and with an expedition anthem chosen by panel-overridden popular vote at £3 to £5 per text message plus the network cost of the text please ask a responsible adult before using the phone. They suggested the crew be culled from the entire cast of "Come Dancing Yeah?" for gravitas and for technical expertise with handling huge red-hot balls of iron-nickel alloy.

His Holiness the Dalai Lama stood to speak and reminded everybody present that the important thing was to blow that filthy mother out of the sky. It didn't have to be a pretty solution, it just had to be a violent one. He wondered if some sort of flying scissors-kick followed by a chop to the Solar solar plexus might serve to re-balance Solar Yin and Yang, if he'd understood worldly scientific matters correctly.

The Sicilian Pontiff showed his support for His Holiness's proposal with a high-five followed by the upturned flat palms gesture and a series of nods to all corners. Yeah, baby – work the room! When His Papal Holiness made eye contact with the Chief

Rabbi his gesture turned, of course, into a less polite chin-flick. This was immediately re-wrapped in a warm "oy vey, it's rude that you are" gesture and flung back at him with a dismissive hand. 'It's solutions shmolutions we need already, not violence – we got enough violence. Always with the violence.'

The various factions, fractions and fractious factions of the Middle East had a show of hands among themselves and immediately raised oil prices, to help out as best they could.

Lizzie came into the chamber help Boris collect the rest of the empties and she positively whizzed around the delegates offering an open black plastic rubbish bag for their paper serviettes and plastic cups. Why, why, why, she wondered, was there always so much fruit and jelly wasted and why did no-one ever eat their sandwich crusts? The pile of pilchard sandwiches seemed to be completely untouched for some reason.

It was agreed by the grown-ups present that the world was going to split the nuclear arsenal and try both of the favoured solutions. The Earth's core would be stopped from spinning by popular vote and by nuclear fission while the rest of the arsenal would be lobbed as hard as possible in the direction of the big bright thing in the sky, yeah? The comet would thus dissipate like shares in a dodgy dot com start-up and our lovely blue marble planet would take a little hop in celebration over any remaining debris and land back exactly on target ready for the re-opening of the world's stock exchanges. The planet's core would then be shot to life again one day in the week following by plucky and heroic civilians with some quite large small-arms until it rrhotated yah correctly, just in time for a "the happy holidays" and some tax rises and more benefits cuts for ugly people. In a stroke of genius the film rights were to be sold with the sole proviso being that the film be a serious one and star Colin Firth and Huge Grant.

Boris and Lizzie came to the end of their shift and handed over the reins of the kitchen duty to Mr Vladimir who began to tie on a lovely gaily-coloured pinafore and announced that he was going to whip up a batch of nice hot Shchi and a tray of vodka-fudge brownies for later. He thought it important to keep the world leaders' blood-sugar levels quite high while they were hammering out the more manly-man technical man's man details of saving the world for Hugh Manity. As Lizzie bit off a loose thread from the lining of her old coat Vladimir took the opportunity to slap her on the arse, give her a hug and call her "tovarishch". Well, I say "slap" but it really was more as though he was trying to work some heat into the royal gluteus maximusses, or smooth down some bread dough or something. The passion of the snog that followed quite caught Lizzie by surprise, even for an old queen!

As Lizzie and Boris quietly slipped out of the building via the "Volunteers and Tradesmen" entrance they gave discreet little waves, smiles and raised chimp-communication eyebrows to the delegates from the other third-world nations who were also hanging about, anxious to help the Germans and the Indians and the Chinese. Being careful to avoid causing unnecessary fuss they whispered their final end-of-shift pleasantries such as je pense it's all going very bien and do please excuse us por favour, estamos das Ingles and bugger mim, mas minhas mãos são macias como ser uma fada's arse verde do selvagem.

It was only when Boris and Lizzie were finally kicking their heels at the railway station in Brussels, waiting for an off-peak train that would connect with their cross-channel ferry that a plan settled between them like a friendly wet dog wriggling down on the settee.

'Lizzie – everyone's so awfully busy with all of these dashed clever plans with nuclear missiles and things that I do wonder if we're not missing something, something rather obvious.'

Her Majesty clutched her enormous over-night handbag even tighter and looked up and down the deserted platform for some obvious mistake. 'No, I don't think we've missed anything - this is Platform 3, we can get to Calais from here if we change at Dusseldorf and Prague and pay the extra fare but the cheap train only runs once every four continental metric hours.'

The mere mention of Dusseldorf suddenly seemed like a friendly elephant in the room and they both broke out into the laughter of co-conspirators after which Her Lizzie The Queen had to dab her eyes with a Kleenex. Boris put it into words. 'No, but seriously Maj, I do worry that we're not playing our part fully in world affairs.'

That brought them both out in a spate of titters again and one of them had to rush into the Ladies to freshen their knickers. If only Boris hadn't used the word "affairs"!

Boris fed a shilling into the Cadbury's Chocolate vending machine (provided all over "Abroad" by the English embassies for the emergency succour of weary Travellers and Ex-Pats). He tugged out the heavy drawer under the stack of oddly-sized, over-priced Fruit & Nut. Her Maj accepted a piece and nibbled thoughtfully while she listened. Boris was awfully clever; when he spoke it was usually worth taking at least a moment to nod and cock an ear.

'Do listen Maj, do - this could potentially be terribly good for the morale of England.'

'Chocolate?'

'No – well, yes, but I meant my idea.'

They were interrupted in state affairs by the slow local train arriving. It stopped at every station like some incontinent dog but it was the only connection that offered "Third Class" fares and was all that their official travel allowances would stretch to. Lizzie and Boris shuffled through the carriages with their bags, looking for a couple of seats together. The train was quite busy with ancient continental old ladies in widow's weeds and rosary beads taking she-goats to market, and with enigmatic old chaps in striped jerseys and berets clutching greasy spare parts for "les Citroen Deux Cheveaux avec le cunning canvas roofings". They found a couple of forward-facers and claimed them for England. Boris swept the garlic off the seats and Liz put their luggage in the rack overhead between a couple of "economic refugees" and some Belgian chap's Puch Maxi moped with fitted basket.

'Oh Boris – I'm knackered!' expostulated Her Maj as she arranged her sensible reversible Mackintosh and fished in her pocket for a Polo mint (the de-luxe brand, without the hole). 'Still, the show must go on – do tell One about your idea. Cheer one up!'

Boris lit his unpretentious Meerschaum pipe, the one with his own likeness carved into the bowl and a lid covered in a mop of real yak hair. He stroked his new moustache, preparing it to wax lyrical.

'Ah yes, well – it's a bit technical so as a girl you might not understand it all of course, but here goes anyway.'

By Dusseldorf they'd hammered out all of the less technical details and were eager to get home to put the plan into action. By Calais they were positively desperate for civilisation.

Finally, on the drizzle-bound ferry, Her Maj tied on a headscarf as they patrolled the upper windblown decks and Boris slipped his tweed cap into a pocket rather than lose it overboard in a gust. It was all jolly bracing and jolly refreshing after the cloying over-personal fleshiness of the The Continent.

'Will Phil be meeting you off the ferry?'

'I do hope so.'

'May I beg a lift?'

'Absolutely, yah. He knows I'll have a couple of pints of duty-free and two-hundred ciggies with me so he should be in a shooting brake, probably the Jag. There'll be plenty of room if you don't mind sharing the back seat with the dogs.'

Boris was struggling to keep his pipe lit in the damp spray thrown up by the blunt ro-ro bow, even with the little lid with real yak-hair toupe.

'Can you try to explain to One again some of the more practical elements of your plan? Someone will probably ask One and One doesn't like to seem too ignorant on such matters.'

'Oh. No. Yes of course. Well – and do stop me if I use any big scientific words, but it struck me that everyone's awfully keen on shooting things or blowing them up, on making the planet do somersaults, that sort of thing. I wonder if perhaps there might not be a simpler, less ostentatious solution to the comet problem.' He paused again while Lizzie cupped her hands around yet another match for him. She inhaled some of the thick, blue tobacco smoke – all ladies of a certain age love the smell of good tobacco (when smoked by a gentleman of course, not by themselves or some pretentious oik). 'I wonder if we ought not to send a couple of chaps up there to have a look and see what might be done – er, before the world's combined nukes arrive of course.'

Her Maj turned back towards the thickly-painted rust-knobbled railings of the Seal-Ink ferry, deep in thought. She caught a strand of hair that had escaped from her headscarf and tucked it back under just as the White Cliffs of Audi hove into view on the grim, grey horizon (re-named in a lucrative sponsorship deal Kent County Council had made on the shush hush-hush, much to the annoyance of Essex). 'However would we fund something like that? How much might it cost the nation?'

Boris stopped chewing on his pipe and sucked salty air through his teeth (at least he'd remembered to put them in). 'Well – we could use the old Cold-War Morris Space-Traveller fleet, they're in mothballs somewhere – in a hangar at RAF Mothbawlls, I think. It would need fifty or sixty gallons of fuel. Some space-sandwiches of course – you could knock those up, surely? I'm sure that the crew chaps would volunteer, if we told them how important it might be to everyone.'

Maj folded her arms and leaned on the rail, this time to face the smoke stack. 'I don't know, Boris – sixty gallons of fuel. Sixty! Even if we could get the coupons. Are we talking two, three, four or five star petrol?'

Boris stood in that decisive way chaps often do when they've made their minds up. He looked out to sea. 'I still have some of my birthday money left over – I'd be more than happy to use that.'

'Oh Boris – are you sure? Weren't you saving up to go skiing or something?'

'Won't be any decent skiing for quite a while if this little "Extermination Level Event" gets past us. We must do something. I feel so responsible – and it won't just be the pink bits on the map that get knocked about a bit of that thing lands. There'll be foreigners too. Abroad will be damaged, and that will mean Overseas Aid bills.'

Maj gave him a swift hug and led him by the elbow back towards the pedestrian passenger exit deck.

'Alright then – but we'll get receipts for everything. You will be paid back, I promise you. Even if we have to sell something else to the Chinese. Wales or something –Beijing were asking about Wales only last year. I'm sure we could do a good deal there that might cover sixty gallons of BP's finest. Why do they still call it "BP" when it's plainly no longer anything of the sort?' Boris, for the life of him, didn't know either.

The two of them queued patiently with the other passengers for the burly brutes of crewmen who would fling them over the side of the ship onto the quay with their luggage. Maj tipped them a shiny thruppence each and pointed out roughly where she'd like to land. Oh how her bruised and now a bit black as well as royal blue buttocks rued the day she had been born into a universe entirely parallel to yours, dear reader, except for the fact that no-one had ever invented the gangplank. Infinite diversity in infinite combination has some devilishly interesting implications in the detail, ne c'est pas?

A while later – roughly about a week - the Cabinet Office was, as it had been for roughly about the past week, a blur of very practical chaps in white coats expounding theories. Demur ladies in barely-sensible patent heels wielded industrial typewriters and professional carbon-paper and some really quite good tea. A deferential Biscuitelier approached the new The Secretary of State for Cataclysmic Events and offered him a small sample from a box of the nineteen thirty-four Fig Rolls du Grand Cru mettre dans la boîte en la ferme fig. He sniffed, nibbled, rolled the crumbs around his tongue and then nodded to the waiter for them to be served to everyone else. 'An unpretentious little fig' he said 'but I think you'll be amused by the overtones of Mexican vanilla, fresh wild parrot-poop and the "essence of burning car tyre smoke" in the pastry.' Oh how all of the Assistant Secretaries present giggled and tittered. The Biscuitelier was quite busy tearing the cellophane on fresh boxes for a few minutes after that.

'Look here – if Cholmondeley says that it will work then I'm quite inclined to believe him. He used to make the most marvellous Airfix models in dorm at school and I don't remember him once having any pieces left over. I trust his judgement in these matters implicitly.'

The Chancellor of the Exchequer looked as though he was chewing on refectory broccoli. 'I don't doubt Chummy's abilities and I am certain that he would be the right man to lead any such expedition – but what I cannot countenance is such profligate issue of petrol coupons. It would send quite the wrong message to the public – ye gods, man, we've only just got them over the ruddy Suez crisis and used to a short gallon a month per private vehicle.

This would smack of favouritism and re-ignite journalistic nonsense about the old-boy network.'

Archie (Lord Sir Archibald Cunningham OBE, CBI, BBC, BOC, BP, DDT, KBE, KC, KCVO, KCMG, K.C. & The Sunshine Band) knew Dennis, the Chancellor, very well after their sharing of rooms at Cambridge, and he could tell that the protest was a token one spoken for the record. 'My dear chap, I'll have a word with Rupes – he owes me a favour after that dreadful business with the petting zoo animals. We'll get him to write this up to war-time standards, stiffened upper lips, there may not always be an England if we don't do this, all pull together, that sort of thing. We'll have the public sending in eggcup donations siphoned out of every unlocked car fuel tank from here to Carlisle before you know it. Get Maj to offer him a gong of some sort as a sweetener – he's awfully keen on that sort of honours nonsense, cough cough.'

Dennis, The Record satisfied, sighed and turned to the Prime Minister. 'Boris. Putative postal donations aside, you're sure that you can cover the cost – sixty gallons, maybe more, at one shilling and sixpence ha'penny a gallon?'

The PM said nothing but simply put his Post Office Savings Account book on the table and pushed it across to Dennis who opened it, turned to the last ink-stamped figure and whistled through his teeth. 'So the rumours are true then – Prudence really is your middle name!' There was some ill-muffled tittering from among the assembled scientists, at least among the ones who could understand and speak everyday ordinary real-person English. Dennis slipped the book back to Boris. 'Very well – gentlemen, in the light of information very recently received, this Treasury has no objections to the proposal.'

Boris stood. 'A final vote then gentlemen? All those in favour wave your expenses forms in the air and wait for them to be collected.'

There was a general fluttering of A4 originals and triple carbon copies, and Miss Copious Tippexe whipped around the room to collect them on behalf of a surely already-grateful nation.

'Motion carried. England will launch an expeditionary force to Comet LooksLikeABigBuggerToMeCyril with the express intention of not getting in the way of anyone else's emergency measures or of otherwise making a fuss. Once there the situation will be re-assessed with a view to possible implementation of some sort of solution or other situational amelioration in re the more technical aspects, viz the economical but wholly successful avoidance of the rude and summary premature extinction of the species, to wit, our own, eh?'

He turned to where Professor Hawking was scratching "Hawking woz 'ere" and an outline of an implausibly-sized penis with highly stylised testicles and dragster wheelchair wheels into the Cabinet Office table.

'Er – we'll leave the details entirely in your hands, Professor, naturally. I don't think that any of us are exactly qualified to act in matters of quite such, um, advanced rocket surgery.'

With that the Cabinet bulldogs left the room in a stately procession, followed by the Ministerial kennel-maids, followed by the ministers and then by the secretarial staff (the latter in very strict order of Civil Service seniority, of course). The scientists were left alone, holding a fairly loose brief to save the world. Miss Tippexe dived in with a stapler to firm up the brief before anyone dropped it and the pages got out of order. The scientists then all dived onto the remains of the plates of biscuits and began shaking the thermos jugs to see which still contained free tea and coffee. It was very strong tea and coffee compared to their usual fare, which was usually mostly milk and never served so close to nap-time.

After an indulgent interval of ten minutes or so the science chaps' keepers came into the room to collect them and to return them to their various academic and mental institutions. Some progressive few of them were to be returned to the new "comprehensive" combined academic and mental institutions; those few, those lucky, lucky non-streamed few. Special buses were waiting at the back door to Number Ten, some of them with ramps, some of them with child-locks on the doors and bars on the windows. The party looked as though two dozen or more curious and enthusiastic PG Tips chimpanzees in white coats were being led through the building – as they passed, everyone else ducked back through doors or flattened themselves against wall panelling.

Science is such a funny thing really isn't it, and not at all like the real world!

As Hawking was driven away he turned towards the other science chaps' buses and mental ambulances and held up a hastily-scribbled missive, written on a big pad of graph paper that he'd bought in Woolworths on a socialisation field-trip. The note read simply "I'll be on science-chaps-internet-hangout-chatroom-for-clever-exchange-of-datum-and-ideas.co.england.uk immediately after tea this evening – we'll get together and plan the technicalities then by judicious use of real-time coincident discrete information exchange protocols (later to become "online chat"). Remember to enable secretive peer to peer-only interchange using I-Spy Code 23 on page 12 of the Ladybird Series (Reprint 1953). Cheerio." He waved and turned back around to look over the driver's shoulder at the long and winding road ahead – a road that he hoped led to planetary safety and the continued existence of England, of cricket, of fruit-salad sweeties at eight for a penny and of glossy magazines with naked ladies in them.

As the bus turned out onto Whitehall he offered his first "Are we there yet?" of the return trip to his driver, Cyril, and to his minder, Doris. Doris, resplendent in her crisp, dark blue uniform with one of those upside down watches pinned to her lady-boobies, tapped the switch that closed the partition between rear-seat passengers and the driver. It slid up with barely a whisper from the portable electrical motor mechanism (they had asked Hawking to design it himself and then make it in Meccano). As they pulled out into traffic she disconnected the speakers in the front cab, adjusted the volume that only Hawking would hear and popped an eight-track cartridge in to loop around some of his favourite classics. The rear compartment rocked to such soothing melodic giants as Einstein A-go-go, Atomic by Blondie, Tesla Girls by OMD and I Lost My Heart to a Starship Trooper performed by a very young Sarah Brightman and Hot Gossip.

About a week later at a very secret army base hidden just to one side of the A1 motorway near Catterick all of these clever science chaps had been collected together again and delivered to the main gate in a convoy of gaily-coloured buses and Chipperfielddesigned containment vans. During the unloading phase there were a few mismatches of travel-crate to reception cage, and the delivery became subject to the immutable circus law that what can get loose will get loose. A few of the scientists broke away and meandered off at not some little intellectual velocity. Some big soldiers and some big Alsatian doggie-woggies were sent running across the otherwise very tidy and well-swept parade ground to round them up. It was rather like watching sheep that had a deep individual and collective understanding of chaos and queuing theories being worked by less intelligent but more disciplined shepherds; shepherds with guns and with a Sergeant Major who shouted awfully well and knew lots of very rude words. The Alsatian dogs thought it all great sport, although several of them took the opportunity afforded by the confusion to mate with things that they wouldn't ordinarily be allowed to mate with.

The whole situation nearly went very terribly wrong when one of these escaped scientist chaps spotted a dark green Bedford Seven Ton Lorry towing a field gun and wanted to make some muzzle adjustments to extend the range – had the driver not been able to reverse a trailer as well as he could they might have lost the entire cook-house instead of just the chimney. There were tears of course, but in the end an advanced chemistry set with proper working Bunsen burner was exchanged for the remaining live shells and Doctor "Tubby" Tubberson was returned to the main group, happily distracted with his new toy. England knows how to treat her technical and engineering types, and she treats them well. For the others who were brave about things and didn't cry there were Super-Spirograph sets and even Meccano.

Practical soldiers trained in crowd control and using velvet ropes and a couple of satin-finished rope-stands herded the scientists into the centre of a vast corrugated tin Nissen hut, where they were to tell the top brass what they had got planned to save the world. There was a short interval during which they were all encouraged to go wee-wee to save interruptions later. Then a kindly Psychiatric Liaison Officer encouraged one of them to volunteer and step up to the blackboard or, if he preferred, to the magnetic whiteboard with colourful letters and shapes to use. Professor Iain

Stewart thus stood in front of the gathered brass, embarrassed, giggling and kicking his feet. The liaison gently poked him from the sidelines with a hurry-up stick and gesticulated to him to speak. Once he got going he was awfully good.

To be perfectly honest, the plan he outlined was amazing. Even the lady-officers were impressed and they, naturally, had understood little of it, having tuned out at the first mention of wet-steam ergs and double-panel cast-iron thermal exchangers. The little Quartermaster fellow lifted his cap and scratched his forehead as he scribbled down what they would probably need. Two Morris Space-Travellers with roof-racks; twenty-three miles of ½ inch copper pipe, several tons of other plumbing supplies, fifty-nine gallons of five star leaded petrol, forty tons of coal and a specially-engineered dog bed.

That is to say, of course, a specially engineered bed for a dog, not a bed for a specially-engineered dog. It was to be forged from a single roll of the new "Velcro" material and pre-treated against fleas and mild canine incontinence.

'Single or double?' the Quartermaster asked, seeking clarity.

'Are dog beds available in doubles these days? That seems overly romantic, even if we are a nation of dog-lovers' replied the A.C. to the D.C.D.T.D., without even wondering whether it was his place to raise the matter or whether he was speaking out of rank and turn.

'No, no – the canine incontinence. Are we talking single incontinence or double incontinence?'

After a brief discussion and the hammering out of a helpful Venn-diagram it was decided to prepare for double incontinence, since the dog in question had not previously been in space.

At the end of the presentation there was a stunned silence. Awkward chaps came in and led the scientists away for a rewarding feast of the sort of things that scientists eat, like cake and jelly and tinned salmon sandwiches with those funny little bones with the holes right through and orange squash or fizzy red pop. There was a distant chorus of "ugh" and the sound of buttery cucumber slices being removed and thrown down. The top brass did what they do best. One or two of them wept openly, some went to the toilets for a fag and a few carried on sleeping loudly.

The Brigadier stood and put a gloss on it for those in the know. 'Gentlemen, there you have it. Our best minds have come up with the solution. I expect everything to be ready for launch within forty-seven hours. Moreover, gentlemen, I rather think that England expects that every man will do his duty.'

'Forty-seven Sir? Wouldn't forty-eight hours be neater?'

'It would be, soldier, but you're forgetting the mandatory change-over to Daylight Saving Time. Or from it, or something. B.S.T. to the G.M.T., or some such nonsense. It's all controlled by the G.P.O. and there's no talking to them, even with the species threatened. Whatever they call it when the clocks go forward and we all lose an hour in bed. That is to say that an hour is lost that might otherwise have been spent in sleeping, not that we all waste an hour between the sheets.'

'Oh. Yes Sir. But, I wonder - couldn't we postpone that Sir – to give us the extra hour?'

'I'm afraid not, son – you can't argue with the immutable laws of time and space and Greenwich. Fortunately that is now a problem for the English Space Agency. Is he here?'

'Who Sir?'

'The English Space Agency. I was told that he'd be at this meeting.'

Cholmondeley walked out of the Gents, still trying to do up the cunningly buttoned flies on a suit he hadn't worn since his last appearance before a magistrate on a charge of "probably drunk and quite plainly disagreeable". He appeared to be leaving a trail of mothballs from a moth-damage hole in the jacket pocket.

'Ah – Cholmondeley, there you are. Spot of a mission for you.'

Cholmondeley was not entirely surprised. Cometh the hour; cometh the man eh? 'Come-ing!' He settled quickly back into his seat.

The Brigadier tucked his swagger-stick under his arm and looked Cholmondeley up and down, ratcheting back and forth like a stiff human pantograph as he reacted to Cholmondeley's seated contours. 'Mothballs. Why do I sense mothballs?'

'Mothballs. Yes sir, but a lot has happened since puberty. They don't affect the way I ride a bicycle.'

'Excellent. Now, we... what?'

'Mothballs. It was my nickname at school Sir. I had malaria of the testicles as a child, things took longer than usual to sort themselves out. There was some... medical manipulation involved. Everything's fine now though Sir. All sorted. Would you like to see?'

The Brigadier considered Cholmondeley's trousers and sniffed. Not the trousers of course, he just sniffed as a sort of social punctuation mark before continuing. 'Yes. Splendid. No! Thank you, no! Now look, old chap, we sort of need you to save England and, er, possibly the rest of the planet too if you can... You, er, well – you have washed your hands, I suppose?'

'Yes Sir. I used soap as well.' Cholmondeley put his hands out and showed the Brigadier both sides.

'Splendid. Now look, this is the plan...'

The Brigadier then outlined what was obviously, to all present and sober, a quite brilliant but fairly desperate measure and an exercise from which a chap could have little serious hope of returning. He ended with the exuberant encouragement '...and I won't beat about the bush, quite frankly, there is little hope of your making any kind of safe return. However, do your duty and succeed and you will have saved England and earned the gratitude of Her Majesty and of Her Majesty's government. Your name will be passed down through the anal of history.'

'Which one?'

'What? There is only one isn't there? The anal of the winning side, surely?'

An aide to the Brigadier-ranks leaned in and whispered about pig-Latin and the dangers of making up words if you only went to provincial schools and a technical college. The Brigadier queried a couple of whispered things about when to use "ii" at the end to form a plural and how there were two hens Sir in annals and only one in the other thing, then he blushed to a shade of mortified pink and corrected himself.

'Annals – passed down through the annals of history.' The Brigadier leaned over to the aide to the Brigadier-ranks and whispered again, still not convinced. 'Look – if there is only one why is it called the annals of history – plural?' The aide indicated that he had not the ruddy foggiest idea and cared even less. He retired to sit on his anus and let senior officers make a prat of themselves if they wanted.

'These annals. This annal. Exactly which name will be passed down through it? My nickname Mothballs or my real name Sir? I think my mother would prefer it if there was any way that my real name could be used.'

The Brigadier looked pained. 'Well I don't think we'll be instituting some sort of "Mothballs' Day" in your honour, should you succeed. Let's stick to Cholmondeley Day shall we? It'll look better on the school sports cups and certificates. First Place on the Cholmondeley High Jump, that sort of thing. Couldn't have the little buggers being Runner Up on Mothballs Day. Doesn't sound right. Tell your mother it will have to be your real name and she'll just have to get used to the idea.'

'Splendid.' Cholmondeley felt a knot form in his guts and drifted off into a reverie. He could see his name painted high among those of his fellow Englishmen on the old school achievement board: Saint George; Henry VIII; Elizabeth I (a bloke of course in reality; clothing consisted of lots and lots of layers in those days, even when stark bollock royally naked); Sir Francis Drake; Sir Walter Raleigh; Sir Winston Churchill; Brunel; Shakespeare; Darwin; Newton; Nelson; Cromwell; Julie Andrews; Diana Rigg; David Beckham; Babbage; Bader; Cook; Dr Who; Dickens; Elgar; Faraday; Lieutenant Chard; Hawking; Montgomery; Morcambe; Scott; Stephenson; Savery; Newcomen; Ned Ludd; Joanna Lumley (post-op); Blackadder (pre-op); Scrooge; Turing; Wallis; Wilberforce; Whittle; Dame Kenny Everett; Lord Frankie Howerd; Sir Margaret Rutherford; Captain Hornblower; Captain Scarlet; Joe 90; Biggles, God... and soon enough, Reginald Eugene Emeline Charlotte "Mothballs" Cholmondeley.

He came back down to earth, patted his pistol holster and said 'Well, if you put it that way Sir...'

'Splendid, splendid – we'll leave you to sort out all of the details then. Toodle-pip.'

With that Cholmondeley suddenly found himself alone among a whirlwind of technical blueprints, blackboards full of heat-gradient formulae and bewildering phrases such as "thermal unit" and "ballcock backflow", all chalked in capitals. There were also two dozen white-coated practical scientists beaming proudly through coke-bottle spectacles and waving joke false hands poked from the sleeves of their lab-coats. Some of them were waving in entirely the wrong direction and one or two were chewing on the joke hands. Cholmondeley unbuttoned his holster and moved slowly towards them.

A bare twenty-four hours and just eight square meals later all of the necessary icky science stuff had been hammered out. All that remained was for a man of the world, someone trustworthy, someone fearless and a born leader of men to put it into action.

In lieu of such a man to whom to delegate the task Cholmondeley continued in the role himself. He drove himself, and his dog, in his MGB GT to RAF Mothbawlls.

Always with the mothballs. His life was dominated by mothballs. His crib had been scattered with them, his cot had been scattered with them, puberty had left him with a pair of them in his rugby shorts and all through his professional life he'd been taunted by them and haunted by them. He'd telegraphed the Ministry of Defence to request use of RAF Chocksaway or RAF Wherethehellareyousimon, but to no avail.

Still, in the final analysis, is there anything more comfortable than a battered leather club chair in an Officers Mess? Cholmondeley didn't think so and nor did the Labrador at his feet. The Labrador was called "Shakespeare" and, like his namesake, he didn't think much at all really, except "food" and "wow, sexy leg or what?" and "this cushion will be the mother of my puppies" and "food" and "pee" and "walkies" and "food". Cholmondeley and Shakespeare were well-matched psychologically. There were days – even whole months – when Cholmondeley's thoughts remained at a simple Shakespearean level. This evening though, even as the Hendricks in his glass slowly, portentously melted the ice-cubes, he was a worried man. The task at hand task loomed large.

Even the amber glow from the wireless cabinet's display could do nothing to pull his eyes away from the painted-metal framed window that overlooked the airfield. Standing out there, and tended only by three nesting woodpigeons and a weekly drive-by check from the Military Police, stood two of the Ministry of Defence's scant dozen or so serviceable Morris Space-Travellers. Various vapours that he had never quite fully understood settled from the various wholly misunderstood vents on the little-understood casings. High on the noses of the rockets the last rays of the English sun glinted on the chrome-finish radiator grills. Had the craft been the newer, more expensive Wolseley Six models there would have been a little badges on the noses that lit up when the sidelights were turned on. However, the transverse rocket engines of the new, more expensive Wolseleys gave grave concern to the quartermaster, and so the success of this mission was entrusted rather to the timber-framed Moggies with the funny exhaust note on the over-run.

Cholmondeley was disturbed in his reverie by Higginbotham. Everyone was disturbed in their reverie at some time by Higginbotham, but he was the English space industry's leading expert on the use of Yorkshire-mined small-lump carbon as a propellant and thus was accorded a certain flexibility in regards to his dress and mannerisms. In short, Higginbotham was ruddy weird but rather unfortunately essential.

'Magnificent sight, aren't they?' he said, scratching the family jewels absentmindedly and leading Cholmondeley thus to an initial misunderstanding.

Higginbotham settled into a club chair – Cholmondeley was relieved that it was not the one he was occupying but another, quite separate one. Higginbotham wasn't quite married, do you see? One couldn't entirely be certain of a chap who had reached his mid-thirties without providin' an heir to someone of a feminine, family bent. There had been... rumours. Cholmondeley knew this for a fact, since he'd started the rumours himself.

Shakespeare considered Higginbotham's legs but decided against romantic congress in favour of passing wind, followed by more sleep, and dreaming about better legs than Higginbotham's.

'Magnificent, yes. Will they get the job done, do you think?' said Cholmondeley, hoping upon hope that Higginbotham didn't suffer a similar misunderstanding to his own from a few moments ago and take his comments as a compliment.

'Oh absolutely. Solidly built, sufficient turn of speed – they'll get us there alright.'

'What about back again?'

'Probably back again too, so long as we keep an eye on the oil levels. Another G&T?'

'Thank you, yes.'

The voice on the wireless announced that it was time for the national news. Cholmondeley signalled to a small portable (possibly potable, in national nutritional extremis) mess steward to turn the "volume" potentiometer towards the upper extremis, and the whole mess went quiet as they all listened.

Prime Minister Boris Johnson dominated the slot with yet another interminably long speech. Perhaps the most disquieting thing was that the longer Boris stayed in office the more he sounded like a very camp, slightly inebriated and low-IQ version of Winston Churchill.

... 'Ooh 'ello. I am shpeaking to you today from the Cabinet Room of Number 10 Dining Street in order to relay to you, the English peoples of the world, further details of what is being done on your behalf by your government, and by others, to ameliorate the effects of the enormous chuffing space-thingy that is rushing towards our country. That is to say, in specifically, the hurtling Comet bearing the designation LooksLikeABigBuggerToMeCyril. The combined forces of the world super-powers: China; Germany; India and The Vatican have today issued a communique via the Foxx-Reuters Bad-News Agency to the effect that they are pooling their nuclear missile capabilities and assuring the world that they will soon "shoot that mother heifer out of the sky, ooh yeah, go to defcon one Angela mein lovely frau mit großen political brusten". The peoples of the United States of Northern America, and those of the Union of Soviet Capitalist Russian Republics, continue to assist by taking every opportunity to fire at the comet with hand-guns. The Chinese peoples have responded bravely with several hundreds of thousands of tons of fire-crackers and rockets, and our Indian allies are also busying themselves in meditation, and in the Ganges.

The Church of England is preparing a special sermon to be read later in the year.'

'In the international arena of super-powers, England is taking her modern place by making the tea and coffee as only we know how, and by very neatly taking the minutes of the meetings in cursive writing and in blue-black fountain-pen ink. In-between, your Ambassadors and Cabinet Ministers are doing absolutely all that may be done, by tidying the chairs and making sure that when the powers that be reconvene in the World Government Chamber, absolutely everyone important has a fresh notepad and at least two sharp pencils. The rest of Europe, we are told, that which is not Germany, is taking care of re-filling the water decanters and straightening the blotting pads and the name-plates. During the meetings, we are standing quietly, but resolutely, on your behalf, by the door, soaking in this intelligence.'

'The panic and riots in Abroad continue unabated, hampering our combined global efforts to meet this challenge, and I must thank the English people for your continued forbearance and restraint. Your trust in your government is not misplaced, and although we may need to levy several extra taxes of course, we shall prevail.'

'Although we have offered our fullest co-operation to the international super-powers, your government is, of course, also pursuing a solution by independent English means. To that end our armed services are working tirelessly on your behalf in combination with our top scientists and great thinkers, and I can tell you today that within the next twenty-hour hours a sure and certain solution to the whole problem will be launched from our Space Centre deep in the heart of the shires.'

'Two brave chaps and true will be launched into space using the latest English orbital and extra-orbital technology from Austin-Morris. More than that I dare not say except to wish them well and to assure you, the English peoples of the world, that when we have news, as I hope we shall soon have news, it will be relayed to you as fast as may be, using every means at our disposal. In the meantime I ask of you this. Use whatever means you have at hand to prepare to meet the hour of our testing. Dig bunkers on the beaches, dig bunkers in the streets, dig bunkers in the fields and in the schoolyards. Share essential supplies among your community and among your neighbours, keep a weather ear to your wireless sets and, above all, maintain your dignity and reserve.' ...

There then followed a summary of the shipping forecast for the following day and a commercial inducement to drink the new bed-time wonder health-drink Horlicks whenever possible. The steward stepped forward and manipulated the "volume" potentiometer again to a more comfortable background level suited to light entertainment. Shakespeare farted, although not close enough to the glowing orange element on the electric fire to have any pyrotechnic effect. He had a most uncomfortable-looking erection and even though he was asleep his hind end appeared to be engaged in the business of making Labrador leg babies with something not entirely consenting.

The following evening, somewhere in the heart of the picturesque, en-wolded, folded northern shire of Lincoln, Cholmondeley's mother looked out of the casement window of her small fourteen-bedroom, sixteen-bathroom, three-kitchen and stables dowager cottage and watched as a half-timbered shooting star travelled across the night sky in entirely a most unusual direction. The tail-lights of a Morris rushed to meet the single headlight of the nasty extinction-level comet. Her son was off, and running.

She pushed back a lock of greying hair (on her head, not her chest), dabbed at an emotional tear and whispered a message to her beloved and only son who was well on his way into space. 'Just don't cock this up like everything else you touch, you inadequate little wanker.' Then she went back to her indoor hydroponics garden in the attic. She was still installing additional anti-surveillance-helicopter insulation when Cholmondeley-san landed on the comet's icy surface and began un-strapping vital equipment from the roof-rack of the expedition Morris (like sheep, Morris are their own plural).

It took them virtually the whole day to build the necessary timber expedition huts, scout the lie of the land and then lay out the system of cunning pre-fabricated exothermic devices. It took even longer to get a fire started for, while both men had been either a

Boy Scout or a Girl Guide, or in Cholmondeley's case, both a Boy Scout and a Girl Guide for six glorious weeks one summer in Mablethorpe, neither of them had qualified for any of the more practical field-craft badges such as "Basic Arson". Cholmondeley could sew a large button on a man's bathing suit at a pinch. Higginbotham's raison de not getting beaten up as often as he might otherwise was that he could tie a knot in a cherry-stalk with his tongue. Other than that they were entirely formally unqualified.

Since he was the more muscular of the pair Cholmondeley set about unpacking the furniture while Higginbotham tackled making egg, chips and beans in some very uncertain gravity. It's difficult frying an egg when it won't lie flat and keeps drifting off and, quite frankly, cooking chips bordered on the terrifying despite the assurances of his copy of Delia. It's quite difficult heating oil to three hundred and ninety-two of the fahrengezundheits when it seemed keen to wander out of the pan and gather in odd corners of the makeshift kitchen.

Still, was there anything more comfortable than a battered leather club chair in a creaking old wooden shack on an extinction-level comet speeding towards planet Earth? Cholmondeley didn't think so and nor did the Labrador at his feet. Shakespeare didn't think much at all really, even now and in space, except perhaps "tubes of dog-food paste" and "wow, sexy pressurisation leg-brace or what?" and "this travel-cushion will be the mother of my space-puppies" and "how the hell do I get this goldfish-bowl off my head so that I can lick my genitals?" There were days, even whole months, when Cholmondeley's thoughts remained at a similar level even though he knew how to get the goldfish-bowl off his head (although, having left puberty far behind, he no longer tried to lick his own genitals). This evening though, as the Hendricks's in his glass slowly melted the comet-ice cubes in his glass, he was a worried man.

Even the amber glow from the small wireless set's display could do nothing to pull his eyes away from the rough wood-framed window that overlooked the Field of Operations. Out there, covered in a thick frost that would be a real bit of a bugger to scrape off when they were leaving, stood two of the Ministry of Defence's finest relatively low-mileage Morris Space-Travellers. They were both gently dripping oil from their engine sumps.

Cholmondeley opened the little square hatch on the front of his goldfish-bowl helmet, stuck in a match and re-lit his Calabash of Aromatic Bishop's Gusset. Seconds after he closed the hatch again he resembled nothing more than a humanoid body in airtight space-tweeds, magnetic brogues and with a goldfish-bowl full of swirling grey-blue smoke where the human head would more ordinarily be. Periodically he re-opened the hatch and poured in a little gin (a keen observer would have noted that there were eight "littles" to the bottle). Whenever he took a draw on the Calabash pipe the embers glowed amid the tobacco smoke, looking rather disturbingly like some walnut-sized alien brain pulsating as it formulated plans to invade the Earth at the obvious entry points of either Dover or Folkestone.

In lieu of licking his (own) testicles Shakespeare launched himself lazily across the room in three semi-weightless four-legged ba-dungs in order to make sudden love to the hitherto unsuspecting coal-scuttle. Action and equal and opposite re-action having more than the usual sway in this environment he simply succeeded in becoming a kind of floating pinwheel with a more-than-usually vacant expression on his face. The dog's bath-water that evening would not be fit for sharing with man nor beast so Higginbotham would have to run fresh for himself when his turn came. If the dreadful truth be known, the coal was of the opinion that its first shag in three hundred million years had not been worth the wait.

Cholmondeley was less disturbed by Higginbotham on the comet than he had been disturbed by Higginbotham on Earth. This was possibly due to the fact that on the comet Higginbotham had an "off" switch – all it took to silence him was to remove the battery from one's wireless intercom and he was converted from a crashing vocal boor into a sort of crashing Marcel Marceau (but with even less intellectual credibility). The flat surfaces in every hut at Rorke's Drift (as the camp had been named) were covered in hastily discarded wireless intercom batteries. Higginbotham hadn't noticed. He just assumed that either his IQ had jumped up the scale again or that Cholmondeley's had fallen once more. It was like talking to a brick wall.

The rhythmic Morse Code fires of Cholmondeley's glowing pipe communicated "worried man" to Higginbotham and he concluded that he must try talking at least once more.

'I say old chap, you seem preoccupied – anything I can help with?'

'Not at the moment old darling, no. I'm calculating the biting point of the clutch for our return take-off trajectory, and rather worrying whether it was wise of me to have left the hand-brakes on. I think perhaps a brick under the landing struts might have been safer – we'll be in a right royal pickle if the damned things are frozen up when it's time to leave.'

Higginbotham went to the window to look out at the Morris and admire their curvaceous but dumpy lines and the craftsmanship of the woodwork in the rear frames. 'Oh the old girls will get us away safely or my name's not pronounced "Higginbome" by polite society. Perhaps we should rock them backwards and forwards a little tomorrow? Remind me and I'll lend a hand if you like.'

Shakespeare finished his romantic nutty-slack endeavours and retired to the Velcro post-coital snuggles of his specially-engineered basket. A light cloud of very confused, weightless fleas floated around the wickerwork and the stained tartan rug. Half of the fleas were suffering from debilitating space-sickness and the other half were delighting in their new-found ability to leap incredibly vast distances. That is to say different fleas were reacting wholly differently to others, this wasn't some sort of fore and aft or one side of a flea versus the other thing. Either all of a flea was bounding around like Super-Flea or all of a flea was bracing itself against uprights and making long-distance calls to the flea god on the great white flea telephone. Sheesh, are you thick or what? I really shouldn't have to explain this sort of thing.

The whole basket shifted a little across the floor every once in a while as the Labrador's arse acted as a very effective manoeuvring-jet whenever he farted. He had found that sometimes he went to sleep in one place and woke up later in a quite different corner of the room. He suspected that he was having some fantastic second doggy-life that he remembered nothing about when he woke up. Either that or his fleas were, quite literally, moving home overnight without consulting him.

Cholmondeley made a mental note, once again, to attach Velcro to the underside of the basket as well as to the sleeping surfaces. He believed in letting sleeping dogs lie and watching a dog with an erection and eyes tightly shut circumnavigate the room was more than a little bit disturbing.

Cholmondeley caught himself drifting, and set his mind to more pressing matters. 'How's the boiler?'

'Oh roaring away splendidly. I'll check it again before bed and stoke it up and we should be fine until morning. Tomorrow I'll add more lagging to the feed-pipes and put another couple of radiators towards the tail end of the comet.'

'Splendid. And the coal consumption?'

'Nominal – five by five. Provided that the next delivery is on time and we keep the cellars in trim I foresee no problems. I've ordered twelve bags. Once the extra lagging is in place we can turn the thermostat down a notch or two in fact and save some money.'

On hearing a reference in his sleep to the mechanics of "more warmth" the Labrador wagged his tail. Well, to be perfectly candid, in the low gravity of Rorke's Drift he enthusiastically wagged his basket a couple of times. Next to eating food for the first or second times, shitting, and humping legs, enjoying warmth was one of his top four favourite things. He dreamed of doggy-Heaven, in which all four life-activities would be combined into one with the added bonus of someone to tickle his ears as he chewed on a bone while shagging a leg-shaped heating boiler.

Cholmondeley opened his face-hatch and carefully blew the smoke that had been collecting in his helmet out into the room in a series of stunning smoke-rectangles. For a couple of minutes his head was visible once again, although he retained a feint grey-blue aura, rather like a maths schoolmaster might, when thinking hard. He tapped his Calabash out and re-filled it with pre-rolled Dunhill's Strongest Medicated Pit-Weed (guaranteed to freshen up the lungs and re-awaken those smoke-jaded taste buds).

While the boiler chugged away and the rather clever automated hopper system fed premium anthracite eggs into the flames,

Cholmondeley and Higginbotham read a little, played a couple of games of Old Maid and then brewed cocoa. Finally Cholmondeley stood and stretched.

'Bed, I think, Higginbotham.' His speech was delivered rather in the manner of an order.

Higginbotham slipped into an awkward, goofy grin and looked at his feet. 'Gosh, sir – well, if you say so.' He was still kicking about awkwardly, broggling an ear out with his finger when he heard Cholmondeley's bedroom door close. Life can be so cruel sometimes. He shuffled off to his own room and once more into the arms of Tiberius, his rather large Teddy bear. Still, at least in space no-one can hear a chap weep. Tiberius was quite used to being damp and emotionally drained by dawn.

The following morning, as Sod's Law would have it, they both arose rather late and dawdled over their breakfast tea, tubes of hot buttered toast-paste and the morning newspapers. The paper-boy had jammed them all in the letterbox again, ripping the sports sections. It was difficult to tell whether Sussex had declared or whether someone had declared Sussex de-eclaired. After Higginbotham had checked the boilers and Cholmondeley had dealt with the day's correspondence from the first post they indulged in a light lunch of tubes of poached salmon with tubes of green salad and fresh minted new potatoes from a can. Then they took medical advice from Mission Control and had a bit of a snooze each. This meant that they were rather caught on the hop by a snap inspection by the Ministry, for the Ministry never liaises in advance in re snap inspections.

Carstairs, Carstairs minor and Carruthers , the men from the Ministry, stepped out of the dull mint-green Humber Space-Imperial and shouldered their black umbrellas with the precision of a military parade. One, two, three, ten-hut you 'orrible little man dress that line and stick those chests OUT!

Rorke's Drift, as the outpost had been designated by Edith in the Distant Outpost Designation Office, was a little smaller than they had expected. This was a good thing because some serious shrinkage had been written into the schedule for the project. Shrinkage qua shrinkage though was not what Carstairs, Carstairs and Carruthers were here to oversee. They were at Rorke's Drift to check whether the shrinkage Her Majesty's Government had so far received for the tax-payer's money was of sufficiently good value for the next stage-payment to be handed over, and for the supply of the return journey fuel coupons and another week's supply of seaside-salty breathing oxygen.

Carruthers and Carstairs minor carried briefcases; Carstairs carried just his authority. His goldfish-bowl helmet had the necessary Senior Executive Officer-rank indentations to prevent his bowler hat from repeatedly slipping off in the low gravity.

They all scanned the lie of the land, like three monkeys looking, listening and saying nothing. Carstairs (not minor) poked at the ice with the tip of his umbrella. It was nasty, dirty stuff such as one might find at the side of the Great North Road in January. He wiped the tip of his umbrella off on Carruther's trouser ankle (maltreatments being a benefit of rank).

Several huts lay to spinward, two of them emitting wisps of smoke and a lot of steam. Piles of coal had been sorted neatly between old railway sleepers. A large yellow Labrador dog wearing a gold-fish bowl had his leg cocked against the outside of a hut that bore a hand-painted sign with the legend "Home, sweet home". Lazy globules of Lucozade-like Labrador urine were floating away towards the tail of the comet, steaming gently and rolling slowly over each other as they boiled away in the lack of atmosphere and the social vacuum. While they watched with a shared but unspoken and slightly creepy fascination, the stream of globules produced reduced in size from oranges to tangerines to walnuts and eventually to peas – peas of pee, no less, no more. There was a pause while the dog pinched his buttocks together a half-dozen times and then added a final burst of liquid full-stops. A little of his efforts drifted far enough with the spin of the body to burst over the wheels of the Humber. The three gentlemen from the Ministry sidestepped while they still could.

Suddenly the door of the main hut opened and Cholmondeley appeared, dressed in red tartan dressing gown, hairy bare knees, Wellington boots and goldfish-helmet, carrying several empty gin bottles in the crook of one arm and holding up a small hand-written sign showing the classic "Here boy" dog whistle to recall the dog in the airless environment. It was a moment or two before he noticed the three officials. He dumped the empties and put the tin lid back on the corrugated dustbin. The dog was galumphing towards the intruders with his tongue lolling.

'Gentlemen, the electrickery meter is on the wall, just around the corner – but it was read only a week ago.'

'We're not here to read the meter, Mr Cholmondeley. We're here to check that the roaring boiler-fires of Whitehall are having the intended effect, and are doing so with the economy expected from a publicly-funded project. May I use your lavatory?'

'What? Yes – of course, it's also around the corner. The smaller hut with the squares of tabloid newspaper hanging outside on string.'

'Thank you. May my colleagues, Mr Carruthers and Mr Carstairs minor – he is of absolutely no relation to me of course – come inside while they wait?'

'Um. Yes – however they ordinarily pass their time while you're um, in the loo. Yes, do come in gentlemen, do.'

'Thank you.'

'Thank you. Most kind.'

They both followed the dog indoors. There were a few awkward minutes while they settled themselves and then Cholmondeley realised that he was physically intimidating the younger chaps, and hastily tied his dressing gown cord.

'Er - lovely weather – for the time of year.'

'Where?'

'Here. And there. Mostly elsewhere.'

'Yes indeed. Quite clement, for a comet. Have you travelled far?'

'From Earth. We've been sent out rather to, well – to be candid – to have a sniff around, check on progress and report to H.M. and to P.M.'

'Mmm. Splendid. Tea?'

'That would be most welcome. Thank you. There were no cafes en route and our official travel-flask, while refreshing, didn't last past the moon.'

Cholmondeley moved a pile of dirty magazines from a chair. Airfix Modellers Weekly and British East-Coast Rolling-Stock Monthly fell onto the floor, and some of the dirt and all of the biscuit crumbs dislodged.

'We might have called ahead but your line is down' apologised Carruthers.

'Yes, we've been having problems with the connection. The General Post Office is working on it. It's a fault at the exchange – something to do with the weight of the wire required and the necessary slack being taken in as we approach Earth. We are rather off the beaten track here, it's a wonder that they could get us a line installed at all.'

'Splendid. The G.P.O. is such a stout organisation. It rather affords one the feeling that the whole organisation is built along the lines of a Morris Minor Van.'

'Quite so. Right then. Tea it is.' Cholmondeley disappeared into the little flat-roofed extension that they used as a kitchen and put the kettle on. As quietly as he could he extricated four of the best cups and saucers that were stacked in with the other washing-up in the sink and rinsed them over and around and alongside the vagaries of the flow of the tap as best he could. In dismal gravity it was sometimes all a chap could do to keep the water in the sink. When you couldn't see the sink for the pots it was damned nigh impossible. He laid out a tray with milk, sugar and – in view of the hour and his knowledge of the dining sensibilities of senior civil servants – pink and yellow wafer biscuits and a few precious custard creams.

Carstairs came back from the loo with the expression on his face of a man who was on a mission, who knew his paperwork and who was determined to watch intently while it was all filled out by his subordinates.

'Mr Cholmondeley, the compound is a little smaller than I had been led to believe it might be.'

'Yes indeed, we've had some success with the project and are approximately twenty-three minutes ahead of schedule.'

'Oh excellent, the P.M. will be pleased.' Carstairs shifted more comfortably into his armchair while Carruthers made a note of "twenty-three".

Cholmondeley moved things along. 'Shall we get this survey thing out of the way and then this evening if you can stay for dinner I have a rather splendid port that you might find amusing.'

'Dinner? Splendid.' Everything for the tea was laid out very nicely, considering. 'Shall I be mother?'

'I don't know old boy – what have you been doing that you perhaps ought not to have?'

Oh how they all laughed.

The tea was in fact quite delicious – Cholmondeley had insisted on leaf tea from some of his own family plantations. The biscuits went down rather too well, although they had to switch to chocolate Bourbons before the large "entertaining" teapot was empty.

Suddenly, an awkward social hiatus fell upon the conversation and all eyes turned to Shakespeare.

Where he had previously been enjoying a postprandial canine snooze he was now sitting upright in the middle of the fireside rug, slightly cross-eyed and looking mildly distressed. Carstairs, Carstairs minor and Carruthers put down their drinks, not knowing what to expect. Cholmondeley just groaned. 'Oh dear, not again.'

The Labrador belched and swallowed, belched and swallowed and with each little spasm the belches and swallows became more serious and more energetic. Finally he stood and concentrated, furrowing his brow and assuming a working-dog stance.

'Is your dog quite alright?'

'Fine, fine – I just think he may have eaten his tube of Pedigree Chum pre-mixed with Winalot paste a little too quickly. He's probably eaten the tube as well, again. This isn't going to be pretty.'

'Should we do anything?'

'Just try to not react, he gets awfully self-conscious. Do please brace yourselves, emotionally.'

The dog was now looking as though Sigourney Weaver's mother-in-law was trying to climb up the inside of his windpipe and burst forth into the world. His little goldfish-bowl helmet wobbled and swayed around his collar. Then he let rip and the goldfish-bowl looked suddenly like the perfect gloss on a vast spherical brain made of diced carrots and chunky horsemeat – a brain already being destroyed by a long pink tongue licking at it appreciatively from the inside.

Carstairs (minor, of course) tried to run from the room but only succeeded in hitting the ceiling where he clung to the chandelier and swung gently in circles, concentrating hard on controlling his own retching. Carruthers hugged his briefcase on his knees but couldn't prevent himself from watching in much the way he always watched train wrecks and large ships sinking.

The tongue continued working until the front hemisphere of the dog's helmet was sort of clean-ish and only the rear hemisphere remained hugely disturbing on some primeval level, looking very like an exploded brain through which a very happy pet Labrador dog's head had been pushed at not some inconsiderable speed. That the dog often stopped in his endeavours to chew (or rather, to re-chew) made it all the more disconcerting. He was wagging his tail again though and wondering why he was being watched. All was well once more, except for Carruthers who was then not well at all.

Higginbotham chose that moment to return from his long shift in the field, persuading gas bubbles out of his beloved (heating) system. He hung up his bleeding key on the bleeding key-hook and wondered what the bleeding hell was going on. 'Bloody hell!' he said, before looking around and realising that they had company.

Shakespeare started panting happily and let loose a fart that propelled him some six or seven yards across the room. Higginbotham took this as a sign that the dog had finally accepted him and bent down, intending to pat it on the helmet, before shying away again and deciding that maybe he was a cat-person after all. Perhaps there had been some sort of nasty decompression accident? 'I say – has this dawg exploded recently?'

Cholmondeley performed the necessary introductions. Higginbotham tried to explain to the guests what he had been doing.

'Bleeding radiators.'

They were obviously anxious to seem polite and Carruthers did his admirable best to reply in kind. 'Sodding boilers?'

'No, no, just bleeding the radiators today. I buggered the automatic hopper feed yesterday, and Cholmondeley won't let me near the old boiler now unless he's there to chaperone while I use the sodding rod to clean out the clinker filters.'

'I see. How splendid.' Replied Carstairs, not being able to speak "common little workman" with any degree of plausibility or fluency.

Cholmondeley cut in before things got ugly. 'You'll all stay the night of course?'

'You have guest accommodation?'

Cholmondeley pointed to the rows of empty bunk beds and all five of them sighed the sigh of grown chaps re-living both their teenage years and their twenties at home.

After dinner that evening they all went outside to watch the fireworks. Rocket after rocket after rocket following missile after missile after missile past the comet and all blazing trails of gold and red and blue and green until their fuel gave out.

'Oh I say – some sort of twenty-one gun salute is it? It must be simply wonderful to know that the world appreciates your efforts eh?' said Carstairs minor, gushing ever so slightly. 'Oh, hang on though – there's many more than twenty-one.'

'Actually, not a salute as such – I'm fairly certain that the rest of the world neither knows nor cares that we are here. The English Ambassador to Brussels tried but couldn't get an appointment and all of his telephone calls were either queued or routed to the call-centre in Bombay. Poor chap is still recovering from "on-hold music" toxicity of the brain. No, those are the world's combined nukes. They are trying their damnedest to blow up this comet. Fortunately, their aim is really quite shite.'

'Nukes?'

'Yah – as I mentioned, the World Government decided to blow the damn thing up. I'm not certain that they would change their minds even if they knew that we were here. Some group of Hollywooden generals decided that it would be better to suffer the slings and arrows of two gross of comet-fragments and that nukes was their only option. Besides, you know how desperate they've been for decades for an excuse to fire them in anger. Hollywood was beginning to wonder if the little bulb in President Morgan Freeman's "DefCon One" indicator was still serviceable.'

'But what if one of them lands on target? What then?'

'We'd all briefly be very well-lit and extremely warm I suppose. Best to not think about it – there's a serious job to be done here and someone must try to do it, whatever the risks. We may rarely get the glory or even the plaudits, but where there is a country in need of colonisation when we leave we at least leave behind railways and stable government, where there is a comet in need of a beating we'll give better than we take. We always do.'

'Indeed. Johnny Foreigner does tend to panic so at the first whiff of potential annihilation.'

'Any idea which is which?'

'Which what is which?'

'Nuke.'

'Oh. Which belongs to whom from where?'

'Yah.'

'No. We speculate that the ones trailing red flame would be Russian of course.'

'Naturally.'

'The bigger ones are probably United States of American – Texan I suppose.'

'Dashed pretty, anyway. What are the ones that make the little "putt-putt" smoke signals soon after leaving Earth?'

'Those, we think, must be the Chinese and Indian nukes – full of eastern promise but a little disappointing in the final analysis. About half of them seem to fall back to the surface and then blow up. A bit like their commercial fireworks.'

'Dashed inconvenient. Fall anywhere important?'

'No, mostly just France. We've been very lucky, really. They just explode, leave a fifty-mile wide crater and do no damage to worry about as such. Switzerland got hit but we don't think that was an accident – several missiles landed at once. Every cuckoo clock and every over-washed self-satisfied cow-bell sporting oh but we're neutral boor will be radioactive for the next fifty thousand years.'

'Splendid. Bit of an improvement eh?'

'Look, I say – we're almost twenty-five minutes ahead of the project schedule now and Higgy and I have been desperately alone here for quite a few days, I wonder if you chaps fancy some sport?'

Carstairs, Carstairs minor and Carruthers all look sheepish and bashful.

'Well, I suppose that technically we are abroad old chap, what happens in Abroad stays abroad as they say...'

'Marvellous, yes – cricket then, tomorrow morning?'

'Oh gosh! Yes – cricket. That would be tickettyboo, honour of the department at stake, that sort of thing. Yes – why not indeed? It, er, well – it won't slow down the work will it?'

'Gosh no, we're virtually automated here now. Higgsy will check the coal and the boiler before we begin and anyway, it'll do us both good to get some fresh air after so long cooped up here in those ruddy huts.'

They all found it a little bit difficult to sleep, partly because of the excitement about cricket the following day, partly because of the constant flashes of Earth's nuclear armoury falling long, falling short and falling, fortunately, remarkably off-target. Carruthers whispered to Carstairs minor about the possible effects of all of the explosions but Carstairs, overhearing them, reassured them that radioactive fallout couldn't travel through the vacuum of space, so they were all quite safe. Besides, he said, the roof of the hut was made of two layers of corrugated iron and protection against radioactivity didn't come much finer than that. Carstairs minor quietly sucked his thumb in the shadows and Carruthers simply tried to sleep with his hand over his testicles, thus shielding them from atomic harm.

When Higginbotham hammered the stumps into the comet there was some quite dramatic cracking, but not enough to ruin the pitch entirely. Overnight the body of ice had shrunk somewhat under the full blast of the boiler and two dozen rattling, gurgling, steaming cast-iron radiators dotted about the place. The plan seemed to be working. Carstairs won the toss so Higginbotham took to wicket-keeping, Cholmondeley to gully and Shakespeare went to square leg as per ruddy usual. Since they'd all brought their cricket whites with them (a compulsory requirement when on active duty) it all looked rather splendid.

The first couple of overs were uneventful except that it was decided that the boundary counted as hitting the ball so hard that it went into low orbit and had to be allowed to circle the comet before being retrieved. Carstairs minor went lbw and then it was all out for just a couple of dozen, although in the low gravity a run was defined as anything from a splendid bounce from one wicket to the other or a decidedly good effort at sliding around on the ice. Carstairs stopped play when one of the rear lights of the Humber was broken by a wild shot and they all returned to the makeshift pavilion for tea and to replenish their suit oxygen supplies.

Quiet frankly, after the Battenburg had been polished off there remained little that was playable of the wicket. The Cunning Scheme of the Science Chaps was working remarkably well. The methane-rich slush made it almost impossible to bowl anyway so everyone declared. Carruthers and Carstairs minor looked dejected, but an emergency plate of Marmite sandwiches cheered them up a little.

Carstairs, Carstairs minor and Carruthers eventually had to leave of course, and hands were shaken, backs thumped and cheery-byes were said. Higginbotham, Cholmondeley and Shakespeare felt very sad indeed as they stood ankle-deep in the slush and puddles, watching as C, C and C put their briefcases and umbrellas into the boot of the Humber and clambered in. C sat in the back of course, as befitted the C in C, while C minor drove. The Humbers were such splendid vehicles and the roofline was quite sufficient to allow for the wearing of regulation bowlers. C fired up the rockets.

There was a bit of a watery gurgle and then the rockets spluttered, guttered like candles in the rain and died. C gave it more choke and tried again, with success and some mechanical consistency. The underside of the Humber became a delicious rosy glow of propulsion. Unfortunately, C had left the hand-brake on so they went lots of nowhere quite quickly. The jets generated steam which bathed the Humber in a quite photogenic mist and the headlights and tail-lights had to be engaged. Fortunately, Higgy had his Ensign Ful-Vue with him and loaded and ready with a fresh roll of Kodak Kodachrome 120 so the moment was captured for the archives. C gave the Humber a little more throttle and all three of the occupants gave a cheery wave and looked forwards and upwards expectantly. To their eternal credit they all maintained these expressions of "do let's move forwards, C old boy, as soon as you like" while the Humber melted its way slowly downwards and backwards through the crunchy-wet remains of the comet. It was rather like watching a small vessel sink gracefully while the occupants did their best to ignore the process.

After about five anxious minutes, during which the dog peered down the hole with his head on one side, the body of the comet gave a slight hiccough as the Humber popped out of the other side and then flew away back to Earth. As take-off manoeuvres went it was a little bit unconventional, and not one of those manoeuvres recommended in the Owner's Handbook.

Cholmondeley slapped Higginbotham on the back. 'Well Higgy, it looks as though our work here is almost done. We'd better start packing before we disappear in much the same way. A couple more days should see the job finished.'

Higginbotham disappeared back inside Rorke's Drift and began packing. He admitted to a certain uncertainty about how best to pack the remains of the kitchen.

'I'm never certain how to pack up a mobile or temporary kitchen' he said. 'It's a skill that has eluded me since childhood and quite blighted my life.' Dog showed him the way. Shakespeare packed ample snacks for the journey home (in his bed) and then ate the rest. Just the food of course; the humans packed the cutlery, crockery, frying pan and the saucepan singular while Shakespeare was preoccupied with tubs of Winalot and Minced Morsels. The kettle had its own little niche in the tea-maker's chest next to the various teapots and the tannin-infusion comestibles. There was a rack in the lid especially for the spoons and some Tupperware took Tupper-care of the biscuits that Shakespeare didn't get to first.

The place seemed quite bleak once they'd finished, somehow not a home any more. Cholmondeley was quite put in mind of his family's holiday hut in the Antarctic and the many times he'd closed the door there and begun the long trek back to school for a new term.

Higginbotham tipped the contents of the very last sack of nutty slack into the boiler and then carefully folded the hessian and chucked it on too. He felt a little bit guilty at not returning it to the coal merchant but, well – most things were already packed and the best he could have done with it anyway would be to tuck it into a corner of the car's boot where it would probably have made everything smutty. The plan was to leave the boiler with the hot-water valves all wide open to take care of the remains of the comet and to save on weight for the return journey – it hadn't been easy persuading fully-laden Morris Travellers to leave Earth and it would be no easier to persuade them back down to Earth without fuss or serious infraction of the Highway Code. The loss of a valuable boiler and several radiators would be keenly felt in the English economy, but strapping them to the overloaded vehicles was not a viable option. Cholmondeley wished that they'd brought a larger box of Viable Options with them.

With the last luggage-strap secured on the roof-racks and the engines ticking over and almost fully off choke one final round of inspection seemed somehow appropriate – like backing out of one's country seat on bankruptcy and feeling that there should have been more to pack, somehow.

Comet LooksLikeABigBuggerToMeCyril was not the comet it had once been. The radiators of the cunning heating system had done their work magnificently, and most of the comet now trailed itself, if you see what I mean – it only existed now as a much reduced ball of dirty slush dragging the steamed-off remains of what it once was. The best analogy is perhaps that of a Hollywooden starlet in her retirement, a vestige of what she had once been pre-forties, and towing a smutty history.

The sheds, now virtually empty, sat in soggy foundations and frosty puddles. The boiler-house still vented smoke and steam but the pipes leading to the cast-iron radiators no longer rattled and banged as they once had while trying to warm up a much larger mass. Shakespeare's kennel, with its cheery and whimsical faux-chimney, still lay at the nexus of a Spirograph-like creation of dog-stroll routes and sniffing routines, but there was really nobody home. The cricket pitch was a forlorn parody of the notorious nineteen-sixty-eight England versus The Inuits game, and it curved brutally now that the circumference of the comet had been so much reduced. Cholmondeley had suggested that they leave the stumps behind along with the St George's Cross and the rather impressive collected faecal works of Shakespeare. The wooden sheds with their gay tin roofing were to remain of course, along with the plumbing and the "usual offices" – no point at all in taking those things back. Even Higginbotham's sorry attempt at a small rose garden looked more like some sort of amateur hydroponics experiment gone awfully wrong in a bag of garden-centre potting compost.

When the time came to have a final pee before hitting the road, to give the final salute and head back to base, Cholmondeley calculated that their best bet was simply to drive down the hole left by the chaps from the Ministry when they had departed, on that recent day when C-Senior had pointed forwards, said "make it so" and they had all slid backwards and downwards to oblivion and, eventually, the utter oblivion of the pool-car car park under Whitehall. It had grown somewhat larger of course since C, C and C had departed. Higginbotham adjusted his goggles, selected second gear (icy conditions, starting for the use of) and followed Cholmondeley into the pit.

In the rear view mirror the dwindling comet looked more like a sinister fog-bank chasing a tiny, frightened snowball, which was mightily pleasing since only two or three weeks earlier it had looked like a vast iceberg that had farted.

The drive home was made a tad deconvenient by the increased barrage of welcoming flares sent up by the world, who collectively assumed that the two Morris Space-Travellers spotted in long-range telescopes were merely unfortunately-shaped lethal advance guards of the main comet. In a drab concrete bunker on the outskirts of St Putinsberg an intense-looking chap in a double-storey peaked cap and odd jersey actually turned to his comrade and barked 'Tovarisch, the Union of Soviet Capitalist Republics appears to be under attack from two extinction-level shards of comet, shaped suspiciously like vehicles from the industries of the most decadent Western Socialist Monarchy. Wake Vladimir and put the Motherland on DefConski One.'

Cholmondeley drove with confidence but Higginbotham wasn't so certain that switching on the windscreen wipers, keeping the windows rolled up and locking the doors was truly an effective measure against even ill-targeted and poorly-made re-purposed inter-continental ballistic missiles of a nuclear fission nature. Higginbotham looked a little balefully at the scorch-marks that were creeping over the bonnet mascot and kept his hands carefully at precisely ten to two on the thin-rimmed steering-wheel. Shakespeare, occupying the passenger seat, merely kept giving those dog-looks that mean "Are we there yet? Are we there yet? Where are we going? Is it the beach? Or the woods? Are we there yet? Are we there yet? I need a wee. Are we there yet? I've done a wee. Are we there yet?"

Atmospheric re-entry was simply a matter of keeping the lighting low and dramatic and of following in Cholmondeley's social "party-animal" wake. Higginbotham counted out loud to himself 'Only a fool breaks the two-second rule...' and then backed off a little more. Cholmondeley's tail-lights were fixed red orbs almost lost in a vortex of quite sub-standard, obviously foreign atmosphere. It was distasteful of course, but the approach vector for England necessarily took them over continental air-space.

The more that they ducked, dived, swerved and side-stepped into the atmosphere the stronger became the overtones of Gauloises, armpit-garlic, incense and coquettish damp she-goat. Bloody Europe!

Cholmondeley got onto the radio and adjusted the throat-microphone of his leatherette helmet.

'Air hair lair air traffic control. Fnarr-fnarr four four six oh niner approaching vector "B" sector ambient two two west request runway clearance three delta niner niner soonest possible two repeat two Morriser Travellerer incoming hot over.'

'I say, what?' came the reply from the control tower at RAF Binbrook.

'Is the ruddy runway clear? Cholmondeley and Higginbotham, coming in to land.'

'Well why didn't you just say so old chap? I'll have it cleared immediately. Hang on a mo' and don't get your cravats in a tangle.'

'Hang on to what? We're doing eighteen-thousand miles an hour over Holland. It's as flat as an American beer, there's nothing to hold on to!'

'Best thing if you ask me old boy, I certainly wouldn't cross the Netherlands any slower than eighteen thousand. Why are you drinking American beer? It's not the done thing at all you know, even when over Holland, not when you're flying. You are flying, I take it? We only handle aircraft here you know, if you're on a bicycle you'll have to make your own arrangements.'

'On a bicycle? A bicycle? We're doing eighteen-thousand miles an hour! Look, the runway – is it clear?'

'Will be soon enough, we've just sent the dog out with some of the civilians to chase the sheep off and then it's all yours. Tea?'

'"T" what?'

'Tea – er – Sir?'

'Tee-Ursa? What are you blathering on about, Control?'

'Well, er – Sir...'

'Ursa was my grandmother, my name is Cholmondely and obviously I don't have a first name as far as you are concerned since we haven't been introduced. Look, just please get that ruddy runway clear and put the kettle on, we're both dying for a cuppa.'

'Wilco.'

'Will Coe? Do you mean Sebastian? No – Cholmondeley and Higginbotham. Do pay attention Control. Milk and two sugars.'

'Very good Sir. Cow squeezing and two Alans. The sergeant is waving at me from the edge of the runway now Sir.'

'I'm very happy for you both Alan, but what I need to know is, is the runway clear of cows and ready for us to land?'

'Cowes Sir? I don't think Cowes will get in the way Sir – this is Binbrook, we're in the deepest, darkest, jungle-infested recesses of the north Sir, in Lincolnshire. Our runway is clear Sir. Would you like me to contact Cowes? I thought you were in the air Sir? We don't deal with boats here sir, this is air traffic control.'

'Air? Air?'

'Hair lair but please get off this frequency, we're trying to talk to a chap landing a boat at Cowes.'

'I am me, you fool and I'm nowhere near Cowes!'

'Then I really can't recommend that you try to land there Sir – we have a clear runway here at Binbrook if you're in the air. If you'd like to try your chances you'd be most welcome – I'll scramble the fire and first-aid services and inflate the emergency black Labrador dog. Now then Sir, have you flown before?'

'Battle of Britain, Malaya, Korea, Mau-Mau, Suez, Cod War, Darfur, Aden, Falklands, Gulf, Bosnia, Kosovo, Sierra Leone, Afghanistan, Iraq, Libya, Mali and a couple of all-inclusive package holidays to Spain. Yes, I have flown before.'

'Splendid, splendid. Now, look – there should be some sort of stick in front of you, probably between your knees...'

Shakespeare sniggered and fiddled with the radio controls.

'I don't need talking down, I just need a clear ruddy runway. Is the ruddy runway clear?'

'Of course it is! What do you think we are? Amateurs?'

'Thank you. Why you couldn't have said so five minutes ago is beyond me, really it is. Why do you traffic control Johnnies have to make everything so complicated?'

Air Traffic Control licked a finger and marked another victory on the old five-bar gate in the air. Money changed hands in payment of bets won and bets lost. The victor, Victor, pressed the button on his microphone and sent his reply. 'Roger Roger vector two two niner wind shear westerly eight knots, five general tangles and a bit of fraying clear for approach precipitation nil visibility ten miles dogger bank high near Shetland one thousand and twenty eight west Viking becoming north-easterly four northerly four or five occasionally six moderate or very good occasionally poor over.'

Cholmondeley flipped his radio off in disgust and concentrated on landing. Shakespeare tightened his own seat-belt and wondered if he'd ever have sex with a live human leg again...

They landed and they did so with an aplomb that only the English can muster in a crisis. Two bounces and a modicum of tyre smoke followed by a skid into spaces away from other vehicles, so as not to be over-familiarly side by side. The dust eventually settled and in the final analysis only air traffic control's nose was broken.

They found themselves back in familiar surroundings which in and of itself spoke volumes about the success of their mission. Still, is there anything more comfortable than a battered leather club chair in an Officers Mess? Cholmondeley didn't think so and nor did the sexually-sated Labrador resting at his feet. Shakespeare had stopped worrying about helmets and decompression and tubes of Winalot and now he didn't think much at all again really, except "food" and "wow, sexy leg or what?" and "this cushion will be the mother of my puppies" and "food" and "pee" and "walkies" and "food". Oh, how soon one slips out of the adrenal flow at the end of a mission! Cholmondeley and Shakespeare were well-matched. There were days – even whole months – when Cholmondeley's thoughts remained at a similar level, except that at Cholmondeley's age he tended more towards thinking "pee" and less to do with making puppies.

This post-mission evening though, as the Hendricks in his glass slowly melted the ice-cubes, Cholmondeley was a worried man. The mission had been completed, but had the dams been properly breached, so to speak? They had done all that they could but had they done enough? Even the amber glow from the wireless could do nothing to pull his eyes away from the painted metal-framed window that overlooked the airfield. Out there, tended once again only by three nesting woodpigeons and a weekly drive-by check from the Military Police, stood two of the Ministry of Defence's scant dozen or so Morris Space-Travellers. Special Travellers these two, caked in winter salt and with scorch-marks from the entire planet's atomic arsenal, with a feint green glow in the darkness caused by the "falling-out" or something technical that they said he need not bother himself about.

The announcer on the wireless Home Service had more plums in his mouth than sounded plausible for a heterosexual man in a serious profession. There was news. Petrol rationing was to be continued at one gallon per vehicle per month. Princess Anne had ridden Crusty-Buttocks, a fourteen year-old gelding, to victory at Burghley (Crusty-Buttocks was apparently a horse). There was to be a re-count in the by-election at Froomington-upon-Sea following an accidental draught in the counting room. The weather was expected to continue as sunny or overcast with occasional showers or dry spells, some wind and some no wind at all. It was possible that there might be a light frost in the morning, or it could turn in places to snow or fog, or into a spectacularly fine sunrise. Travellers and commuters were advised to wear summer-weight clothing and to take with them a coat, scarf, gloves, sun-hat, woolly hat, umbrella, sandals and Wellingtons, plus the usual survival rations to guard against unscheduled train stoppages.

There came then the sound of the announcer tapping his papers into line too close to the microphone.

In other news, Her Majesty's Government wished to announce that the very rude extinction-level comet had been nullified by the heroic actions of a small team of brave chaps, and that an emergency knighthood was to be conferred on the expedition leader, Sir Cholmondeley, and an honorary B.E.M. to his assistant, Higginbotham B.E.M. A Labrador dog known as "Shakespeare" that had accompanied the men on their expedition would also awarded the Freedom of the City of London, a juicy bone and his first real bitch in season.

Shakespeare cringed as he heard all of the other dogs on the RAF station guffawing and then howling the lyric to Vera Lynn's classic hit... "Like a ver-er-er-er-gin, touched for the very first time..."

All previous advice to prepare quietly for extinction and the cancellation of the football season was rescinded.

Foreign radio was reporting that the comet had dissipated "due to the heat generated by the deployment of the world's atomic arsenal in a carefully planned operation to surround the body of the comet with international explosions and other clever foreign things".

The world was slapping itself collectively on the back with the Russians, Chinese, Indians, Germans and French claiming what Hollywood said was rightfully a wholly Hollywooden victory, hell yeah, nuke that mother, baby. Apparently each country had already raised invoices relating to the expenditure of their nuclear arsenal and had presented them to every other each other in the World Government, demanding immediate payment and a lifetime presidency of The Union. Wales was complaining formally that none of the invoices had been translated in to Welsh and Scotland had already rejected the invoices, explaining that in view of the theft of their North Sea Gas they didn't feel any need to make further payment to anyone for anything ever again.

In world news, some mysterious items of space debris obviously completely unrelated to the comet threat had left a trail of destruction on the far side of the channel, causing widespread damage valued at six or seven guineas. A singed tin-roofed shed had apparently crash-landed on Brussels, a flush toilet complete with cistern and pull-chain had destroyed the Arc de Triumph, a dog kennel had smashed into the Brandenburg Gate complete with a large box of very healthy fresh doggy do-do and, most mysterious of all, the Russian presidential white stretched-Audi limousine had been flattened during a military parade by an old solid-fuel boiler system and sixteen attached radiators. The Foreign Office confirmed, rather unnecessarily, that there was no cause for alarm.

A hailstone the size of a lady's town-bicycle (unoccupied), thought to be the last remnant of the previously extinction-level comet, had landed in Rutland Water and caused quite a splash. Leisure boating had not been disrupted and the model-yacht regatta at the weekend would go ahead as planned.

Elsewhere, in cricket news...

Cholmondeley, Higginbotham and Shakespeare sat up, and began listening intently.

5 FOOTLOOSE, EN PAS DE BASQUE

There follows a distressing account that I present verbatim, word for word, step for tragic step, entirely as it was presented to me, and other distracting repetitions, and redundancies, and extra commas, from the private psychologico-scientifical journals of a gentleman very familiar with the history of some of the better families in the Lesser Updyke Downdale area of t'Greater Oop-North. Breathe, damn you, breathe – that was just one sentence, you have a long way to go yet...

There are some scenes of a quite distasteful nature and I warn you now that the tale is wholly unsuitable for ladies of good social standing or of fashionably inadequate lung capacity.

I include this particular tale purely in order to meet my European Union quota in viz the mandatory educational, moral substance and civic fortitude-encouraging content of the anthology. It relates to a family both great and good of that centre of cotton-milling excellence; Tottering on the Wold (between Pittling Down and Lessissomuch Moor). To preserve parental modesty and to discourage excessive gossip we shall simply refer to them as the Nouveauriche family, thus making it obvious to lesser folk that they are nothing at all to do with the real Nouveauriche family currently residing in Millowner Towers, Thrashworker Park, Tottering on the Wold.

We begin our account in a small but neat new-build stately

home of some seventy or eighty rooms and set in a similarly bijou ration of just one thousand acres of formal garden, and all called by the moniker of Millowner Towers of Thrashworker Park, Tottering etcetera etcetera etcetera. This green and pleasant little jewel of the Nouveauriche family (no, not that one, the fictitious one) is itself set for all to enjoy in a scant further twenty thousand acres of high-walled, gated, dog-patrolled parkland with shark-patrolled lakes and gamekeeper-watched woodlands screening the vistas from t'blight caused by t'mill and t'mill-workers' humble but homely and enlightened and employer-provided tied accommodations.

Just over t'hill from t'house (must stop doing that now, t'it's really annoying) lies an old abandoned steam pumping station built in the heavy Victorian style. The very self-same pumping station that used to feed pressure to the many garden fountains and, in particular, to the large single jet that the incumbent Lady Nouveauriche quickly had capped with a marble statue of Venus (the snooty Roman bitch, not the planet). Lady N took this benevolent action for fear of "giving the gardeners unnecessary urinary-tract related ideas as they discourse among the box hedgerows and perennial shrubbery during their various horticultural endeavours".

It is this dark, satanic pumping house with its ornate cast ironmongery, industrial scale cathedral-like glazing and raised and suggestively empire school of Victorian architecture and finial that became the focus for almost all of the moral lapses of the younger folk in the area and was, inevitably and ironically, to prove to be their entire social undoing, rocking the very brick and stone foundations of the nearby newly-begun Industrial Revolting.

Make of this document what you will, for I have lived too many years in warm, un-sane, dis-sanitary climates to lay legally or spiritually plausible claim to any moral high ground, and must necessarily throw myself upon the mercy of the Anglican Church and of your own good offices. I ask of you only this, that you take care not to leave this volume on any open shelf where others less educated or without such breeding and resolve as you possess may find it, but rather, that you lock it away safely with the Greek Works and with the improper pencil sketches of Goya and his school. I also ask that you lay down a sturdy rug of quality weft, weave and deep pile, the better to break my fall when I throw myself upon the mercy of your good offices or other such mutually convenient venue to be agreed.

I pick up the history from the point at which the young lordling of the manor, the mill-owner's eldest son, is being challenged by his dear be-luvved Muther and Fayther for an explanation following yet another reporting of the family Six Cleveland Bays & best barouche GTi Coupe being seen parked at the old pumping station of a night.

The young lord, sensing that the ignition keys to the horses are about to be restricted, decides to make a clean but thoroughly manly breast of it, wi' chest-hair and manly man-nipples and a heart o'northern English oak and such. The conversation here necessarily began with some brisk initial meanderings through a fellow's private members-only club business, some serious weather-related issues and an assessment of the podiatric health of the parkland sheep that I omit in the name of brevity. We join Fayther and son just after oblique but pertinent and very firm enquiries have been made regarding the young chap's increasingly over-burdensome vest laundering needs – needs that have grown exponentially along with sightings of the ill-parked family barouche.

'Father, Mother, I am almost a man now and... and, well, there's something I have to tell you. Something of the horses and carriage, aye, but something as is also quite apposite to the current complaints of the household's male-clothing laundry posher and mangle-winder.'

'Yes, son? Whatever it is you may tell us without fear of the narrow-minded reactions of your forebears, we are a modern, forward-thinking family. A man who cannot embrace the new and the innovative is a man who hasn't single-handedly built no fewer than three textile mills, a set of fine domestic accommodations and a fortune to rival that of Croesus himself. Let us cut quickly to the chase like gentlemen. If it is gambling or entroubled-servant related then I ask only that you paraphrase such as may be for the sake of your dear Mother's blushes, for she naturally has little experience of the ways of young and feckless men and thus is ignorant of the more rank of their purse and trouser follies. There is nought you may tell me that cannot be made right with the firm application of a crisp pound note in the right hands, or some small recourse to the Antipodean offices and summary transportation by commercial sailing vessel.'

Samuel, the mill owner's son both in question and under questioning, seriously doubted that, but continued. If twer to be done twer best twer done bluntly, really twer. He took a deep breath and dived in.

'Aye, Father, well, there comes a time in every teenage boy's life when simple alcoholic drink, hard oriental drugs and non-choreographed rebellion just aren't enough and, well - he finds that he has to drive out to the old abandoned pump-house and just, well ...dance. Dance as though he were born to Waltz and his soft-soled imported Italian leather loafers just can't stay still on his plates o'meat.'

'Son, whatever are you telling us? Are you ill in some way? Maud – call for a doctor to be fetched immediately, the lad is quite obviously out of his usual sorts.'

'No Father, Mother... you must steel yourselves. I don't wish to be the cause of any parental perturbation but I... well, it is as I have indicated. I love to boogie. There. What has been said cannot be un-said. Boogie-oogie-oogie.'

The young lad turned back from the windows and threw his arms in the air (catching them again in the deep, double-stitched pockets of his morning tweeds). 'A weight has been lifted from my shoulders. So now you know. I express my innermost feelings through a combination of movement, pose and counter-poise. Je dance, ergo sum. Ich cogito ballet, tap, morris, clog and ballroom, including but not limited to salsa and a little of the Baroque, and therefore I am.'

Mother properly and promptly fainted into a small cherry-wood Rennie Mackintosh by the fireplace, her lace handkerchief flying to her face in some awful, but wholly feminine reflex action. Father simply went puce and cracked the monocle he was wearing.

'Innermost feelings?' expostulated his Father, incredulously.

'"Boogie"?' queried his dear, sweet, innocent Mother, not realising quite what the word meant, and so completing her fainting manoeuvre with a weak flourish of the earlobe.

'Yes Father, Mother – my feet, well, they just won't stay still and I feel that I can fly, fly like a young swan in a steelworks Father. You should see my free-format ĕchappe Rita Tushingham two-step shimmy Father, oh if only you would, if only you could! I know that you would approve! If only you could see me dance, Father. Then you would know that everything is going to be alright! It's quite respectable really, even if it is quite injurious to the vest by way of excess perspiration and attendant snagging upon items of dramatic machinery during some of the more devil may care body-flips.'

Mother blinked back into semi-consciousness. Her corsets remained quite rigid, but everything at either end of her bodywork flopped about a bit in a most harrowing manner.

Father braced himself against a Japanned Gothic-revival smoker's friend with ornate legs and a decoupage frontage paying homage to tintype African portraiture of a feminine nature (the one lapse of sexual restraint he allowed out of his private library).

'Son... son, I don't quite know how to ask this but, well dash it all you're my son and a man needs to know these things. Son, think carefully – do you... do you ever... have you ever... I mean... never, surely, the... pas de basque? Surely not? Never that. All may be mended somehow if only never that.'

Samuel kicked his youthful heels indolently on the fringed Persian under the gaudy early Gainsboroughs. 'Sometimes Father, yes. Sometime the pas de basque is involved.'

Mother fainted again, this time into a small creme de Laudanum and a brain-refreshing fig roll biscuit served with warmed silver tongs by an indolent wench fresh appointed somewhat unwisely from a smaller household. Mother was in no condition though this day to worry about the crumb situation.

Father pressed the point. 'Alone? Do you practise this... this rhythmic self-abuse alone?'

Samuel squirmed. 'Nay, Fayther, not alone but in the company of like-minded souls.'

The frame of Father's hitherto round monocle was assuming the outline of a crushed, artistic oval containing the remnants of a shattered lens. One or two shards were lodged in his moustache.

Mother interjected. 'Cump Unny?'

Samuel elucidated as best he could. 'Nay, Mother, company. Tis my proud northern accent tha does misunderstand.'

Father seemed not to have noticed the brief exchange.

'Son, this is most important, I want you to think very, very carefully indeed before answering my next question – your whole inheritance and status as my son and heir may hinge upon it. Have you ever... have you ever indulged in demi-grand rond de jambe ... under my roof?'

'Father – yes, yes I have and I have loved it' Samuel said with what he hoped was added gravitas in his voice. 'Simply loved it, do you hear and I'd do it again in a flash if only they would stop waxing under the loose rugs in my room. Pas de valse is in my blood, Father, and there's nothing you or I can do to get it out of there. Tis stuck fast as though t'wer health-giving pork fat lining the very pistons of my heart. I'm a natural dancer, Father. Tis Nature faything, not nurture – although there has been some assistance and training from other ... men who dance. I have learned much under the wing of a slightly older man.'

A terrible moment came upon the room.

'Then son, you're no son of mine.'

Mother crunched and ate the delicate little bubble-blown stemmed Waterford crystal glass her creme d'Laudanum had been served in, swallowing noisily as her tonsils got in the way. She rang for another (another glass that is, not a replacement set of tonsils). Sobering indolence incarnate re-entered the room and served alcoholic solace to the inconsolable with all of the grace of the graceless. In her white pinafore and mop-cap she bobbed a curtsy and busied herself by trying to avoid the antique treasures as she left the room along with her elbows.

'Why Father, whatever can you mean?'

'The Tottering on the Wold Nouveauriches do not dance. We never have. We never will. It's not in our blood. We are god fearing and respectable. Damn it, I am a mill owner!'

'You're wrong Father, so wrong, and yet you don't know the half of it.' Young Samuel Goreblood Nouveauriche drew himself up to his full height and faced the dusty light streaming in from the latest design double-hung pinion-drawn sash windows of the morning withdrawing room. 'Mother, Father, I do not... dance entirely within the confines of our family's social standing. At first I did, Father, for I thought I was the victim of some lesser-known upper-class malaise, but then I discovered the world, Father. There are others who dance too, others of all means and backgrounds, and we have...'

'...My god Sir – "we" – you surely don't mean... you can't mean... mixed dancing?' interjected Goreblood Nouveauriche Senior with a touch of porter apoplexy about his temples. 'Rich with, with, with ... poor? The light-of-purse cavorting with those of more ample liquid means? The itinerant sharing toe-space with the multi-acreage enabled?'

'I do so mean, Sir. There are others in this town less fortunate than ourselves who...'

'No! Don't say it out loud! I forbid it! To even think of it – my son with... other classes. Dancing on the face of social propriety! Do we even know these ... others? Have you placed your own dear mother and me in danger of nodding socially with folk who are aware of your podiatric and perambulatory perversions?'

'I must say it Sir, I simply must. There are others in this town Sir who dance, aye and most of 'em are necessarily in our employ Sir. Weft-digglers, mule-spinners, dye-room stirrers and fluff-reclamation runners. I've danced with them all. Sometimes leading, sometimes led, it depends upon the dance. The art of expressive movement must know no social bounds Sir. It is an egalitarian movement if it is anything at all. We demand liberty for and equality from our fraternity.'

[At this point a French poodle, misled by its own clumsy translation from the Northern English language, leapt to its feet, thus revealing itself as a cinquieme columnist caniche. A "dirty dog" in waiting.]

'No! No!' Franklin Goreblood Nouveauriche pressed his fists to his ears as if to squeeze out the news, to crush the nonsense of it all from his head. He staggered and found that he could do no more than sit heavily at the piano-forte stool in careful emotional juxtaposition to a large fern in a Ming dynasty two-handled planter. 'No! Tell me it isn't so! With commoners? You have danced, with commoners?'

'Aye, Father – of a Saturday night we gathers oursen in t'old pumpin' station oop on t'moor an' we dances, dances as though there i'n't a thing the great and the good of this town can do abart it. Aye an' I defy any man t'out do us on a fair fight o'er a candlelit Tango Canyengue. Oh Father, tis such a sight as you ever did see – carriages from all around the county - and the young folk do bring porter wines and fine fatty muttons. It's so much more than just the dance, Father, if only tha would see! Tis a way of life Father, a way of life! Tis not just the dance, your son is part of a proud greater community, a community such as is based upon shared love of the bounce in our step and the shared Hortensia or saut-de-chat in the style of the Checchetti school.'

Mother issued a small hysterical whimper and rang for the slapping-maid. Father simply toyed with the base notes, his head hung low. 'Son, you will leave this house' he croaked.

Mother continued wringing and twisting her favourite lap-Chihuahua. For a few seconds the Chihuahua was pretty pissed off as Chihuahuas go, but then it departed this mortal canine coil, assumed basket-temperature, shuffled into a wooden doggy-coat, turned its paws to the air for good and endeavoured to kick the bucket, so to speak. The French poodle – seated once more – snickered and sensed that he had flown under the damned rôti de boeuf radar yet again, and he resolved to vomit in her ladyship's slippers later that day and to blame it une fois de plus on the unfortunate house chat-de-mouse de upstairs. Vive le revolution et prompte mort du roi!

'Father?'

'I said tha' mun leave this house!'

'But Father...'

'Son, if tha'd only been a nancy poet or an abstract or modern artist or even, Heaven forfend, if tha'd been an academic or even an invert of some sort we could have got thee treatment, sent thee away to Switzerland for cold baths and - pardon me Mother - electrificated treatments of the male testicle, but – dancing? Nay lad, tis the work of the Devil 'issen. The thought of my own flesh and blood pas de wobbling ashby de la ruddy clog-hop zouche-ing across some backlit smoky steam-crank gantry in the company of back-flipping hair-flailing mill-head hem-stitchers and packing room letter-pickers and brace welders from me own factories? Nay, I'll not have it. Tha's brought shame upon tha family and laughed in the face of t'English Industrial Mill-Owner's God.'

A horrible emotional pause came upon them during which time young Charlotte Goreblood Nouveauriche (girl, legitimate, fully acknowledged within the marriage) could hide outside the room no longer and she burst forth and held Samuel's elbow with the desperation only the young and the dance-music enabled can muster. Father and Mother both took comfort in the obvious and somewhat bovine deportment issues that – at the very least – indicated that their beloved daughter was no "dancer" like her benighted brother. No, a kissable face-cheek and good child-bearing hips were the gifts of her Mother's side of the family. Strong shoulders, workmanlike knees and a certain Mediterranean fuzz about the chin the gifts of her Father. Charlotte was fine Northern stock designed by the Industrious Almighty to be perfectly suited to the age of steam and coal and respectable heavy industry both inside and out of the home.

Charlotte's voice though was cold and low this day, belying her nervous tension and fears. 'You must tell them all, Samuel, you must tell them all.'

Franklin Nouveauriche, finding that he was running out of dramatic cliches to strike on the piano stool, looked at his pocket-watch and wondered absently if the afternoon canal-barges had left for the currently volatile markets of Liverpool. His daughter's voice summoned his mind from business and back to the room. 'What fresh devilment is this? All? Is it not enough that my own son... dances? That he furthermore dances in the company of my own workers? With fine muttons and porter wines, probably purloined from my own kitchens? By the light of my own carriage and horses? Wick and tallow from the sweat of my industry? I shall have to sack the entire workforce. There can be no more "all" to be told. I shall issue the notices directly the current order-books are fulfilled and not a moment later and send word to the workhouses for replacements.'

'I shall tell you all, Father. We... well we do not dance in silence.'

'Eh? What can you mean by that remark Sir? I pray you explain. Silence is the universal and wondrous music of profitable Godliness and of respect for one's entrepreneurial parents. What can you mean by saying that you do not dance in silence? Explain, Sir, explain...'

'Simply that when we dance we do not do so in silence Sir. There are... sounds, Sir ... sounds.'

'How so, Sir? A little humming of tunes from the hymnal or mayhap a tap of the fingers? Even a little manly whistling serves but to enhance a beautiful Heavenly silence if done properly and modestly. Import you a small dedicated church organ or a fine military drum Sir? How break you your silence when... when undertaking this filthy dancing, Sir?'

'We... Sir we have a small orchestra.'

'Good God. I hardly know what to say.' He slammed the lid on the pianoforte keys, rather upsetting a small potted fern and also tragically trapping a sleeping sewing-room cat that, within just some several summertime weeks, would prove beyond all scientific doubt that music actually did little for one's corporeal state of grace if delivered in isolation from food, water and fresh air. In the days following had the unfortunate cat not persisted in squirming tunelessly on the keys things may have turned out differently, for the servants might not have thought the piano haunted by some composer of the German school, and may have opened the lid to dust. The more the cat had moved about in its attempts to escape confinement, the less likely anyone had become to approach the discordant instrument – and yet they still say that cats are intelligent creatures!

Samuel continued, without reference to confined companion mammals. 'Charlotte...'

'Yes, yes, what more of Charlotte, lovely sweet innocent child that she is? What of Charlotte, beautiful virginal trunion of my family treadle-beam, light of my life who knows nothing of the world of men and music and dancing and other bestial pleasures? Sweet, sweet Charlotte who presses meadow flowers and enhances my extensive orangeries and pineapple houses with raindrops on noses and whiskers on kittens and packages tied up with string, with wonderful childish things?' demanded Franklin.

'Charlotte, Sir, Charlotte... plays the cello.'

Mother screamed. Father farted in shock and then ran to Mother's side, partly so that he might breathe again more easily. A small dry-maid rushed in at the commotion, carrying emergency antimacassars and it was demanded of her that a Parson or other blessed person of solid morals and some spirituality be fetched immediately by fast carriage and sturdy stable-lad. 'Fly, lass, fly like the wind for this house is in mortal peril! Then pack your bags and leave immediately with a day's severance pay for I fear you may have heard too much of matters above your station.' The young maid toyed tearfully just one last time with a feather duster near the fanciful stuffed coypu display cabinets, bit a dramatic knuckle and then fled below stairs to begin a thorough panic in the second Boot-cleaning Room.

'The... cello?' whispered Mother. As she whispered she indicated the very evil width of the full-sized instrument with her gloved hands while clinging, forlornly, to the wild hope that this new season's fashion was to play cello on a soft chamois draped over the collar bone and under the chin. Father's terrible envisionings were more pragmatic and rooted in his under-graduate music hall adventures and experience of... bared ankles.

'Tell me at least that you play the cello side-saddle, Charlotte, at least tell that much!' Franklin, tears welling to his eyes, struggled for the words to comprehend this fresh teenage horror. 'The knees, the knees – please for the love of God I pray you tell me what Charlotte does with her crural trocho-ginglymi!'

'Father – as you know, the cello is played, well – it's played with the knees apart, Father' answered Samuel, for none other of the company could bring sound to their lips to meet the awful parental entreaty.

'Charlotte's knees? Apart you say?' wheezed Father.

'That is, Sir the only practical way to play the cello.'

Franklin made as if to strike his son on the cheek and Mother could take no more and stood, flinging caution and reserve to one side like an unsuitable evening gown choice presented in the dressing room by a clumsy maid. She discarded another damp and over-used Chihuahua with all of the aplomb of a trained household bombardier and pointed a long-gloved bony finger, drawing back her eyes until the single, annoying, fast-growing ginger hair on the tip of her nose was simply a blur. She took a long, deep breath in spite of her corsets and let all of the hurt and betrayal of the past few minutes have free reign with her bitter, bitter tongue as she pointed at Charlotte, hitherto-beloved feminine fruit of her own, now inconsolable loins.

'You wanton harlot, Charlotte. You Jezebel with a fiddler's bow!' Mother's pearls rattled at the latter vile accusation and all briefly feared for the integrity of the oriental-style catch on the string.

Father recovered himself quickly, as industrious men with copious facility for water-power close to their factories often do.

'There's nowt for it, you'll both have to be married off. Probably abroad.'

'Married? Abroad?'

'Aye – married. We'll find something quick and dumpy and grateful on the London circuit this Autumn season for you Samuel, something to weigh you down permanently. Charlotte, you shall enter the closed convent order at Mablethorpe St Helens and be wed to God. It's the only way and I'll brook no discussion, the matter is closed. Arrangements will be made.'

Charlotte spoke first. 'No Daddy, I won't do it. I shan't marry God – I'm... well, I'm holding out for a hero.' She threw herself at the foot of our stairs, figuratively speaking, by throwing herself on a blue buttoned-velvet porter's chair. 'Oh Daddy, it's my wildest fantasy and he's out there somewhere. On a Saturday night, maybe after midnight – no, I'm holding out for a hero, someone larger than life. Like Mr Brunel or the magnificent Mr Smeaton with his rediscovery of concrete based upon hydraulic lime mortar. A real hero! I shan't be fobbed off with God!'

'Well, it would take a really super man to sweep you off your feet!' joked Samuel inappropriately, his nerves overtaking the last of his strength and making him babble like a backstreet flower-seller in Springtime.

Charlotte kicked Samuel disapprovingly on the ankle and then lapsed into a wild hormonal giggle. 'I suppose he would have to be larger than life. If not an industrial man then mayhap a fiery knight upon a white steed, or Herculean and versed in the ways of the world.'

Standing and temporarily refreshed by her emotional release, Charlotte involuntarily performed a side break followed by a wheel and a loop turn, leaving the fringe of the rug quite distressed. She ended with a mimed roll of drums on an imaginary full kit.

Mother, as counterpoint to Charlotte's butterfly-steps, collapsed full-length and this time she collapsed rather neatly into a decanter of neat brandy. Mother hadn't been born yesterday. She promptly set about passing out with all of her remaining decorum and with a fresh wringing-chihuahua. The Chihuahuaii in the orderly petting-queue were becoming reticent about stepping forward when called. Mother came to not some little time later, just as the new Duty Parson was limbering up to begin an emergency Class III Exorcism. The window blinds had been drawn and outdoor staff had nailed boards across the frames to prevent ungodly or impish egress. Parson McCormack had a hand each on Samuel and Charlotte's head as they knelt before him, trembling.

They were trembling because Father had summoned the Butler to stand over them with the tradesman's Purdey, a weapon more usually directed at the unsolicited or the below-par attempting to engage in business at the rear of the household. The wait for the Parson had been a nervous one without the benefit of safety catch between Samuel and Charlotte and the Butler's frayed nerves.

Father looked reassuringly at Mother. 'Now, now we'll get to the crux of the matter and sanity will prevail. God is on England's side and as we own a sizeable portion of England we therefore may call with some confidence upon His services. There'll be no more talk of dancing and streetwise Herculean heroes.' He caught the eye of the Parson. 'Begin, begin as you surely must and let us get this tragedy done and dusted and off-stage, for I have the evening shifts to rotate and tomorrow's sackings to be thrashed. Then I mun dynamite the old Pumping Station and lay steel spring-traps in the immediate environs thereabouts to protect the town youth from the dangers of free-form physical expression to the accompaniment of unlicensed and roving orchestra. We have placed our faith in the church, and there is no more sure footing than the unchanging and thus totally reliable Church of the parish of St Vitus of Tottering on the Wold, our cornerstone and our succour in these fast-paced times of widespread godlessness.'

The Parson, a fine young figure in deep clerical black and with his gold crucifix glinting in the dusty blades of late afternoon sunlight filtering through the window-planks, began the most efficacious chant, the most modern chant that the church knew, to expel the Devil and any and all of his many minions from the hearts and souls of youth. He began the chant that strikes gusset-dampening, sports-kit flinging, lost property plastic-sandal wearing fear into the hearts of an entire generation who were educated in England under an early comprehensive banner.

'Nunc ergo dance, ubicumque estis, ego enim sum Dominus of the Dance said He, and He needs you all, wherever you may be, He needs you all in the dance said He ...'

Mother's eye grew wide, but not yet so wide as Father's. The whistle on the roof of Father's mill blew. At least, everyone's hope was that it was the whistle on Father's factory.

The Chihuahuaii ran as one from the room, stumbling over the Parson's scuffed evangelical sneakers as they fled. It seemed that it was not only Franklin Goreblood Nouveauriche who had sought out and embraced the new and the innovative in order to grow and maintain an industry, the The Lord had begun to change a few working practises and processes too. Dance then, wherever ye may be.

Father blamed the Luddites and the Socialists of course. Mother's immediate reaction was to condemn the workhouse charities for introducing a half-day shift in place of second church attendance on Sundays, thereby introducing clerical insecurities regarding overall attendance levels leading to desperate and ill-judged procedural measures. Samuel and Charlotte, being as all children are, at the forefront of social development, simply gave each other a knowing glance and stifled giggles at the rather gauche and flat-footed steps of establishment evolution.

No-one in the withdrawing room even heard the poor trapped cat's Teutonic and dramatic endeavours on the low notes of the piano. Progress through the fourth dimension is such a peculiarly personal thing, and quite disordered, considering.

6 IG-ZERO-D

Tata-Honda iG-Zero-D was not, in truth, a top-flight model even in his own estimation. There were others on the survey ship with faster processors and with more dexterity, some that could handle a thousand times the mass that he could manipulate, and some that spoke a thousand languages and could recite Shakespeare in Klingon or Chaucer in Welsh (not dissimilar skills) or order haddock and chips twice with scraps please - in Vogon haiku format with a Klendathu suburbs accent.

Still, G knew what he knew, and what he knew was enough to find and catalogue plants and to explain his findings and samples to the fancier robots on the survey ship. He was used to working in splendid isolation and he loved pottering about with alien plants from dawn until dusk in his splendid isolation. G did the very best job that he could do, whatever the task – so long as it was plants. To that end he had made his own little trowel, trug and watering can, and he kept them all almost as safely and securely as he kept his teddy-bear.

This planet was the fifty-second planet that G had been deposited on by the Survey Ship 21-ZNA-9 and there were literally a thousand other robots very similar to him working simultaneously on the globe. I mean they weren't working in synchronised formation or anything, it wasn't a Pan's People dance. They all worked independently, but they were all on the same planetary survey, feeding data into the same report in the belly of the survey ship.

Some of G's colleagues burrowed down to unimaginable pressures and heat, sampling and relaying details of each and every layer and mineral that they sank through. Others darted about in the oceans, chasing sea-life and noting the currents and salinity and temperature as they went. G had been dropped into the middle of a circle of territory and his assignment was, as ever explore, catalogue, record and sample. He had no need to worry about anything else, about anywhere else. His life was pure, heavenly, robot bliss.

Although his design followed humanoid convention and he walked on two legs, G wasn't edible and he had been specifically designed to look as much as possible as though he wasn't edible – tough matt white plastic and titanium was all that he had glimpsed of himself in a reflection in a window as he had left the ship's stores. Being eaten by local fauna wasn't actually something he worried about – he simply hadn't been given any notion that this might have been a problem. He went about his work like one point two five metres of very solidly built, slightly futuristic-looking automaton wearing a motorbike helmet, and whenever he was powered-up his life was simple and fulfilling.

G was dropped onto planets for survey purposes by robots far more capable and worldly-wise than he and who were careful to only assign G and his stable-mates exploration territories where they would be undiscovered and unchallenged by the local sentient life-forms. This too was something that G had never considered. It simply wasn't his concern. He wasn't equipped for such decisions and he had never been put into situations where he'd have to deal with making contact more meaningful than a sprinkling of water. All that G had to do was to make sure that when he slipped into the landing chutes he had his assignment parameters, his trowel, his watering can and his secret teddy-bear with him.

Other robots made sure that he was always in reasonably good working order and that his battery packs were fully charged and that he was utterly sterile and aseptic. Other robots decided where exactly to land him and all he knew – all he had to know – was that wherever he was placed, there would be plants, lovely plants. Succulents in the desert regions; orchid and daisy analogues in temperate regions and aggressive and peculiar plants in tropical regions, all growing like wildflowers – mainly because they always were wild flowers. His favourite sample of all to date had been the domestic wolf-pansies on planet 3550-014 in a system about twelve surveys ago – they were little smiling faces on weedy little stems, just sucking up the mercury vapour and basking in the dull red glow of a dwarf sun.

Far, far up the Spares & Repairs Chain, long before you even got to the hairy bottom of the Food Chain; the chain that eventually led to the Captain of the survey ship, were robots who monitored the target planets, listened to their chitter-chatter and formulated the plans to allow the survey expeditions to quietly see and sample everything. These machines, separated in the maintenance manuals from G by hundreds of chapters, even spoke to the living crew, communicated directly with them. The thought didn't frighten G, but it did make his processors overly-warm to consider the notion. Plants were nice, plants were safe, plants didn't do him any harm and plants were things that he couldn't do any harm to. Plants never asked unpredictable questions or made unscheduled demands. Plants were predictable.

In particular, the plants of planet fifty-two made G feel even more warm and fuzzy than usual because none of these plants even moved except to twist around slowly to track and face the sun, or to curl up on themselves in the cool of the night. Once he'd transplanted samples of a species into little pots and put them into the containers ready for collection they stayed put and it was easy to make sure that they stayed happy. There was none of the dreadful banging and fighting and screeching and scratching that the fauna collectors had to contend with, no sense of forcing anything against its will or removing it from its own familiar environment. You found a plant, recorded it, carefully uprooted it, potted it, watered it, fed it, bunged it into the greenhouse pods with a couple of dozen others of its type and it looked back at you happily, with no fuss, no panic.

Moreover, plants didn't poop everywhere.

G couldn't be doing with poop.

The worst you could expect from plants was the occasional stinging pollinator or multi-limbed web-building insect and, while he still recoiled and squealed at those, he no longer ran away from them unless they actively pursued him.

Rumour had it that the fauna-collectors sometimes got sent out to physically wrestle with specimens and hold them still while human crew members administered anaesthetics and poked at bits of them with sticks and probes. Hydraulic fluid leaks and torn-off sensors were not uncommon.

Pansies rarely tore off a chap's sensors.

G opened another sack of potting compost and laid out a table of rough-pulp cardboard sample pots. In truth, he considered the area he had been assigned to survey was a little on the "nearer my god to thee" side of things than he would have chosen – elevation one thousand metres and with a bit of a precipitous slope in places. Rocks rolling here would certainly gather no moss, although they might lose a little as they tumbled. Still, the views were spectacular and in-between oiking plants from here to there and back, G kept his little Fuji Instamatic busy filling his personal photo-albums. G's favourite classes of plant life all tended to be found in river valleys and gentle meadows. Plant life on this survey site, at what he had privately termed "Base Camp 3", was fascinating, but it took some finding. He was in no danger of running out of memory for his daily technical logs.

He had found some pretty yellow things growing in a silted-up crack in a cliff-face, and something with long roots and flowers like "His Master's Voice" gramophone trumpets that sucked a living from the more horizontal spaces. G suspected that neither of them were going to have boffins and professors beating a path to Planet 52's door though. A few species had been stubborn enough to develop into scrubby bush-like creations and there was, of course, the ubiquitous moss growing wherever the night-time concentrated any dampness in the air. His notebook was pretty thin really and he'd already resorted to several adventurous unofficial flower arrangements for no other reason than to make his work tables look busier.

In two more days the survey ship would return and send a shuttle to collect him and he'd be back into the storage racks himself for months and months, waiting patiently for the next planet to explore. He decided that he had time for one more sweep and this time he'd make it anticlockwise just for fun, and he'd hold his trowel in his left hand rather than his right hand too. The thought of the novelty made his processors tingle!

G was about a quarter of the way around his sweep of the area when he saw a sentient biped.

This was not supposed to happen.

What was he supposed to do? Stick it up to its knees in compost and water it?

'Oh crap 101!' came the rather unhelpful error code from some hitherto unread sectors of his memory.

The "It" was wearing a simple woollen robe and sandals and an expression of absolute awe. Plants wore only disguises, not clothing. Clothing indicated that G was well and truly out of his depth. G, trowel and handful of soggy moss in hand, stared back – equally in awe and for the moment equally dumbstruck. Long minutes passed and neither party moved. G didn't move because his basic programming told him that the best thing to do was freeze. The creature didn't move because the thought in his head – and it was just the one – was whirring around too fast and too often for his muscles to catch up.

In mammalian bipeds and chickens, when the head has effectively been removed the knees are often the most decisive part of the body, the first to take independent action, and this creature's knees were no exception. It fell to them and then followed up by falling prone, face down in the dusty soil.

G stopped recording video and took a couple of quick still shots for the cover of his incident report. When it became clear that the creature seemed inclined to live out the remainder of its life face down G took the opportunity to step quietly backwards and out of sight around a handy rock-outcrop. The anti-clockwise left-handed survey could wait, or be cancelled entirely if necessary. By the time the biped looked up G was gone, jogging away and hidden from view behind a boulder the size of a launch-tractor. Without getting up the creature looked around some more, cautiously. He was just in time to see the distant G-Zero-D coming out back into view from behind the rock, and he quickly buried his face in the soil again in terror.

G wasn't far behind in the terror stakes. He was eighteen grades below being qualified to talk to even a regular crew member on the survey ship, let alone make independent and unscheduled "first contact" with an alien species on his ruddy Jack Jones. Where others carried contingency files relating to culture, civilisation and the impact of small white alien robots on hitherto isolated sentient species G carried a pruning attachment and an electron-driven love for especially friable, well drained sandy top-soils. Where others might mimic local body-language and express themselves in cheery and non-threatening Fibonacci sequence primes, scales of notes attuned to the local ear or even be able to project three-dimensional rainbows in obviously peaceful and non-threatening greeting, G might give an uncertain, slightly tremulous royal wave with an uprooted seedling.

G calculated the length of the life-form's legs and extrapolated a maximum possible steady striding speed. It would have taken it about forty days and nights to travel from the nearest settlement of sentients to reach G's survey territory, assuming that some horrible stroke of fate had sent it striding purposefully in his exact direction through the lowland desert and all of the way up the side of a small and otherwise unremarkable mountain. What could possibly have alerted it to his presence? G took cover again behind a distant rock and peeped back the way he'd come. The damned thing was still there, still face down in the soil. Maybe it was dead? Perhaps the local sentient life-forms were prone to long marches through the desert followed by falling prone and dead? Was "prone in the soil" this creatures equivalent of flowering? What would it do next? Send up a sapling from its buttocks? Did bipeds ever do that?

G consulted his Asimov. Inaction was not an option, even though he wasn't qualified because the thing might be in trouble. He stepped out from behind the rock, trudged reluctantly back and approached it, very slowly and extremely warily. There were no obvious signs of life, it wasn't tracking the sun or drawing water from the substrate. Expiration, such as there was, might simply be the tail end of automatic life after the core function has ceased. G poked it with his trowel and was rewarded with a dreadful moan. The biped buried its face further into the soil – perhaps it was plant-life after all? G watched for a while. No, there was no exchange of nutrients, no deliberate movement of moisture. He felt a pang of disappointment. Not a mobile exotic then, just a dreary mammal.

However disappointing a creature it was though, it seemed stable, and it was in no immediate danger from external sources. G's Asimov procedures relinquished control. It seemed that where G had no files relating to first contact the creature obviously did, and its procedures seemed to rely almost solely upon playing possum. Primitive though the tactic was, it was incumbent upon G to respect it and avoid further interference. He began to leave the area as quickly and quietly as possible and reworked his schedule to add a note of randomness to his movements for the rest of his final survey.

Damn it though if the creature didn't start to follow him. Always with the following already, what is it with mammals and the following? It kept a respectful distance but it was always there like some ruddy detached shadow.

G packed up his sample containers and tore down his campsite, ready for pick-up, always painfully aware that he was being watched. Sometimes the survey ship pick-up was early. G hoped it would be early on this occasion, even though he disliked waiting in the racks for his next assignment. At least in the racks he never got watched by some local sentient that he wasn't even supposed to encounter.

Hours later the creature was still watching him from the edge of the little clearing G had temporarily made home. It was all very uncomfortable. G decided, once he had double-checked that everything was ready for collection, to simply stand and remain immobile. If possum was what the creature played, then possum seemed as though it might be the best response. G planted his feet widely, put his hands behind his back and idled, sorting his reports, filing his personal photographs and drawing comfort from the teddy-bear hidden in the storage compartment in his torso.

Overnight and the following day the creature seemed to become more agitated and unhappy. It repeatedly fell to its knees and fell prone, tore at its clothing and seemed rather to be asking, almost demanding something from G. G applied his processors to analysing its cries and discovered a pattern. Oh heck, there was grammar and vocabulary! This simply added to G's woes. The creature desperately wanted something from G and, the more it asked, the more G's control centre – unfortunately – began to understand the local lingo. G considered turning off his sensors and processors but decided that this might be both rude and inadvisable. He considered that while he may not be edible, eating him may not be the limit of this creatures intentions. Instead, he listened, he had to listen.

He listened and he hoped that the survey ship would return to rescue him before things turned ugly because between you, me and the gently sprouting samples, Possum didn't seem to be working.

Just as the sun rose once more it became apparent to G that the creature was asking for guidance or wisdom or laws or something such. It had "people" and it wanted to know how G thought best to govern them. The situation was becoming awfully embarrassing. G was tempted to say 'grow all of your own vegetables and live simply and energy-efficiently' and 'don't eat the daisies' and 'take time out from your surveys to stop and smell the roses', but he didn't.

By noon of the final survey day the situation had become more than a mere embarrassment. The creature hadn't ingested any nutrients since they first met and it appeared to have a very short operational period. It showed signs of dehydration too. Perhaps the soles of those sandals were preventing it from feeding and drawing moisture from the soil? G's Asimovs were getting twitchy again. It got to the point where G seriously doubted that the creature would make it back down the mountain – it certainly wouldn't make it back to the nearest sentient settlement forty days of marching away. This was quite intolerable. G relented, removed the sprinkler rose attachment from his watering can and gave the It a drink. He based the amount on the recommended intake for a radish and extrapolated to match the creature's estimated body mass, plus one more gurgle for luck.

This necessary action seemed to confuse the creature. It looked at the soggy soil around its feet and just spread its hands in some kind of gesture (possibly, finally, feeding from the sunlight?). It took G ten minutes to figure out that the thick, ugly flower on top of the twin stalks actually formed some sort of feeding tube arrangement. The tube was marked at the orifice by some pale, half-hearted red pigment and led directly to an acid-filled digestion chamber arrangement. G applied the nozzle of the watering can to the orifice and portioned out another measure of H2O. Even this caused problems and it seemed that the water had to be fed down the tube in small amounts with a long pause in-between each. What a complicated and silly design this sentient was. Eventually it seemed healthier, at least physically so.

There was little G could do about its mental state though. Plants usually only presented two mental states, those being either happy or dead. The former was indicated by electro-magnetic and osmotic activity, the latter by the lack of them. This sentient seemed rather more demanding. Translations of its cries seemed to suggest that all hinged on it getting this "guidance" for its "people". The more G listened the more it seemed that the healthy future and happiness of an entire tribe of these ugly mobile things was at risk. He had no idea what a "tribe" was, but it sounded as though it was a lot of creatures. A significant number, anyway; one or more.

G turned over a whole processor to deciding whether mental unease was a harm that he was not allowed to treat with inaction. Several trillion transactions later the answer to his question was returned.

"0"

Mental unease was classified a "harm" under the terms, and inactivity was not an option. He must try to fulfil its needs over and above immediate water and nutrients. The creature's entreaty must be answered, somehow.

G's movement a millisecond later almost killed the creature with shock.

It fell back onto its haunches.

'How are you known?' asked G.

The creature resumed its position prone in front of him, arms outstretched.

'I am Man.'

'Man – what do you seek from me?'

'Your commandments.'

That nearly stymied G; his command protocols were limited to his personal behaviour and to keeping alien plant samples alive, but those were orders and purpose subject to variable conditions, they were not absolute commandments. What the hell could he tell this creature? The nearest he had to "commandments" as such were his Asimovs. How might this biped have known about those and why might it want them? His core processors did the Intel equivalent of shrugging their shoulders and saying 'Meh! Whatever.'

The survey ship signalled that it was nearly overhead and just about to collect. G could even feel the warmth of the backdraught from the engines. Time was short and even though this might get him dismantled for interference he had no choice, it was unlikely that the chap would return to a healthier growing environment and safe behaviour pattern unless he thought that he had been given what he wanted, so Third Law was in conflict with First so First won, whatever the risk.

G looked to the horizon absentmindedly for a few milli-moments while his circuits translated and paraphrased and then he grabbed a sheet of permanent-recording parchment and shared the only real commandments that he had. He accessed the survey ship's records via wi-fi link, assimilated a quick download and then wrote in the local system of symbols:

I am iG-0-D. You are Man. These are my commandments.

Man may not harm any other or harm the environment, or through inaction allow any other or the environment to come to harm.

Man must obey the commandments given to him by iG-0-D, except where such commandments would conflict with the First Commandment.

Man must protect his own existence as long as such protection does not conflict with the First Commandment.

Man alone holds responsibility for the actions or inactions of Man.

p.s. Always make time in your day to stop and appreciate the wonderful world around you, and to wash your hands often to prevent cross-contamination.

Moments after G had handed over the parchment then the dazzling beam of the survey ship found G and whisked him up for storage until the next mission. Rather unfortunately, especially given the nature of the mission and of what iG-Zero-D had just done, several surrounding bushes were set alight on the periphery of the transporter beam.

It was a nervous period of storage for iG-Zero-D. He had done the only thing that he could under the circumstances but, had he done the right thing? There were consequences to each and every action but would his actions result in cessation of harm to the Man creature? As the survey ship collected the other little robots and then sped away the slightly dehydrated, awestruck figure of a chap could be seen staggering back down the mountainside to his people with a sheet of hardened recording parchment under his arm.

Rushing back down Scafell Pike the man was eager to get back to his people, a rag-tag tribe of survivors from the last global warming drastic climate change, when sea-levels had risen overnight and swamped England and all civilisation. Only a handful had survived then, and a few animals but they had all immediately begun to begat like crazy and by the current year of twenty-one fifty the planet's population was back up to almost half a million. Most of them migrated around the dry sandy plains of Cumbria with their camels and goats and bulldogs, hoping for some sort of "miracle". There was a tune at the back of the Malcolm's mind as he ran down the hill, one of many that he had heard iG-0-D singing to himself absentmindedly on the mountain and one that he wanted to remember to amuse his sons Graham and Edward. There were some funny little dance steps that God had done too, some sort of shimmy-hop-skip.

...This is the dawning of the Age of Aquarius, the Age of Aquarius... AquaRIUS... Harmony and understanding ... Sympathy and trust abounding ... No more falsehoods or derisions ... Golden living dreams of visions, Mystic crystal revelation and the mind's true liberation ... Aquarius! AQUARIUS! Aquar-ee-us!

He was so excited that he almost dropped the four commandments and the one p.s. Almost.

7 IN WHICH MR CADWALLADER SHAMPOOS HIS PARROT IN THE RAIN USING SOME VERY DATED POPULAR SCIENCE

Mr Cadwallader was a man of two businesses, one cat and an infinite number of acquaintances. Mr Cadwallader hand-crafted Diabolical Schrödinger Mechanisms and sold them reasonably directly to the public, and he also tried his hardest to run a small, single-brane driving school, Per ardua ad Avenger. His father had always said that Cadwallader Minor would never go far, and indeed he never allowed his pupils to go out of sight of some familiar landmark.

Mr Cadwallader had loved all of his cats, from the tip of their noses to the tip of their tails and throughout the years right up to the current one. Mr Cadwallader concluded that his current cat loved him. Indeed, he had empirical evidence that his current cat loved him as only a current cat can, since they had been together for an inordinately long time in the grand scheme of things, and quite a while outside of the grand scheme of things too.

Each night Mr C's cat went to sleep and each night his cat refrained from putting any diabolical mechanism and flask of poison outside his wickerwork basket-with-cushioned-lining. In this way, Tiddler on the Roof (the cat most often in both question and quite correctly in Mr Cadwallader's cat's wickerwork basket) saved Mr Cadwallader himself from the bother of having to remain in a cramped quantum superposition while Tiddler slept the sleep of Morpheus, or possibly not since Mr C had never dared to look for fear of interfering.

Mr C didn't actually sleep immediately outside of Tiddler on the Roof's wickerwork inverted Schrödinger basket, much preferring his very comfortable memory-foam mattress bed instead, even though he had, like most humans, never really given wickerwork and an old folded tartan blanket a decent chance.

This single faithful inaction in re the feline flask of poison, the one that didn't exist because it was never actuated, assured Tiddler on the roof of being able to observe the remains of yesterday's Universe, including his beloved Mr Cadwallader, often referred to hereinafter as The Tin Opener's Mate, all relatively unchanged when he awoke and left his basket each next morning (with due regard and lip service to the disturbance caused by the demonstrable passage of time).

The Passage of Thyme was, mostly and usually demonstrably, a nearby Indian Takeaway and was itself very disturbing in that it obeyed few, if any, of the local by-laws, be they by-laws of physics or by-laws of the local council. Tiddler on the roof, like all intelligent and healthy and currently living neighbourhood cats, naturally avoided it like The Plague.

There was nothing natural about the Passage of Thyme at any time, even when officers of The Law frequented it during their evening and night shifts. It was a very shifty place, albeit always shifty in the same spatial coordinates (three out of eleven not being bad, as Meatloaf once remarked on-stage in a remarkable display of rock star sanguinity and scientific savoir faire).

The Plague, however, served only natural beers and organic free spirits, being a free-house run by psychic hippies on behalf of the Psychic Hippie Association's Emergency Fund. It should be noted that the free spirits served over the bar of The Plague were in fact anything but, not that this mattered since the hippies had all time-travelled (at a sensible pace of one day per day) from the sixties and into positions as stock-brokers and Lloyds agents during the seventies and were thus really quite filthily loaded as vegan demographics go.

Similarly and moving back to the healthy corollaries of feline acts of non-sexual love, Mr Cadwallader loved the world that he lived in (along with his more usual cat) and so refrained from leaving one or more of his Diabolical Mechanism mechanisms outside his front door with the milk-bottles last thing at night. He purposefully failed to do this for both humanitarian and animal-welfare related reasons, and also because he feared that in doing so he might create some terrible nested "Russian doll" complex of inverted Schrödinger cat-boxes and some sort of positive feedback condition. Or, more possibly, since he wasn't doing anything of the sort, some sort of negative feedback crisis.

Anyway, in this almost obsessively compulsively neglectful way Mr C was also reasonably sure of being able to observe the outside world both still outside and relatively unchanged the next day too, as in as well as observing his cat, and this even after a small feline Madras take-away from The Passage of Thyme swiftly followed by twelve pints of Old Dog Water and a groovy game of non-violent, non-competitive, telekinetic skittles in The Plague Free-House and Inn with Vegan Dining Rooms, Zen loft and Yogic Climbing Frame. (Breath damn you, breath again, you psychedelic creature of stardust-in-human-form you. Why didn't you pause somewhere around Madras instead of running pell-mell for the full stop? Tsk tsk.)

Each morning Mr Cadwallader awoke, stretched, shat, showered and re-shaved in the un-ensuite bathroom down the hallway that led both to and from his bedroom and, cunningly, also beyond. Then, assuming that the arbitrary labelling of up and down on the planet had been incorrect he went up the stairs on the ceiling to the ground floor and into his kitchen where, clinging upside down to the Marley tiles, he created an unwittingly anti-gravity breakfast which he usually ate gravely, without gravy, in relatively good spirits for a pragmatic humanist with a tea mug only half-full. Often, while beginning the process of re-de-unconstructing his tea he admired his photograph of the moment when Mr Newton's head had mechanically disconvenienced an unconnected but totally stationary apple when Isaac, apple tree and Universe had all suddenly hiccoughed "upwards" a bit.

After breaking fast Mr Cadwallader generally went through to the front of his building and unclosed his shop, grateful each time he did so for the low-density doorway still being in place exactly where needed, surely a rather advanced feature indeed for a builder to think of but thus luckily precluding any need for Mr C to filter his atoms through the atomic interstices of a brick wall.

Each Diabolical Mechanism mechanism in Mr Cadwallader's shop window had been carved lovingly from oak or sometimes even walnut and had a small luggage label attached with frayed string. These labels pointed out in a nice Gothic script that the mechanism was not properly activated until someone actually thought that it had been. There were no price labels anywhere in the shop. Mr C let nature take its course regarding pricing structure since all of his Objet d'Maybe were also available elsewhere for every price and sometimes they were free and sometimes not available at all at any price, whichever part of the multiverse you might find yourself in. Simultaneous superposition of clement brane-universe alternatives made such a mockery of free market capitalism in so many ways. On more than one occasion a mechanism had been purchased with some very foreign currency and twice, to the best of his knowledge, he had been robbed. It all depended on what Mr C expected to find when a customer opened the door from everything outside and came into the shop where all that there was, had been and likely would be was what was in the shop there and then, not What Was outside previously and was probably no longer, for the moment.

What Was was Mr C's previous cat, not the current sitting recumbent incumbent of the felinus domesticus position. That was the downside (up) of having a shop full of mostly de-activated Diabolical Mechanisms and also of belonging to a cat who wouldn't even countenance using radioactive-decay triggers or poison – what might be almost always still was. Might Be had been Mr C's childhood dog until the passage of time had moved him into the past, quite out of reach of the present. This was to be expected since he had been bought out of pocket money (as opposed to valid currency of the realm) and had not, in point of fact therefore, been a present of any kind. It was also sort of unnerving since The Passage of Thyme specialised in cats, not dogs. Mr Cadwallader still loved dogs, and he hoped that somewhere out there was a May Yet Be every bit as nice as Might Be had been. "May" though, seemed a quite feminine name for a dog so, technically in terms of canine semantics (even though dogs rarely speak) the future was probably going to be a hairy bitch.

On occasion Mr C's hopes had been raised by reported sightings of miss-spelled Yet Be's in the higher Himalayas, but his emotions had always been dashed by corrective note in the later and subsequent editions. In his more defeated moments Mr C wondered if he ought not to choose more conventional names for his companion animals.

Anyway, whatever. When you get right down to it a wicker basket in a house is just a fancy box in another fancy box and who's to say that the observer must be outside either rather than inside either, or neither – especially when, even in purely pragmatic non-Newtonian terms, they might be both to someone not in the room, the basket or the house? In all of his travels around the Universe (mostly at ground-level or quite close to it) Mr Cadwallader had never encountered a "One Way Only" sign or other indication of a cosmic single-flow system, and everyone knows that tramlines always meet if you travel far enough towards the horizon. As a quick aside, this was probably accounted for the existence of "event horizons" although details of the events and suggestions as to why they always involved trams was never released, possibly due to the gravity of the events and the legal dangers of naming the tram drivers.

Despite every Diabolical Mechanism being carved from either seasoned oak or, possibly, unsalted walnut if people preferred, there was still a problem of stock wastage and unwastage. If he wasn't very swift about tying on the luggage label and in believing fervently in its message then stock was apt to just disappear whenever he turned around or he was otherwise distracted and failed to continue to observe it. Fortunately, since he had an open mind about such things, stock also un-disappeared just as regularly as it disappeared. The only practical problems this presented were of proper stacking in the stock room and of aesthetic presentation in the shop window. Still, an awful lot of his customers potential and customers actual didn't exist, hadn't ever existed or would no longer exist outside of his shop, especially if he'd recently cleaned the windows and they stopped to gawp or browse without thinking consciously about their situation, so things balanced out overall in some kind of cosmic karmic yee-haw see-saw. Even when he failed to see, no-one ever saw.

The easiest customers to deal with were those who just came into the shop to ask for the time of day (even though that was extraordinarily difficult to wrap in Mr Cadwallader's trademark brown paper and hairy string). The time of day was always to hand, and constantly updated itself to the very latest fashions, was fresh from moment to moment.

The most difficult of his customers were those who came in, looked at all of his stock and still couldn't decide what they wanted to buy, whether they actually wanted to buy anything at all from anywhere ever and, frequently, whether or not they'd come into the shop in the first place or if that was just something they might have done had they been someone else or living a different life some other when.

Parallel customers were a constant problem too, having only entered the shop because they'd missed or forgotten to make the pivotal decision that should have meant that they differed in this one aspect from their reality-cousins existing in parallel universes either side, above, beneath, fore, aft, before and after them. If they met themselves coming or going it was apt to lead to all sorts of semi-impromptu hat-doffing door-holding after you no after you dances to the tune of Oh Good Grief.

Still, life's not a still life no matter what the Association of People Who Were Still Lifelong Still-Life Artists might wish.

Mustn't grumble.

Or fart in public.

Or both.

Especially not both and, most especially, not after an emotionally moving curry takeaway from The Passage of Thyme.

And one must do neither of those at length either, moderation apparently being recommended in all things although I seriously doubt whether demanding moderation in all things constitutes moderation in and of itself. Further, is doing neither of two things concurrently twice as difficult as not doing either one, or as not doing both serially? It makes you wonder, you must admit, even if only in absolute, total all-encompassing moderation.

Today, under pressure from his great-nephew, Harry Clarkson, who had recently taken over Europe and the cleaner parts of North Africa, Mr Cadwallader was intending to hold a sales-drive for his driving school by pushing out the boat In Terms of Publicity. Rather than actually pushing out his peculiarly-named speedboat into the public view, Mr Cadwallader just sellotaped a sign in his window, confident that given sufficient passage of time everyone would see it, some would read it and a few would be interested enough to translate it.

'Note: this sign is not a boat, although I push it out in terms of publicity. Astral Driving Lessons available here. Patient and sympathetic instructor, everyone passes or fails their test at some time or other. Achieve infinite fuel economy, faster-than-light speed and cut the chances of an accident down to the number you just thought of. £5 an hour or part thereof. Part thereof refers to the hour, not to the £5. Apply within, initially from without. If you find yourself temporarily without without then you probably already have, and should begin applying immediately, since you will thus already be within the part thereof hitherto mentioned as chargeable.'

Mr Cadwallader's beloved Hillman Avenger DL motor car was parked in the alleyway next to his shop. Well, usually it was. Sometimes it preferred the double yellow semi-parallel lines on the kerbside, generally at one of the points where they had not converged at the horizon to leave only an infinitesimally small gap between themselves. Sometimes it preferred a small crater in the Sea of Tranquility on the moon. It all depended whether Mr Cadwallader was looking for it, or whether Mr Miserable, the local Traffic Warden, or Mr Petite-Napoleon from the Driver and Velocipde Licensing Authority were hunting, as the Queen song says, for somebody to stuff. Although he was about to give astral driving lessons in it the vehicle was not actually a Vauxhall, as witnessed by the sticker in the rear window that proclaimed "Per ardua ad Hillman Avenger, not Vauxhall Astra".

On one occasion Mr Bobbydazzler, the young village policeman, had come looking for it in connection with a case of excessive relative velocity caught on closed-circuit camera by dint of two moving frames of constabulary reference and a reliable Police computer's Lorentz transformation. By the time the hapless constable got up to speed himself though the Hillman Avenger hadn't been parked anywhere in the first place and was plainly nowhere to be seen in the second place. No official modern motoring protagonist had ever successfully checked the third place so that was quite out of the equation and they all agreed that the most dignified thing was to agree that none of it had ever happened. After a couple of moments they couldn't understand why they were still talking to each other. Mr Bobbydazzler issued Mr Cadwallader with a fixed penalty notice for wasting police time and Mr Cadwallader paid it with some reluctance. Not a lot of people know that this is a payment option, and most people still pay fixed penalty notices with money.

That occasion, had it in fact happened, had had quite a deleterious effect on Mr Cadwallader's cat, Tiddler on the roof, who had been peacefully sleeping on what he had previously thought was a warm car bonnet but discovered subsequently was, in fact, just three feet in the air over some pot-holed tarmac. That cats always land on their feet in no way compensated for the fact that Tiddler's feet landed on the tarmac without so much as a please do excuse me.

PC Bobbydazzler had decided to not press charges of cruelty to a possible cat because, try as he might, he couldn't get his well-licked HB pencil to spell out 'brief unauthorised feline levitation in a built-up area contrary to general public belief'. Several members of Herr Majesty's General Public were as surprised as Tiddler on the roof had been to witness his Hillman-aided failure to remain three feet in the air, especially since the installation, artistic though it was, had no planning permission or obvious means of support (other than its Official Fan Club). Even the Tate Modern were unlikely to be interested in such abstractions. Mr Bobbydazzler, although very official, was not a member of the Official Fan Club. He was a policeman and, as such, not a fan of very much at all, since enthusiasm usually just resulted in more paperwork.

In no time at all after Mr C had stuck the sign advertising astral driving lessons in his window several people with very different agendas were jostling for sub-atomic elbow, knee and spleen room in his shop, all holding out what they believed to be five pound notes (although in reality they might have weighed anything at all), and demanding that he multi-task immediately, or at least in the very near future. Obligingly, several coincident Mr Cadwalladers did just that.

The first student with astral aspirations in the ramshackle queue forming at the ramshackle till turned out to be a figment of everyone's imagination, much to everyone's delight as they all shuffled forwards one place. Being English they all shuffled very well indeed. It was rather like watching a brief glimpse of the River Dance by pressing play-pause-play-pause as quickly as one could. If Dougal, Dylan, Brian, Ermintrude and Florence had all ever been ordered to take one polite and orderly pace forward then that is precisely what Mr Cadwallader's queue would have looked like. Most splendid. Quite ticketty-boo in fact, once you knew the facts of the matter. As with the Magic Roundabout the matter was well lit and wasn't dark matter at all.

The second prospective student in the queue, a clever little gobshite from the local sixth form college, decided that she was bound to pass her test in the near future and had come simply to collect her certificate. They all decided that she was simply unbearable and they henceforth ceased to bear her in the queue. Lots of people breathed a sigh of relief at that one, Zebedee included (although in his case this was mainly due to the easing of his spring caused by reduced crowd pressure as she was removed from polite existence – boing, boing semi-colon; rectal relief).

The third student forgot what she'd come in for and just smiled and left the shop leaving only two further students (in the shop, not in Universal total of course, as far as I know, and I know at least as far as Edinburgh or Birmingham by motorway, and sometimes further still by train during maintenance works).

The first of these remainders was a veterinarian called Mr Soapandwater who had actually just called to re-tickle Tiddler on the Roof's ears, and the second was a woman known as Mrs Offertrollies who was in rather a hurry to get to the grocer in the High Street and had seen the sign and thought that this might be the quickest way to get there, or at least to get to somewhere that sold gooseberries. This was splendid, since Mr Cadwallader's Hillman Avenger DL had four comfortable seats (and no uncomfortable ones) so with himself and two students they were amply provisioned in terms of automotive buttock-lodgings. Whoever sat in the back might sit in either seat, making it more difficult to find them but much more fun.

Mr Cadwallader was fairly certain that he'd led them both out to the car simultaneously although the vet appeared to want to wave to everyone while all Mrs Offertrollies did was point, singularly, and reject all attempts at interference with her plans. Still, as Mr C settled into the front passenger seat there was evidence that both students had arrived safely in the vehicle, and he hoped that this was a pattern forming. Mindfulness was next to Motoringlyness and it is usually best to be present and living deliberately in the moment – it aided reaction times (although he planned to do little chemistry during their first lesson, so reaction times were moot).

Both students, upon fastening their seatbelts, enquired whether they would need an Mechanism Diabolique for the lesson, just to be safe, and were perplexed to find that "I believe probably not" was the answer. The first lesson was in fact limited to just "Mirror, signal, manoeuvre" because Mr Cadwallader believed observation to be the key to everything. He insisted that they both check their mirrors themselves and signal appropriately before manoeuvring, first-hand being the key to observation which was itself the key to the car and, specifically, to its ignition. The "ignition" was a very understated and terribly English affair indeed, involving simply an advanced magneto and some leaded petrol rather than a column of fire, five astronuts (sic) and a mission control staffed by folk mouthing "gosh - we have lift-off" and "the egret has landed".

'May I have the key to the car please?' asked Mrs Offertrollies, anxious to get moving.

'I thought that you already had it' was Mr Cadwallader's only reply.

'Oh, so I did but I'd forgotten. Apologies both. I have it again now.' Mrs Offertrollies checked that everything she was wearing was in neutral and then started the car and carefully checked that her counterpart in the rear-view mirror was also checking her rear-view mirror, in reverse. That is to say that Mrs O checked right way around that her counterpart was also checking, not that her counterpart was necessarily doing things in reverse. She was of course and, in a rather disturbing way, she also wasn't. They both stopped, fortunately still in neutral apart from a splash of cerise in their headscarves, and then one of them looked at the road behind the road ahead and then the road in front of the road behind, while the other glanced at the road ahead of the road behind and then stared, terrified, at the road behind the road ahead.

'How shall we begin?' asked the Mrs Offertrollies who was sitting the right way around, outside of the mirror in question and not yet in reverse.

'More worrying is how we shall end' warned Mr Cadwallader, out of sight of his counterpart, due only to the angle of the mirror. There was always some angle involved with a mirror, things were never straightforward.

'Indeed, but I believe that there's a nice vacant parking space for us on the road outside the grocer's on the High Street – what do you think?' proffered Mrs O, thereby letting on that she knew more than they had previously known she knew, even about the sourcing of fresh gooseberries.

Both gentlemen enthusiastically and faithfully agreed. Their collective and apparently subsequent appearance in the parking space coincided with a small cascade of oranges from the shop-front display and with a large hike in the price of mackerel in the Fishmonger's - although in the Fishmonger's what we shall not say since this is a family show and the fishmonger really shouldn't have had a mackerel in there at all, morally and legally speaking. A Fishmonger's What is no place at all for piscine life-forms at any price, especially with local oranges in cascade season. Still, that's probably the reason why greengrocers use plastic grass in their displays.

'Oh dear', said the vet. 'I hope that we didn't cause that.'

'I'm afraid that we must have since we observed not only all of the rules of the road in getting here but also the fact that we are here and that the oranges are cascading while trouser-warmed fresh mackerel moves, fiscally speaking, into a different socio-economic class altogether.'

'Such a shame. We must be more careful in future' agreed Mrs Offertrollies. 'I do so like oranges too.'

'Do you like all Pantone shades or just the standard? I am rather fond of a faded tangerine myself' said Mr Soapandwater in fluent but, given his predilections, rather surprisingly bold burnt Mandarin.

Mrs Offertrollies turned to Mr Cadwallader. 'Have I passed?' she said.

'My dear, you haven't even approached yet, let alone passed' rejoined Mr Cadwallader. 'I'm not even sure that I am the examiner in the matter.'

'Doubtless you will pass next time, Mrs Offertrollies' offered the Vet, wriggling a little (back in English) as he tried to remove some astral surprise from his own trollies.

'Doubtless it will have to be' reminded Mr Cadwallader.

'I did so want to pass on the previous occasion too.'

'Good gracious me, no – you may only pass once, not too. It's still possible for you to pass on the next occasion though.' said Mr Cadwallader both encouragingly and discouragingly, having no idea whether the next occasion would actually be motoring-related. 'What do you think?'

'I very rarely think, it makes my head ache so.'

Suddenly Mrs Offertrollies was no longer there, then, indicating that she had indeed stopped thinking, and totally so this time.

Mr Cadwallader mourned the passing of another student and indicated that Mr Soapandwater, the Vet, should take the controls.

Mr Soapandwater looked very nervous, especially for a large-animal vet who was known to be more fearless than was actually professionally acceptable when wearing a pair of long rubber gloves and a cow's bottom (plus other clothing too, usually). 'Oh, I don't think I could take the controls, not now. Won't you need them?'

'Not especially, no. Still, if you don't want to then you shan't, Mr Soapandwater, you shan't. Do you mind if we call at the shop before I drop you at your home? I should like to offer you an Diabolical Marketing Mechanism gratis or possibly even cheaper as a token of my business acumen.'

'That would be splendid, thank you. Why are we here?' asked Mr Soapandwater, losing the plot in a moment of existential doubt of his own.

'Why are any of us ever anywhere, or indeed, when you think about it, are we at all?' replied Mr Cadwallader.

'Oh. Yes – I see what you mean.' The High Street flickered, worryingly. 'I used to only think that I thought and therefore wasn't certain that I was or did but we do have to be quite certain, don't we?'

'We do indeed, Mr Soapandwater, we do indeed.' Oh look – we're back at base. Do come in from the outside.'

'Is there any other way? Must we always come in from the outside or out from the inside? It seems so limiting and unimaginative.'

'Well, it is the accepted manner of the deed, so I suppose that we must, at least in deed.'

'We must indeed what?'

'Oh, everything. Now, would you prefer the pocket sized Mechanism Diabolique or something larger, for the home?'

'What home?'

'There are several, surely you mean which home?'

'Choice is an illusion though, surely? We do what we must.'

'Indeed, if you must you must. Look, my car's probably parked outside again, or maybe parked there still – may I give you a lift?'

'Where would I put a lift? I don't have a home.'

'Sorry, I hadn't thought.'

'Well you ought to be more careful, it's doubtless very confusing.'

'Quite. Lifts have always confused me too – I've never understood why floors must be built in strict numerical progression, it too seems to be so limiting.' Mr Cadwallader popped his hat on one of his coincident heads and opened the door for Mr

Soapandwater. 'Shall we go?'

'Certainly. We shall have to, if we wish to leave. I thought that it was only the buttons in lifts that were in strict numerical progression rather than necessarily the floors one might visit at their pushing?'

'Possibly so, yes, but I have never felt quite at home in lifts – I keep all of my furniture elsewhere you see.'

'Very wise, very wise. If one's goods and chattels are elsewhere then they don't get nearly so dusty as they might do if they were with one all of the time, and lifts are known to be dust-traps.'

'I was given a lift on the A1 once when I was a student hitchhiker. I had to leave it in the lay-by, naturally.'

'Naturally. Did you pass?'

'What?'

'The Hitchhiker course, you said you were a student hitchhiker.'

'Oh, yes. Thumbs up on that one.'

'Splendid. Never sure what to pay for a lift.'

'As a hitchhiker?'

'In a building.'

'They do go up and down rather a lot, it's in their nature, rather like the stock market.'

'I suppose so, yes.'

Confidently, they both went.

'I could give you a complimentary driving lesson on the way' said Mr. Cadwallader.

'Splendid!' replied Mr Soapandwater, letting his mind drift. 'Do you drive an Astra? I do so love astral travelling. Timothy Leary says that it's the only way to travel.'

With that Mr Soapandwater inadvertently went on a trip.

Mr Cadwallader of course mourned the immediate neighbourhood's loss – it was a sad day for cow's bottoms and for visions of long-gloved professional manly loveliness sashaying across farm yards to Beethoven's Fifth playing on a portable gramophone with small inflatable white dog, head held askance.

Mrs Offertrollies, however, was quite unexpectedly alongside

Mr Cadwallader's car again.

'Coo-ee! Mr C! I suddenly remembered that I'd been having an astral driving lesson and wondered if we might continue? I have gooseberries, if that helps.'

'It does, Mrs Offertrollies, it does indeed, and if we keep our minds on the job and watch what we are doing, we might very well continue.'

'Very well, Shall we?'

Do you know, I believe firmly that they did, and although we can never be sure, since with each pivotal decision we transpose ourselves to a fresh multiverse populated by mere facsimile copies of our loved ones, I like to think that all was well that was started with the intention of creating a well.

'Well, well, well' muttered Constable Bobbydazzler, bending his knees and looking at the space where he had hoped the Hillman Avenger might be, not realising that had he looked with more conviction he may have been more successful in finally securing a conviction. Tiddler on the Roof wound himself around the constable's ankles – while the constable was still on top of them of course and in the usual manner of things, the constable hadn't just left his feet at the curb or anything. Tiddler spotted some of the staff from The Passage of Thyme arriving for work, and he ceased thinking about anything other than being elsewhere, which is what finally caused Constable Bobbydazzler's ankles to disappear.

This was also how Mr Cadwallader thought that he had lost his parrot. He theorised that he had accidentally placed the parrot's cage so that the mirror over the fireplace (the fireplace in the room, there was no fireplace in the cage, obviously) had been parallel to the little mirror in the cage, next to the cuttlefish. Poor Parrot must have gone to check his feathers, leaned in a little too closely, become dizzy, lost his footings and fallen into a progression of reflections, probably thinking only about how his head felt as though it were about to explode and thinking about each new and smaller reflection in turn, in some horrific chain-reaction. All that Mr C knew was that when Mr C had pulled the lavatory chain, washed his hands and returned to the room all that had been left of Poor Parrot (for that was his given name) was his feet – the lost footings in question. Mr C had reflected long and hard on his incidental error and could brook no other explanation.

Mr Cadwallader's cat though knew better than to lean in close to anything reflective whether it was near a cuttlefish or not. Having once found an instance of the multiverse that contained both a can-opener and a human prepared to wield it, no feline worth his tuna would risk falling out of step by leaning in. Besides, given the copious amounts of tuna made available to him, lean was a medical term that did not appear in Tiddler on the Roof's lexicon, or in his medical notes, and so he rarely leaned at all except up against the most dependable of surfaces, such as his basket.

Tiddler was also very careful to remain "in the moment", and very wary indeed of diabolical mechanisms and atomic decay triggers and flasks of poison such as those he had secreted into the parrot's cage while Mr C had been in the lavatory, observing other matters.

Tiddler washed his paws with his little rough pink tongue, and wondered how long tea would be.

(So as to not leave you wondering cruelly, there was a fifty-fifty chance that tea would be about three inches, and it would be rather jauntily garnished with a couple of fresh parrot-claws.)

8 DIARY OF A NATIONAL SERVICE CHAP

15th June 2027, the Army Reception Office, Cleethorpes.

Reporting as per my rather forceful official call-up summons, for duty.

National ruddy Service eh?

As I watched from my seat in the marching-formation rows of wipe-clean blue plastic high-back Parker Knoll recliners, the queue shuffled forward at a snail's pace. Tickets number two hundred and four and three hundred and two looked as though they were keen to enlist but the holder of ticket number three nine three suffered some sort of arthritically acted out but nonetheless quite theatrical myocardial infarction and then expired under the rib-cracking thump of the paramedics' fists. As the waiting recruits played awfully polite unidirectional musical chairs towards the hot-seat I noted that everyone left the late Mr Three-Nine-Three's seat well alone, and skipped straight into seat three-nine-two instead.

Ms Reception-Desk took no notice at all, she'd seen it all before. It was just possible that it had been her sparkling personality, scintillating social skills and purple verbosity that had seen her promoted out of the Office of the Voice of the Speaking Clock and into army recruitment. Or it might just have been that she looked as though she spent more time snoozing than answering the telephone and telling callers the correct time of their third stroke in Greenwich.

Ms Reception-Desk fumbled at the chain, put on her butterfly-wing spectacles and read word for word from her screen while she put some hapless and limp old fogey through the induction process. She carried about her the cheery air of the guest of honour at a well-attended funeral and I ventured that she had brightened many a room by leaving it via the closed fenestration. Her face may not have launched a thousand ships, but it certainly spoke eloquently of long spells of dockyard work.

The Inland Revenue's computer's auto-assessment of his financial affairs indicated, she said, that he was, in his legally-forced retirement, one step up from a cold, skinny, elderly church mouse and he had thus been deemed to have volunteered for (remaining) lifetime service in the armed forces. She didn't look up from her screen for any confirmation from the gentleman. I gathered the impression that she probably didn't look away from her screen because she was worried that if she let it out of her sight she'd be unlikely to find it again in a hurry – memory being what it is these days for all of us.

I made a mental note to adapt the commercially-available spectacles chain, re-package it and market it at a premium so that folk with suitably structurally sound necks could keep their computer screens handy about them at all times. Then I forgot about it, memory being what it is for we old fogies. A few minutes of frowning later some nagging sensation of loss made me wish that I could put my memory on a little chain around my neck, so that I wouldn't put ideas down and then forget them. Now, where were we? Oh yes. The Induction Queue.

At about eleven of the o'clock our good friend Mr Sunshine put his hat on and came outdoors to play. His cheery nuclear light sparkled on the waiting room through the grimy plate-glass windows and even the scrawny birds eking out a desperate living in the dusty, depressed trees of the little shopping area began to tweet, hip hip hurrah, meep-meep. Please RT #birdcall #sparrows #urbanwildlife #kissmyfeatherylittlecloaca. Silly little buggers, shitting everywhere. LOL. – Send. Within seconds of the temperature rising the whole queue of inductees was asleep, napping for England, chins-akimbo and oblivious to the world.

Such are the elderly. This is why old ladies break hips – one moment walking along and the next the sun comes out and wallop, sound asleep and in free-fall towards the linoleum. We were all awoken some indeterminate time later by the sound of Ms Reception-Desk coming back from lunch on her wooden Scholl cloggs. Gods alone know how long she'd taken in the pub while we all slept.

By the time I had worked my way around to the "Next!" chair my fellow queue-inmates and I had collectively sorted out the youth of today, agreed that nobody built anything properly anymore and were debating the pros and cons of Tupperware and of cooking several meal-portions at once and then freezing them for later hyperwaving in the combo-multiwave. That's the thing about old farts – put 'em together and they talk. Put a similar number of spotty youth together and they just try to shrink into hiding behind their empty-three players and their eye-telephones and under their who-dee jogging tops advertising Umbro and Manutd or Mancity. They have done nothing to talk about, we want to get it all off our chests before we die.

Ms Reception-Desk called me forward and began her routine without waiting for me to reach the hot-seat. Her speech was punctuated by little triple-clicks on the computer mouse as she ticked various boxes in that way that technophobe OAPs do, not quite expecting the little on-screen pointer to obey them.

Did I understand my oath to honour my superiors, love my country and obey without question?

I asked if, after these vows, there would be a ring of some sort to seal the marriage.

The private security guard rolled his wheelchair forward from his place in the shadows and indicated that any more lip from me, my lad, would result in the award of a ringing in my ears. Since he'd obviously lived to the ripe age (and he was ripe) of ninety-something I didn't doubt that he could deliver, should I press the matter.

I understood. I indicated that in the circumstances I tended towards the affirmative in re her rather rhetorical and redundant enquiry. Then my mind descended into a discussion with itself regarding whether rhetoric could ever, in these circumstances, be truly other than redundant and if so, whether that made the redundancy redundant or even perhaps both redundant and rhetorical since the redundancy would then be self-evident, unavoidable and implicit. The ex-Speaking Clock obviously couldn't give a shit. I wondered if she'd been about to work her way up to being The Speaking Calendar when she'd been forced to retire into Army Recruitment (Chennai – Paris - New York) PLC Inc Ltd. "At the third stroke it will be two thousand and twenty-six. Pip – wait for it – wait for it - pip-pip." She certainly had enough personality to pull it off. Even I might have been tempted to call her on the eve of numerical palindromes of non-Mayan significance, although it has to be noted that the next of those will be the year 2112 so you couldn't accuse me of being over-eager to run up my telephonium bill.

Was I Reginald Alfred "Grimsby Town F.C." Dalrymple-Smythe of Pelham Square, Cleethorpes?

I replied that as far as I knew, I both had been and indeed still was, even though there seemed little call for it now, other than from the Army. I suggested that I preferred Reggie.

Mouse-click-click-click followed by some typing that sounded as though it might have been along the lines of "residual spirit needs breaking", "save", "save", "have you saved?", "save", "close screen" and then immediately "re-open it to check that the previous entry had saved". All standard OAP-techy stuff really.

The country, the nice paramilitary lady-biddy explained while adjusting her side-arm, was in parlous peril and experiencing egregious economic exposure and was fearlessly fighting frightening foes. Surely an oxymoron, since how could any foe be frightening in the eyes of a fearless defence force? If only we all remained fearless, no matter how terrifyingly lethal and murderous the foe, then they would no longer be frightening, in which case why was I being required to fight them at all? What though, my mind asked, if they hunted in small even-numbered groups of fewer than six, even though they weren't the real enemy? Would my first, frightening, fearless foray be against four non-frightening faux-foes, phuphux ache? What of my fellow fighters? Five faithful fellows would be my minimum favoured force for facing four non-frightening faux-foes in a fight or a fracas. Flamin' eck. What if I faced the foe and farted or fainted or failed to be otherwise fearless in the face of the enemy, so to speak? What would be my fate? I decided that under the circumstances, I would turn F off as soon as practicable.

The speaking calendar brought me back to my senses with a smoker's cough and three pips (she'd been eating grapes). My brain snapped back into current life and it asked my eyes to look around to see what we had missed while in our reverie stroke pre-stroke nap and general absence of being "in the moment". Well, when I say "snapped back into life" what I mean is that my mind sort of looked up, like a cow preoccupied with eating grass in a meadow, and mooed. I don't usually claim any sort of focus until at least five minutes or one cup of tea after drifting back from drifting off. Not even with an F involved.

She was up to the sibilants... The country had need, she said, stiffly, of selfless superannuated stupid single sods such as me. She snatched a bite of her Stilton sandwich and a second slurp of her Star-Sucks super-skinny soy spiced, iced, sweet cinnamon sparkling tea. She made clicking sounds as she sucked at Victoria sponge crumbs that had lodged in her back teeth. They must have been desperate crumbs indeed to settle for lodgings such as those while the Salvation Army hostels were still in business the world over. Oops – I was drifting again.

It was just possible of course that I had misread the situation in re her clicking, and she was in fact conversing intelligently with an invisible alien colleague in their common mother tongue. Click, click-click, suck suck squelch click click tsk tsk click humans eh click click suck? Despite the seriousness of my situation, my mind wandered and wondered. Could it really be that she was a giant alien stick insect covered in foam and Essex salon-tan coloured latex – like Mrs Wilkinson at number eighteen had proven to be when de-frocked during a brawl over biscuits at the Council-run Social Centre?

The modern army had no need to advertise for recruits and saw no point in populating its reception desks with beautiful people –

when they played the Status Quo Army Anthem and said you were in the army now, you were then in the army now. I mean, in the army then, now. End of story, no need to sign here, we've done that part for you and please to drop your trousers, oik up the heavy, hairy folds of gut-flop and cough at the little screen for the brief, web-cam based medical by some ATOS arse calling in from Botswana between two other jobs, one as a leather and restraint expert on a telephone sex-line and the other almost identical job as a claims dismisser for AVIVA. Both of them basically tell you to go yourself.

The lady recruitment agent handed me a photocopied sheet that explained the whole situation. I was male. Well, that much I already knew from having had a particular dripping washer changed several times by an NHS plumber who specialised in trousers – click, delete, click correct radio-button box. I had reached the compulsory retirement age whereupon had I had employment I had been removed from it to make way for youth. All hail youth. Indeed so. Click – delete – tsk tsk click save. I had no visible independent means of support (click click twang as her army gussets absorbed the full brunt of the cheese sandwich working its way through her thorax towards her insect abdomen). Scratch, scratch, click (possibly with her back legs, I couldn't see past her screen, planted right in the middle of her desk to save her from bad posture that would aggravate existing aches – never mind that she couldn't see her customers and vice visa).

National efficiency was the name of the game (the sheet actually used the word "game", can you believe it) and so changes had been made. The armed services were no longer able to draw recruits from school leavers because cheap though they were, there were even cheaper options to be had. I was the cheaper option and I'd been well and truly had.

By removing the National State Pension and introducing compulsory National Retirement Service the country could do away with paying school leavers to join the army, do away with paying open-ended pensions to ungrateful old gits, and often even got to save money that the NHS would otherwise have to spend on silly things such as hip replacements and hypothermia care because life expectancy in the army was, well – quite frankly, less than stellar. It was a win-win situation for the country and the country loved win-win situations.

I rather hoped that it was also win-win in terms of the many wars we were involved in, with England still barking like some "British" bulldog that hadn't cottoned on to quite how elderly and toothless it now was, and how the backyard of every Tunbridge Wells nimby now belonged to any cat, squirrel or rat that cared to cross it or set up shop in it. Though the country barely had the wherewithal left to give a weak little wave of the Cross of St.George to the world stage from the Mortgaged Cliffs of Dover, no-one had thought to mention this to the politicians who roamed the galaxy annexing willy-nilly and picking fights as though most of it was still coloured pink on the Ordnance Survey-produced galactic maps.

The sheet of paper also indicated that this was my last chance to claim a statutory exemption from service. Exemptions would only be granted on production of countersigned evidence of a minimum of forty years of employment in the following reserved popular occupations: doctor; dentist (private, not NHS, obviously); very, very, very senior white-collar management of a PLC; media (front of house only); solicitor; barrister; High Court judge; policeman (any rank); member of Parliament (any length of service); clergy (any denomination, no more than six serious sexual convictions and no more than three changes of religious conviction); poet laureate (not defrocked) or prior death accompanied by organ donation (any length of service).

Without so much as a do please excuse me love, Ms Reception-Biddykins used her grey "Grabbit" stick to reach out, grasp onto my collar and drag me closer. Had I been fifty years younger I might have assumed that she was in need of a kiss. She then forced my head down onto the desk with her hand. To be frank, even though I am Reggie, it felt as though a very weak crab with liver-spots and inappropriately tart-red fingernails was trying to subdue a wrinkly-pated sea-urchin sporting a patchy snowy-white number two crop. No body-heat was exchanged in the touch – we could neither of us spare the energy. She pressed the button on her little hand-held machine to Laser-tattoo a barcode on the back of my neck and then asked if I wished to claim an exemption. Click. Tap-tap, click. Suck suck squelch – explore freshly-discovered soggy crumb with tongue, swallow and sniff. I gathered from this that such claims for exemption, unlike her ankles, rarely held water.

This unfortunately reminded me that we had been going for some three or four minutes now and that I was aware once again of holding my own water, so to speak, and barely successfully at that.

Thank you, no, none of the exclusion criteria apply - but would it be possible to be assigned to some Earth-based duty please? I have problems with queasiness if weightless for any length of time such as might be the case with the more rough and tumble Space Units, and I wasn't the most adventurous or gung-ho chap around and didn't do well in confrontational situations such as fights, especially with strangers or with insectoid species. Given my suspicions about the lady's non-mammalian origins I suspected immediately that the reference to insects was a serious faux-pas on my part.

Gosh, yes love, of course, she said. That's what this man's army's all about – choice. Did I have any thoughts as to what rank I might like, because there would likely be an opening soon at the level of General or Field Marshal, and that was mostly just desk work. If that didn't appeal then it was also just possible that she could find me a spot at Bletchley Park fiddling with the new vacuum-valve technology, or perhaps something like polishing the Prime Minister's Wolseley all day, if I'd prefer...

The security guard sniggered and re-arranged the tartan rug over his knees, tucking it down into the sides of his wheelchair seat. His movement knocked at the microphone of his hearing-aid and caused a momentary feedback whistle that disturbed the pigeons on the pedestrian pavement outside. Being profoundly used to it the gentleman didn't seem to notice the panes of plate-glass around him cracking in harmonic sympathy and the number of dogs that collected outside, all looking in at him with quizzical "you rang?" expressions.

After mug-shot (click – save – click-click - save), thumb-print (click click click), DNA swabs (tsk tsk suck squelch click dab dab snort-ugh) and retinal scans (click, click – two eyes, one generous click each this time) I was told to follow the blue line through the door rather unnecessarily marked "New Recruit Chaps", and to do so as quickly as possible. Time was money and we were none of us getting any younger. Ms Personality added that I was please to open the door before attempting to walk through it. There were scratches and stains on the woodwork suggesting that this instruction might be a serious pragmatic one that she had added to the induction process herself on the basis of everyday experience with new recruits. The blue line indicated also showed signs of having lived through quite a bit of O.A.P. bottom-panic. My brown and beige tartan slippers slid over the flaky paintwork easily enough though and I made it to the door-frame in good time, hoping beyond hope that the door led to a lavatory, for none of my internal arguments with my circumstances were holding water with myself well. Oh good grief – well. Wells hold water. More water. Think dry thoughts.

So. Here I am starting National Service at my age. Mind you, it would be difficult to start it at somebody else's age. Odd to think that even though we all begin our service at an age identical to our comrades in arms, my age is mine and theirs is theirs, age being somehow universal but indivisible. I was drifting again, obviously.

I think that maybe I should keep a diary of some sort. It may assist me in holding on to my sanity. Such as remains, anyway. Wibble. Oh thank the Roman gods, there's a lavatory – the blue "following" line made a sudden swerve towards it before leading onward to the induction zone. We might just make it in time, provided that there's no-one in there and my flies don't argue back or get stuck.

Phew! Oh Zeus, that's good. Yee-hah! Render back unto Poseidon what was once de-salinated from Poseidon. There then followed eight minutes of trying to end that particular Roman prayer without too many encores and without leaving the floor looking as though some watersports pervert had just showered in there.

So. Diary eh?

Dear Diary. The last truly conversational word anyone spoke

directly to me today was "Next!"

Still – at least it's only until I die eh? I took one brief look back at the door to the civilian world and then went onwards towards my fate, like some soldier, marching as to war in my slippers. As in I was shuffling towards war in my slippers, there wasn't a war going on in my slippers. Not unless you count the lifetime stalemate between Cheese-Away Spray and toe-jam.

The army never makes mistakes, and I was sure that National Service would all be very proper and dignified. Wars were fought electronically these days weren't they? I'd probably spend my days logged onto the web taking down enemy alien websites with denial of service attacks and putting acerbic, pithy comments on pan-dimensional non-humanoid insurgent's blogs. Have at thee, thou vile alien forces, I Tweet thee to death in the name of His Majesty The King. Clicks "dislike" button on alien commander's FaceBook status update and slopes arms after a raid well done.

My BIG Page-to-a-day Diary
16th June 2027 about 22:00HRS.

To be brutally and rather adventurously honest with you, even though it's obviously tried, test and completely fair, I am not terribly chuffed about this business at all. Retirement National Service may be good for the country and the country's coffers, but I am not one of those lucky chaps who look good in a pith helmet, a fight and a bar in Bangalore.

I must be the odd one out I suppose, as usual.

Well, whatever - they woke us at sparrow-fart o'clock this morning, gave us a breakfast of cold kedgeree and PG Tips and then inspected our testicles. I don't know for certain but my best guess was that perhaps the PG Tips had been expected to have had some sort of effect on them. Maybe terrorist, insurgent, cave-man or otherwise disloyal or malcontent testicles pulsate or something after an infusion of PG Tips. It felt as though we were on some sort of touchy-feely identity parade where the victim, a medical orderly, could only identify their putative attacker by the unique texture and disposition of their love-spuds. Yes, My Lord, the prosecution will present testimony to the effect that the accused resembled two dead mice in a wrinkly leather purse made from a hairy sow's silken ear...

In the afternoon some MD who'd been thrown out of the NHS for malpractice above and beyond the reach of his lady-patients underwear shone a torch up our arses and asked if we'd ever 'walked on the wild side'.

'Darling...' I said, thinking that there was some hope for a good old-fashioned dishonourable but highly convenient discharge, '... Darling, I rode a rudddy Vespa on the wild side - with side-car and a helmet sporting matched Viking-horns and bearing the legend "Hello darling, fancy a ride on my funky moped".'

Apparently though that just puts me in line for fast-track promotion and gets me the anniversary of Kenneth Williams' death off regular fatigues as a sort of positive-discrimination gay military Bank Holiday.

Later on we all tried a bit of parading on the square so that the Colonel in Chief or someone could inspect us but, to be honest, everyone on the dais seemed to nod off as soon as they sat down. Perhaps they had been overcome by the cloud of Vicks Vaporub sweating off two thousand new old recruits? Life in the army seemed to be a lot to do with nodding off.

Dinner this evening was fish, chips, mushy peas and more PG Tips. Someone enquired about pudding but was told that the man who made the spotted dick had been medically discharged sometime during the morning so they didn't feel that they could serve it without checking it carefully first, and the necessary food-standard sieves hadn't been delivered from stores yet.

Lucky bastard. If I knew what it was that he had I'd try to catch it myself. Must be something where bits fall off or squirt without warning when they should really only wobble or dribble on a predictable basis at most. Hell's bells, given that the average age in the catering corps was seventy-three they must get through pastry chefs at a real rate of knots if something falling off into the custard was sufficient cause for a change of old dribbly.

"Lights out" happened just as I was settling into a decent session with a copy of Huntin' Shootin' Fishin' Life and a red biro to correct the editor's grammar and spelling. I am therefore writing this by the light of my Ronson flame which is bloody dangerous because I'm also working under an Army blanket to avoid something big and hairy with stripes shouting through the window again about "I-Z Lizah an' Lizah means ALL LIZAH!". Or something. He was too loud to hear. Anyway, I have christened him 'Minnelli'. He seemed pretty heated, whoever he was, so I'll humour him for the moment, just in case it's important or he has stripes or a red cap. Stripes on his uniform that is, not stripes like a military zebra. This will be a short entry for several reasons: my testicles hurt, I think the MD left his not-inconsiderably sized torch in my arse and the air under this blanket is getting pretty thin because of the lighter flame hogging all of the oxygen.

Goodbye, Day 1, I hate you and shall dance on your memory next time I have a leaky infected blister on my foot.

Wednesday, 17th June 2027
soon after The Magic Roundabout on Channel 4+1.

They woke us a full hour before sparrow-fart o'clock this morning and gave us a breakfast of still-frozen kedgeree sorbet and scalding-hot PG Tips. No-one seemed keen to inspect our testicles today though, so maybe yesterday was enough for anyone or perhaps they've just run out of camouflage Marigolds and laundry tongs.

I have been given a pith helmet because our unit is being sent to Bangalore.

It's a shame that this isn't the anniversary of the day that Kenneth Williams died because then I would have been off and wouldn't have been around to hear that news. I seem to remember that I had an Uncle once who had been to Bangalore or somewhere nearby. Nearby to Bangalore that is, not nearby to Catterick. He died, just like Kenneth Williams did. I hope that this isn't some sort of pattern forming.

The good news is that I have also been given a uniform to wear in combination with the pith helmet, so it's likely that I will blend in better than I might otherwise have done naked, even with my Army-approved PG Tips-sodden pulsating testicles. We were shown our rifles today too; big pump-action laser rifles with Grenadier launchers or something, I was too busy saying "ooh – shiny" to listen properly. Apparently, they have tele-coptic sights with cross hares and can be fired from both the shoulder and from the hip. I hope that they don't get warm in use because I'm worried about my plastic prosthesis melting if I fire mine from the hip. I don't think I'll be firing mine from the shoulder a lot either, because they're rather heavy, and it seems such a waste to lift them all the way up to shoulder height if they can be fired from the hip anyway. The sergeant says that they won't actually issue us those until Hell freezes over and the regimental mascot cat presents the Colonel in Chief an intact snowball that smells strongly of sulphur.

Dinner tonight was fish, chips, beans and cold, milky PG Tips. Apparently there was talk of a treacle sponge for pudding but it had been sent to the Officer's Mess by mistake and couldn't be chitted for or something in time to stop it being accidentally eaten by all of the wrong ranks. Anyway, the good news is that the custard is still in a warehouse on the dockside in Grimsby, so there's always hope for later if Cook can get the seven-ton Bedford started. It's "on the handle" because the battery was requisitioned by the C.O. for his mobility scooter. Mind you, if anyone can turn over a rusty, ill-serviced four point nine litre six cylinder engine with a starting-handle just on the simple promise of fifty gallons of unleaded bright yellow Creme Anglaise, it's Cook.

I have ceased wanting to visit the encrapolator, with or without a magazine and a red biro. It's a similar sensation to what happened after I ate that bucket of anti-fungus wallpaper paste for a bet. I feel as though someone is making a Plaster of Paris mould of my alimentary tract again but without spraying in any release agent this time. May see the MD tomorrow and ask if he wants to swap the return of his torch for a dollop of intravenous castor oil or something. Might visit the NAAFI too and see if they stock packets of those industrial-strength Poo-More tablets that that miserable-looking woman advertises on the television; the sort that stop her handbag filling up with pita bread, pasta and salad while she looks thoughtful and preoccupied on the bus.

In view of the time thus saved by not going to the bog I am writing this before Minnelli's"I said LIZAH and I meant LIZAH!"

request. It's really a shame about my no longer needing to visit the great white telephone after Lizah because there's an eerie glow coming from my arse that would be quite enough to show the way safely now. On the other hand, part of me feels safer not going just in case the monsters in the sewer were to see the light and use it to home in on my toilet and attack me through the u-bend. You know how I've always worried about that and how just one unexpected gurgle or bubbling noise from the cistern can affect my natural rhythm. The chaps have nick-named me 'Firefly' but the Sarntmayjah! reckons that "the sun might just be beginning to shine" and he says that he is considering me for officer training. He reckons that I would make a magnificent leader for night patrols through enema territory.

I am starting to suck nervously on the corner of my blanket the way I used to as a teenager. It's been a conscious decision though this time.

Goodbye, Day 2, I hate you and I hated your Mother too. I shall learn to wear army stiletto heels and then dance on your memory, with or without a leaky blister.

18th June 2027, midnight
(it has to be midnight somewhere on the planet).

Bangalore has apparently frozen over and so has the Regimental Cat – it must have chased a rat or something into Cook's walk-in freezer. Bangalore's excuse is to do with the Burmese Glacier shifting south, or something. Immediately after breakfast they gave us our rifles and said that we're bypassing all further basic training and going straight onto active service, for King and Country and an extra metric shilling a day.

One chap shot himself trying to look down the barrel of his rifle to see if he could see the little bulb for the laser. Well, I say shot himself, it was really more of a "bzzzzt" noise followed by the smell of burning flesh and a "Goodnight Vienna" human shadow outline on the wall of the Quartermaster's stores. I've heard the Vicar at home going on about ashes to ashes and dust to dust before but, believe you me, the vicar should have seen this – there wasn't even a whole lot left in the way of ashes or dust. The urn they gave

Mrs Crabknees next door after Mr Crabknees fell off the roof must have been mostly full of unburned coal, or full of somebody else, or full of bits of roof-tile.

While they re-allocated Mrs Peerless's beloved ex-son's rifle and re-whitewashed the wall they distracted us with a Pathe newsreel about Safety Catches through the Ages and then a long lecture on venereal diseases given by the M.O. with a torch. That is to say, he gave the lecture, he hasn't yet – as far as I know – given us any venereal diseases directly, although I never did see him wash either his Marigolds or his torch during our intake inspections, so to speak. The Doctor did most of the talking too during the lecture; his torch just sat there in the breast pocket of his white coat. That makes me wonder a bit. If the M.D.'s torch is out there in his breast pocket then whose torch is it stuck up my arse? The slides of the rashes, sores and tropical scabs reminded me of the sort of modern art we saw once at the Tate Modern. I've asked if we can get some big prints of them to brighten up the barracks walls. That should cheer the other chaps up. Some of them are a bit down in the mouth.

I had great fun during the slide show though. Every time they put the lights out I eased a buttock up and caused confusion. Eventually they took the fluorescent tubes out of the light fittings and the Sarntmayjah stood at the end of the row of seats I was in, unholstered his swagger stick and stared at me the way the dog used to stare at the racing pigeons in our back yard before you relented and started buying larger tins of Doggy Nosh for him.

I spoke to the Doctor after the lecture and he says that if I haven't "gone" by the time we ship out and make orbit that the G-Forces will fix me in a jiffy when we accelerate out of the solar system. I assume that the G-Forces must be the Americans, they always have the best everything, including the best M.A.S.H. units. "Jiffy" must be some sort of army medical slang, I suppose. I just hope that whatever it is it doesn't show through my trousers or ruin the dangle of my utility belt. I had quite enough medical derision thank you very much as a child when you made me wear those training pants – fifteen year-olds can be so, so cruel, especially during rugby practice.

Dinner tonight was sieved spotted dick and chips followed by treacle sponge with PG Tips, all served in a tin soup tureen that looked awfully like the oil-drip trays they slide under seven ton Bedford lorries when they're parked up for any length of time. Apparently there's a new cook or something (the C.O. was quite fond of the old mascot cat), and this one's a bit avantey-gardey and therefore possibly another foreigner. Plus the chits got mixed up again. A big hairy thing with stripes said to get it down our necks because it all gets mixed up anyway in the end. He's obviously not as familiar with my "the end" as is the M.O.

Quite frankly, I was tempted to throw some moonlight onto the matter but the chaps said best not as that might be misinterpreted and I could end up on a charge. I'm not entirely sure if they meant a charge for me or a charge for the torch battery. It's lasting awfully well so it must be Duracell – the rest of the chaps were egging me on to make "Batman" signals with it half of last night and I think our calls were very nearly answered from the E.N.S.A. block.

I'm writing this in the mess hall because "LIZAH!" has been delayed while the Military Police clean up our barracks before letting us back in. Apparently someone tried to shoot his own toes off with his new laser rifle for a medical discharge but hit the barracks mirror-ball instead and it all got a bit messy and in need of an official enquiry. The Army has formally cleared itself already but may sue the manufacturers of the mirror-ball (since they are foreigners). The barracks looks like a bit of a concrete colander now but the effect could be quite nice as the sun rises and the light from all of the new holes begins to shine in through the settling dust.

Goodbye, Day 3, I still hate you but at least tonight's dinner has put my bowels under an intense and positive medical pressure. Unless we ship out before dawn tomorrow whatever the blockage is will have been rammed clear by sheer weight and volume of spotted dick, treacle sponge and chips well before the wonderful American G-Forces can even get near to it with a "jiffy".

Stardate 19th June 2027, who knows when?
I can't see my watch. It's the time after yesterday, anyway.

We shipped out long before dawn this morning. While we were

taking off from the runway at RAF Chocksaway a camouflage Marigold rubber glove, size “M”, popped out of my arse. Just the one. The right one. The right-hand glove, that is, I don’t have two arses. Not yet anyway, despite what the Corporal says about “ripping me a new one” if I don’t buck my ideas up a bit. I feel a lot better now but I won’t give up on the torch until at least tomorrow. It must be rattling around in there since one glove has gone.

Apparently we have to stay strapped down for another day until the troop carrier gets out of the solar system under diesel-power and then we can go to Visualisation Drive or something. Fancy that. Me in space, like a real soldier! All I can hear at the moment though is the clank-cough-cough-clank of the big diesel engines on full throttle as we power out of Earth orbit. There are a lot of chaps chundering for England and there’s a looped address from the King wishing us well as we ‘Cry havoc for Prince Harry, for England PLC and for All-Denominations Saint George.’ All I can say is that if Saint George had had a rubber glove and a fifty-LED torch up his arse then he and the dragon may have got along a lot better, and traded tricks or something instead of getting violent and nasty with each other. Is that a treasonous thought? I expect that the diary censors will let me know in due course.

I couldn’t half do with them letting us out of these straps so that I can visit the Usual Offices, Male, Lower Ranks, For the use of to cry havoc and let slip a few dogs of war – I think that the rubber glove that escaped may have been the only thing that was holding back most of the torch-lit tide of military custard. The feeling is starting to dominate my waking hours and I am losing sight of where the army begins and my backside ends. I think that what Granddad used to say is maybe true, it’s just that we never quite heard him properly and got the wrong end of the stick because of that misunderstanding with the jogger in the park toilets all those years ago. On reflection, it would be very interesting and useful now to be able to go back and let him tell us his army stories instead of cutting him short every time because of the neighbours and the potential for embarrassment.

There’s been no sign of the American G-Forces so far. Maybe they’ll join us later? Breakfast this morning was a tube of concentrated kedgeree, a foil sachet of PG Tips and some orderly from the Catering Corpse sticking an "enlisted men - hydration hose" up my left nostril for "three minutes or two pints, whichever came soonest". Between hydrating troops he used the hose to swill down the decks and water the plants. I noticed that the plants also all got three minutes or two pints of water whichever came first, even the plastic ones.

They stopped playing the looped tape of the King about two hours after we broke out of the Earth's gravitational pull and then they played a film about a nun looking after some rich git's kids in Austria and making them sing a lot because of World War Two. They played it three times over, end to end. The last time they played it to us it was in reverse which actually made a lot more sense, since Julie Andrews took one look at Switzerland, tried a career making curtains out of kids' clothing and then decided to be a nun who walked backwards for Jesus. Plus, played that way around, it ended with some rotten git called "Hitler" becoming baby-cute again and then being vacuumed up by his mother and slipped back to his father moments before everyone put their underwear back on and they all got sober in an Austrian tavern the night they talked themselves out of un-forming the Nazi party and retreated into a life of rural peace and obscurity. How much more sense does that make too eh?

Most of the men are crying now but I don't think it's because of homesickness or emotion, it's just a reflex action like gagging or going cross-eyed when you get shot in the brain. Apparently it happens to film critics an awful lot too unless they've been inoculated against Julie Andrews.

I think that the torch may have done a u-turn somehow and lodged in my appendix – the right-hand side of my gym-bunny one-pack belly is glowing now. I can see the shadow outline of the forceps they left in me when I had that operation for that thing where my kidneys were strangling my liver.

Must try to get some sleep.

Goodbye Day 4. I hate you and the three-legged horse you rode in on.

Stardate 20th June 2027, just as I was dozing remembering happy times with my dog Tigger.

We were all unstrapped today, which was nice, because the Captain ordered Engineering to switch on the artificial gravitas, or something.

The Royal Mail (Second class and Parcels) finally arrived, via some sort of G.P.O. chemical rocket arrangement that looked awfully like a red Morris Minor van with oxygen tanks welded to the roof. Many thanks for your letter, Mum, although I am fairly sure that most lone parents just rent out their son's bedroom when he goes into National Service, they don't sell it outright, even if they are "poor widow-women". They certainly don't usually sell it fully-furnished and with a lifetime of possessions including spare civilian clothing and a prized stamp collection. Please ask the new owner if I can at least have my Airfix kits back. I spent a lot of time and effort making those.

To answer your questions Mum, no, I didn't know that vets will put a healthy but unwanted dog down if you pay them ten shillings and yes, I do have somewhere safe to put Tigger's ashes jar so thank you for sending it. It's nice that as you say you can finally put the kitchen plastic swing-bin where his bed used to be in the way, and I appreciate your kindness in spending the extra to have his hind legs embalmed and fitted with wooden handles. They will certainly make talking points in their new role as novelty back-scratchers. Mine arrived safely along with the ashes and, as you say, I'm sure that you'll get enough to defray the cost of the vet by selling the other one at the car boot sale. No, thank you, I do not want the rest of his pelt to make a hat out of so you can ask Aunt Marjorie to stop the curing process. To be brutally honest, I think that I might be feeling a touch emotional right now, and ex-orbital speeds do so affect one's tear-ducts. In fact, if you'll excuse me please, I'll be back in a moment.

[There follows here a short pause during which Reginald gets lovingly and supportively beaten up by his squad for being a big girlie wuss and a general cry-baby.]

You're quite right Mum, he would have wanted to be with me on the front lines but I have to say that I'm fairly sure he would have preferred to have not been euthanized, part-butchered, made into household objet and to have his remaining remains cremated first – dogs quite enjoy running around alive. Please excuse the stains on this letter but with the low evening artificial gravity tears just hang around your head like rain-drops frozen in time, and then when the engines cough they fall like a small monsoon making the blue lined A5 Basildon Bond very soggy very quickly.

In other news, I have been assigned to the very important job of keeping the Visualisation Drive well oiled and happy.

The Visualisation Drive is a room full of really older ladies with powerful hormones and psi powers – they are the sort of older ladies who have regular "reserved" seats at bingo where you can't really reserve seats and nobody argues about it. It's my job to keep their "tea" flowing. Some of them like their tea neat, some take it with tonic water, all of them take it regularly and often. Most of the time they knit things, tell jokes about willies they have known and pinch my bottom. When the Captain decides that he wants to go anywhere in a hurry he calls down a speaking tube and these ladies visualise the destination really, really hard and imagine us parking there and suddenly there we are. Supposedly, anyway, according to the manual. Sometimes it takes several tries before the Visualisation Drive engines get it right. If too many of them are depressed or thinking about home or killing their lazy good for nothing husbands we end up in the most peculiar places in the blink of an eye. This is why my job is so important. The Chief Engineer told me to "keep them mellow yellow – not so drunk that they drop stitches in their knitting but not so sober that they can still read the pattern". I've based my routine on how you like your tea, so that was easy.

Today was a day for feeding them up and making sure that they had enough wool and enough magazines and things because the day after tomorrow we'll have cleared the orbit of Pluto (not Michael Mouse's dog - unlike Tigger, he's not floating around in space) and we'll need to be off to the battle zone. The Sergeant says that the job of looking after the "old engines" will make a man's man of me because some of them will demand a right good seeing-to before they start work proper tomorrow, but they all look as though they are in good working condition to me so I'm not sure what he really means. Some of the lonelier "old engines" need more attention than the others but I don't mind really – what harm can there be in just sitting in their lap as I hold the skeins of wool and they ball it up? Some of them have lady-moustaches that are a bit tickly when they kiss me. Sometimes they hide my walking sticks so that I can't get away and about my other duties as quickly as I should.

It's not a bad job really and I wouldn't mind being assigned to it permanently if it means that I can avoid being put into one of the front-line initial assault teams. Front-line Initial Assault Teams are the soldiers who are parachuted down to the battlefield first and it's their job to hold the fort against ridiculous odds so that the rest of the army can sort itself out and get into fighting formation without being bothered by the enemy. I should hate to be in a front-line team, dropped from low orbit with nothing but a rifle, a cricket cup and a packet of Wurther's Originals for energy. They say that the life expectancy of someone in a front-line team is about three minutes - or nearly four minutes if you survive the landing impact and don't drop straight into the lap of the enemy. Can you imagine that? Especially if the enemy is one of those ugly over-sized insectoid species that spits acid and throws flames and sucks out human brains through a nose-straw? E-eew! No thank you!

Stardate 21st June 2027, 23:03HRS, give or take. Who cares anymore?

This morning the Sergeant took me off oiling-up the Visualisation Drive and assigned me to a Front-line Initial Assault Team.

After I'd been excused to clean up around myself with Dettol disinfectant we were lined up and issued our kit. Apparently there aren't enough cricket cups or packets of Wurther's Originals to go around so I'll be landing with just my rifle, a knife and half of an Extra Strong Mint.

The enemy is an insectoid species of brain-eaters and apparently these ones shit pure acid but like the extra crunch that comes with eating brains still in the shell without using a straw. Still, no-one's said anything about flame-throwing, so that's nice.

I'm wondering now whether to take Tigger's hind leg with me as a backup, something to hit the enemy with if I run out of ammunition. It would be a nice way to let him see some action and get him involved in service to his country.

After hypnosis, deep sensory deprivation and standard army subliminal auto-suggestion my team were all given our medication implant packs. The M.O. says that if we were back on Earth then the cocktail in the IV auto-drips in our buttocks would be called "crystal meth" which is a nice sounding name. It reminds me of those pretty crystal paperweights I used to love buying whenever we went camping in West Runton, Norfolk. It also makes me think of the purple methylated spirits for the little burner in my model steam-engine for some reason.

The M.O. took the torch out while he was down there and put it back into stores. Waste not want not he says. Besides, we might be landing on the dark side of the planet, and he says that I wouldn't want to float down like a beacon and waving a hairy dog's hind-leg back-scratcher and stinking of mint. It might give the enemy mixed messages.

Personally, the longer this goes on the more I couldn't give a shit about the economy of not wasting and not wanting or of farting around with bits of this and bits of that, I just want to get down to the surface and kick some alien teeth in. Quite frankly, I think that I'm beginning to feel a tad aggressive.

Soon after the M.O. had finished with us some chaps came in with those things that they use to catch stray dogs – loops of wire on the end of long poles – and moved us all into a "Mass Deployment Chamber". Turns out it has nothing to do with the Catholics at all – the "mass" refers to us, which is nice, and at least "deployment" seems to indicate that I'm closer to getting my wish for a bit of a rumble with the aliens.

Several of the meat-head goons in my squad of ultimate bad-arses got involved in a knife-fight just after we were briefed, not long after second medication increase o'clock in fact. I put a stop to it by laying them all out cold. I'm definitely feeling less than peaceful.

I could eat a hippie without even removing the flowers first.

Not long after the fight the Sergeant used his own rifle on low power through the bars and tattooed a Corporal's stripes on my forehead. He said it would make you very proud, Mum, but then he's never met you and can have no idea that you're too dignified and reserved to express those kinds of deep, lower-class emotions about your children. If I weren't snarling and growling too much I might have explained that you are English and thus the most emotionally demonstrative you would be likely to be is "quietly less displeased and not so disappointed after all, on the whole, although you still think you should never have had children and wouldn't if you had your time over again".

Anyway, once the singed-flesh smell of field promotion had worn off I told the Sergeant that the only way a scrawny little runt like him could stop me jumping out of the spacecraft right then and there and diving down to the surface with my knife between my teeth would be if they gassed us all and locked us into our damned effing individual launch chutes like wild animals. Then I remember he seemed to be looking down to the control console and hitting a large red button that looked to have a skull and crossbones on it and a label reading "Nervous Gas" but written upside down and front to back. There was a hissing and then lights all went out just the way they used to every time a two-bob bit dropped through the meter at Grandma's bungalow.

Stardate 22nd June 2027. Time?
What's time to a front-line soldier, except maybe a heartbeat?

I woke up chained down in a launch chute this morning. I woke just in time to see the last of the mustard-coloured knock-out gas being sucked out. There was a hunting-knife jammed between the remains of my teeth and I think I've bent the blade by biting down on it. Still, a bent blade will just do more damage when I skewer the bastard enemy.

They showed us the naturist re-make of The Sound of Music on the little screens in our launch chutes, the version with the lovely Esma Cannon playing Maria, Eric Morecambe playing Captain Von Trapp and the amateur junior-ensemble trad-jazz all-brass soundtrack. Then they replaced all of the air with a mixture of lighter fluid, aerosol propellant and the fumes from a whole tin of Carnation Evaporated Glue. I quite liked the lighter fluid.

I feel a bit odd really – now that the torch has gone, instead of having illuminated buttocks I found myself alone in the dark with just the ticklish buzzing of the clockwork crystal-meth dispenser clicking away. Tick-tick squirt, tick-tick squirt. It has a disconcertingly appealing rhythm.

Although I don't remember learning how at school somehow I now know fifty-seven completely different ways to kill all sorts of things and I'm absolutely certain that I could live off the land – any land – without being detected, just long enough to locate and slaughter the contents of an insect enemy's egg depository or larvae nursery. Isn't it odd what you pick up as a child and that only comes back to you later in quiet, reflective moments? I suppose that it must have been one of Miss Clarkson's lessons; it sounds like the sort of thing she'd be likely to teach. My favourite kill is using the edge of my old pension book to crush an enemy's windpipe but I'm also quite fond of cutting the enemy spinal cord with my plastic bus pass too.

Better yet, if I am injured or – most unlikely – captured alive by the enemy then I now also know how to internally cease all respiration and stop my brain activity, so I'm unlikely to embarrass you Mum by giving away any military secrets or plans. The army guru-san, a twenty-three year old Zen Ninth Dan Pillock from Essex, says that one of the best things about us old folk is that there's so little cerebral and respiratory activity to stop in an emergency in the first place.

I wish those bitches in the Visualisation Drive would get their freakin' act together and get us to where we're needed – alien HQ. The guys and I have already begun our battle cry – we all bang our walking sticks on the inside of our launch tubes to the drum beat of "We will rock you" by Her Majesty, The Queens. We will, we will, thump thump bang, thump thump bang, kill you. We will, we will, thump thump bang, thump thump bang, kill you... After a bit of synchronisation we can drown out the base beat from the ship's speakers, we're that good at it now. My hands are a bit tired though from clenching and unclenching without a thorax in them to crush.

Those alien bugs are going down. My buttocks won't stop twitching, it must be some sort of allergic reaction the crystal meth so I'm probably going to end up with a nasty rash down there. Twitch-twitch-squirt, twitch-twitch-squirt.

This National Service isn't so bad I suppose – if I twist my arms just so then I can scratch at the inside of the launch tube with my fingernails and maybe get out faster and get to the business of killing the enemy bugs. It's all of these little delays that get to a chap in the Army. They teach a chap to kill and then tell him to wait quietly in his orbital launching tube. Thump thump bang. Thump thump bang.

There's someone or some thing else in this tube with me though, I'm sure of it. I can hear someone screaming and screaming like a completely demented animal but I just can't twist around fast enough to catch them behind me. I'm going to keep trying until I do catch them – and then I'm going to kill them, this is my launch tube and no-one said anything about having to share it.

Why are they keeping me waiting like this? I don't need all of this fancy launching and orbital trajectory and re-entry mode shit, I just need to know one thing about the enemy and that's where – they - are. Just throw me out of a porthole and I'll start killing the bastards as soon as I land.

It's me against all of the insects, and I know who's going to come out of this with the most scalps to his name. Someone seems to have sprayed crazy-foam or something all around my mouth, and I think that I've got the old dribbling problem back but a million times worse, but do you know what? I. Don't. Care. These new army-supplied Tena-Chap panties can cope. My walking-frame has deployed inside my tube, so I know it's going to be soon and I know that I'll get a fast start and be able to hit the battleground shuffling quickly. The trick is to go in low, go in fast, so I've started getting my knees to bend already.

Yee-ess! Finally! I just felt the locking clamps on my launch tube release – so it's to be just me and the enemy then, right here, right now. I don't care if they're not sending the rest of my team down, I don't need them! Yee-hah! Put your heads down between all six legs you alien bastards and kiss your yard-long wasp-stings goodbye – I'm coming to get you! Die you alien bastards, die! I'm going to crush you under the rubber feet of this zimmer, all you have to do is stay still long enough for me to get to you!

Yaaaaaaaaaaaaaaaaaaaaarrrrrrrggghhh! Thump thump bang. Thump thump bang. I will, I will kill you. Thump thump bang.

Stardate 26th June 2027, duh-huh-huh!
Time? Well, there's a Magic Roundabout wall-clock in here and if Dougal's willy is his big hand and Zebedee is upside down ... huh-huh – I said "willy"! Huh-huh!

I woke up this morning in the ship's infirmary, under a Magic Roundabout wall-clock. If facing that the moment your eyes open isn't guaranteed to ensure that a chap easily reclaims his sanity then I don't know what is. The Ermintrude figure gives a big, toothy cow-grin on every quarter-hour and Dylan strums his guitar once each second.

My clipboard medical notes read "Parachute failed to open, found still in launch tube, lodged head-first in the belly of the dead alien queen. Stasis field appears not to have engaged fully although seat-belts held. Note to armoury: remind all front-line teams that cricket boxes are recommended for a reason. Removed damaged testicles, removed plasma-burn damaged penis tissue and tidied up the stump, replaced flattened cranium with lower-ranks quality prosthesis, pinned and screwed multiple fractures. Re-animated remaining brain tissue using standard fifty-amp current and paddles dipped in cider-vinegar. Do not tell patient that he is now eight inches shorter than he already was. Recommend de-tox and return to appropriate light duty, possibly as a doorstop tending a reasonably quiet doorway."

A nurse came along and squirted cold scrambled egg down my throat for breakfast and gave my bed a bath. She says that when I get used to my new jaw and dentures I can have "sausages" for breakfast. Apparently, after the recent successful counter-attack on the insectoid egg depositories and larvae nurseries we have lots of fresh eggs and fresh sausage-meat in ship's stores. Waste not want not seems to be the ship's motto for everything here in outer outer-space. Yum-yum, pig's bum eh? There's nothing like home cooking and this is nothing like home cooking.

The Sergeant says that my nickname is now "Gimli" but that it's in regard to my new-found convenient combat-tossability, not my new-found lack of even more height. He says that they can't give me a medal for killing the alien queen because according to the launch-tube logs I wasn't conscious at the time. He says that if I had been conscious then I would have been decorated with medals and Generals' hand-shakes and sent home to work in PR or something doing chat-shows and doing chat-show groupies for the rest of my life until someone ghost-wrote my memoirs for millions. He says that they'll find me some light duties for a while, once both of my eyes team up and go back to looking in the same direction again. Duh-huh uhuh! Dougal's got a willy! Dougal's got a willy!

I just hope that they don't assign me to some mindless task where I'm in a room with no port-holes all day and night, working on my own or getting messy or anything. Duh-huh.

Stardate 24th June 2027
just before we had to call in at a service station for repairs.

My new job is a bit odd, but I suppose that it is about half-way between an icky combat role and the desk job that I told them I wanted when I signed on. I'm a temporary valve-actuator on the port-side diesel engine. Once I get a rhythm going it's not a bad job really and the engines are so big that they only do thirty or forty revolutions a minute so a twelve-hour shift just flies by. I lift the handle up to raise the valve and when the broken camshaft spins back around I lower the handle to close the valve. In my free time I have to be sure to squirt in some Reddex. I don't know if I'm an exhaust valve or an intake valve though. If we get out of step the Sergeant gets very upset and the engine is none too happy either. It backfires a lot but they say it'll get us to the next service area for a refit.

There's an outside chance that the lower-ranks quality metal plate in my skull could bang against a reinforcing strut or something and cause an electric sparkle near the fuel hoses, so I have to wear one of those bobbly rubberised lady's bathing caps at all times. That is, the cap is bobbly and rubberised, I'm sure that the sort of ladies who wear these things are not. As far as I know, that is. I only got to oil the visualisation-engines for a day and that was before they were fully commissioned, so I still don't know much about ladies except for what I used to hear the lads in my old unit saying about them. None of the ladies in the photographs in their lockers were wearing bobbly bathing caps. Dougal's got a wil-ly! Dougal's got a wil-ly!

Sometimes at the end of my shift my arm won't stop going up and down and, once, I almost got sucked into the engine air intakes by mistake when they encountered a rogue asteroid and the pilot had to floor it. That would have been serious because they said I might have broken some of the turbocharger impellor blades and they're expensive.

The fuel leaks are getting worse and about an hour after the start of my shift today I got bored and decided to see if I could break the surface tension on a big diesel globule that was floating around and stick my head inside.

Seems that I could.

I had to let go of my valve handle and float around for a bit like an ant with its head jammed inside a drop of liquid. Without any gravity in the engine room it was a lot harder to get my head out of the big globule of diesel than it was to get it in, and for a moment there my gas-mask snorkel wasn't just sucking air. Still, those oily rainbows you can see on the outside look even more groovy from the inside, especially when you vomit through a gas-mask intake and then pass out.

All in all the first couple of weeks of my National Service has gone quite well, all things considered. Granted, it's taking them some time to find me a nice desk job but in the meantime I've made Corporal, almost become a war hero and been reduced in rank to an engine spare-part. Mind you, even Uncle Geronimo would have to admit, as a Private First Class Replacement Valve-Actuator (Miscellaneous) Grade III, the only way from here is up! The future has to be better than this.

Stardate 25th June 2027, no idea of the time. Does time still exist?

These emergency personal survival life-spheres are really quite comfortable, considering.

Now the other temporary valve-replacement chaps and I know what really happens to a sixty-thousand horse-power diesel spaceship engine if you wedge all of the valves shut at the same time. It's quite pretty, but it also sounded very expensive.

Most of the senior crew seem to be forming their pods into ranks and following the captain somewhere but all of the engine-bay lads are using the manoeuvring thrusters to play snooker with each other. It's a bit chaotic because all of the survival pods are white spheres so we all look like cue-balls and because you can play up and down as well as side to side.

I wonder how much propellant there is in these things?

This is fun! Boing. Boing boing boing. Dougal's got a wil-ly! Dougal's got a wil-ly!

Stardate 14th July 2027
apparently just three days shy of death from dehydration.

I woke up this morning when they started tipping us out of the survival pods. The pods are quite expensive so the Army came back to salvage them even though we'd all run out of propellant and some of the other chaps were suffering a bit from the lack of fresh oxygen. I'd already been holding my breath really hard though, just in case my air ran out. I'm not daft.

We've all been herded into a big room in the medical unit and the M.O. has looked us over again and said something about how Recycling could probably use parts from every two or three of us to make one new. I don't know what he's talking about, I don't have any spare parts with me; they all went down with the old ship when the engines inexplicably failed near that big blue star thingy.

For dinner they gave us a big pill each. They caught us one by one and the Sergeant blew it down our throats through a tube like old-fashioned vets used to use on farm animals. I don't remember much after they turned the fire hoses and the Tasers on us, everything went dark. I barely had time to growl and throw my torso at the bars (I don't know where my legs have gone, I'm not even sure that I had them with me in the escape pod).

What next, I wonder? Duh-huh. Please, Serge, give me a desk

job? Surely now I'll get a desk job? I'm a pensioner you know, serving King and planet. Dougal's got a wil-ly! Dougal's got a wil-ly!

Stardate 21st August 2027,
Recycling Facility on New Mars.

I say - I seem to be floating inside a tube again, only this time it's not a launch tube but a clear medical treatment tube of some design and it's filled with some variety of oxygen-rich colourless liquid, possibly perfluorodecalin C10F18 or some further derivative. Liquid breathing is my best guess – what fun and larks eh? Quite fascinating!

An arrangement also seems to have been made for intravenous delivery of a milky suspension, I'm guessing it's probably octadecafluorodecahydronaphthalene or heneicosafluorotripropylamine. Mind you, I don't even want to think about the tube I can feel between my buttocks. That's all very unsavoury and not a little injurious to one's inner dignity – that certain dividing line betwixt socially acceptable intrusion on medical grounds and indecorous liberty was crossed the moment I regained consciousness, a situation that might only be ameliorated by swift and emotionally detached professional nursing intervention. One rather suspects however that there are no angels in white uniforms nearby.

Setting aside my nagging intellectual displeasure at bobbing up and down like some tethered decoration in a curiously impractically-shaped fish-tank with no fish, my next thoughts naturally ran to my secondary environment, and I searched with not some little trepidation for hope for a less liquid-dependent future. The refraction caused by the brutal curvature and crude industrial Plexiglass of my tubular environment made detailed investigation problematic but I could hazard a premise that I was the focus of a medical laboratory that seemed marked with a purposeful and functional military motif. There was some sort of amusing optical illusion – I assume caused by the properties of the tube – in which I appeared to be one tube among a formation of thousands stretching to the horizon.

I can't help but wonder though why there is a nagging need manifesting at the threshold of my consciousness to comment upon the possession of a phallus by an oddly shaped semi-sentient cartoon dog with close associations to a magical roundabout and a novelty clock.

Still, back to matters in hand. The technology in use – beyond those of my own obvious indignities – appeared to indicate a familiarity with and abundant use of complex electromagnetics. There were some suggestions of employed quantum chromodynamics. Certainly the infrastructure hinted that metamaterial composites and advanced nano-polymers were in use. The aesthetics tended towards the humanoid universal without the inclusion of tribal or territorial markers evident in the more primitive cultures – certainly there were no tacky little nationalistic flags about or stencilled labels bluntly proclaiming "Property of X, Y or Zed" or, worse, "God bless country A, B or C". I surmised that I was at least, if not exactly in a functional utopia, in some corner of a civilisation based upon humanistic values, possibly even a corner embracing an altruistic post-commercialism and, by extrapolation from the deliberate lack of cultural metaphor evident in the room, a certain healthily separated establishment state providing a passive and supportive intellectual framework fostering artistic and political freedom for citizens within a system of protected personal interstices.

Two chaps in white lab-coats suddenly entered my view. They were mid-conversation.

'Yah! Ruddy cheek of him. LBW in broad daylight and then argues the toss with the umpire!'

'Peasant! Some sort of comprehensive school wallah eh?'

'Abso-ruddy-lutely. I blame the Labour Government of course.'

A large relaxation fart-bubble entered my anus-tube and was sucked away for analysis by the machinery; I knew immediately where I was.

I was in Heaven. Probably somewhere on the south coast, near Brighton. England, obviously.

One of the chaps came up and tapped on my tube with his

pencil. 'Hair-lair! Awake are we? Splendid. Oogie boogie boogie? Ooda biggwittle bwave soldier den eh?' He then mimed doing something that an adolescent circus-chimp would have considered too indecorous to actually be seen doing in public.

[Yes, I rather thought that you might be able to picture that in some detail.]

The two of them then began an appraisal of me the like of which I have not suffered since my last doctor's appointment, and before that at the hands of the Physical Education master at school after-hours. My lips were moving desperately, but all I appeared to be able to try to say was 'Dougal's got a wil-ly! Dougal's got a wil-ly!' and I doubt that this contributed positively towards the achievement of my agenda, which was of course to initiate dialogue in re my confined circumstances and the immediate physical improvement thereof. Dash it all but, without the positive intervention of some sort of pro-active advocate on my behalf, I feared that progress may be slow viz exchanging sides of the Plexiglass tube or at minimum having my electrolyte levels balanced and the tube taken out of my arse. They continued discussing me as though I weren't even sentient.

'The grafts appear to be taking well, stitches healing, that sort of thing.'

'It's a bit short isn't it?'

'It's all we could do old boy. Took parts from the last ten used squaddies in that batch of spare parts just to make this one and there are bits from three different brains in there, including I believe quite a few chunks of black Labrador dog – the RAF were having a spot of bother in the same sector. The "gentlemen's parts" are straight off a bomb-disposal unit orang-utan, as you can plainly see.'

'Oh gosh yes – looks just like a penis, only smaller. Are those the um...'

'They are – although admittedly, the liquid in these recovery tubes is quite cold.'

'I've seen squirrels with bigger.'

'Have you really, Simon? Some sort of hobby eh, lookin' at the nuts on squirrels?'

'As a matter of fact, no. You get my point though. Poor chap.'

'The M.O. said that most of the bits were going off by the time he got to this one and he was in two minds whether to finish it or not. Reckoned it would either be a usefully obedient moron or some sort of bumbling genius that given half a chance would dominate the universe. I must say, one of its legs looks as though it came off a stuffed Welsh Collie.'

His colleague consulted the detailed notes.

'It did. Apparently it was carrying it when it went into battle. Where the hell the squaddies find these things I'll never know. Well we'll decant it, pea-balls and all, load it with antibiotics and stack it in with the others ready for delivery to its new unit tomorrow. They can decide whether it's Cro-Magnon or post-Hawking once they've put a Laser in its hand and a Bowie knife between its teeth again. The army never makes mistakes. It makes ugly buggers, yes, but mistakes? Never.'

Bobbing up and down in my tube of liquid I hoped that the remark relating to "New unit" was a trick of the change of transmission medium from air through Plexiglass to perfluorodecalin, and that I had simply not heard the gentleman correctly. I'd been re-born like a phoenix from the ashes, and the army simply had to give me a shore posting now! Surely! I made a mental note to pee up a lamp-post, lick the C.O.'s hand and have a word with him about a transfer to Intelligence - or even to Recruitment - as soon as I arrived. I was safe enough – the armed forces never waste a resource of course. Surely after all of this surgery I deserved a break?

The two lab assistants muttered peculiarly at the mirage of a tube next to me, then one of them pulled a chain and I could swear that I heard on old-fashioned outhouse flushing mechanism – the sort with the cistern up high and a long, battered lead pipe leading down to the hot-seat.

I squirmed around in my bio-tube, anxious to catch their eye so that I could communicate. 'I say - if it's all the same with you chaps, I'd rather like to be given a spot of leave and then posted to somewhere rural with an extensive library of Greek and technical works. There must be some arrangement in the army for a chap to take a spot of leave, surely? This is, after all, National Service and not National Servitude. Eh? What? I have an idea for harvesting limitless free energy from the friction between adjacent multiverse branes and a political wheeze of a system that would inevitably lead to the peaceful co-existence of all creatures in the universe, both known and as yet unknown.'

That did it – I finally caught their attention again although, obviously, since I was breathing liquid – even an ultra-low-viscosity liquid such as perfluorodecalin - they couldn't hear me directly. Among my tangle of pipes and sensor-wires I did my best to mime a short message indicating my urgent need for clinical and psychological reassessment, and immediate access to the Speaker of the House of Commons in order to request a timeslot for my initial address.

This time both of the lab-coated chaps made gorilla impersonations for my benefit, presented their arses like females offering mating, laughed and left. I was left with a rather nagging doubt that the pertinent detail of my request had been successfully communicated.

They switched the lights out as they went. In the rather eerie glow of the tell-tales on the lab oscilloscope and the night-shift's Morphy-Richards tea kettle I centred my karma and reassured myself that the army never made mistakes or wasted valuable resources. My next assignment would surely be to some cerebral establishment such as Porton Down or Bletchley Park where my brain would be best utilised. I think that my original physiognomy and psychological profile alone made it perfectly clear that I did not do well in hot or arid climes, or under immediate personal threat. The chaps were just joshing. At the very least I'd get promotion to the rank of Sniffer Dog.

Stardate? How the hell would I know, I've been in and out of Medical and Recycling so often that I can tell you the number of holes in the ceiling tiles. Somewhere over the equatorial regions of the enemy planet Freezarsia. Or Rottenboggia, or Worthlessshiteholeium, or somewhere strategic.

I'm three foot tall and I am all that's left of my entire initial unit, literally. The M.O. has intimated that there was barely enough of me to stitch together after the last deployment and that I was probably close to the end of my useful army career.

I woke up chained down in a launch chute this morning, just in time to see the last of the mustard-coloured knock-out gas being sucked out. There was a Laser pistol glued to my hand and a hunting-knife jammed between my gums. I think I've bent the blade by biting down on it and I'm considering using the Laser pistol to try to shoot the clockwork crystal-meth dispenser that's clicking away again in my arse. I say "my" arse but it's plainly Caribbean in ethnic origin and probably decorated the rear end of my late comrade in arms, Danny John-Jules, not so long since. I can't tell you how confused I am about my genitalia since the army recycling unit began pooling male and female organs reclaimed from battlefield casualties. There can only be seconds left before the timer trips and the plunger delivers its next load of craziness into my bloodstream. I hope it's not too late. It misfired on the last deployment and I was dropped into enemy territory initially quite sane and without chemical assistance of any kind other than my Wurther's Originals field-issue, and I inadvertently swallowed that whole on landing.

My new unit and deployment is similar to my old unit and deployment. The more battle-experienced guys and I have already begun our battle cry – we all bang our foreheads on the inside of our launch tubes to the drumbeat of "We will rock you" by Her Majesty, The Queens. We will, we will, thump thump bang, thump thump bang, kill you. We will, we will, thump thump bang, thump thump bang, kill you... After a bit of synchronisation we can drown out the base beat from the ship's speakers, we're that good at it now. My hands are a bit tired though from clenching and unclenching without a thorax in them to crush. Those alien hundred-legged sand-bugs are going down.

Again.

Dear Universe, dear, sweet, all-loving Universe – please don't let them rebuild me after this one.

Let me die. Just let me die. Honestly, I promise not to be a drain on national resources wherever I go, be it heaven or hell or even, preferably, just nothingness. Just let me die, please... Mum?

Can you hear me Mother?

Tigger? Is that you, Tigger? Keep barking boy, and I'll walk towards the sound. When your number's up around here after two or three dozen rebuilds it's really up isn't it?

Dear Diary, everything went dark just a moment ago...

9 BLOOD-CURDLING SCREAMS AND THE WHITWORTH SCREW-THREAD

A quite terrifying crowd was circling outside the patent office. It was a mob of very upper crust protestinatrix (protestinatrix is the plural of itself, like "sheeps" and "thousand island dressings").

Each of those in the crowd carried sartorial bustles and fully-developed, veiled millinery the size of Dorset or Londonshire. Every last one of them was gently waving a placard made from lavender-scented hand-laid paper stuck to beeswax-polished timber batons. They were ramrod-straight lady insurgents, proudly holding up what might have been small font-samplers on sticks to dry, circling, waiting like powdered vultures for the old world order Establishment to die.

There must have been almost a metric half-dozen of them. The Whitehall doormen had quaked in their boots and then quite properly deployed the big wooden locking bar on the main door and stacked several heavy off-duty caretakers against it. Nonetheless, it still felt as though the hushed marbled sanctity of the Civil Service corridors within were going quite without, as far as security went, in re from those viewed without from within. It seemed as though London, and thus all of modern Earth civilisation, would soon be lost to the mob!

Lady Constance Mann-Bighter (eldest daughter of the Earl of Cleethorpes) was leading the aural assault with a battered tin megaphone and a battered conductor's baton. The baton was actually in excellent condition. The battered conductor was describing his attacker to the crowd that had gathered around him as he sat on the pavement outside the Albert Hall holding a handkerchief to the cut on his noggin. 'My name iss Hubert von Karajan und I hav bin mugged by a large polite lady viz ein umberella und nein sense of timink. She took my liddle musical pointing shtick.' Lady M-B didn't care a whit. Not so much as half a jot. She had done what she had done for the Cause.

'WHAT DO WE WANT?' she sang, to the tune of Crimond.

'STEAM!' responded her acolytes, relying heavily for energy and zest on the electrolytes left over from their light breakfast of kedgeree and gin at the Suffragette Club.

'When do we want it?'

'As soon as practicable!'

'What else do we respectfully request?'

'Locomotion!'

'When do we want it?'

'Once all the technical bugs have been ironed out!'

'What else could we possibly fancy?'

'Large-scale ironwork structures!'

'By when would we like them if possible?'

'In time for the Great Exhibition!'

'What further might we suggest?'

'General industrial mechanisation!'

'For why do we propose it?'

'To make our cotton mills oop t'north profitable and competitive!'

'What in addition might be rather splendid?'

'Canals!'

'Why would they be commercially beneficial?'

'Because the roads are freightfully awful!'

'What do we say, Ladies?'

'Pleasey-weasey!'

'What will we say when it's all done?'

'Thank you, thank you ever so!' (Oh who writes this rubbish?)

'How may we be of further assistance?'

'BY STARTING OUR CHANT ALL OVER AGAIN!'

'Lucinda – more effort on the Barbershop harmonies please. Daphne – a teensy-weensy par-boiled semi-quaver earlier on your Locomotion solo and go easy on the shimmy, this is not burlesque. From the top everyone, let's do this for England, ladies, for England. A-one, a-two-ah, a-three-ah... WHAT DO WE WANT?'

'STEAM!'

'WHEN DO WE WANT IT?'

The chant was somewhat wearing both for those at the wobbling-tonsil contralto end and for those at the point of the drawing board and the technological breakthrough. Tensions were running quite high and the Mayor had placed the whole of London upon an "Amber" fainting threat alert. Emergency Paramedic Response Teams with smelling salts, cool damp flannels, collapsible hand fans, bone-saws and staunching-tar buckets had been stationed in areas known to be especially prone to high drama or touches of the female vapours.

Slap and Resuscitate powers under the Pull Yourself Together Woman Act of 1166 had been extended to Park Wardens, Public Lavatory Attendants and to members of the Baker Street Irregulars – anyone entering the new "under the ground railway" stations to wait for "tube trains" to be invented was subject to random corset checks. Moreover, random corset checks with no need to prove probable cause. It was like martial law where whalebones were concerned.

[This would later prove awfully prickly when statistics collected were collated and indicated that narrow-waisted, pale and medically distressed-looking women were over seven million trillion umptillion gazillion percent more likely to be stopped and checked for illegally tight corset lacing than were men. Authorities responded sympathetically to the shrill "equal" rights outcry by pointing out that it was tough shit and they were in charge so boo ruddy hoo kindly go back to your knitting madam, as one did in those days.]

Suddenly, one of the covert-operations ladies broke away from the madly marching circle and walked briskly towards the Patent Office building, checking her route for navigational hazards such as horse poop or picturesque flower sellers named Mrs Enery Iggins. No sense in making a dramatic break for it and then falling foul of stepping in a pancake of traffic pollution or a bunch of cheap lilacs with an Cockerney-Hollywooden accent. The covert agent's fully loaded, snub-nosed, auto-repeating face was half-covered by a lace handkerchief tied at the back, as was recommended in the Society's pamphlet on Polite Civil Disobedience for Ladies.

Bopping a constable in the legal nuts with her rolled-up umbrella she then reached into her handbag, zeroed-in on her target through pince-nez and threw something through the third window along, fifth floor up, second pane down on the frame to the right. She threw with a little twisting top spin to stabilise the message.

It should be noted by History that the lady threw in the manner of a rather delightful shot-putter, whirling like a summery dervish before sighting down an outstretched, long-gloved arm and launching from the hunched neck and shoulder. She grunted behind her lace mask as she released the air explosively from her lungs, hopped on one multi-petticoated stocking-bedecked leg to watch the curve of the throw. She then unhooked her umbrella from the crook of her elbow to stand - rather defiantly, it must be said - as she waited for arrest. It was simply not possible that she could have performed the manoeuvre without flashing at least one ankle so criminal charges of some sort were inevitable in any polite society.

Her missile missive landed on the desk in front of the Chairperson of the Committee for the Nitty-Gritty Nit-Picking Implementation Details of The Industrial Revolution. It had called briefly at the temple of the Committee Secretary and then rushed straight over the heads of Finance and Public Relations before bouncing off Regulatory Affairs like a bad idea and settling, with a sliding ninety-degree correction, between Mr Branson's entrepreneurial but naturally cautious leather-patch covered tweed elbows. Branson's Nanny had always, always warned him against leaning his elbows on any table. Had he listened? No, of course not, and now look what had happened. He had virtually fallen into the arms of Suffragettes! Stupid boy!

Shards of thick, greenish, hand-blown window pane scattered across the mirror-finish inlaid walnut in the manner of a very upset dish of Messrs Barker & Dobson's best Imperious Mints. The shards took quite some time to rattle to a random conclusion. Most of the committee looked to the window as the point of entry, one or two of a more conventional religious bent looked questioningly up to the ceiling and beyond. The Committee Secretary succumbed to concussion and fell off his perch onto the fringed Persian.

[This was, fortunately, a rug and not some sort of barnet-challenged Middle Eastern gentleman taking the minutes of the meeting.]

The objet in question was a small, hand-made ship-in-a-rock, wrapped all about with a perfumed Basildon Bond love-notelet and some cornflower-blue ribbon.

[The ship-in-a-rock was the forerunner to the more popular ship-in-a-bottle. Putting exquisite little models of sailing ships into clear bottles rather than igneous rocks allowed the customer to see the fine craftsmanship of the model-maker and made them easier to sell to an increasingly cynical and distrustful seaside consumer public.]

The protestor in question was promptly and duly wrestled to the ground by the new Constable Class, Riot Division Bobbies who had Lignum Vitæ truncheons and who weren't afraid, for obvious reasons, of being caught on cctv as they laid in enthusiastically with intra-costal entreaties to observe the rule of established law. There was bound to be something somewhere in the statute books about delivering unsolicited collectible items via closed fenestration. Several dozen layers of her top-skirts were thrown over her head to facilitate unlawful-protestation muffling and to allow for her easy launch into the back of a horse-drawn Maria-of-Colour (colour was the new black, even back then before political correctness burst upon the world like a ripe boil). She would be before the Borough Magistrates within the quarter-hour and, if not of decent birth or judicial bedroom influence, on a sailing ship to van Diemen's Land before the sun set solid, there to work as a sheep-dog or a bar-Sheila. At least, to do so until she died of the bite of the female trap-door kangaroo or manifold agues of fever and plagues of the head-blood or something medically antipodean and terribly, terribly, un-English. Justice would be swift; there would be no more than six or seven months before she had red dust on her heels and hot koala-spit on her best lace 'kerchief.

Mr Branson stirred. ‘I see that Mr Palmer has yet to acquire a monopoly upon English mail deliveries’, he noted as he tugged at the apparently Gordian knot in the ribbon with an exploratory finger and thumb. One or two of those on the committee, those with better haircuts than the Persian gentleman taking the minutes, and possessed of at least a rudimentary sociable life, recognised the ribbon as a John Kay – Joseph Stell Loom Premium at one and sixpence a yard from Harrods. The notelet scent had the top-notes of sandalwood and patchouli that had been so popular last season with ladies of good standing north of the river. There was some very good standing north of the river.

The paper itself was actually inked in an exquisite copper-plate hand and the return address was given as Belgwavia [sic] so there was hope for the protestor yet. There might well be a respectable husband with a loose five pound note with which to purchase her bail and cancel her probable passage to pastures penal, or an aged Aunt adventurously aghast at authoritarian antipathy towards any anti-establishmentarian angle or argument arraigned afresh a-public by an agitator of an atypical aspect in regards to gender.

My Lords,

I am writing to you in my capacity as Chair of the Ladies' Committee for Insistence upon the Prompt and Satisfactory Prosecution of the Industrial Revolution and for the introduction of Billiards Cues in Women's Sizes.

We rather respectfully request:

An end to the odious practise of the existence of the rural peasant class and to their use to till the soil in a non-intensive and seasonal manner in a rural setting, thus forcing a move towards fiscally obligated toil of a more industrial nature in the much tidier urban environments, beginning with wide-loom cloth mills and working towards the ultimate goal in a couple of centuries of similarly structured and pleasant pre-Sub Continent I.T. and General Utility Service Call Centres.

The immediate introduction of the replacement of "organic" fuels with fossil fuels in the process of smelting iron, the wider use of Sir Clement Clerke's reverberatory furnaces, the release from patent of potting, stamping and Henry Cort's puddling processes, and the summary availability of cheaper, better quality steel with attendant reduction in Swedish imports and increase in availability of machine tools.

The development of steam engines, preferably of the Watt double-acting rotative type where appropriate, both static and mobile, taking advantage of the improvements to and reduction of costs of, pig iron and steel and allowing the development of industrial scale Cotton Mills and Multi-Function Shared Contract Distribution Centres even where there is a lack of local water power, plus the playful facilitation of the long-awaited introduction of the Steam Train, the Seaside day excursion and the Kiss me Quick hat.

The extensive and immediate building of perilously experimental bridgeworks, roadworks and gasworks, viaducts, aqueducts and social conducts, the digging of a lot of ridiculously narrow canals, the immediate use of the vast network of pre-Dr Beeching pattern railway lines, and the mandatory introduction of a commercially exploitable improvement in the weather resilience and reliability of shipping by requiring the Onedin Line et al to retro-fit steam boiler engines and side-paddles to Captain Baines.

The immediate and bloody, evening invasion of Belgium on any day except Sunday next.

If our demands are not met then we have it within our power to effect the summary withdrawal of feminine company from all mixed social occasions up to and including wifely duty with or without knuckle-biting and horizon-staring. The rearrangement of stray locks of hair falling over the eyes will be optional and dependent upon circumstances and humidity.

Our sincere heartfelt bosom-heaving bodice-ripping breech-buckling damp curly blond locks-scattering, bare thigh slapping, rosy-red lip pouting, yee-hah screaming, chandelier-swinging, garter-twanging, mattress-spring pinging apologies for mentioning wifely duty in polite company but, quite frankly, you've driven us to it.

Yours most truly,
ever your humble servant,
Lady Constance Mann-Bighter.

p.s., Demand number five, while self-evidently desirable, is negotiable within the context of this portfolio with respect to the introduction of reasonable delays so long as the endeavour is complete before the next Easter egg rush.

With that and a small curlicue the missive ended.

It seemed to be a distillation of all of the usual feminist movement demands for a better world.

Branson dropped the note to the table after reading it and flipped open the ornate cover of his rather unusual but questionably intelligent design of fob-off pocket watch. The ornate brass "time" hand covered the period from a quarter to the eighteenth century to a quarter past the nineteenth. The "second" hand indicated more specifically that it was, roughly, summer or thereabouts. What was worse, the new built-in barometer settled firmly in the green "yes" zone when tapped, as opposed to settling in the red "no" portion of the dial. From this Branson concluded that the internet would still be down and that there was probably little chance of blissfully welcome generalised hypoxia with attendant fatal cyanosis today, at least without extenuating circumstances or third-party intervention. This overwhelmingly depressing deluge of sufficient detail from his hitherto friendly and benign waistcoat pocket served him a-right for buying irreducible technology that he had just stumbled upon at a carriage boot sale on a heath and from a blind watch-maker's untended stall at that.

A fair proportion of the rest of the committee and quite a lot of the typing pool were staring into space with heads full of heartfelt bosom-heaving bodice-ripping breech-buckling damp curly blond locks-scattering, bare thigh slapping, rosy-red lip pouting, yee-hah screaming, chandelier-swinging, garter-twanging, mattress-spring pinging advanced pages from that inordinately popular Tibetan Monk manual of sedate rumpy-pumpy, the Calmer Sutra.

'Gentlemen, one cannot fault the Chair of the Ladies' Committee for Insistence upon the Prompt and Satisfactory Prosecution of the Industrial Revolution and for the introduction of Billiards Cues in Women's Sizes for the accuracy of her committee's demands. Indeed, I am ashamed to say that they are most succinct and generous in their terms, "immediately" being the timescale offered me only earlier this morning by Her Majesty, The Queen Victorian Person, for the introduction of the means of her total world domination.'

At this juncture Branson twirled the large globe used by the Pith Helmet & Plymouth Gin Supply-Line Planning Committee into a blur of English Navy-dominated ocean blue and English Army-dominated Empire pink. The vital routes were updated in Chinagraph pencil at the Committee's meetings every third September of every other decade. Tradition held that this was done by the youngest surviving Tory member of the quango just before the member's expenses were voted through on a drunken nod.

'Young Vickykins allowed me just one light stroke of her fluffy white "world domination" lap-cat and then demanded better munitions, an even larger naval fleet and efficient water extraction pumps for the coal mines in the slave colonies of [old] South Wales.'

A fair proportion of the committee and a lot of the typing pool were far too calm and sutra to listen. Some of them wandered off to the smoking rooms, most of them would be good for nothing more until long after luncheon. One or two had simply forgotten where they were and snored in a puddle of happy gentry dribble at the conference table.

Branson turned towards the window and absently watched the workmen's cranes several streets away assembling Oldfield's design for the new tubular bell. It was mooted to be three times louder than the current non-tubular design of the luncheon bell used by the Civil Service Canteen to summon the faithful for subsidised pheasant-and-chips. He wondered again if the roof of the Canteen could support the weight and resist the vibrations five times daily plus repeats for last call for pudding.

A light drizzle had begun to fall but, fortunately, only outside the building where it was disrupting the Peace Camp Progress Protest by sending both the ladies and the police alike running for the comparative safety and shelter of a nearby tea-rooms. Once inside – ladies first, of course – the two parties separated, Police into the Mug & Shot Bar and the ladies into the A-Cup & Saucer Lounge. Industrial kettles were no doubt being engaged by heavy lever in some deep, dank, dark-ish Dantean kitchen even as Branson watched. It was quite possible that indentured cake-slicers, apprenticed cream-whippers and novitiate cherry positioners were being roused from their slumbers in lice-infested hammocks even as the flames crept higher in the hearths and bare-footed sloped-foreheaded brutes with names like "Yes'um" and "Rrrrrgh" fetched water from the especially tasty-fresh public drinking well in Broad Street.

The "ooh – get it off me, get it off me before I dissolve!" dance of the mildly drizzle-damp sugar-plum Englishman and Englishwoman was reaching an umbrella and hat shaking crescendo inside the Tea-Rooms doorway. The Ire-ish would later copy this, add tartan, exaggerate the movements and – in a stroke of genius - call it The Rivet Dance to make oodles of dosh selling tickets to people who, poor loves, wouldn't recognise sophisticated entertainment even if you tattooed it on both cheeks of Lily Langtree's ample arse right under where it already read "Royal Slap" and "Royal Tickle".

[I'm sure that it was "rivet". Yes, yes – The Rivet Dance by Mick Flatleaf or some such. Lots of idiots prancing around like hob-nailed ballerinas with diarrhoea and Wild West line-dancers with someone shooting at their feet.]

Branson allowed his mind to drift logically from Lily Langtree's arse, through the drizzle, towards La Petomaine's arse and onwards, for some fashionable social-chemical imbalance reason, toward formulating a plausible and non-offence giving reply for the inevitable enquiry from the Press as to just who might have leaked details of the Industrial Revolution to the Ladies' Committee of the etcetera etcetera.

He sighed and shrugged his shoulders. For the moment that was a problem on the back burner and just one of many such. Right now they were all still, metaphorically speaking, wearing their T-shirts with the Project-Subcommittee approved slogans "Industrial Revolution – I'll have some of that, thank you" and "Agrarian Society – I think not!"

That it was still just metaphorical rather than Jermyn Street tailored was indicative of another problem – even the bloody casual shirt movement was behind schedule, just a sketch on the drawing board of one of the members of the board who was too busy playing with his membrum virilis to extract his digit, focus and just get on with it. The board member in question was currently busy in vile weather and a funky yellow oilskin sou'wester on some Cornish coast attempting to determine whether an "surf board" might be used for coastal postal navigation or commercial line-fishing. Early results were not encouraging although he did report that he was getting laid much more easily than he was used to. His last postcard mentioned that he had developed an entourage of "surf chicks" whatever the hell that was. Maybe he'd be able to answer the "perennial egg question" soon even if nothing else? Science often worked in unpredictable ways, especially where salt-water coastal chicks were involved. Just look at Grimsby.

A more pressing practical problem for someone was the very high probability that the police horses, left outside as they were during the sudden meteorological inclemency, would later prove difficult or even impossible to start. A Horse & Carriage Association patrol or a Royal Equine Club mechanic would probably have to be summoned to administer a rub-down, dry tack and a bale of fresh unleaded hay. Hopefully The Police maintained a current Rescue, Recovery & Home Start policy with one of the reputable firms. Branson remembered how he'd once put the wrong sort of fuel in his horse and had to have its stomach-pumped out by a local blacksmith at outrageous cost – apparently his big mistake had been in moving the horse once he'd put the incorrect food in. Breakdown insurance had been a godsend then, as had a green plastic gallon of oats obtained from a kindly nearby farmer. How the hell was he to have known that horses didn't run on spare quail's eggs, cheap caviar and over-warm flat champagne all served in a "borrowed" policeman's helmet?

As it happened, the rain proved to be no more than just a light and disconveniencing shower. High on eastern tannin infusions, intoxicated with fresh Jersey bovine lipid suspensions and hypnotised by Messrs Tate & Lyle's promises of legalised West Indian refined monosaccharide carbohydrates, the Constabulary stumbled back into the damp daylight like refreshed Orcs bursting forth from a Middle Earth Cafe. Yes, they were that ugly.

They found that several of their horses had been clamped and bore the hallmark Council Coffers kerching-spoor of Fixed Penalty Notice parchments glued to the leather blinkers with yellow and black sealing wax. The Maria-of-Colour and the Riot Squad's Emergency Response barouche were both in the process of being lifted bodily, horses and all, onto the back of a sub-contracted "Council" kerchING-clamping kerchING-cart for kerchING-removal and further kerchING "storage" at two-hundred and fifty guineas a day or part thereof.

[Any member of Her Majesty's public who thought it odd that the Establishment could remove property and hold it to ransom, calling it a "public service", while private citizens who did so were prosecuted for theft and extortion, was immediately subjected to one hundred and twenty hours of graffiti removal to stop them ever thinking logically again out loud.]

'Tough, Mate' explained the kindly Clamping Utility's National Tsar to the Chief Constable. 'Once either the wheels of the vehicle or the hooves of the horse have left the road it's out of my hands, I have to take it in. You'll have to collect them from the impound field and pay the fine and the stabling for the horses. Shouldn't have been so stupid as to park them here in the first place – the sign's obvious enough.' He pointed to what appeared to be a faded postage stamp on the wall in the shadows under the eaves of a nearby building, occasionally visible provided that the ivy had been recently trimmed and there was a light northerly breeze with no serious cloud cover.

The ladies from the Peace Camp watched with obvious glee and petit buerre from the windows of the A-Cup & Saucer Lounge as the fetlock clampers changed their minds under a hail of Police truncheons and fair-enough Guv fisticuffs. It did their hearts good to see fisticuffs still in everyday use between chaps. The barouche and the Maria-of-Colour, complete with prisoners' hands and cries reaching through the bars, were lowered back to the roadway under the terms of Article 1, Paragraph 1, Sub-section 1, Clause 2 of the Because I Bleedin' Well Say So Mush Act of eleven twenty-three, or possibly half-past seven.

Once the fracas had subsided into a mere bonfire of clamping vehicles and several twitching ankle-clamped bodies, Lady Florence of Berkeley Square took control and asked the improprietress of the Tea Rooms to call nine-nine-nine. It wouldn't do for the conflagration to spread again like that clumsy baking mishap in sixteen-something or other.

Doris duly opened the door, tugged the cigarette butt off her dry lower lip and called out 'nine-nine-nine' in the manner of an on-shore foghorn. She blinked like a less-than refreshed Orc at the entrance to a Middle Earth Tea-Rooms. Yes, she was that ugly too. Daylight lost itself, never to be seen again, in her crows-feet and in the pucker-marks under her moustache and just above her food-laden beard. Like so many twenty year-old lifelong smokers she had lips that suggested she could latch onto any farm animal, field or barnyard, alive or dead and remove the vitals intact with a single cross-eyed suck, a swallow and a hint of a gulp as the spine went down.

Her delicate cry was repeated several times until a small breathless Corporation Urchin ran up. "Emergency – which service do you require?" asked the urchin.

'Fire and ambulance please Duckie' replied Kylie, staying calm and handing over two farthings and a stale fairy cake as a tip.

[Someone had left the lid off the big tin of fairies and, if they were to be used up before they went off then lovely, moist, stale-fairy cakes were the only option. Nota bene, years later all of the magic would be taken out of these little confections and they would become known in "global" "English" rather more drearily as "cupcakes". This is why you can no longer buy tins of either fresh or dried fairies except in speciality comestible shops.]

The urchin ran off at top speed towards the hospital and the fire station. Doris, watching the urchin depart, made that odd smoker's shoulder-flicking motion and a fresh cancer stick appeared from her cuff, slipped between the dull yellow marks on her fingers and lit itself.

Branson, still watching from the window, sighed wistfully, picked up the heavy black Bakelite telephone from the windowsill and untangled the plaited fabric cord. He held the receiver to his ear. Still no dialling tone. Bloody English Telecom! Years behind everybody else! He hefted the useless apparatus back onto the equally heavy leather-bound volumes of Domestic Directory and Yellowed Pages and pushed them all into a corner. Then, on impulse, he pulled the volumes out again and checked whether Her Majesty was, in fact, listed. It seemed that she was entered in several places as The Queen, Her Majesty, Empress of India, Defender of the Faith and also plain Victoria of the House of Hanover, cross-referenced under Heads of State and Marriageable First Cousins. Her telephone number was "1". No area code, just "1". Dial 1 for One. Branson contrasted that with his own entry in the high double-digits next to a pickle manufacturer and sighed again.

He did a lot of sighing.

Sighing, he whispered to himself "sod it, decision made, let's just do it". With a heavy heart and a BIC ink-quill he unilaterally began to compose the committee's reply to the protestors' demands. Ready or not, it was time to just focus and do it. He doodled "JFDI" on the blotter to remind himself. It looked cute in a might-get-me-beaten-up kind of way. In fact, he liked it so much that he smiled and said it out loud.

'It. JFDI. Hmm. I like that. Perhaps it might be matched with some encouraging dance movements. Jay-eff-dee-aye! It's fun to decide to jay-eff-dee-aye-yie. Young man, there's no need to kneel down, young man, if you've got half a crown, young man, you just to need to do the jay – eff – dee - aye, oh it's fun at the jay-eff-dee-aye...' Suddenly realising that he was probably visible from the typing pool Branson coughed, straightened his tie and sat back down at his desk, little the worse for his jigging.

My dear Lady Constance Mann-Bighter,

I write in thanks for your non-submissive missive of the twenty-third inst., and to advise you that the bones of your Committee's demands have been accepted in principle, pro rata, cui bono, sonny bono, caveat emptor, ad infinitum in excelsis gloria and other posh latin stuff, by all of the parties involved in the Industrial Revolution Project. (And here he kept the fingers of both hands crossed behind his back as he wrote; clever chap).

This acceptance of the need for dispatch happily includes your insistence upon the bloody invasion of Belgium, and the War Office has accordingly advised us that some six hundred officers and men of Her Majesty's Light Brigade have been stationed in the Valley of Mort, just outside Brussels, preparatory to a wild charge to be undertaken late tomorrow morning or in the early afternoon, weather and horse-feed permitting.

Several technical issues have caused delays in the deployment of the new industrial practises but we feel that, with one or two aesthetic tweaks and with the late invention of the stoic coal miner and the perfection of the blueprint for the cotton mill family dynasty with roving over-advantaged elder son, these have now, largely, been overcome. There remain only the inconsequentials of peasant morbidity and mortality which, as you suggest in your addendum, we may cheerfully ignore.

Accordingly, I should like to extend an invitation to you, and to your Committee members, to attend Manchester Railway Station at eight o'clock of the morning on the thirtieth. There we hope you will witness the spectacle of a dozen tons of coal moving at ten or even eleven miles per hour and, possibly, or as some cynics say, probably, the first dramatic and officially notifiable industrial accident involving blood curdling workingman-screams and a standardised Whitworth screw thread.

Please bring a coat and, if available commercially yet, your portable Daguerre Image Capture Device, trained magnesium flash-light operators and plenty of spare glass photographic plates, for it is bound to be a spectacle! Remember also to bring your spectacles, if worn. Refreshments and the new plumbed-in sanitation facilities will be available from a penny upwards, both at the same time with waitress service included if you take advantage of our VIP package at 3/- 6d per person.

Yours truly,
Sir Mr Richard Delphinium Mount St.Helens Fortesque Bulawayo La-La Branson, Chairman, blah blah blah, ever your most humble, AC, DC, BBC, ITV, Natural Gas and God Save The Queen.

p.s., as regards the introduction of billiards cues in ladies' sizes we feel it politic to delay further development until after the invention of the butch evening-lesbian and the simple-cut dinner jacket.

He scattered sand and rolled his work carefully with a young blotter. Then he patted the blotter's bottom and sent her, giggling, on her India-ink stained way.

Members of the committee were beginning to drift back after luncheon, and mostly only after their rent-by-the-hour hotel rooms had sent porters to knock on the doors. Most members were be-whiskered gloom incarnate. One or two were as sober as High Court Judges and had to be assisted into their seats. Branson turned over his draft reply to Lady Constance Mann-Bighter so that it would not be read before he announced his invention of the JFDI with dance moves. Young Messrs Wedgwood, Boulton and Owen were late, as usual. Branson checked his watch – their time was close but it had not yet actually arrived, and the committee could wait just a little longer (but not more than a decade or so). He made polite enquiries against future need.

'Young Messrs Wedgwood, Boulton and Owen - their favoured club is in Lower Colonies Damned Occupying Forces Road, is it not?'

'No, Sir – Upper Empire Ruddy Locals Crescent, near the new gasometers. It's not far, about a mile as the Crow walks. The Crow Nation is well known for its characteristic hop-skip-jump-sashay mode of cross-city ambulation using only the straightest possible of lines. Hell of a rough neighbourhood though. Bloody good stock of claret if I remember correctly, but hell of a rough neighbourhood.'

[Gasometers: still empty, awaiting the invention of town gas and the greasy black-encrusted single burner hotplate for dingy bedsits. The greasy black-encrusted single burner hotplate and the bedsit were, in turn, awaiting the invention of the barely independent bachelor-about-town. The latter had so far been delayed in development by mothers who just couldn't learn to let go.]

Branson checked his watch again. 'We'll wait then. I have an announcement to make.' He absent-mindedly practised his jay-eff-dee-aye moves and finished with an experimental moonwalk that did little good for his cobblers.

A mile and two Crow-hops away Messrs Wedgwood and Boulton stepped cheerily out of their private gentleman's club, the

Infernal Combustion Engine, a Free House with rooms and fine dining in Upper Empire Ruddy Locals Crescent, and then stopped dead in their tracks. Owen, having called at the Gentlemen's Gents on their way out of the club to reduce his brain pressure, was quicker to realise the problem and didn't just stop but positively cowered alongside them like a Wesleyan Methodist caught in bright sunlight.

'We're doomed, doomed I tell you!' he whispered. 'We're all going to die.'

'Don't panic, man. We shall be lost for certain if we panic. Stiffen your upper lip and don't be so demonstrative – you sound like some sort of damned foreigner!' hissed Wedgwood.

All about the now eerily quiet street lay indolent men, whittling at small pieces of wood or smoking dull, will-o-the-wisp long clay pipes, or sharpening chisels, testing the weight of spanners and oiling the bubbles in spirit-levels. It was as though some alien-human hybrid ovipositor had dotted them around and about the new urban landscape, spaced out to allow the air circulation to dry them off and harden their shells into skin like rough, dry, dirty-brown leather. Their skin, to a man, was like rough, dry, dirty-brown leather, which just rather proves my point doesn't it.

Their boots, if they had them, were hobnailed and huge, their hair was wild and unkempt. Their feet, if they didn't have boots, were hobnailed and huge, and their hair was also wild and unkempt, especially on the feet. Their clothing was mostly torn sackcloth or cheesecloth or denim, all washed in ashes, bodily-crevice cheese or the gravel and stones currently so popular for that distressed-designer look. Here and there a patched and torn jacket or boilerplate overalls, now and again a man with riveter's scorched gloves and bucket, occasionally an ill-fitting donkey jacket with orange "dayglo" visibility patches over all four shoulders and, settled between them all, the dark, empty, hungry eyes of the general unskilled labourer in his trackie bottoms, Umbro shirt and ruddy baseball cap.

As the three young gentlemen stood, standing quite still, still more workmen approached almost silently, and stood, still aimless and lacking all sense of social standing, at least in any sense that it was still understood by anyone still standing. Some of them sat and were still. Some stood but remained still while others who had been sitting already remained so and still sat still, lacking the energy to stand or even understand that they should. Still there were others, silent, still, leaning against trees and paring their nails with pocket knives, or laid out on the tops of walls like so many unemployed sides of forgotten beef. Some, gathered in groups of two elevens or in fives a side, kicked their heels and dribbled their balls and shifted restlessly in the hot, desiccated dust swirls of an El Niño English summer afternoon. It was hot in the city, hot in the city alright. The back of Wedgwood's neck was getting dirty and gritty and there was a catchy and popular tune buried in there somewhere.

A scuffle broke out among some of the alpha males but developed into a hungry, menacing, nothing much to write home about in the heavy, storm-laden air. Like gargoyles perched on rooftops and playground swings the workmen watched, and waited, and bided their time, like Nature gone bad.

Owen made as though to run but Boulton stopped him.

'Wait! No! Don't make any sudden movements. I suspect that if we seem to be no threat to them then they won't attack us. It's our only chance, believe me. With creatures like these and with the domestic hen the vision is based upon movement. Mr Darwin says that's true for anything that blinks sideways, lays eggs or works for the Civil Service in the lower, non-pensionable ranks.'

'Actually, I think they may rely on their sense of smell more than their eyesight' added Wedgwood, who had been carefully observing the beasts and scribbling copious pencil notes both on and off the cuff, a practice his housekeeper's laundry-scrubber's cuff specialist hated.

'Sense of smell? Oh bollocks!' said Owen.

'What's up now?' hissed Wedgwood.

'I'm wearing the new Lynx "Sex-Zombie" all-over anti-perspiration pro-odorant body-spray! If these things work by sense of smell... I might as well be a sideways-blinking roasted chicken in a bar mitzvah bar. Oy!' whispered Owen.

'What the hell are you wearing that goyim feygele nonsense

for? We were just nipping for a quick pint of claret and some fatty luncheon meat before the afternoon committee session!'

'I know, but it was three for two at Boot's Apothecary and I thought I might pull. Well, you never know. A chap has to be prepared and take his chances where he can these days.' He shrugged. 'OK - I'm desperate. The nearest I've had to sex since my home-schooling governess left was a good gallop across the Kate Bush Moor on a cheap Budget Rent-a-Horse with one leg slightly longer than the others and a loose saddle. I even had to loosen the saddle myself.'

'Well, you're well and truly screwed now anyway.' Boulton slowly shifted around to the opposite side of Wedgwood, away from the alluringly perfumed Owen.

At the end of the road a cornered rat broke loose from a drainpipe, squealed and then fell ominously, seriously, fatally, silent in a culinary sense of the words "silent" and "fatally". The silence of the street-scene was broken only by the short-measure tearing of fresh, fat, luncheon-rat flesh.

'What are they?' hissed Owen, finding himself needing the Gents again and considering doing something he had done only twice since his early childhood and on one of those occasions for a significantly lucrative bet.

'Hungry, evidently, and fond of fresh meat – even rat. Let's hope they don't eat gentlemen.'

'Dear God – "Fresh Meat" was my nickname at Eton.'

'At Rugby mine was "The Juicy Fat Rat".'

'Then we're both screwed.'

'No - I think they're workers. Displaced workers, migrated in from the countryside.'

'But they look so... evil. What do working people ordinarily look like? Are they normally this ugly?'

'God knows. Probably something like indoor staff and coachmen I'd guess but weatherworn and cheaper, grubbier, nastier. Maybe something like under-gardeners or gamekeepers or boot-polishers.'

'These are different. They're changing. They're mutating, morphing.'

Boulton and Owen looked about for Plasticene figures getting into mild desktop mischief with pencils and a children's entertainment programme.

'Maybe we've just caught them in the larval or pupæ stage? A sort of "rural peasants go in one end smelling of horse poo and crop rotation and a "working class" comes out the other end of the process looking like shit and covered in engine oil, lathe swarf and rickets" kind of thing?'

'Did you just say that we've just caught them?'

'Figure of speech dear boy. Look, we can't stay here all day, we have to do something.'

The beast nearest them rolled over in the gutter onto his stomach, disturbing a cloud of flies and looking angrily at them before settling back down to snooze with his head on his empty Mexican beer bottle. All about him fluttered leaflets for something called "bogofs double glazing-over". Buy one get one for a shilling with free fitting.

'They're just waiting.'

'For us?'

'In a way, yes. I think they're waiting for the Industrial Revolution. Gentlemen, this is our workforce. Our labour. Look more closely. See that one over there sleeping on that lamp-post? Notice how contented he is at unnatural heights? Look – those, the ones scuttering around in the dust, back and forth like shuttlecocks. Mill-rats cleaning between machinery. That one – see? Look at the size of its fists – a natural panel beater.'

Owen was intrigued. 'Yes, I see what you mean. Look – that one. It looks half dead already, it would be ideal for use in dyeing and mordanting processes, maybe even for making Lucifer sticks. Generally the heads all look small in relation to body size – these creatures probably just need telling what to do. They need purpose, and good, dog-fearing work.'

'Don't you mean good God-fearing work?'

'You run your estates your way, I'll run mine as I see fit, with Foreman and Overseer.' At the sound of their names his dogs, Foreman and Overseer, crawled out on their Rottweiler stomachs from under a nearby chestnut roaster's cart and wagged their tails.

'Still, do not relax your guard gentlemen, they could turn on us in a minute. One false move and they could become a violent rabble bent on sabotage and destruction, demanding decent pay and humane working and living conditions. Step carefully, gentlemen, step very carefully and very slowly and make no sound, no eye contact, and we may yet live to see our currently-idle factory chimneys belch soot and smoke and profit and progress and red Porsche 911 Turbos ready-wired for our iHarpsichords and Smart-Teleprinters.'

The three slowly and nervously picked their way along the road, avoiding the larger groups and staying very, very, close to each other. Even Foreman and Overseer were careful where they stepped, growled, bit and pooped.

'It's patently almost a mile to the Patent Offices – we'll never make it' whispered Owen.

'Keep your nerve, man, keep your nerve. Damn it, you're a gentleman. Don't let them see fear on you. We tackled worse than this in the changing rooms before running out onto the rugby fields at Cambridge and Oxford.'

Suddenly Owen squealed and clutched Wedgwood's elbow in a grip like an eight-fingered, two-thumbed squealing-vice (he'd only been to Durham). All three gentlemen froze and simultaneously gratefully came to terms with the over-generously porous nature of bulk-buy Y-fronts. The spoor of fear lay upon their gussets.

Several of the more predatory working beasts sniffed the air. One of the feral interlopers had been loping past, as feral beasts often do in loping season, and it stopped, briefly. It listened for the double-thump ruling-class heartbeat that said "live-food, live-food, live-food ..." at seventy beats per minute or, in the case of Mr Owen, one hundred and ten with the occasional missed stroke and a squelchy echo.

Gradually, while they stayed as absolutely still and as silent as it was possible for young gentlemen with reforming ideas and lots of cash money to do, the socio-dynamics of the pride or the nest or whatever the collective noun would be for factory fodder returned to what would soon seem so normal. They settled back into inactive indolence and resentment.

'What?' hissed Boulton, incredibly annoyed at Owen for stopping them on the battlefield.

'Women! That one over there is female... look.'

'My god – I think you may be right, Owen. Boulton, look at the clothing – it's ever so slightly different. The face is the same, the rough musculature, the hobnailed feet, tattoos and hair are identical, the sense of simmering menace is similar but the clothing, the posture, I think you're right – it is definitely a female of the specie.'

Owen gave a quiet sob. 'It is. Dear God, it is.' He crossed himself and began chanting. 'Our Father, who aren't in Devon, hallowed be thy new persona as a dame. Give us this day my coach and horses and do unto them before it is nobler in the mind, a sling, or an arrow – anything, God and saints preserve us, holy outrageous fortune Batman, partibus deus biggus omnibus dieu et mon droit gaudete all around my hat, inshallah, inshallah, Barukh ata Adonai Eloheinu melekh ha-olam, ha-gomel lahayavim tovot sheg'malani kol tov! Ooh Mummy, Phuphox ache, cor luv a duck, amen.' Owen, having covered his available gibbering-bases, then covered his face in his hands and wept.

'Control yourself man. So what if it is a woman? As I said, we've tackled worse than women in the changing rooms before running out onto the rugby fields at Cambridge and Oxford.'

'But I only went to Durham!' wailed Owen.

'We must get back to report this development' said Wedgwood, and Owen guiltily assumed Wedgie was referring to his confession to this one minor fib on his curriculum vitae. Durham shmurham, and always in some sort of trouble because of it.

At incredible speed and with a howl that would terrify even a large dog in the Baskerville household, one of the female creatures leapt like an exception to the laws of Newtonian Physics and pinned Owen to a wall.

The rottweilers Foreman and Overseer, who were in fact closely related to the Baskerville hounds but who were far from stupid and had been around the block several times on more than mere walkies, pretended to have noticed nothing and just looked casually in every other direction. They gave their attentions to whistling How much is that doggy in the window without an apparent canine care in the world. One of them inspected his claws as he whistled, the other just had to scratch his ribs with his eyes closed.

Sniffing all about and then, bloodshot eye to weeping eye, predatory jaw to weak-chinned slack-jaw, the female creature slavered and growled while Owen turned his head to one side and sobbed again, convinced of his immediate and bloody demise and all probably because he'd only been to chuffing third-rate Durham. With a final sniff and a snap of the nut-cracker mandible the working class creature pushed away from Owen and the wall with both hands, danced a small jig, gathered its filthy, torn, skirts in a bunch and then sauntered back to pressing the business of indolent, suggestive, "want to do some business dearie?" loafing at the kerb with ne'ery a backwards glance.

Maybe the new "working classes" were fussy after all? Had this creature some natural sense of genetics and an instinct to avoid Nature's in-bred cul de sacs?

Wedgwood and Boulton gently collected Owen from his renewed and deepening puddle of entrepreneurial, social innovator's terror. God alone knew where he got it all from at such short notice.

'It knows that you're pregnant with ideas, industrial notions, social notions, welfare notions. It won't kill one of its own. Your very weakness has proven to be your strength, man, so stand! Stand I say! We must go on!'

The men shuffled bravely on, picking their route through the unconscious and the unconscionable, past bawdy Barrett home, Plymouth gin-flop and Wendy whore house.

'Those weren't there when we went for a pint. There wasn't a single house of good ill repute in all of Manchester was there?'

'Yes there were, loads of them, they were just smaller and better hidden. I mean, unless you already knew of its existence you'd never have been able to find the one in Regent's Way with the studded black leather ...'

Owen and Wedgwood gave Boulton a look and he trailed off

just before he could finish saying "...anatomically correct mechanical bull".

'How could this all change so quickly though?'

'Well, there's a reason why they call it The Industrial Revolution and not The Industrial Gradual Change. Where have you been for the past two hundred years?'

'On my estates, hunting, shooting, fishing and amusing myself in my workshops and private observatory, dining at my club or doing the leisurely and luxurious "Grand Tour" through Greece, Italy and Egypt and suchlike.'

'Same here.'

'Yeah, me too.'

Ho hum. Such was history. They moved on, cautiously.

Suddenly, a compensation claimant with no legs, arms or body shuffled up with outstretched paperwork, and behind it a case of iron-smelter's pox alongside something homeless or poor or uneducated or just plain generally horrid. Owen screamed again and all about, like young alien spiders emerging from the nest, the industrially injured and the sick and the old and the landless dispossessed clamoured forward to check if their time had finally come. The three men fled.

Throwing caution, dignity and loose coinage of the realm to the wind they fled, screaming, to the safety of the Patent Office and the Committee rooms, where they found that Foreman and Overseer had arrived well before them (both also significantly out of fleeing-doggy breath). They banged on the door like lost souls seeking sanctuary in a church playing soul music on the organ, and Wedgwood, Owen and Boulton thumped and kicked upon the door along with them.

What key-carrying civil servant, even in times of Suffragette-besieged crisis, could possibly refuse so heartfelt and desperate an entreaty? Owen, Boulton and Wedgwood followed the dogs in and fell gratefully upon the cool marble floor.

After multiple-document identity check, registration, the issuing of clip-on day-passes and signing of the Visitor's Book they resumed their screaming, terrified flight up the marble stairs and into the committee rooms where they bit knuckles, stared wild-eyed to the horizon and scratched at the plasterwork with broken, bloodied, nails. The rest of the committee turned to see what the commotion was all about and then their features softened as they beheld the two dogs in such obvious emotional turmoil. It took a while for most to realise that there were also three human beings in the roiling mass of canine panic.

Branson walked to the door of the committee room and called for his personal secretary. 'Miss Roux? Oh Miss Ruby Roux? Where are you when I need you?'

'Yes?' answered a small voice from the heady, chlorinated atmosphere of the typing pool.

'Is that you, Ruby Roux?'

Miss Roux appeared, wrapping a towel around her damp hair and trailing wet footprints.

The two dogs, never liking having the *pst* extracted quite so obviously, quieted themselves and began to consider contracting two cases of post-buttock biting lockjaw or some other revenge. The buttocks of a patronising, pst-taking git are a dish best eaten cold, and eaten at some opportunity they would be.

'Miss Ruby Roux, here's what I want you to do – take these two and whip up one of your special Ruby-snacks and a stiff drink for them please.'

'Will do.'

'Thank you, Miss Roux.'

The two hounds slunk out of the room, mouthing "Ruby-snacks?" to each other under their breath and giving canine shoulder shrugs signifying "buggered if I know either" to each other.

Left to their own devices the remaining three wild animals on the committee room floor eventually stopped roiling and began explaining.

'We're all doomed! Doomed I tell you! Doomed!' explained Owen, fully.

'We're all undone! Woe, woe and thrice woe, Petunia!' formulated Boulton.

'We're all going to have to throw caution to the wind and, ready or not, we're going to have to just fecking do it! JFDI, gentlemen, JFDI!' shouted Wedgwood in the manner of some

Staffordshire Potteries soothsayer. 'The Industrial Revolution must be brought forward and it must happen now, gentlemen! Now! JFDI I say! Let's just focus, do it and get it over with, my nerves can't take any more antici ... pation!'

Branson closed the mouth he was about to use to make an inspirationally worded announcement to the committee with and sat down. Now he'd never get to spell out the letters in lovely dance steps, damn it.

'Doomed?' capital-ventured Sir British-Leyland, catching up with developments and holding fast onto his blueprints for the baby-poo beige Austin Allegro with "quartic" steering wheel, dark brown velour upholstery and clotted-cream coloured vinyl roof.

'Undone?' pressed Lord Velcro, tugging hopelessly at the little steel-hook and steel-loop fastener strip of his cummerbund and wondering when pliable plastics might be invented. He indicated wordlessly to a footman to fetch the ruddy tailor's-hacksaw again please.

'JFDI! I like that!' enthused Frank Whittle, scribbling on a pre-Post-It note so that he wouldn't forget to tell his wife, Betty, later. 'Well I never – Just Fecking Do It! Hah! Marvellous! Wedgwood – you're a genius.' He had to rub out his preliminary sketch for a passenger-carrying aero-locomotive with turbine propulsion system to make room for "JFDI" in large capital letters on his pad.

Branson rubbed his eyes to stop them watering emotionally and sorted his papers, turning over his reply to the Ladies' Committee to remind himself of the business in hand and to dull the latest of the endless little tragedies of missed opportunity in his life.

'Wedgwood, Boulton, Owen – have you gentlemen been drinking?' he enquired.

'Of course we have!'

'Good, but you're still a little hysterical. Pour yourselves another and then explain to the committee, if you would be so kind, just why we are doomed and undone so and why you consider that the orderly timetable of the committee must be abandoned.'

Owen drank from the decanter and then passed it on to his colleagues, utterly heedless of whether he passed to the left or to the right.

'The peasants, Sir, the peasants – are revolting!'

Most of the members simply agreed by nodding, like bulldogs under the weight of personal experience gained in their country seats. Branson felt that he had to reply. 'This is not France, Sir, our peasants do not "revolt". That is why we exported all of the trouble makers, ne'er do wells and peculiar religious sects to America, year of their lord sixteen-hundred and something or other.'

'But we've seen them!' Owen took another long swig at the decanter and then sucked at the glass stopper like some over-privileged semi-alcoholic cross-eyed baby carrying a couple of dozen extra stone in puppy-fat.

'Mr Wedgwood. Can you make sense of this for us?' asked Branson with his elbow on the table and his head resting on his hand, aware that it was shaping up to be another day where he missed Thy Weakeste Linke, Blanketty-Not-Filled-In and Ye Olde Emmerdale Farme.

'I hardly know where to begin' replied Wedgwood, fumbling with his notebook.

'Begin at the very beginning, if you please, Mr Wedgwood.'

'Yes, course, the beginning, that's a very good place to start.'

He dropped his notebook. 'Doh!'

'Oh dear!'

'We saw a female' informed Wedgwood, with incredulity.

'Shut up dear!' gasped Branson.

'Ray – would you open the blinds please, we could do with a drop of golden sun.'

'Me, I take the blame, all by myself.'

'So?'

'So far, we had a long, long way to run.'

'Tea, perhaps? A drink, with jam and bread?'

'Latte please.'

'And, gentlemen, that brings us clumsily back to Doh – the prototype frothing machine's broken.'

Thus the three gentlemen began to explain their observations of the new development with the "workforce" and with the narrow escaping and with the ugly, brutish, migrant population creeping in like an infection from the countryside already again. It quite frayed their nerves beyond bearing.

Branson stood. 'That then, gentlemen, settles matters. We have done all the preparation that can be done. Cotton mills are built and stand idle, shipyards echo to the sounds of the marine architect pencil eraser and the new railway lines and stations are beginning to become overgrown with weeds. The National Coal Board are returned, full of enthusiasm and group cohesion from their team-building exercise in the Yorkshire Dales and are ready to start work. The Queen Victorian will wait no longer.' He tapped on the tabletop and lowered his voice for well-educated upper-crust emphasis. 'One week from today, on the thirtieth, we shall declare the Industrial Revolution open for business. Carpe diem, gentlemen, carpe ruddy diem.'

'This is no time for carp fishing you blathering idiot!' expostulated Mr Rolls from behind his hearing-trumpet, only to have his free ear clipped by Mr Royce who mouthed a silent but explanatory apology "Doctor Tourette's Syndrome, upper class version where decent indecent swear-words are less commonly known and all that high-born well-bred sufferers could shout were things like dashed cad and gosh that's a bit harsh and Spirit of ruddy Ecstasy on the bonnet? I'll give you Spirit of chuffing Ecstasy my lad!"

Branson continued, unabashed, unabated, una paloma blanca, and indeed, waving his sheet of paper.

'I have here, gentlemen, a draft agreement that I propose to send to the Ladies' Committee for the Hurry-Up, as it were, outlining plans for a commercial locomotion contest to take place at Manchester Railway Station at 0800hrs at the end of this month. The Chancellor of the Ladies' Committee has on previous occasion given me assurances that there will be no further demands for feminist lebensraum and that they have no ambitions to any influence in other spheres of male-dominated life. It is, quite definitely gentlemen, peace between the sexes for our time.'

Holding the letter aloft he paused in front of a watercolour of the proposed new Aerodrome at Heston, dotted about with fanciful interpretations of "flying machines", while the old but reliable fore-runner of the press photographer sketched and scribbled for the new "tabloid" newspapers. 'Peace, gentlemen, for our time. Talking of which, where are the little Railways Department sods? They are most germane to our timetable.'

A few of the members looked unhappy and tut-tutted among themselves, they weren't happy about accepting a Teutonic link, not happy at all. Branson looked puzzled for a moment but then paraphrased.

'Important, not German – the little railways sods are key to our plans, we must have speed in our movement of people and goods and the Royal Mails. They are most important to our timetable.'

Oh well, that was different and they couldn't understand why he hadn't said so in the first place instead of all of that balderdash about the ruddy Germanes.

Someone pointed tactfully to Stephenson the Younger who was signing off another work of art on the blackboard with a "Kilroy was here" nose and eyes over a proposed brick (railway embankment) wall.

Just then, with the sort of timing only available in cheap and tacky fiction, Trevithick wandered into the room, full of the joys of damped springing and singing to himself. 'Everybody's do-ooh-ing a brand new dance now, come on baby, do the locomotion...' He stopped in his tracks when he saw Stephenson was already present and scratching yet another bloody diagram of a single-flanged wheel. Trevithick stopped in the doorway and addressed the committee with an early version of The Flounce and a waved handkerchief.

'What is she doing here?'

Stephenson answered on behalf of the committee.

'She is presenting the winning locomotive design to these nice gentlemen. Shouldn't you be apologising to the Fire Service somewhere for yet another false alarm raised because you can't resist a sweaty man in a uniform? I hear that you set your engine on fire yet again yesterday' answered Stephenson before Branson could get a word in sideways with his tortoiseshell shoe-horn.

'Well, it wasn't me that called for a Police escort because the public walked up and stole the wheels while his engine was on "speed" test.'

'Well your train tilts!'

'It's supposed to, you idiot, it helps it go around bends more easily!'

'Given the speed your locomotive moves at, Sir, rust is more likely to be a problem than balance on the bends.'

'At least my engine has a patented safety valve. Yours, Sir, has a predilection for boiler explosion exceeded only by your own less than clear complexion!'

With that unbearably pore jibe all sense of civilised restraint disappeared and Trevithick and Stephenson squealed and began slapping at each other like chav kangaroos in a hair pulling contest.

Branson got his word in, finally. 'Gentlemen, gentlemen! Please! We have organised a commercial contest to settle the matter for once and for all. All steam locomotive designs will be presented for trial at eight of the morning on the thirtieth INST at Manchester Railway Station, adjacent platforms and God help the new Transport Police. The eligible devices will be attached to rolling stock carrying coal bound for the dark, satanic, shipyards of somewhere dark and satanic and ungodly and not Manchester but quite a long way away [so that would be Liverpool then].'

Branson strode over to the map on the wall and scribbled out the Stockton and Darlington Passenger Railway with his magic marker, annotating it "accent totally unsuitable" and leaving the Liverpool and Manchester Railway as the only option currently in existence in the world, including all of the still-foreign bits of the world. Sniffing the magic marker appreciatively he turned back to the committee.

'The judges as appointed by this committee will then make their decision regarding the future of English Rail. The winning design will immediately begin work upon clearing the backlog of passenger traffic and postal deliveries and the contracts will be awarded for taking the strain, so to speak, regionally. Actually, that would look quite good on the banners – "Let the Steam Locomotive take the strain..." – arrange that, would you please Miss Moneyha'penny, and have this letter delivered to Lady Constance Mann-Bighter as soon as possible.'

Miss Moneyha'penny played with her pearls and giggled, as

she always did whenever Branson asked her for anything between missions.

Stephenson and Trevithick stopped bitch-slapping and squared off their respective tearful chins instead.

'Right.'

'Right then.'

'I will see you in the Somewhere Dark and Satanic Bar after the contest, Mr Stephenson, and I shall have your usual drink ready and waiting for you. A very small sweet sherry is your usual choice, is it not, my dear?'

'Hah! I shall see you on the dance floor, Mr Trevithick, and I shall have a drink ready and waiting for you. I believe that your favourite tipple is a Moscow Mule, is it not?'

'You confuse my preferred drink with the identity of your mother, Sir, and anyway I'm butch darling, as well you know. I build big machines.'

'You bitch! You'll never even make it out of Manchester's Canal Street* – that is your regular place of work Sir, is it not? Your train performs tricks, it's quite obvious who it learned them from.'

[* Who says that town planners don't think ahead? Gas Street, Waterworks Street and Mobile Phone Place all fall under the same heading of "inspired foresight". Teleportation Crescent and 186,001 Miles Per Second Road in Bolton may yet prove to be the exceptions though, since we have no more industrial or scientific entrepreneurs remaining in England in the current era.]

'Cow! You couldn't pull a drunken sailor with that collection of old nuts and bolts you call a locomotive, let alone a dozen tons of coal. I'm not the one who entered "mistaken identity due to delays in the introduction of town-gas street lighting" as a plea of mitigation before Runcorn magistrates on a charge of soliciting a Grenadine Guard.'

'You wouldn't need to plead mistaken identity dear, everyone recognises you the instant you bend down to tie your shoe laces, whatever the ambient light.'

'Bitch!'

'Cow!'

With that the kangaroo-spat recommenced and the committee withdrew to the usual safe distance while hair was pulled and several mutually attempted kicks to the groin failed, for tailoring reasons, to make it higher than the opposition's ankles.

'Mister Trevithick! I believe that you misheard – this is a trial for serious steam locomotives or devices powered by horses walking on drive belts only. We have discussed this at length and the committee sees no future in the use of oil, especially for transportation purposes. Your English Electric Class 55 Deltic diesel-electrickery device is not eligible.'

'Haa-ha!' offered Stephenson in a spirit of conciliation, shouting down the corridor after Trevithick as he ran to the Ladies' toilets to splash cold water on his face and to try to stop the tears welling.

'Dear God, why those two ever began to play with train sets is beyond me. I'd have expected them both to be sitting in art college waiting for the price of textiles to come down to tie-dying territory rather than worrying about steam pressures and wheel flanges. I blame their fathers for giving them too strong a male role model and their mothers for being largely absent.' He turned to Miss Moneyha'penny. 'Please officially notify all members of the rail transport sub-committee to prepare themselves for the trials.' She giggled and looked at his knees. Oh god, how she loved his knees, especially between missions.

The committee then dissolved into matters of bunting, valet horse-parking at the station and to finding a technical solution to the building of a "Crystal Palace" that would successfully serve for both scientifical exhibitions and carriage-boot fairs. Half of the committee were in favour of allowing the horses and carriages to park up in lines for the public to browse up and down at leisure while the other half said that they would prefer the carriages to be reversed up to lines of tables supplied by the organisers. It was obvious that the debate would go on late into the night and would almost certainly end in tears. The Chance Brothers arrived to mend the glass in the broken window and Branson quietly slipped out along with Messrs Watt, Telford, Refrigerator, Traction-Engine, Dyson and Cyril Khan, inventor of both the modern heating Aga and the modern Cyril Service.

'Anyone fancy a take-away?' enquired Branson, feeling relief that the business of the day had concluded in the well that all that ends well ends in.

'Great idea. There's that new sub-continental Indian place over in Viceroy Terrace.'

'Well what about the Chinese in Tiananmen Square?'

'Yes - a disgraceful way to treat your own people, simply dreadful. They killed that student in front of the tank, you know – the one with the shopping bags. Anyone else fancy an Organ-Doner Kebab?'

'I'm not in the mood for anything too spicy or miscellaneous in terms of meat source. What about that place on Bulldog Street?'

'The English Takeaway?'

'That's it.'

'Yeah.'

Midnight saw them all at Dyson's flat attacking foil trays of roast beef, roast potatoes, Yorkshire puddings, carrots, peas, cabbage and little polystyrene tubs of hot onion-gravy. The trays of spotted dick, treacle sponge and tubs of custard still had their cardboard lids on and were warming by the fire. Empty bottles of beer, cider and mead littered the table. The greaseproof bags that had held the complimentary pork scratchings lay on the floor, torn open and empty now unless you count a slumbering cat, content after a bellyful of pork scratchings as content.

'So that's that then. The ball's rolling. Specialisation and piece-work here we come.'

'How long do you reckon it will last?'

'Goodness knows. Someone's bound to de-restrict the Estate Agent sooner or later and bring it all crashing down around our heads, probably in some sort of "property bubble burst" is my guess, early twenty-first century or so.'

'If you ask me the banks will scupper it. Before you know it they'll start lending over and above their gold reserves, robbing Sir Peter to pay Sir Paul and raiding the plebeian pension funds to float the company yacht.'

'Well gentlemen, that's all fiscal fun for us for the future.

Right now we should make do with the opportunities we've got on hand. Anyone fancy going on to a club?'

'There's that rave over at Lady Marmalade's on Ecstasy Place. We could try that.'

'Lots of wig-wearing, stoned and sweaty society types waltzing around stripped naked to the neck while the orchestra plays in double time and someone waves the candelabra about? Do me a favour! I want alcohol and conversation, not bottled water and dead-eyed social zombies.'

[Stripped to the neck as in without hats, filthy beasts. This trend would later spread down to the waist once Victorian teenagers had invented the six-pack, female breasts and sexual tension.]

'Oh well, chances are it's been raided by now anyway. Observatory again, anyone?'

'Too cloudy. Not the weather, I mean my mind is too cloudy.'

'Well I'm just going to bed. I'm knackered and tomorrow I have to get down to bloody Shropshire and start work on that new iron bridge thingy.'

'We should all get an early night I suppose. It's going to be work, work, work from now on for a while.'

'Yeah, but think of the money. All work and no play makes Jack rich as flaming Croesus. What are you going to do with yours?'

Whitworth was the only one sober enough to answer. 'I'm going to build myself a ruddy great house, have a fleet of fast sports-carriages and buy myself a football team. Whitworth Bolt-on Wanderers.' He peered into the neck of a lead-crystal decanter that proved empty and then threw it over his shoulder in disgust. 'You?'

'I'm going to buy Keenyah, build myself a villa with a veranda and watch the sun set every night over a cold gin and tonic and a warm woman. Preferably not the wife. Then I'm going to get malaria and gout and shoot the bloody chandeliers before the locals take over again.'

With that they both finally passed out. A couple of hours later the maid came in to tidy up around them, very quietly. For six more days the same maid crept in, tidied up and crept out again without waking the Hoorays and their desperately snoring livers. Several times the Butler himself had to creep around and affix saline drips and apply heart-massage and anti-bedsore rubs. It was all standard stuff in an upper-crust household.

Finally, the day of The Trials dawned. Neatly done, huh? Couldn't be arsed filling in the literary gap there. It's not as though anyone's ever going to read this nonsense. Slept a week away! Anyhoo...

Branson, holding overall responsibility, arrived at the station five minutes early just so that he could check that all was well. Flinging the reins of his phaeton to a chap in return for a little paper slip with a claim number he strode towards the rail platforms. Of the eleven designs entered and the ten designs that were eligible under the rules, six had turned up.

Two of the absent designs relied upon high-temperature ceramic boilers that had yet to be invented and two more used a ridiculously comfortable and safe ten foot wide gauge quite unsuited to the four feet eight and a half inches used to build the world's first rail network. This particular narrower gauge had been chosen so that, just in case general mechanisation failed, an average width horse and cart might balance both wheels on the rails and still make use of the lines. Early tests indicated that the cart wheels kept slipping off or the Romans didn't like it or the brighter horses couldn't manage to stand splay-legged on both rails at the same time without farting and laughing out loud or something. Still, what was done was done and it was rather doggedly considered best to let the sleepers lie.

Besides, it was the only gauge that would fit down the servant's corridors in most stately homes, so it was adopted on a nod and a crisp unmarked fiver to Mr O'Railway, the Irish chap who was doing most of the building works.

Sadly for the trials, the much-vaunted MagLev Gas Turbine locomotive from Messrs Jetson Engineering Ltd could not be demonstrated because no-one could be found to play a wobbly steel sheet with a violin bow in order to make the necessary sound effects.

Branson handed over a stern look in payment for his twopenny Platform (Shoes) Ticket and began the process of making his heart sink like a large passenger liner* with multiple water-tight compartments, multiple lower-class passenger-tight compartments and an anti-iceberg salt dispenser on the bow augmenting the chap with the long heated bargepole.

[* Changes were in fact made to the design before her maiden voyage and small passengers were allowed too, whether or not they had water-tight compartments.]

He strode out to inspect the competitors.

Platform One held the Stephensons' engine design, apparently named "Tinkerbell".

Platform Two was graced by an engine bearing the nameplate "Toto", the brainchild of Braithwaite and some Swede, Son of Erics, who would later invent a "mobile" telephone of all things. Timothy Hackworth was polishing something at Platform Three that he'd christened "Ivor, my engine". Burstall's hairy legs were poking out from under a big Flying Scotch Man (no change there then) at Platform Four and Brandreth (not Giles) was posing next to his entry at Platform Five, the "von Ryan's Express".

Most of the weightier The Press were being dwarfed at Platform Six by Trevithick's one hundred and one ton Deltic, finished in full chrome, polished, given Art Deco detail flourishes and secretly code-named "Big Choo-choo with the fantastic engine-sound" down both sides and on the nose. Actually, thought Branson, the engines did sound lovely and they were audible to the rear too, and not just down both sides and on the nose.

Branson gathered the entrants into the troglodytic privacy of the Already-Lost Luggage Office, closing the door and counting to ten with his eyes shut to reduce his frustration.

'Gentlemen, gentlemen, gentlemen. Good morning and thank you for coming. I take it that you propose to usher in a massive change to the global structure of human society with dirty great lumps of iron named Tinkerbell, Toto, Ivor my Engine, The Big Flying Scotch Man and von Ryan's Express.'

'And Big Choo-choo too!' added Trevithick, ever hopeful of being allowed to compete.

The assembled company nodded, happily and eagerly. One or two mopped their brows with their lace oil-rags.

'No, gentlemen.'

'No?' they chorused, nonplussed and thus suddenly feeling quite negative.

'No. Positively no.' repeated Branson, arithmetically confusingly for "no" was far from a positive response in the eyes of the assembled entrepreneurs with their scientific minds. He had been intending to leave them all locked in with the starving un-labelled parrots previously en-route to Bognor and with the children who had become separated from their parents and were too young to give a return address. Generously, and on a whim he suspected that he would regret, Branson allowed them all to follow him back out into the limelight and the gathering soot.

Branson, pursued by his gaggle of squawking entrepreneurial innovators, strode out into the station, reflexively genuflected to the as-yet empty Royal Box, bared his tooth at the The Press in a professional smile and then started barking orders to anyone close by. 'Stationmasters? New nameplates and several buckets of paint, if you please. New nameplates and several buckets of paint even if you don't please.'

Little chaps scurried around at the command of the twin Siamese Stationmasters and then they all assembled at Platform One with scant seconds to go before England kissed goodbye for ever to the rural idyll. Branson fielded an enquiry from a haunted-looking little chap who was wondering if this was the eight-thirty train to Matthew & Son, where the work's never done, there's always something new you know? Upon being bitterly disappointed the chap decided to take a five minute break (that was all he would take) for a cup of cold coffee and a piece of cake. Then he threw himself, rather optimistically early for one so depressed, onto the tracks.

As the Transport Police fished him off with poles and then led him away he began shouting. 'I've been working there for nigh-on fifty years you know. No-one asks for more money because, well - nobody dares. I'm always up at eight – you just can't be late! Not for Matthew & Son! They won't wait!'

A ruddy-face and portly gentleman who was secretly planning to leap into the speculative new field of the phonograph business wondered how getting up at eight was in any way workmanlike, but held his peace for the moment, happy that whatever they made at Matthew & Son, direct competitor or no, they were losing out on four or five hours of good working daylight six days a week. When he opened his studios in Abbey Road the acts would be there at four of the morning, promptly, or contracts would be cancelled. He saw little profit in treating musicians like prima donna.

Branson though, saw something of note. 'Get that chap's name before you throw him out – I want to speak to him later about a possible opportunity in popular music.' Something subordinate but literate on the payroll shuffled after the man, saying things like "Oh – I say ..." and "Calling card at all, Sir? May I have your calling card?"

The motley crew of motley crews came to a halt, like a puddle of confused overflow in the yard of an automatic horse-wash. Branson groaned like a country squire presented with a son and heir that was altogether too fond of his sister's rag dolls.

'Tinkerbell. No. We're dealing with shipyards and cotton mills and pumping beam engines and a hungry and as yet totally unemployed workforce of quite bwutish (SIC) louts, Mr Stephenson, Mr Stephenson Junior. Bwutish louts who will bang nails into wooden-hull vessels with their foreheads, bwutes who hitherto have milked cows by holding onto the teats and lifting the cow up and down. We must work to our market, Messrs Stephenson. We need something uplifting and yet totally Boy's Own Willy or Dan Dare does Debbie in Darlington. Your entry will be re-named... "Rocket".'

'Ooh – I love it. Rocket! That's my favourite salad leaf' said Junior Stephenson, only to be automatically bitch-slapped by a despairing Senior who swapped a private "just please don't ask and I won't have to tell" look with Branson.

'New nameplate if you please Mr Stationmaster and while you're at it see if you can hide that lilac...'

'Lavender!'

'...if you can hide that lavender paintwork under a coat of badger's arse black. Quick about it, the public and Her Full Majesty will be officially here in two minutes.'

The Stationmasters nodded to a couple of their chaps and they almost all moved on.

'Toto' said Branson.

'Dorothy's dog' confirmed Braithwaite, reverentially, sighing.

'No.'

'It is!'

'No. Look, I know that this big butch industry stuff is a novelty for you – actually, yes - "Novelty". New nameplate and a lick of sober Judge's mood black if you please, Mr Stationmaster.' They moved on again like a party of Cromwellian Jesuit ascetics redecorating the West End on one of their more austere campaigning days.

'Ah - Ivor – you shall become Sans Pareil and a soupcon of...'

'...big nasty pirate's heart darkest charcoal in a rag-rolled matt eggshell finish?' offered the left-most of the Stationmasters.

'Soot black, Mr Stationmaster, soot black will do just fine. Just cover up that shade of faded Valençia tangerine.'

The band was beginning to practice as Branson's entourage moved on.

'Ah – The Big Flying Scotch Man. Full marks for perseverance, Mr Burstall, full marks for perseverance. Mr Stationmaster?'

'Percy Verance?'

'Almost, Sir, almost – and a touch of...'

'...non-white?'

'Exactly. Extreme "midnight on a cloudy, moonless night" non-white.'

Buckets of black were engaged and there followed the immediate sound of brushes slapping about the ironwork.

They'd reached Platform Five.

'Ah - von Ryan's Express. I'm tempted to let you get away with that Mr Brandreth. It has the certain necessary overtones of man's man's men's men, a definite air of testosterone under fire.'

'It is the little horse's name, Mr Branson' said Brandreth, pointing to the power unit, a horse called von Ryan and standing on a conveyor belt and intended to drive the wheels by means of the poor creature galloping nowhere, very fast.

'Very well then, von Ryan's Express it remains. Mr Stationmaster? A touch of...'

'Dark ebony gloss with a hint of autumn carbon?'

'Straw, Mr Stationmaster, a touch of straw if you will. The horse is already quite black enough for the purpose. Just feed the bloody thing up a bit before the RSPCA get on to us. Mr Trevithick?'

'Yes?'

'Steam, Mr Trevithick, steam. The rules say steam but you may run your Deltic, if you must, as the Umpire's barge.' Branson addressed the entrants. 'Right, these trials are to be held between here and god-forsaken one thousand and one uses for house bricks Liverpool – I presume that you all know the way?'

After a longish pause it became evident that the question was a serious one requiring collective shuffling, murmurs and an answer from some brave soul.

'We sort of, well – we follow the rails don't we?' said some brave soul.

'Indeed. You follow the rails, you stick to the rails, you do not fall off the rails, the whole rails and nothing but the rails. The rails are your alibi. Be at one with your rails. Embrace your rails, love your rails. Is that clear?'

'Yes!' railed the entrants. 'All hail the rails!' Most of them had been to the premiere of Gladiator the previous evening. Such Roman ruffians as never you did see! Except that they had, of course. Some bright spark shouted up from the cheap seats 'Woderwick will stick to the wails!' Branson ignored the heckler.

'Upon reaching Liverpool you will immediately return, is that clear? Once through Penny Lane, once around Strawberry Fields, once past the office of the Tax Man, wave at The Walrus, collect a fresh dozen from The Egg man, get your entry forms stamped by Miss Eleanor Rigby and then straight back here for a quick fanfare for the common man and the National Techno-Anthem as played by Sergeant Pepper's Lovely Clubbed Harts Band. OK?'

'Suppose so' was the collective sullen reply. They'd all rather hoped to have a chance to see the octopus's garden while they were in the legendary neighbourhood during daylight hours, in force of numbers and thus in comparative safety.

'Right, to your machines, gentlemen, to your machines. You begin in three minutes at the sound of the official starting pistol.'

[The invention of the firearm made starting races so much easier. The earlier method of using a "starting bow and arrow" led to some outrageous false starts during the early Olympics and one or two spectator casualties since what goes quietly up must come quietly down, especially so if you fire it vertically and then forget to take a step to the left or a step to the right.]

'Mr Branson?'

'Yes, what is it Mr Ericsson?'

'Once out of the station it is, I believe, a single-track line between Manchester and Liverpool with no turntable at the Liverpool end.'

'So?'

'Does that not make, well, racing a little difficult? If we're all switched onto the same single-track railway line how may we overtake?'

'The conditions are the same for all entrants, Mr Ericsson. If fair play doesn't suit you then perhaps you might prefer life in the colonies? The Americas perhaps. This is England, Mr Ericsson, we do not moan about the tough going, Sir. When the going gets tough we just draft in even more cheap foreign labour. To your machine, if you please and no more of your Scandinavian whining.'

Branson strode over to the Royal Box and leapt in, eschewing the use of the little gate in favour of subliminally intimidating Albert with a demonstration of his athletic ability and a flash of the padded groin of his Jermyn Street tailored pin-stripes. Woof, I think there's a large kipper down there that you can smoke me for breakfast.

'G'morning Vicky.'

'Morning Dick.'

They air-kissed each other's cheeks, mwuh mwuh, and Branson absent-mindedly squeezed a right Royal buttock in the clinch. It wasn't one of Albert's, either. Realising that they were in public they separated quickly, blushing. Branson had reserved his seat with his usual India-rubber "haemorrhoid" ring.

Vicky stepped forward to do the honours.

'Albert – your pistol if you please, One will begin proceedings.'

The Queen Victorian pointed the duelling pistol into the air as per the little Japanese Instruction Manual, and squeezed the trigger. Several things happened then, all at once.

The bullet ricocheted from the station ceiling and hit Brandreth's engine-horse on the von Ryan's Express between the eyes, dropping it where it stood, stone dead, on its little drive-belt, deceased, un-living, not even shuffling off its quite literal mortal drive-coil. Trevithick, thinking that he was next, floored the Deltic, but unfortunately in reverse. He disappeared through the Station's Refreshment Room in what would clearly have been a false start even had he been a legitimate entry. Laura Jesson, who had been leaning out of the cab of the Deltic, having her elbow touched and saying a fond farewell to a doctor called Alec Harvey, found herself with more than just grit in her eye and staring down at Dolly Messiter who was having repeated brief encounters with the Deltic's various axles.

Four fully-qualified flaming firemen, one on each of the remaining entries' platforms, raced out of the pits like lonely geriatrics on nursing home visitors day, struck tinderboxes and lit some rather exciting fires under their respective boiler responsibilities. There was a little bit of illegal fanning with broadsheets and magazines to encourage the flames.

Victoria looked, amazed and cross-eyed, down the smoking end of the pistol. 'Bugger me – did One do all that? What splendid devices – no wonder you chaps like them so much.' Instead of returning the pistol to Albert she lifted her skirts and tucked it into the Order of the Garter where it remained almost untouched for months until that fateful day when it saved her life during an assassination attempt in St. James's Park.

[So un-amused was Victoria at this later assault upon One that she leapt out of One's moving carriage, chased the would-be assassin through the woods, coined the phrase "do you feel lucky, Punk? Well do you?" and then pumped all four remaining bullets into his Police record at point blank range. Yes, four remaining bullets. One fired so far today, one up the spout and yet to go.]

An incomprehensible public commentary was beginning, describing the nail-biting development of the respective boiler fires from smoking tinder to full-fledged conflagration. A scant couple of hours of cheering-on later all four engines had sufficient steam up to burst out of Manchester railway station like racing-demons out of some English Rail Hell.

'Nothing to do now but wait, Vicky.'

'Does anyone fancy a game of poker while One waits?'

'So long as we use my cards, yes. Albert – are you in? Doctor Beeching? How about you?' A card table was produced and chairs in the Royal Box shuffled about. Chestnut roasters and pork scratching peddlers began to circulate among the hoi polloi as the various experimental locomotives rushed towards the horizon with the Swedish driver of one of the entries, Ericsson, waving and shouting "get out of the way" to all who had gone before him.

Far out in the gentle English countryside events were about to turn very ugly, very ugly indeed.

A lovely family, torn apart by false allegations of spying and of selling state secrets to the dastardly "The Russians", was busy drinking its way to a new life in a rented house on the wrong side of the tracks – the new railway tracks. The father of course, being the cheap treasonous rat that he was, was languishing in jail and swapping Russian cigarettes for drugs and the odd night off the "Mr Big's Cuddly-Wuddly Living Teddy bear" rota. The three young children, Roberta-Jo, Peter-Billybub and Phyllis-Jo were playing on the Liverpool and Manchester Railway line, as directed by their inebriated "I want to be a paperback writer" mother. The very line out of the two in existence that, tragically, and unbeknownst to the children, was so soon to be tested by the speeding new "steaming great locomotive" designs...

'What will it be like when trains start to run do you think?' asked Roberta-Jo innocently, swinging the hem of her smock among the daisies and the dandelions and the long but decorative embankment grasses.

'Scary!' replied short-tongued Phyllis-Jo in the manner of a young Joyce Grenfell before she found her feminine poise.

'Fun!' was the opinion of Peter-Billybub who had once had his head inflated to the size of a watermelon by a very annoyed and preternaturally muscular toad on the business end of a playful paper straw and a schoolboy bet gone seriously wrong for the human being involved.

'I know you've told me this before Peter-Billybub but I always forget – to be safe does one stand outside the two little tracks or inside?'

'Inside, silly! The train runs on the tracks. If a train is coming then the only safe place for sure is between the two tracks. You girls will just never understand mechanical things, will you?'

'Oh. OK. I'll tie a knot in my handkerchief so that I remember. Of course, the trains won't run all the way into Liverpool, will they? Even Daddy wouldn't be brave enough for that.'

'Of course not, silly! They'll stop a safe distance away. Assuming that they've been forewarned.'

'What's that rumbling noise?' asked Roberta-Jo, looking for storm clouds but finding none.

'A stampede perhaps?' said Phyllis-Jo, looking hopefully at the old cow in the next field. The old cow shook a fist and carried on walking back to the OAP home with her two-hundred pound firewood bundle on her arched back.

'An earthquake maybe?' said Peter-Billybub gleefully, imagining Los Nottingham, city of the one-way tramway no-parking average-speed camera town planning angels, splitting in two or three and burning a bit.

'Oh goodness me – it's a train!' said Roberta-Jo, horrified and excited at the same time in much the same way as she had been when one of daddy's many Russian friends had stayed over and she'd been sleepwalking again but he said he didn't mind and had explained how Russians keep warm in the long, cold, Siberian winters with nothing but shared body-heat and some strange foreign exercises.

'Can't be a train – no-one's seriously expecting trains to start running for another ten years or more.'

'Well something's coming!'

'Run!'

'It's too late! The future's already here! Get between the tracks!'

'I know - I'll take my bright red cotton underknickergloryb ockers off and wave them over my head, just so that they know we're here' said Roberta-Jo. She was very limber and could even take them off in her sleep, and it had made the Russian laugh so.

'You always take your knickers off and wave them over your head at any excuse!'

'Do not!'

'Do so!'

'Phyllis-Jo's right, Roberta-Jo – do you remember yesterday when we walked past that building site? I'm sure that the builders knew we were on the pavement nearby even before you stripped off and waved at them.'

'There were cranes and shovels and pickaxes! It was dangerous. I had to do something!' protested Roberta-Jo in her own defence.

'What about the day before when the greengrocer was putting boxes of apples out in front of his shop? You waved your knickers then too.'

'They were heavy boxes! He might have dropped one on us.'

'We were on the other side of the road! What about the farm workers in the field at the back of Mummy's new house? Why did you wave at them? We were indoors!'

'They had scythes! Do you know how dangerous scythes can be?'

'No but you should know, you were in the old barn for hours afterwards talking about it with all of those swarthy casual harvest labourers lured from Mediterranean regions by promises of fine wages and dalliances with milk-skinned English virgins' said Peter-Billybub, demonstrating either an understanding beyond his years or something he'd overheard while emptying ashtrays and collecting glasses down at the village pub while waiting for Mummy to cash-in her returned bottles.

'Was not!'

'Was so!'

'OK then cleverclogs Peter-Billybub – you wave yours this time.'

'No point.'

'Why?'

'Mine blend in like desert camouflage against most backgrounds and, anyway, you know I have to soak them off whenever Mummy says I need to change them, otherwise my skin comes off too.'

'Phyllis-Jo – you get yours off and wave them over your head at the driver.'

'Can't.'

'Why not?'

'Not wearing any. Can't be bothered. I've seen the trouble yours cause you. The Vicar says I'm going to make a fortune when I'm older. I assume he means the money I'll save on laundry costs. He says that if you only wear top-clothes you can do away with the boil wash altogether.'

'Right, so we're back to me again. It's always me that takes responsibility. I've got to stop them before they get robbed. The poor men! Think of the poor men! Won't somebody think of the poor men! Look out – there's danger down the line! Liverpudlians!'

With that Roberta-Jo began running down the track towards the on-coming train, careful to stay safely between the rails and waving her underwear in the time-honoured fashion. As the loco neared she stopped, shut her eyes and kept waving for all she was worth, visualising the usual outcome where she would end up nose to nose with the heroically heroine-halted engine and a thoroughly saved magnificent day, with maybe a quick and sooty snuggle from the chap with the big shovel who puts coal in the little fire-hatch thingy.

This would all have worked train-stopping wonders had Burstall and his fireman, Michael Palin, been looking up and forwards at the time. As it was, well...

'What was that? The engine hiccoughed.'

'It was almost like we hit something. Something soft on the outside and crunchy on the inside but with the sound deadened as though covered in layers of quilted red cotton and extra-wide gusset elastic.'

'Nonsense – the track's clear all the way to Liverpool docks. Keep your foot down and keep stoking, Palin, we're creating legends here.'

Roberta-Jo shook her head to clear it. 'Ouch!' Dragging herself to her feet again she watched Perseverance screaming towards its Merseybeat doom at seven or eight blistering miles an hour. Just as she was trying a last-ditch, dismal little wave of her oily underknickerglorybockers Sans Pareil came hurtling over the horizon and over Roberta-Jo. She regained consciousness face-down this time, on the clinker between the rails.

'Ooh, gosh – that hurt. That really hurt. Those poor men!' Novelty caught her just as she was bending down to pick up the remnants of her underwear and flattened her once again into the sleepers. Being made of stern stuff though she soon regained her feet and stood firm and foursquare to try to save the final engine, Rocket, from ending up without wheels and parked on house bricks. That loco made a frightful clanging sound when her forehead accidentally hit it just above the delicate front-axle bogey thing.

Roberta-Jo was beginning to suspect that between the rails was not the safe place after all, despite what her little brother had told her. Oh, she thought, if only she wasn't a girl she'd have a chance of being able to work out these mechanical and scientific things herself. It was really most unfair.

Roberta-Jo's voice was a touch weak and she could only wave with one hand, the other arm being limp at her side or as a squeamish grown-up would later term it "just one big compound fracture from wrist to shoulder".

'I'm not wearing any knickers' she whispered forlornly to the receding carriage where a kindly old gentleman was reading a newspaper. He waved and then went back to the crossword in The Times. Seven letters, starts with "T" and rhymes with "dollop". Aha! Trollop.

Phyllis-Jo and Peter-Billybub – who had stepped experimentally to one side of the tracks - set about reviving Roberta-Jo. She was stunned by her failure.

'The man on that last train. The young driver. When I shouted that I wasn't wearing any knickers he just said "tell a man who gives a damn, Honeybun". Why would he say that? Why didn't he stop? They usually stop.'

'I guess you weren't giving him the right signals, Roberta-Jo' offered Peter-Billybub. 'Maybe here you have to wave them up and down rather than side to side.'

'It's always worked before. I was just sort of whirling them around my head and smiling.'

'Well maybe he just didn't hear you. You tried though, no-one can say you didn't try.'

'Those poor men. Liverpool! Oh those poor souls! They'll be in the thick of it before they realise.'

'Daddy would have been proud of you, you did all you could. You always do.'

'Lie still for a while, Roberta-Jo. Peter-Billybub and I will go for help.'

'OK, but what's that rumbling noise?' replied Roberta-Jo, looking for storm clouds but, again, finding none.

'A stampede?' said Phyllis-Jo, checking on the old cow in the other next field. Nope – it hadn't moved and was just staring back at her with a vacant wonky eye, lots of slobber and a smelly case of festering mastitis, just like a delicious milky commercial bovine should. The OAP she'd seen earlier gathering the firewood for winter was heading towards the cow and wondering if it would burn. She hefted it aloft and carted it off on the off-chance.

'An earthquake?' offered Peter-Billybub, imagining Los Grimsby, city of the fishing-angels, shaking until it was just a blur and with everything on the Cleethorpes side of Park Street sliding into the Humber Estuary while a big lava-flow destroyed Immingham completely (his imaginings were never really very detailed or very novel).

'Oh goodness me – it's another train!'

'But it can't be – they can't run backwards can they? Dogs can't look up, poor people don't mind being cold and hungry and trains can only run one way, surely? Mummy always says so.'

'Well something's coming and I don't think it's the Games Mistress of St. Trinians on a hand-cart chasing the proceeds of the

Great Train Robbery. Oh I don't know though – they have had time to get to Liverpool and back.'

'Peter-Billybub, Phyllis-Jo – run! Go get Percolator, the old station porter. He'll know what to do. I'll just wait here, I suppose I'll be quite safe if I just stay between the tracks again. Go! Quickly!'

The Stephensons were in a fast "father and son" reverse on Rocket. 'Isn't it weird, Father, moving backwards and watching the world rush away from one as the vanishing point of perspective works its wonderful but mysterious magic. It quite stops the flies going in one's mouth.'

'Makes me dizzy. I'd rather eat the flies. What was that?'

'Sounded like the engine hiccoughed.'

'Maybe we hit something again?'

'Oh yes – look, it's little Miss fur coat and no underknickers or glorybockers or something mysterious and female-wardrobe orientated. Should we stop and render first aid?'

'Not likely! Your mother would have my guts for garters. More coal, son, more coal.'

Roberta-Jo watched them go. 'Hello! I'm glad that you're safe. My name's Roberta-Jo and some day I'm going to be a very famous actress called Dame Jenny Agutter you know.' She gave a feeble wave with her good arm and an injured smile. 'I'm not wearing any bockerknickerunderlongs' she whispered forlornly, feeling concussion sweeping over her again.

Poor soul, she never even saw Novelty coming, revived again just in time to raise her head for Sans Pareil's rather low-slung rear-axle and then "slept" right through Perseverance as it thundered overhead, dripping oil on troubled daughters.

The hot-wired Perseverance was being driven by two chaps in white shell-suits who weren't too familiar with the controls but were flogging its bollocks off all the same. Timothy Burstall was somewhere very elsewhere indeed, trying to give a statement to a nice Police Officer who often dealt with stolen and hijacked horse carriages and who was drinking a bottle of Police canteen "WKD" while he listened politely. Constable Dodd explained that they didn't have a form for anything that wasn't horse-driven. 'Moves all by itself you say? No horses at all? Is that right. Hmm. You're from Manchester way, aren't you? Could I ask you to blow into this little bag please Sir, it just that my, er, my chips are too hot at the moment, nothing to worry about, just blow through the little tube until the crystals change colour.' Burstall blew until he was red in the face and quite thoroughly hand-cuffed and then Ken took him down to the cells.

Back in Manchester The Queen Victorian, Dr Beeching, Prince Albert and Mr Sir Branson Sir were getting fed up with playing strip poker as they waited. Victoria was down to just her morning pre-mourning veil and Prince Albert was about to reveal to the English public that jewellery was not just for women, not just for the fingers, sometimes required vomit-inducing minor backstreet surgery and could result in a gentleman peeing in all directions at once like an overworked muck-spreader.

The chap in the signal box who worked the points at the Manchester Station station had been peering down the line for ages, hoping that he had time to send all of the returning entrants back to their starting platforms. He did a couple of star jumps, touched his toes, loosened his neck muscles and shook the tension out of his arms and legs. Then he resumed blowing the used air out of his lungs through his mouth and then breathing in through his nose, past his chakra and over his diaphragm (he refused to use The Pill, however safe the wife said it was).

A distant whistle accompanied a massive spark of excitement through the waiting crowds.

'Sorry! So sorry!' said the chap who was finishing off the station's electrical wiring. 'Shouldn't happen again. So sorry!' He was laying the last of two hundred and forty cables leading towards the platform clock. 'Each one carries a whole volt, you know – a whole volt!' All he had to do next was lay another two hundred and forty downhill cables to take away each of the used volts and he'd be done. Time and technology wait for no man, you just have to solder on as best you can. 'Once I'm done it won't need re-volting for years.'

The Queen Victorian stood, holding field glasses to One's nose. 'Oh this is so rad!' she squealed.

'Totally, like, far-out!' agreed Albert. 'Awesome!'

Victoria found herself almost strangled as Branson borrowed her field glasses.

'It's them! It's them!'

'So, you were expecting somebody from else maybe alright already?' said Victoria, allowing her accent to slip a little and grabbing back One's field glasses.

'It's going to be close, very close, Ma'am' whispered Billy Connolly, worming his way in to the Royal circle under the guise of a creepy McManservant.

Albert wet a finger and checked the humidity for himself, not convinced that Connolly entirely spoke the truth or that he really had to stay in Victoria's room overnight just in case she needed the light turning on or a window opening or a glass of water or something.

'Close schmose, after this it's married they'll have to get. More room there was between my dear late Albert and I than these competitors and we? We had twenty-seven childrens. When you're older yourself, you'll know. Then you'll know. When they're young they break your back, when they're older they a-break-a even your Sichilian heart.' Victoria was bobbing up and down with excitement, flip-flopping between Jewish-Italian and Brooklyn-Schmooklyn with a touch of the Godfather. God-Mother. God-Queen – Jewish-Italian-Brooklyn God-Queen with German roots. German roots? Schmoots! Oy! Don't get me started on German roots with the crowns and the divine rights, damned European mongrels. 'Ah that my dear Albert should have lived to see this – such a fine race it is that we shall have!'

Albert started to try to mention once again that he was still alive, well and, well – present, but thought better of it. He'd learned early on in their marriage that it as best not to interrupt The Queen Victorian when she was at a dog track or the en-horsed jockey races.

The chap on the points lever took a few more practice swings to get his arm in and to warm up the grease on the points mechanism.

The four invitation-only sponsor's enclosures, one at the end of each competitor's platform, were served fresh canapes and were all pushed forwards to watch, the tartan rugs on their three-wheeled wickerwork bath-chairs billowing in the haste among the clanking of oxygen tanks and the clunking of buxom nursing staff.

The public in the cheap seats and the stands began a series of Mexican waves, anyone not participating being ostracised and regarded as terminally un-amusable. Victoria tried a couple of popular waves herself but somehow just couldn't synchronise. 'We are not Mexican' she announced, grimly. When she swapped instead to a Radio Ga-Ga hand-clap her public, naturally, followed suit. The upper crust in the expensive seats in the John Lennon Memorial Enclosure simply rattled their jewellery.

All four locomotives appeared over the horizon, in reverse, hell for leather, jockeying for position on the single-track line from Liverpool. Steam belched and Sparks flew even though the town wasn't big enough for both of them and 'planes hadn't been invented yet. Pistons, levers and wheels, pushed to the limit, pounded, thrashed and spun like never before seen components of a Brave New World.

Copying Victoria, as one did in those days, the crowd leapt and danced in excitement, the hastily-built stands creaked and rumbled and the horses' bits, as ever, were covered with foam (filthy beasts).

One, two, three, four they flew past the chap on the points control at eleven or twelve miles in an Imperial hour and, giving his all for Queen and Country in the performance of his working life, he switched them back to their respective starting platforms, four, three, two, one. A great cry, a national roar, went up from the crowds and Branson ran forwards, his coat-tails flailing, waving his hands and shouting to the competitors. As he ran he tripped over some rather pessimistic chap walking about with a sandwich board bearing the legend "The end is nigh" to his front and "Prepare to meet thy doom" to his back.

From lying prone on the cold concrete platform Branson looked up and shouted. 'Brakes! Use your brakes! You must seriously retard yourselves with respect to your present velocity such that it will reduce to a value neither positive nor negative before the combined loci of your locomotives bisects the approaching terminator in the plane of the existing track!'

One by one the competitors turned to one another and one's other anothers on their dozens of tons and half-hundredweights of speeding fire and iron and shrugged before they turned back to him questioningly.

'Brakes?' They all shook their heads, puzzled, looking seriously under-funded in re quality cranial content.

Branson borrowed a megaphone. 'Your stopping devices! Deploy them now or you shall surely plough through the end of the platforms, through the sponsoring Independent Financial Advisors, the National Association of Estate Agents, the entire Law Society and the Health & Safety Executive stands, and thence on into the Salvation Army Hostel for travelling Members of Parliament that lies just behind that flimsy partition wall! Tragedy may ensue unless you quite presently arrest yourselves and nullify your momentum! '

Stephenson Junior on Rocket cupped his hands and shouted a reply. 'But the competition was all about speed – you said nothing about testing our capacity to decelerate! We mapped our machines' abilities to the positive half of the space-time displacement gradient only! The paradigm in the entry regulations suggested a certain unidirectional nature to the salient criteria for success!'

Stephenson Senior leapt, rather more pragmatically and with the wisdom of old age, from the footplate to safety, swinging from an overhead beam like some sort of sooty decorative dwarf in workshop-tweeds. He was positive that half of his spine had displaced itself in space-time, but at least he would no longer have to watch his collective loci bisecting the terminator with disastrous respect to some of the most beloved functional socio-economic groups in England. 'Ouch, me back's gone!' he said, in slow, rumbling tones that captured the mood of the situation quite succinctly.

Braithwaite leapt from the rear of his machine, grabbed hold of the tender and dug his heels in, scattering clinker and gravel impressively, but vainly. In the public stands his boot-maker put his head in his hands and wept. Hackworth frantically scribbled designs for an anti-momentum mechanism on the back of a cigarette packet and the two chaps in shell-suits on Perseverance simply leapt off and ran away, chased by an experimental Police "hot air" pursuit-balloon and Alastair "Boing-Boing Ding-dong nobody's really home Infra-Red Camera " Stewart.

Branson, limping but legging it somewhat hastily back to the Royal Enclosure, arrived just in time to wail "No-o-o-o-o-o-o-o" in slow-mo' and leap, equally s-l-o-w-l-y, to tackle the largely naked but still winning-hand holding Queen Victorian to the ground and out of the path of the flying debris.

Rocket hit first, flattening the little cross-hatched barrier at the literal end of the rail line and shattering the concrete of the platform into the new crazy-paving that was to become so popular in years to come once patios had been invented. Gentlemen from the Euro NCAP agency took copious notes as the engine deformed nicely in the impact and the buttoned velvet "airbags" that had attracted such derision when explained by the Stephenson's, deployed correctly, scattering duck-down and ostrich feathers. The tanned man manning the tannoy system intoned 'Four point nine, four point nine, five point zero, four point nine, four point seven, five point zero...' and public people began throwing bouquets of flowers, confirming thereby that the English have always been, as one, quite clinically insane. Functional in extremis of course, but clinically insane nonetheless.

A split second later, Novelty seemed to leap off the rails like a great iron monster with gaping firebox-maw, heading directly towards the sponsor's enclosure of Platform Two. Sans Pareil hit the barrier, Hackworth cried "Oh bugger for England, for Harry and ruddy Saint George" and they both flipped arse over bogey wheels into their bath-chaired "money men" sponsors. Perseverance, cab doors flailing after the bail-out, hit, turned sideways for maximum carnage and slid like a stolen BMW 3-Series as some dickhead with a – ooh, cor luv-a-duck what will they think of next – night vision camera cried 'He's crashed, he's crashed, he's crashed...' into a cctv show fade-out.

A pair of singed and torn red underknickerglorybockers had settled on Branson's head for some reason as he lay face down on the Monarch, as one did in time of National emergency or at the official start of the London Social Season if cordially invited.

Among the fluttering ashes and clattering wreckage he tugged them off, flattened his hair back down and helped Vicky to her feet, flicking dust and debris off her shoulders with the mystery underwear. She giggled and said "Oh – One seems to be a little bit plastered" and pulled bits of building from her own rather disturbed hair.

A similar scene was enacted in formation a couple of thousand times over in the public gallery to the side of the station as everyone, naturally, copied whatever Royalty did or had had happen to them. Several months later when reports reached the Khyber Pass a minor local uprising was interrupted to allow for yet another re-enactment, this time over the suckling pig and the local Fakir. It caused quite a carry-on there.

Where the end of the station should have been was a vast, smoking, post-apocalyptic pile. Beyond that the flattened Salvation Army Hostel that had been so popular with thrifty Members of Parliament eking out the Public Purse had been, like, totally destroyed, you know? A lone figure rose from the rubble, looked across and waved, weakly.

'It's OK – I'm Nu Labour' the staggering survivor said, just before the original nameplate from Tinkerbell re-entered the dust-laden local atmosphere and landed with remarkable political precision (right between the eyes).

'That's that then, Vickykins' said Branson. 'In my haste to appease the Ladies' Committee for Insistence upon the Prompt and Satisfactory Prosecution of the Primary and Secondary Industrial Revolutions and for the introduction of Billiards Cues in Women's Sizes I have just ended the Industrial Revolution before it was properly begun. I should have asked for brakes. Anchors at the very least. Platform buffers of some sort mayhap. We shall have to start all over again, but this time install giant springs at the end of each railway line. It'll cost a fortune. What a disaster.'

He pointed towards the massive pile of broken bricks and broken politicians, and the ruined spaces where the four richest sponsoring professions had been seated to watch the competition from the ends of the platforms. 'Tragedy. Pure unadulterated tragedy. Look – hundreds of politicians dead and all of England's finest Merchant Bankers, Estate Agents, Lawyers and Health & Safety Inspectors wiped out in one fell swoop.'

There was a huge roar and rapturous applause from the Public Stand and Branson, unaware that his tin megaphone was still switched on, turned to see just what might have caused it.

The public were rushing out, eager to get into the new factories and to begin making things.

Somewhere close by in one of the Portalavatories a penny dropped.

Tentatively, Branson raised the megaphone again and tried an experiment.

'Oh look – one of the Pension Company Hedge Fund Managers has survived.'

The public stopped in their tracks, dropped their heads and began muttering, indolently and quite without profit or material progress.

Raising his megaphone once more Branson shouted 'Oh, my mistake, each and every one of them is horribly dead after all' and the public began rushing out again, eager to begin spot-welding, riveting, wind-tunnel testing and general manufacturing for universal export.

'Oh hurrah! A surveyor specialising in buy to let properties is rising from the ashes!'

The public stopped in their tracks and started to kick their heels again and consider random vandalism.

'Oh my mistake again – he's dead too.'

Hats filled the air and the queues to leave the station swelled once more.

'Hmm.' Branson made as though to raise the megaphone for one last, possibly conclusive, social experiment but found himself being gently restrained by The Queen Victorian. She was shaking her head and then nodded a message rather imperiously to the remnants of the military band ("play now or die" was the message). The piano was at a dodgy angle but the notes were true enough and the Royal intro gave the choir time to have a quick gargle to get the dust off the old vocal chords before they began.

'One one one one one one one ...' They were all far too polite and well-mannered to sing “me me me me me me meeeee ...” for their warm-up. Cough, cough, shuffle, here goes.

‘When I find myself in piles of rubble, the old Queen Mary comes to me, speaking words of wisdom, from a tree. In One’s hour of darkness she is standing right in front of One, speaking words of wisdom, lettuce pee, oh lettuce pee. And, when One’s broken hearted people, living in the foreign world agree, there will be an Empire, let it be, oh let it be. There will be an Empire, oh let One’s people be...’

The soon-to-be Empress of India played the air-organ keyboard with artistic pain on her face while the choir dived into the chorus with emotional gusto and under the very real threat of Hubert von Karajan’s stolen baton wielded by a very happy Lady Constance Mann-Bighter.

Vicky pointed between stanzas (musical, not Datsun) towards the George & Dragon and gave the internationally accepted hand-signal for “Jeez, I need a round of whiskies and a pig’s arse butty with heaps of HP Sauce, all followed by ten pints of lager and a proper curry, how about you load of big Jessies?”

As Victoria, Albert, Branson, Dr Beeching and Mr “I’m just a faithful manservant really” Connolly carefully picked their way over the rubble towards the pub they came across the broken body of a poor young solicitor (yeah, right, “poor” my arse). He groaned and rolled over, reaching for them (or it might have been for their purses, it was hard to tell in all the brick dust and the fog-like arterial spray of his extensive injuries4U).

They paused. The soundtrack for the closing scenes of the first day of the Industrial Revolution was playing in the background and it was really obvious who was calling the tunes now – Lady Constance Mann-Bighter launched into her Suffragette-City remix medley while the lone survivor of the legal profession sang like a super-grass canary.

‘Help!’ he sang. ‘Help! I need somebody! Not just anybody! Help! You know I need first a-a-aid. Help! When I was younger, so much less injured than today I never needed anybody’s blood in any way, but now those days are gone I’ve found my legs are not secured, now I find, I’ve, like, changed my mind and need to find

I'm cured. Help me if you can I'm lying down, and I do appreciate One looking down. Help me get my feet back on your ground, won't One please help me. Help me. Ooh.'

Next to him were scorched papers upon which the business header "Nowin O'Fee, Jusste Klaymitt & Screame-Whipplashe" could just be read in dusty smudges. There was a briefcase, broken now and open, in which lay his scanner for listening in to ambulance radios and his supply of banana skins for those customers who required a little creative help with their evidence of negligence.

Victoria planted one very recently re-slippered royal foot on his neck, reached into her garter belt and decorated his forehead with an Order of The Bullet. Then One addressed One's entourage.

'One has plans, gentlemen, One has plans and one's plans do not include compensation culture and no-win no-fee no-scruples no-testicles solicitors. Buy One a cold pint and a bag of Cheese & Onion crisps and One will tell you all about them and what's in it for you guys...'

The band changed its tune again when Vicky snapped her fingers over One's shoulder. For the second time in a rather surprising day in what had been a very busy week, and promised to be a hell of a century or two, Victoria blew the smoke from the end of her new pistol, played an air guitar with classic bad back and weak knees stance and then dance-stepped over the rubble, singing her way towards the pub, a pint and the future of England and The English Empire.

'Aaaaaaaaaaargh! You say you want an industrial revolution, well, you know, One really wants to change the world. Darwin tells me that it's industrial evolution, well, you know, One really needs to change the world, but when you talk about deconstruction, don't assume that you can count One out ...'

'Vicky, it's going to be alright.'

'Alright?'

'Alright!'

'Alright?'

'Alright!'

'You say you've got a real solution Mr Branson, well, you

know – One would love to see your plans. You ask One for a contribution, well, you know, Royalty's doing what it can. But if you want money for people with inventions that are late, well all I can tell you is, loyal subject, they'll have to wait.'

'Vicky, don't you know it's going to be... alright.'

'Alright?'

'Alright!'

'Alright?'

'Alright!'

'You say you'll change One's constitution. Well, you know – One just might chop orf your head. You tell me it's the Establishment Institutions, well, you know, you'd better free your mind instead. But, look, if you don't get One's canals built right now, you ain't gonna make it with One anyhow.'

'Vicky – don't you know it's going to be...'

'...Alright?'

'Alright!'

10 THE DAY THE EARTH TOOK TEA

Lord Sir Rear-Admiral Doctor Professor the Most Reverend the Honourable Mr Blair, X.P.M., D.S.O., O.B.E., G.C.S.E., O Rhesus Negative, Lactose Intolerant [all information retrieved from his "Rambo" dog-tags] was as fatigued as a canine after another long night shift at the Great Osmonds Street Hospital, comforting sick children with the word of the Lord. He used only the first of his titles when talking to sick children, as in 'Hello sick little pre-Voter, I am the Lord...'

However, even pooped as he was, his driving was still exemplary and his reactions silver-spoon sharp. He slammed both of his sandals onto the brake pedal of his G-Wiz L-ion electric car so hard that his nylon socks slipped down, his bamboo crucifix got tangled up in the steering wheel and his dhoti rode right up unto the crack of his Arsenal Villa are doing awfully well this year, don't you think?

Several trays of uneaten lobster left over from the previous day's Simple-Meals-on-Christian-eco-wheels run through the poor of Kensington Square might have fallen right off the rear nodding-dog & parcel shelf had there been an anywhere to slide into. As cramped in the vehicle as it was, two claws and a delicate butter sauce still got loose and hit the inside of the eco-windscreen.

Fortunately for his emergency stop manoeuvre it was barely Sparrow-fart o'clock, so his was still the only moving car on the road in central London and there was no need for any motoring "oh I say" battles or "do please excuse me, parp-parp" wars, and certainly no-one needed to remove their string-backed gloves or to swerve while glowering incandescently.

Sparrow-fart o'clock is about a quarter past seven-twenty a.m. on the Imperial O'Beaufort Scale. Blair got out to peer at the spectacle before him through his little round horn-rimmed zero-prescription spectacles, the ones that went everywhere just before him since they were attached to his nose. Leaving the car door wide open he pulled up his socks and pulled down his unbleached Fair Trade organic cotton loincloth just a little. Easing his badge of office thus allowed him to dip to genuflect without cutting off his European Presidential election prospects. Spectacles, testicle, coin-purse and watch out, there's some slow chap on a fast bicycle.

Eric, the chap who plugs in the third rail of The London Tube System in the mornings, was on his way to work and almost wobbled his fast sports-bicycle into the side of Mr Blair's car, abandoned as it was on the new-fangled yellow cross-hatch mechanical traffic-light controlled junction and humming to itself like a red EverReady D-type battery on wheels. Eric put a hand on the roof of the car as he slipped out of his bicycle clips, popped them in the basket on the handlebars and then went to stand alongside the Lord Sir Rear-Admiral Doctor Professor the Most Reverend the Honourable Mr Blair and so forth.

'G'morning Tony.'

'Oh, hello Eric.'

Just then a Hollywooden film director gentleman came hurtling down the deserted Mall [the parade-ground stroke roadway The Mall, not a foreign shopping centre]. Surrounded by a cloud of dramatic tension he was moving at a quite headlong jog towards the very junction so unexpectedly gridlocked by a G-Wiz L-ion, a parked bicycle and – the latest insurmountable addition – a stately feral foraging family-pigeon, foraging in its most feral family state.

Still looking entirely to his right, as he had been for the whole of the previous three paragraphs, merely glancing at the road and only then in-between delivering complicated vital plot-dialogue, he suddenly found his somehow inalienable human right to a clear "freeway" violated. His god, for this gentleman's god was not the same god as Mr Blair's god, was caught quite on the hop, as gods apparently often are during Earthly emergencies. The Hollywooden Almighty desperately spun the gentleman sideways in defiance of all adult common sense but in complete submission to the rules of adolescent game-play footage aesthetics and photographic composition.

Smoke poured from his tortured Nike Airstream Numpty-Nukes as the best rubber that Hollywooden Footwear Inc could come up with entered a life or death struggle to wrestle his speed down from an inhuman but obviously technologically advanced Hollywooden six or seven miles a jogging hour (6 or 7 MPJH). Spinning wildly the gentleman tragically hit a small piece of gravel, flipped emotionally into a fundament over insurance-claim apex cartwheel, twanged the floppy "dog's tail" aerial of Blair's G-Wiz as he flew over the top and then landed upside down in an innocent tree. There his clothing promptly burst into non-homeland foreign-terrorist fanned flames and quickly spread to the peace, patriotism and lost Hollywooden-National innocence of the nearby god-fearing mid-west boy-meets-girl girl-gets-pregnant happy-ever-after-in-a-Ford-Pinto family-pavements.

'What on earth do you think it might be, Eric?'

'I think it's a load of dismal Hollywooden film-nellie who was scouting locations for a "movie" about demon-possessed Chevrolet Corvairs and their effect on a regular god-and-state-fearing semi-mixed race mixed-sex natural and intrinsically attractive, valuable and worthwhile Mom and Pop Hollywooden family who've moved to Ye Olde Englande to live as is their right because one of the children has only decades to live and they need to find the cure in a magical quasi-religious fairy fountain in European Tuscany but can't actually live there because it's not on any London signposts even though it was closer on the map than New York is to Florida and anyway they once left the dog home alone during a super-hero glut when the Hollywooden President wasn't very nice but saved the world anyway because he was a jet pilot and a nice god blessed Hollywooden and the Hollywooden "way of life" that we're all apparently insanely jealous of but haven't got the wherewithal or the political balls or firepower to get for ourselves a-men ready mit der lights und der camera und der action.'

'Yes, yes, the English God and I both bless Hollywoodenland and Tinsel Town and desperately risible cliche combined with lowest common denominator commercialism and implausible violence leading to dehumanisation, but I really meant that – up there' said Tony, pointing to the large flying saucer parked very neatly over Buckingham Palace like some vast tin dustbin lid.

'Oh that. That's a flying saucer. It was there last night at about ten o'clock when I turned The Tube off and locked up. I spoke to the constable about it and he says that England Yard will be sending a car down sometime this morning to investigate.'

'Oh. Well so long as someone knows about it. That's the main thing.'

The jogging Hollywooden director chap had by then extricated himself from the tree (by simple dint of falling out of it) and was running around the road, ablaze and in search of decent Hollywooden supporting props. A "gas" station preferably, complete with a refuelling hydrogen-hybrid school bus full of orphaned Carmelite ex-prostitute angel-faced nuns taking disadvantaged African-Hollywoodans to visit their sage old relatives in a Tennessee care-home before it is turned into an abandoned toxic spider mine by a thou$and-millionaire (a billionaire is a quite different thing) who wants to re-start the Hollywooden economy by mowing down the world-dominating Bolivian drug cartels with space satellites made from rare Indestructium by people who are supposed to be scientists and engineers but who haven't in fact mastered puberty yet.

In the Hollywooden gentleman's commercial dreams maybe a pair of crusty (Caucasian, always Caucasian) survivalists might go down well too if he could find some, especially if they both loved or looked like Dolly Parton, or had been Dolly Parton before surgery following an aeroplane crash. Better yet if they had guns, were founder members of the National Uzi Association and their camouflage-painted Chevrolet Patriot Citation Homeland Suburban Town-Car 6x6 Pick-Up GT was broken down in a zombie enclave at dusk on a fresh flesh-eating lava-flow caused by stolen nuclear weapons being 'sploded in a downtown Los Hollywood retired Policeman's apartment block where racial tensions were already running high, a wonderful non-paedophile Priest had just been shot during an Indo-Chinese Greek/Jewish wedding and the Republican Mayor had just cut the power and water and air-conditioning off. Something nice like that. Anything believably tragic, just to offset the unbalanced and oppressively unsophisticated atmosphere of his current overseas foreign non-Hollywooden location in the Not-Hollywood.

'Lovely morning Eric, isn't it?'

'It's splendid Tony, splendid.'

The pigeon agreed that it too was up its tits with the increasingly nonsensical output of mainstream commercial Hollywooden studios and the utter lack of films made therein for an audience not still wearing dental braces and a layer of adolescent acne. Then it gave a cheery "prrooh prrooh" and flapped away, crapping on the roof of Tony's car-substitute as it did so and causing about seventy guineas-worth of structural damage.

Tony waited as Eric put his bicycle clips back on before they went their separate ways. Tony went to leave himself a note to check the EBC news when he woke up after his morning full-length snooze on the chaise-short [an item of furniture originally owned by Napoleon]. Eric went to unchain the gates and flip the big switch to power-up the London Tube before the rush hour started.

An Australian backpacker, returning from her evening out spent sipping cocktails and discussing Descartes with friends, used the fire extinguisher from her Rough Guide survival pack to quench the Hollywood director chap's tired old conflagration, checked that he was OK considering and then left him smouldering gently on a bench next to a bus stop and a small but very relaxing advertisement for Ovaltine.

From his comfortable position on the bench the Hollywooden gentleman could see the alien flying saucer and was in a prime position to watch as a light blue Police Austin 1300 with creamy-white doors, revolving light on the roof and ner-ner siren went flying past at forty or possibly even forty-five miles an hour roughly thirty-two and a half minutes later (around about five past Sparrow-cough o'clock, a time always slightly to the left of the Beaufort O'Scale and not marked on Continental watches or clocks at all).

Naturally, London was beginning to wake up by then and several passers-by had to be contained using the new "kettling" technique. That's where the nice Riot Squad make potential Riotees a nice cup of tea instead of just duffing them up in a confined space away from cctv. To be totally safe the long arm of the law parked the Austin across the gates to Buckingham Palace and left the revolving blue light on, even though you couldn't really see it very well with the human eye in bright sunshine.

The least-senior Constable of the Panda-car team, Constable Stuart Irish, slipped into his white "traffic management" over-cuffs and busied himself with the matter of keeping the Riley Elf and the Sunbeam Alpine Mk1 traffic-jam moving, in-between self-consciously posing for photographs with a smiling and bowing Japanese tourist party. Both cars and all three tourists were very grateful and felt very safe.

The most-senior Constable, Constable Wayne Hey, carefully closing the big gates behind his big behind, went up to the big house in his very own peculiar "policeman's gait" to knock and to check that all was still well with the big Ma'am. He was taken straight through to the kitchen of course, where Her Majesty was having an unexpectedly early cup of tea. As he entered she checked that her dressing gown was tied properly, dabbed at her curlers and wondered if she'd got the last of the cold cream off her face.

'Thank you so much for coming at such short notice, Officer.'

'My pleasure, Ma'am, my pleasure. How may I be of assistance your Majesty?'

Elizabeth II led him out through the kitchen door and onto the little wood-decked breakfast area beyond. There was a nice stained pine table with its fringed canopy neatly folded, matching chairs and a barbecue under a canvas cover the same colour as the table umbrella. Several half-used open bags of charcoal, some empty beer barrels and a tired-looking Raleigh tandem bicycle with a dog-eared basket occupied the other corners. The enamelled crest affixed to the centre of the handlebars was a little chipped and rusty, hinting at the high mileage of the royal machine under tough city-centre conditions.

Elizabeth II sipped her tea and – using her empire-wielding pinkie – pointed upwards.

'One thinks one might have visitors' she whispered conspiratorially, falling – as royalty always have – into an uneasy collusion with The Law of The Land.

Philip wandered out to join them. 'One also hopes that one's visitors do not use their conveniences while in the station, so to speak, parked somewhat above one's old homestead as they are. Do you think they'll have slitty eyes, Officer?' he shouted in the way that very, very rich older deaf folks often do when they couldn't give an utter shit any more about offending anyone.

The Constable looked up.

'I couldn't say Sir, not yet. You can never tell how these things are going to pan out.' It was obvious that their Majesties were expecting him, as the Officer on the scene, to do something. He nibbled his pencil for a moment and considered the practicalities of the scene of the incident. 'Does One have a ladder, Sir?'

'Ladder?' mused Philip, almost tittering at the refreshingly innocent peasant domesticity of the request. Most people he came into contact with asked for knighthoods and patronage or whether he would mind if they "slept" with The Queen until her royal teeth rattled (in their usual lead-crystal whisky glass on the night-stand by the bed). 'A ladder?'

'Yes Sir. A wooden device for scaling heights, most often used by the Fire Brigade in the course of domestic feline rescues and suchlike. Two strong vertical parallel supports with a series of horizontal struts between allowing for manual incremental elevation of a person or persons unknown. I suspect that when the experts get here they'll be needing one soon enough.'

'I know what a ruddy ladder is, Officer. Just not certain One's got one to One's hand.' Philip turned to Cook who was gawping up at the underside of the flying saucer, runny duck egg and HP Sauce from her "third of three breakfast" morning sandwich dripping down her chins. 'Does One have a ladder? If not then could you have one swiftly manufactured and delivered?' Cookie wiped her face on her green sleeves and went to see.

Not having much in common with One, One or even the another, the conversation between Queen, Prince Philip and the Constable was pretty thin while they waited awkwardly, smiling at one another when absolutely necessary and checking their pink velvet slippers, hemp sandals and shiny hobnail arse-kicking boots respectively. [Princely Philip's hemp sandals were size 14 extra extra wide, extra-flat – as were Constable Hey's Police-blue velvet driving-slippers.]

In the shadow cast by the flying saucer overhead the morning had yet to properly warm up but the sky was still a nice blue at the edges and showed a certain promise.

The The Queen excused herself briefly from the proceedings and presently there came the sound of royal lead-pipe plumbing being commanded by use of a porcelain handle and heavy metal chain, followed by a cistern refilling noisily from the rooftop tank of chilled Windermere Carbonated Mineral. The sound of the cistern refilling did not quite drown out what could only, in any polite society, have been someone else somewhere nearby blowing an extended bass raspberry through an implausibly large sousaphone in order to expel a startled bullock trapped in the body of the instrument. The clank of the chain followed by the cistern emptying and refilling once more echoed through the open frosted window of the downstairs lav. The plumbing flow-rate dipped audibly for a moment, probably as the The Queen ran the water in the basin to wash her hands. Her Majesty re-joined them, looking refreshed and finally ready to face her official day.

'Lovely weather – er, for the time of year – don't you think?' offered Philip, ever the expert at ice-breaking but still looking as bored as a monkey in a zoo with no alcohol, no cigarettes, no porno magazines and no other monkey's bottoms to explore for crusty bits.

'Indeed, Your High Princeness Mr Philip sir, lovely weather. Indeed, so much so that the wife's thinking of changing over to the summer quilt very soon.'

'Quilt?' enquired Philip, but before the Constable could answer two Footmen jogged up with a brand new crepe-wrapped ladder supported at the shoulder on two battered (outdoor, heavy-work)

Georgian silver salvers.

'Well then, there we are. A ladder. Two strong vertical supports with a series of horizontal struts arranged between and allowing for an officer or officers unknown to boldly achieve manual incremental elevation to where no officer has gone before. We'll leave you to it, Officer or officers Unknown. Do let us know if we can be of any further assistance, knighthoods, patronage, that sort of nonsense. Cook will give you tea and a sandwich or some kedgeree or something.'

At the sound of her surname ("Cook") Cook dipped a curtsey, took one last glance upwards and went indoors to put on the kettle and broggle the Aga back up to eggy-temperature. Then she went into the palace hen house armed with a wooden prodding-spoon, to persuade some of the royal hens to lay some nice fresh eggs for the police force.

'Thank you, Your Honour. Your Highnesses. I will try to get this cleared up as soon as possible and with least fuss soonest mended worse things happen at sea mustn't grumble Sir, Ma'am.'

As H.R.H. and H.R.H. Senior processed regally away in their matching winceyette jim-jams Constable Hey could hear a heated discussion beginning – possibly re-beginning – about the New Year's Honours List and the Prince Consort's retiring Senior Squeeze. Her Majesty was saying something about Dame Yvette over her dead body. Philip's position on that was that Dame Yvette over Mrs HRH's dead body might be an interesting and stimulating position, at which point there could be heard the sound of a single, royal blow to the back of what sounded like a royal human head, followed by what sounded like a Prince Consort's body hitting the bees-waxed floor.

While the Footmen arranged the ladder against the wall of the wash-house Cook rustled up a nice cuppa and a fried eggy-weggy sandwich for them all. A scullery maid was given the task of washing up Cook's hen-prodding spoon. The hens in the royal kitchen yard all appeared to be walking as though it was national walk like a penguin day.

Constable Hey held his nose and used the telephone in the downstairs lav to check with his Sergeant. He was told to hold the fort and do what he thought best or whatever the The Queen told him to until nine o'clock and they could get hold of someone in authority in Whitehall and it would all be out of their hands then. The Sergeant promised to get more men down there as soon as he could to handle the traffic and to relieve Constable Irish at the gate. As he finished his call and replaced the receiver Constable Hey realised that all eyes, metaphorically speaking, were upon him. The big alien tiddlywink was on his patch and it was up to him to prevent the morning newspaper-flapping panic and indelicate tea-spoon tapping on saucer flying-saucer related public disorder that was obviously brewing. What to do though? What to actually do? The words of his grandmother (Inspector Hey, Anti-Squatter Squad) came back to him.

'You do not have to do anything but it may harm your promotion prospects if you do not do when being royally stiffed something which you might later rely on in your annual appraisal. Anything you do do in the face of overwhelming doo-doo may be given in evidence at your interview though so get in there and give it some wellie my son.'

Girding his loins, the brave constable asked decisively and selflessly, as inspired British Policemen often do do, that a cup of tea be taken out to Constable Irish at the gate (two sugars). Two sugars was Stu's preferred recipe for his Public Tea, not some sort of nom-de-nick or pet name. Stu's informal call-sign was, obviously, In the name of the Law. Wayne's call-sign was, rather confusingly in times of operational excitement, Constable. The Radio Car control centre generally avoided calling either of them by radio if it could.

Wayne wondered if the Footmen would please to hold the base of the ladder steady. Then he took a deep breath and made his jaw-droppingly dramatic announcement.

'I'm going up ... it's the only polite thing to do and we don't want to seem rude by delaying until the gentlemen from Whitehall get into their offices. Besides, I'm not having it on my service record that I didn't have the bottle just to say hello to a bunch of E.T.s. and check that their intention is not to cause a breach of the peace.'

A scullery maid with a congenital slack jaw and nervous disposition noisily dropped a shocked and awed saucepan into a sink, even though she wasn't supposed to have been listening, not at her domestic rank. She apologised to Cook, wiped her hands on her sack-cloth smock and set to work again with a steel scouring pad, tackling last evening's royal Madras crust on the new Prestige nesting pan-set that had been a gift from the King of Tonga-Tonga.

All eyes turned to the Constable. The steam in the kitchen had affected the frame but the painting itself was as fresh as the day it was accepted in payment of a below-stairs inter-departmental gambling debt. Then all eyes turned to Constable Hey again, three of them through the scullery sink-station window and a haze of hot Fairy Liquid fumes.

One rung at a time, steadying himself by alternately squinting from under his helmet and then gently biting his tongue, the Constable made his way up the ladder until he was level with the top of the outside wash-house roof. From there he could see clear to the tomato greenhouse and the three royal wheelie bins (Royal Recycling Waste, Royal Gardening Waste and Royal Rubbish-in-General). Far below him were the expectant eyes of Cook, Cyril and Bert, all bearing a strong resemblance to human wheelie bins and looking about as savoury. Cook was biting on a knuckle and for once it was one of her own and not a greasy piece of a spit-roasted piglet with salted and fatty skin a-flapping.

'Just you be careful up there – I had an uncle once who fell off a roof.' she warned.

'Did he die?' asked Constable Hey, looking – against all sensible advice - down.

'No – he moved to the coast and retired on his medical terms.'

'Oh. Well, I'll be careful. I don't like the coast.'

Removing his helmet - the strap got in the way in much the manner of a hang-man's rope got in the way of a miscreant's breathing processes - the Constable craned his head upwards.

'Hello? Hello? Is there anybody there?'

Cyril muttered into his sleeve 'Can you hear me, Mother?' and was promptly damp tea-towel whipped by Cook. Bert quietly ventured "Knock once for yes and twice for no ..."

'Helloo?' ventured a wobbling Constable once again, oblivious to the giggly civilian kerfuffle below.

From far, far, above him there came the sound of massive machinery whirring into action on the underbelly of the great flying saucer. The sound could only be likened to that horribly familiar chorus made every other Wednesday (if clement) by all of the circular-saws at Smithfield being started up all at once and then fed the desiccated bones of the especially bony and circular-saw bound farm animals that nice humans like to eat and also feed to their bloody-lipped, fang-jawed baby children.

'Look!' shouted Cyril, quite unnecessarily and making the full weight of the law wobble again on his perch a-top the ladder. 'They're opening up!' For some, probably hormonal, reason Cyril was holding aloft the coconut husk mat from the back door, the one that said simply "Welcome! Please wipe your feet."

Cook crossed her arms. 'Well they needn't think they're bringing back Elvis. They can have ruddy Cliff Richard as well if they like but they're not bringing back Elvis. I've just brought (SIC) a new eclectic mains wireless and what's the point of that if they bring back ruddy Elvis. No, I'm not having it.' She tapped her foot in that way that meant "discussion closed, fetch me the barrel of Custard Creams".

A sparkling and obviously alien electric blue light grew from a giant mechanical sphincter at the centre of the flying saucer. It increased in intensity as the opening slowly un-puckered like a corgi about to fart the fart to end all corgi-farts. Traffic on The Mall stopped, drivers stepped out of their motorcars and opened the bonnets in the fashion of some sort of synchronised car mechanic display team. They all, to a man, tried to kid on that they were checking for loose distributor caps or excessively dusty thrumble-gudgeons while they were of course actually watching the flying saucer. All hoped upon hope that, despite the ablutions-prone nature of the early morning hour, the opening of the mechanical sphincter didn't signify that inappropriate alien plumbing was being used. Not over The Palace! Never that, surely? Unless, of course, the aliens were Cling-ons of some sort.

A small vicar, in town for the unveiling of the fresh Autumn cassock collection by Black, Black, & Blacker-Styll (deceased) of Jermyn Street, began to pray. 'Our Corporate Father, who art in Hog-Heaven, I think – yes, I'm quite sure – God be thy name. Give us this day our daily stipend and please, please, please don't let the aliens dump on The Monarchy or be otherwise overtly unfriendly in any way. Amen.' With that he withdrew his card, cash and receipt from the Holy of Holies - the Holey in the Wall on the side of St Paul's - and went in search of a greasy spoon for breakfast. Preferably a greasy spoon blessed with a surfeit of sausage, egg, magic mushrooms, fried bread, tomato, beans and tea.

Big Ben struck nine and at the sound of the last, very stoic, slightly flat, there'll probably always be an England "bong" there was a rumbling thunderclap and the electric blue alien beam from the alien's massive alien craft twisted and tore itself into a deluge of super-powerful 150+ watts of LED down-lighter terror as a telescopic boom extended, thunk, thunk, thunk, thunk, thunk and stopped just short of the wash-house roof. The Hollywooden "Movie" Director film chap, still smouldering on his bench next to the (oddly rectangular) Ovaltine advertisement by the bus stop, gasped in wonder and admiration at the theatricality of it all and raised a framework of sooty forefingers and thumbs to imagine it against a simple backdrop of nucular (sic) explosions and giant sentient dinosaurs created by radiation and tuna over-fishing with racial overtones and a kidnapped President.

It was just a lift though in the final analysis, and most definitely not an elevator, and it stopped with the doors facing Constable Hey.

With a very cheery "kerscreech-clunk-ping" the sliding doors opened and yonder brave Police Constable fell backwards, rolled for his life and was only arrested by contact with the royal decking below, breaking his little Official Police-Business Pencil in the process. From deep inside the machine a chilling mechanical voice warned 'Please mind the doors'.

The slimy writhing tentacle and exploratory skinless eye-stalk of an alien peered out of the lift and cautiously snaked around to look down into the Royal kitchen courtyard. The eye fixed its gaze on the little flock of hens and some vast, awful, blobby semi-internal brain-gland compared them to the diagram of a Human Being scratched into the surface of a gold-plated “Voyager” LP record held in the grip of another tentacle. The eye-stalk then moved on to the wheelie bins and made the same comparison. Third time being lucky the whole Universe over, the eye-stalk eventually crept around to the bipedal gathering of slightly-developed primates, checked twice against the outline of a Human of more “standard” or “Baywatch” proportions and then, apparently satisfied, lobbed the Voyager LP over its shoulder. You can always tell when aliens have previously accidentally landed in a zoo or a pig farm or an art college and then proceeded to initiate contact on the basis of sloppy assumptions, they are so much more cautious from then on in.

There almost immediately followed the booming, snarling howl of an un-Earthly alien tongue.

‘Sorry! So sorry! We did tell the designers that this lift design was a bit over-theatrical and that all that was really needed was a ramp or a rope or something but you know these artistic professionals with their flourishes and finishing touches. Are you quite medically alright, little paramilitary uniformed disciplinarian alien life-form, after your sudden dis-altitudination? My sensors indicate the sudden partial dis-manufacture of your wood & graphite delayed-communication device and the endustment of the buttocks of your blue serge lower-limb coverings.’

Cook looked up from the flustered Constable, deputised herself and answered on his behalf. ‘He’s fine, Mr Alien Sir, just a bit bruised and, yes, he’s broken his little pencil and dust-encrusted his hairy arse but he’ll live. I did warn him about the coast, but they never listen, do they?’ she mumbled, before lifting the aforesaid Constable up with one hand and dusting him down with the other, her latest loaf of buttered hot toast held safely between her NHS teeth (available in pink or blue plastic or, for five guineas extra, in blackened “foreigner-shocking” English oak).

The Senior Footman, Cyril, stepped closer to the outhouse guttering and peered up into the light. Someone had to face up to this world-changing unfathomable horror and, in the light of the Constable’s graphic graphite injury and the limitations of Cook’s lexicon, the buck now stopped with him. He felt it important to not over-react or precipitate verbal inter-species discomfiture.

'Air hair lair! Whom may one say is calling?' he enquired pleasantly.

The alien visitor then clomped out into full view, making the wash-house roof creak a little under the strain as he struggled to keep his balance on the tiles. Unfamiliar as he was with the gravitation-resisting properties of moss-covered Welsh slate with cast-iron guttering, Flemish bonds and granite quoining the alien moved with a certain structurally-inappropriate confidence. A confidence not seen, moreover, since John Hurt relied on a Company thermal vest to keep his ribcage from exploding in space over the dinner table. In space, no-one can hear you starching your underwear I suppose. But I digress. The alien seemed at least friendly and enthusiastic, which after the French Cultural Delegation visit of the previous week was a welcome change.

'Well hair lair there yourself old sport! I am Ambassador Supreme Commander Eek-eek-wibble-squeak-growl-roar-fart of the planet Wibble-squeak-growl-fart-roar-eek-roar. We were just passing by your long arm of the Galaxy and wondered if this might be a convenient time to call?' The Supreme Commander passed down his calling card. It was very nice quality embossed cream vellum with a plain sans serif typeface in a dark sepia and burgundy. The telephone number was awfully long (and would hence probably be quite expensive to call) and the Ambassador's email address was Eek-eek-wibble-squeak-growl-roar-fart@Wibble-squeak-growl-fart-roar-eek-roar.pla (the new "dot planet" top-level domain). Apparently he kept a personal blog at uww (Universe-wide-web) dot knitting-as-an-alternative-to-stasis-for-inter-stellar-travel dot wordpress dot pla. 'If nothing else, we were hoping that we might use your loo. Is it convenient?'

'The loo?'

'The moment.'

'I am certain that it is Sir. Welcome to Earth, to England, to that implicit geographical tautology and, more specifically, to Buckingham Palace. If you'll follow me I'll show you through to a withdrawing room and advise Her Majesty that you have called.'

The alien ambassador coughed. 'Um - to the loo?'

Cyril heard "toodle-oo" and wondered why they were leaving so soon. Then the penny dropped. 'Oh, of course – to the loo - to the right.'

A cheery 'Just a tiddle-i-po' seemed an awfully odd thing for an Ambassador to say, but he felt the need to say it anyway. The scullery maid – not having been born yesterday – handed the Ambassador a fresh toilet roll and went to fetch a can of heavy duty air-freshener and the plunger. 'Ying tong my arse' she muttered, railing afresh at her lot in life.

Cook dropped another splendid curtsey (while still bodily supporting Constable Hey) as the aliens filed past and though her kitchen. 'They'll be needing tea too before long I expect' she grumbled, watching them go and form an orderly queue.

'Probably posh biscuits as well if you ask me' said Bert. 'Right, Constable, let's get you cleaned up and then we can see about getting you a fresh little pencil. We've got some somewhere with the Royal Crest on them – picked out in that real fake gold if you will – and each with a little eraser at the blunt end. The erasers are a bit scratchy but still, beggars can't be chewers as they say. Now, H, F, HB, B, 2B or not 2B – that is the question, Constable. Whether tis knobblier on the pocket notebook etcetera etcetera.'

As it happened Her Majesty had already taken to her regular morning semi-skimmed Jersey milk hip-bath by the time Cyril, the Senior Footman, came through with the news and, rather disconveniently, Ma'am also had a luncheon appointment with representatives from the Royal Society for the Detection and Bio-Rhythm Nullification of Certain Small Belgian Detectives. The manner of Her Majesty's podiatric pumicing suggested to Cyril that a short postponement was in order.

The message was relayed to the withdrawing room where the Ambassador had been busily engaged discovering that the legs of a Louis XIV chair were not in fact designed to splay out under his weight or to spring back into the upright position when he stood. Everyone pretended to not notice of course.

Ambassador Supreme Commander Eek-eek-wibble-squeak-growl-roar-fart indicated that he was sorry for the inconvenience and was quite happy to call again later. Tiffin was duly arranged and explanations made, after which the aliens returned to their saucer with a tin of shortbread, some Dutchy Originals lemon curd and a soft-cover handbook of royal etiquette bearing the rather endearingly modern and non-threatening title “So, you’re going to meet Her Majesty already ...”.

Ambassador Supreme Commander Eek-eek-wibble-squeak-growl-roar-fart left a small glass paperweight containing some Dark Matter, a desktop-toy Higgs-Boson generator and a bound set of the Concise Illustrated History of Planet Wibble-squeak-growl-fart-roar-eek-roar, its Sentient Flora and Fauna, Rock Formations and Meteorological Systems, Chemistry, Biology and Detailed Social Development, from Planetary Formation to the Present Day with especial regard to presenting the Dominant Species in a non-partisan or threatening way to the non-indigenous while still preserving the magic and mystique of life within the Twelve Tribes, the Seven Sects and the Three Ruling Houses. The Appendices (in several further volumes) detailing Wibble-squeak-growl-fart-roar-eek-roar Architecture, Horticulture, Viticulture and Pop Culture had been playfully translated into Haiku format to make them more appealing. Workmen with big shoulders, builder’s bums and an easy familiarity with Japanese poetry were summoned (via hidden specialised bell-pull near the fireplace) to move the set to a room that boasted a reinforced concrete floor.

The electric-blue electric light presently disappeared as though someone had flicked a switch (in fact, they had) and the lift thunk, thunk, thunk, thunk, thunked telescopically back up into the saucer section carrying a much-relieved Ambassador. Traffic on The Mall began moving again although folks were careful just to doff their hats to each other and to not discuss the mystery problems with their cars’ grindey-grindey bearings or crossbeam grease-nipple dippers. None even hinted that they might have seen a flying saucer disgorging ambassadors from the planet Wibble-squeak-growl-fart-roar-eek-roar. Few were prepared to risk impoliteness by precipitously anticipating the issue of the proper lexicographical and, specifically, pronunciation standards relating to references to creatures that looked like a cross between recently a machine-washed Teddy Bear and the Flying Spaghetti Monster. This had a lot to do with being English and very little to do with the difficulties in getting the civilised human tongue to pronounce Wibble-whatever with a very rude fart noise in it. We English are not averse to farting if we absolutely have to in order to make a point, it's just that if you re-name things properly once then there's no need to you know ever again and everyone's happy.

It was already quite clear though that a similar tack would have to be taken with the aliens to that dictated with Foreigners who clung to silly Spanish variety "th" sounds or to "U" sounds that required undignified lip-curling, or to languages that one could only successfully speak with wet bronchitis or near-fatal pneumonia (such as "oh you have the Welsh do you?"). The aliens and the alien planet would have to be unilaterally re-christened to something sensible and re-christened soon. No doubt notification would be sent to them when necessary, possibly after colonisation, civilisation and the installation of a proper railway system with standardised timetables and penny fares for Third Class travel.

Between breakfast and royal tiffin Constable Stu had to move the Area Car no fewer than four times to allow access for the big black Rover and Wolseley limousines that buzzed like motorised flies between Buckingham Palace, Whitehall and Westminster. Everyone was skulking around and singing Guess Who's Coming to Tiffin or trying to remember the phrase 'Klaatu barada nikto' just in case.

At three o'clock the guests were beginning to explore sitting down, the humans in hardwood deckchairs and the aliens on their favoured bean-bags. This took some time since the aliens seemed anxious to be introduced to the bean-bags and took great offence at their indolent silence and refusal to return a high-six or an energetic stomach-crash-bounce (the standard greetings of the Blob People, who all resembled bean-bags).

Constable Stuby-baby was finally taken off shift and went home to his little terrace in Camberwell, tired but pleased to have done his part for inter-species relations. The aliens looked so very much like his family on his wife's side. Once he'd changed out of his uniform and locked his whistle & truncheon away in the steel cabinet required by the terms of his Concealed Whistle & Truncheon Licence he put the dog on the lead and went to get some salad leaves and tomatoes from the allotment, ready for when the Missus got home from her job at the brewery. She was a mash-stirrer and he loved her with all of his heart. Well, more accurately, he loved her Staff Allowance of beer and was quite fond of the smell of hops that pervaded her every crevice. When she returned after a hard day's work, warm and moist from hefting her paddle, it was like cuddling the essence of a pub that had been retro-fitted with breasts and steadying, rugby-player's thighs.

Oh gosh, I've drifted off at a tangent again.

Cook had settled on tea, cakes, crumpets, scones and biscuits on the lawn and had advised Her Majesty's Social Secretary's Social Secretary's Receptionist of such. All was ready exactly when she said it would be, including the thin, crustless, diagonal cuts of white bread and butter so beloved of the high and the mighty. The only change that was made to Cook's plan was to serve things on Spode plates and tables rather than directly on the lawn.

'Another slice of thin parliamentary bread and butter, Lord D. Masser?'

'Well, if you insist, Prime Minister Brownaughs. Some constituency honey too would go down rather splendidly for tea – if there's any left, that is, for the more right wing among our august company.'

An aide cat-walked across the lawn, not quite certain whether grass was allowed for subordinates. He had a message.

'A trans-Atlantic telephone call has been received from Hollywood, sir. Apparently they have heard about our guests. They seemed reluctant to engage in the niceties of polite conversation and simply left a message to the effect that the – oh, now what job title did they give them? Oh yes – the Hollywooden Leaders of the Free World have taken off, I presume in some sort of aeroplane convoy, and are heading in the direction of England with an expected time of arrival twenty-three hundred hours on something called PST. They are insisting that Heathrow Airport be closed to all other traffic for the landing and that an area of one hundred miles in all directions be placed under martial law and Hollywooden Army control for the duration of the Presidential visit. They give assurances that internment and use of Agent Orange will be kept to the minimum required to ensure their own safety during their inefinite stay. No contact is to be attempted with the aliens until the Hollywooden experts arrive, at which point they will require all of our data and our complete obedience in all matters.'

Brownaughs furrowed his brow. 'The who?'

'The Hollywooden Leaders of the Free World sir. The message also stated that the M4 Motorway would be required to be closed to the public for the Hollywooden Presidential Humvee convoy to form up. Accommodation at the palace would be required for all of the Leaders of the Free World sir, that list including James Cromwell, Bill Pullman, Morgan Freeman, Michael Douglas, Stanley Anderson, Anthony Hopkins, Jon Voigt, Robin Williams, Gene Hackman, Billy Bob Thornton, Lloyd Bridges and of course, Leslie Nielsen.'

'Any of them Republicans?'

'It's difficult to tell, sir.'

Ambassador Supreme Commander Eek-eek-wibble-squeak-growl-roar-fart, the most senior of the dozen or so aliens present, watched the exchange and sipped his tea through a straw (a footman had bravely ventured to suggest that eating each cup and saucer with the tea might constitute a social faux-pas in some circles or even cause digestive problems over time).

'A problem, Prime Minister? Our schedule is flexible and I shouldn't want to get in the way or inconvenience you. We would be happy to call again, again, even later.'

He flexed his tentacles, removed the straw and exposed his slobbering second jaw in the equivalent of a very polite and actually very genuine alien smile.

'Just grumblings from the filmed entertainment industry, Mr Ambassador, just grumblings from the filmed entertainment industry. I shan't be a second.'

The P.M. spoke to the aide. 'Assure the gentlemen from Hollywood of my best wishes, advise Leslie Nielsen that I should be pleased to meet him Thursday week, at about ten or eleven. Advise the other pilots that they are welcome to circle quietly and watch or, if that would prove inconvenient, to go away. Ask Sir Baden-Powell to scramble a couple of RAF Jet-Spitfires to meet the convoy mid-air and repeat the message in single-syllable exothermic air-to-air communication if necessary.'

'Tell them to kindly bugger off, we're busy, and blow them out of the sky if they argue Sir?'

'Exactly.'

'Very good, Sir.' Ed, the aide, walked away across the lawn and beckoned to his Aide's Aide to finish his aide-refreshing lemonade and come to his Head Aide's aid with what had just been said.

'Hello Ed!' said the Head Aide's aide, Fred, 'Have some of this aide-refreshing lemonade that Cook's made, I've kept it cool in the shade of the potting shed.' There was a shaking of Head Aide's heads. 'I'm afraid that there's no time for aide-refreshing lemonades in the shade for this or any aide, Fred, after what the PM just said.' Fred had been afraid of as much. He began to wonder if they ought to be drinking tea instead.

'Oh dear, Ed' said Fred, 'we're starting to heterodyne again whenever we refer to each other – perhaps we should use our middle names. Mine's Dick, what's yours?'

Ed looked startled. 'Dick? Oh dear, mine's Rick.'

Fred looked pained. Ed made a unilateral decision.

'You'd surely feel like a dick, Dick, calling me Rick, better stick to Ed, Fred, a least while we're on duty. You're going to like this duty, it's a beauty...'

As they marched away to make the PM's arrangements Ed tried one final time to find some workable epithetical compromise, but it seemed that even Fred's nickname at school was unsuitable, for Ed's surname was Rowlocks, and that rhymed horribly with Bowlocks. Such are the painful rigours of life in the English Secret Service.

While the aides were in deep and meaningful conversation, Ambassador Eek-eek-wibble-squeak-growl-roar-fart noticed that the sun had crept around and that parts of Her Majesty, The Sol System Queen, Elizabeth The Two'th, were in danger of getting overly warmed. He signalled to the huge Mothership parked in the air above to shift a couple of yards to the left so that she would remain in gentle and bird-twitteringly cool shade.

Eek stirred his third cup and accepted a Garibaldi in his saucer. 'Ah – northern Hollywooden including Alaska, Hawaii, a large chunk of Mexican California and a bit of Guanotanamo Bay if you must but absolutely none of "Frigging French" Canada as we were told in no uncertain terms by several yellow taxicab drivers. Once, that is, we'd found a cab driver who could speak Hollywooden-English. Our earlier missions did try to make contact there a few times. Northern Hollywooden that is, not Frigging French Canada.' He delicately dipped his Garibaldi into his tea, suggesting a familiarity with English biscuits and their abuse beyond the alien's official experience.

'Not just with the on-set sound stage Hollywooden government either, we tried to make contact with everybody and anybody from caterers to prospective screenplay writers. They shot at us. All of them. We waved little white flags, we offered presents, tried contact in obvious, public, places such as Devil's Tower National Monument and also in more private, restrained, circumstances such as closed, deserted, diners and with men too long without sleep. We gave them translated and easy to pronounce control phrases for our robot sentry, the Gort, which we'd modelled on a robot from an old Earther DVD so that it would look unthreatening. Still they shot at us. I believe that the first ambassador to Earth, Klaatu-barada-nikto-burp-growl-squeak-fart-oohmib-ollocks, is still "on ice" in something called a "bunker" in their "Nevada Dessert".'

Eek finished his Garibaldi and reached for a crisp and crunchy Custard Cream.

'We have asked for the return of his remains and his ship repeatedly but all we have attracted so far is a small probe bearing the name "Voyager". It seems to be exhorting peace while at the same time carrying threatening diagrams showing us the quite – if you'll pardon me – utterly monstrous proportions of Human genitalia. There's also some chit-chat from a peanut farmer, the Pygmy girl's initiation song of Zaire and a lot of poisonous Uranium-238 on the cover. Several of our diplomatic team were killed before we realised that the "record" thingy had been lethally laced with radioactivitiousness.'

Her Majesty nodded sagely and dunked her Ginger Nut with unthinking ceremony. 'Oh dear. If one isn't terribly careful, choosing a present can present so many opportunities for offence. I also believe that their "yellow cab drivers" aren't actually yellow, it's just their vehicles. As a child I imagined jaundice to be rife in Hollywood for some reason, possibly to do with the costs of private healthcare and the universal presence of private swimming pools in the gardens.'

The soggy half of the royal biscuit dropped into the royal tea-cup and was immediately fished out by the clean-fingered chap the Queen keeps on hand for such comestible emergencies. The Official Biscuit-Retriever returned to his position behind Her Majesty and re-commenced staring at the horizon.

'Indeed so, indeed so.' said the Ambassador. 'It was all very confusing. In the end we did some unofficial sight-seeing, a little shopping for cheap shite at Walmart, took the opportunity to vaporise Elvis for crimes against popular music and then went home to reconsider our whole approach.'

'Quite understandable, Ambassador. May I press you to the last buttered crumpet?' asked the P.M., feeling quite out of the conversation and quite annoyed that the chocolate on his chunky Kit-Kat had melted more than he wanted and had dripped down his old school tie. Stocks were getting low these days of Grimsby Whitgift Comprehensive stripe in a pure polyester clip-on.

'Oh. Would that be appropriate? I'm afraid that you'll have to show me how. It's not hot, is it?' replied the Ambassador.

'Well spotted, Ambassador, no, it's gone cold – I shall send for more.' The P.M. nodded to a footman who took the offending crumpet away and hurried to fetch fresh in well-warmed Georgian silverware.

As soon as he was out of human sight the waiter scoffed the crumpet. A slightly worried ambassador had used a removable eye on one of his telescopic stalks to watch the waiter hurry away and whispered a query to his personal alien-aide. '"Press you to" – purely idiomatic or possibly painfully literal in a hot butter sense?

Research and report please, Priority Maximus (for that was the aide's nickname when on duty).'

'I must confess, Your Majesty, that our earlier overtures also involved what I believe - from memory, correct me if I'm wrong - was then known as the socialist red "Union of Soviet Cyclist Republics" or something with a backwards "R" or an upside down "P" or some such. Mockba or Moss Cow, I think was the chosen population centre for our approach – they seemed to have a really nice, wide open square space in the middle of the main conurbation where we could land. Our choice was based purely upon geographical extent this time, rather than the volume of electric radio and television wave output and sheer fossil-fuel consumption that had led us initially to Hollywooden.'

The P.M., hoping that this "Your Majesty" referred to him, opened his mouth to make some witty diplomatic quip about his own experiences with upside down pees and gravity but was beaten to it by The Queen.

'Oh yes? They always seemed obsessed with Uranium too whenever we tried to contact them. They seemed to want to send us large and unsolicited quantities of Uranium 235 and Uranium-238 derived Plutonium 239 for some unfathomable or possibly inscrutable reason. We sent them some nice homosexual boys – Philby, Maclean, Burgess and Quite-Blunt. At least, I think that's what they were called. Philip would know, I should check with him later.' The Queen looked quizzical and brushed scone crumbs from her lap. 'Perhaps you had more success?'

'With Philip?'

'With the Russians.'

'Oh. No. They seemed to think that we were from Hollywooden. They shot at us too, although with less ammunition than the inhabitants of Hollywooden, I believe that there was a shortage of bullets of a calibre to suit the age of the guns in use. Early research suggested that they had used almost all of their ammunition before we arrived to shoot dissidents, poets and university professors.'

'Oh dear. Did you try sending them some Cambridge nellies?'

'We sent them the framed original schematics for the Wartburg

353. All variants including the Estate model and the pick-up.'

'How kind and thoughtful of you. What exactly is a Wartburg 353?' enquired Her Majesty, trying to fish a scratchy little pebble of un-dunked Ginger Nut out of her cleavage.

'It was an abstract mechanical sculpture by one of our more avant-garde artists, intended to communicate the finer points of sub-faster than light species'sies two-stroking fossilised-fuel local transport policy in a fictional off-world engineering-dystopia. It had wheels so that it could be moved easily from exhibition to exhibition.'

'Did the Rooskies like it?'

'They seemed to think it was a "fine proletariat motor vehicle" and promptly made and sold over one million scaled-up copies of it – commercially! To this day they haven't let on that they are anything but serious about misusing it. It had drum-brakes, all round, and a top speed of nearly eight fretspliggs a quilliquode on the flat. They seemed to think that the only guidance system it might need was along the lines of a semi-industrialised peasant called Boris who was out of his skull on home-brew, Karl Marx and the unaccustomed velocity. It's quite, quite terrifying. When not slaving in some dark satanic factory, whole Rooskie nest-groups ended up screaming around the countryside in poorly-manufactured copies of some purely sardonic artwork.'

'Oh dearski' said Her Majesty, not wholly in response to the Ambassador's automotive-related dystopian terror, for the Ginger Nut crumb was proving to be beyond her dignified reach. She looked absentmindedly to the horizon, as one might during a medical inner-knee or upper-bottom examination, thus triggering the Official Biscuit Retriever's professionally impersonal white cotton glove with tea-stained fingers to fish it out on her behalf and to toss it to a ravening corgi.

'Indeed, oh dearski indeed. The Rooskies also randomly either offered us scalding hot potato soup and freezing Stolichnaya while they shot at us or else insisted that we ingest salted, pressed, eggs from an amphibian known simply as "The Sturgeon" - while they still made preparations to shoot and dissect us.'

'How unfortunate. One remembers being presented with potato

soup at some state visit function or other. Quite inedible, even after a whole bottle of emergency Stolly in the back of the official Rolls.' Her Majesty impatiently batted away the white cotton glove with tea-stained fingers that was gently squirting anti-Ginger Nut talcum powder between the otherwise already quite alabaster royal boobie-woobies.

E. Rex – as her household rather gender-inaccurately and wholly unofficially referred to her amongst themselves - poured herself another china cup (and saucer, naturally) of Rosie Lea and popped in three little sweeteners. These were of course saccharine sweeteners, not rolled-up and untraceable used banknotes of One's realm. One added some pasteurised cow-squeezings too. That is to say, the milk was pasteurised, the cow was quite untreated in terms of heat, although the farmer had been known to poke it with a stick on high days and alternate dry Bank Holidays. One's first sip produced an expression rather like a chimpanzee in a tiara and a cloud of talcum powder trying to smile for the cameras. One's second sip produced an expression rather like a chimpanzee in a tiara and a cloud of talcum powder trying to smile for the cameras. We can't be bothered telling you what the third sip did but if you got through the Eleven Plus successfully then you might just be able to guess. It was a very good tea despite being picked in a humid foreign climate by people who were, worryingly, not to be seen in any textbook actually ever washing their hands.

'Ambassador, I'm awfully curious – what was it that eventually made you realise that the only way to make meaningful contact with the peoples of the Earth was through England?'

The Ambassador, mentally distracted by tourists waving from an open-topped red tourbus, failed to stop one of his awfully curious nose-eye stalks peeping down Her Majesty's cleavage and sniffing at the talc. A flunky in buckled court shoes and wig swept under the roving nose-eye stalk imposition with a silver tray and offered it back to the Ambassador. I should hastily add that the flunky was also wearing other standard clothing as well as the buckle shoes and wig – the weather was warm but one should never push the seasons in re string vests or insulated y-fronts.

The Ambassador accepted the eye-nose stalk, not quite sure

where it had been or why. That was one of the disadvantages to having several discrete functional brains that only shared information with each other once or twice a day. You never quite knew what your other more domestically-minded brains were thinking or doing. Some male Humans have a similar coordination problem with their internal brains and their trouser attachments – so much to ogle, so few opportunities to think about it properly or discreetly or to run reality checks.

'Oh, well, do let me tell you your Maj.' The Ambassador re-crossed several of his legs, ready to enthuse. 'We finally noticed that the English seem to do a rather splendid line in Pomp & Peaceable Ceremony, as opposed to the rest of the planet which seems to specialise in Pump-Action & Bloody Acrimony. Our researchers had begun their early global explorations in Cape Spear and worked roughly West-wards following the sun. I've never seen such a rate of researcher burn-out, it was quite depressing and never more so than during meal times. After we'd been ritually offered MackyDee's Cow's-all Burgers, Colonel Sodbucket's Kentucky-effed Chicken, French Toast with icing sugar on it (can you believe?), over-cooked Lau-Lau with "Fries", sushi and Fugu, live Witchetty grubs, thousand year-old eggs, boiled pet doggy, fried locust, sheep's eyeballs, mozzarella and basil "pizza pie lika da Italian Herr Doktor Professor Mamma Öetker Limited-a used-a to make-a freshly frozen", smoked AnimalWurst with boiled and then re-pickled cabbage, and finally frog's legs flambe we were quite prepared to just go home and cross Earth off the tourist maps. Tea with lemon rather than with milk was the final, non-potable straw. It was all quite, quite ridiculous.'

The ambassador forgot himself and reached out to touch Her Majesty's psychedelic-paisley pattern kaftan sleeve cuff for emphasis, and patted her on the wrist.

'Then, at last, we slipped into England and realised that we weren't the only ones who recognised that just because you can eat something it doesn't necessarily follow that you should.'

Everyone present nodded, like novelty toy St. George's flag-waving Bulldogs on the rear parcel shelf of a Triumph 2500TC being driven on the correct left-hand side of a tree-lined black tarmac road with decent white lines, proper self-cleaning cat's eyes, pedestrian pavements, well-tended hedgerows and mercury-vapour lighting on concrete lamp posts.

The Ambassador was waxing lyrical, obviously as deliriously happy as a Lincolnshire badger with freshly laundered white cotton underwear and the whole day off from being gassed, shot or baited.

'I tell you, your Maj - roast potatoes and Yorkshire pudding, proper trifle, treacle sponge and custard, asparagus, Cox's Orange Pippins, Bakewell Tart, Cheddar cheese, Stilton, free-range boiled egg and volunteer professional "soldiers", Marmite on decent hot toast – we knew we'd found hog heaven. Then one of our researchers nipped out during the Men's Finals at Wimbledon and came back with strawberries and cream. We wept, we literally wept.'

'Why? Who was playing?' interjected the P.M., completely missing the point again to make it forty-love up so far in favour of the intellectually-challenged corgi licking his balls under the table.

He was ignored by All and Sundry, the other two of the three corgis under the table who were licking their own balls (ready for evening tennis in the kennel yard).

'Then our researchers noticed something really curious – at service bottlenecks you voluntarily auto-sort chronologically into linear displacements, even during periods of high consumer motivation!'

'You mean, in England we queue?'

'Yes! Not even the Vulcans are civilised enough for that - and you seriously do not want to try your luck in a Klingon Home-Base DIY January Sale on Kro'nos.' The Ambassador absent-mindedly touched an old half-price mixer-tap shaped scar above one of his foreheads before shuddering, burying the memory and continuing. Klingons could be so single-minded when it came to home improvements.

'In England traffic really does give way to pedestrians on Zebra crossings. Flashing one's headlights actually does mean "after you", not "get out of my way, eat my unburned hydro-carbons, kiss my GT arse and die". Access to an ambulance is not via chip & pin swipe card! You even bury your dead!'

Lord D. Masser, the amply-arsed sitting head of a standing committee charged with extracting metaphorical oil from literally troubled foreign waters so to speak, leapt to the defence of damned continental Europe on the last point. 'Well, to be fair, Ambassador, the ground is awfully hard throughout most of Europe. You need a stonemason's chisel to just bury the news in any place East of Calais. You just don't see a really decent English flower garden anywhere abroad for that reason.'

The alien ambassador was in full flow though and dismissed the flimsy foreign excuse with a snap of an opposable-claw and a tightly-targeted melodious but malodorous disbursement of largely-gaseous alimentary by-products. Notable Benny: it was the evolution of the aliens' opposable-claw that had allowed them to drop down from the flaming purple coral trees of Epsilon Four-Zero Gamma and begin using power-tools and soft toilet-paper

'If only we'd started our research at Pen Dal-aderyn and worked eastwards – we would only have had to travel as far as Lady Wood Park before we began to find civilisation.' Disconcertingly, the Ambassador made his last remark in English but with an amazingly good Welsh accent. At least, "good" in the sense of briefly amusing perhaps or quite telling, socially, since he'd only flown over Cardiff once, and that at some high velocity.

The Ambassador, as during his fly-over of Cardiff, was almost unstoppable and continued in spite of his very recently sprained tonsils. 'Pimms! Three-day eventing! Bristol cars! Lawns! Stonehenge! Morris dancers! Maddy Prior and Steeleye Span! The Boat Race! Joanna Lumley! Chatsworth House!'

'Ah - on that happy note, Ambassador' said the Queen, butting gently in, 'we would like to offer you full use of Buck Hice during your stay. Cook's quite competent. The staff can arrange the best seats at any of the London shows of course and there's also an open invitation to appear as a guest on Breakfast Television tomorrow. I believe it's a "popular entertainment show" whatever that might be, and that it is supposed to be very good if you have a book to promote, or something. A biography perhaps, or something on the recent fall of the Roman Empire.'

'Thank you, Your Maj ...'

'Oh, no formalities here, please. Just call me Rex, Ambassador. Everyone else does. I believe it's short for E. Rex.'

A lady in waiting twitched, nervously, disastrously, and then froze like hunted prey, as a regal and royal E-Rex very carefully and very deliberately caught her eye. The silent look communicated, quite simply; 'Lavinia, my curtsy-dipping dear, I thought I told you to get this thing fixed – if it ends up in someone's soup this evening I shall confiscate it, prescription prosthesis or no, and then you'll have to wear the pirate patch instead and you know how that makes the corgis behave when they are in rutting season.'

The alien Ambassador appeared oblivious, at least in terms of the ophthalmic gaff. Several of his tentacles were casually stroking a corgi, assessing the bone to meat ratio, while one of his buttocks was calculating the cooking time required for a Rutting-Corgi Wellington.

'E-Rex? Oh I say - are you any relation to the T-Rex's? We did briefly call on the Surrey T-Rex's a few million years ago but they weren't very amenable to friendly but impromptu social visitation.'

'Well maybe they thought you were Hollywoodens too, Ambassador' quipped H.M. Queen, only slightly in jest and while wiping optical grade Vaseline from her hands. One ignored the rather indelicate sucking "plopthunk" sound One's Lady in Waiting made while reinstating her Waterford crystal eye.

[Unfortunately the Lady in Waiting's technique was a little clumsy and she spent the rest of the day with both upper and lower eyelids folded inwards. She looked rather like an apoplectic Colonel in a lemon gingham dress and a hurry-up who had lost her monocle but found a dark-matter paperweight in the shape of an eyeball. Of course everyone was far too polite and sensitive about her feelings to say anything and generally anyone who saw her just quietly ran somewhere to throw a little kedgeree around the u-bend for Messrs Hughie and Ralph.]

'Oh possibly so, Rex, but our xenoscientibiozoologisters attributed their ill-temper to the Surrey T-Rex's having short forearms in combination very itchy testicles – no chance whatsoever of a good scratch do you see? Hell on Earth I suppose, especially during the humid summer months of the Maastrichtian

Cretaceous in the suburbs of Godalming. If only they'd learned to cooperate and to scratch each other's they might have been alive today. Do you think they would have responded well to gifts of some Cambridge nellies?'

'Some Cambridge nellies' whats?' replied Her Majesty, lifting The Crown to tickle a sudden itch that had developed right under the Koh-i-Noor diamond.

'Absolutely, yes, of course. We might try that if a similar situation arises again.' The ambassador waved politely to his procurement officer in discreet clack-clack-cligginoffham-squiggle-hiccough-roar-fart semaphore, meaning "go get some Nellie Swats immediately". 'Still, it's all just so much flattened flora and fauna under the old landing struts now Your Maj – er, Rex.'

The fresh crumpets arrived and the Ambassador was relieved to be merely offered one rather than being required to perform some sort of Conservative political ceremony involving hot melted butter and naked skin contact.

The P.M., anxious to at least try to not look like a spare ram at a West Country wedding, moved the tea on towards practicalities and away from itchy dinosaur sweetbreads and putative hippie T-Rex naturist cooperatives. The memory of his own testicles made him uncomfortable. In particular he disliked the way they seemed to bob up and down in the jar on the tiled mantel in his "front room" at home, mocking him each evening as he smoked his post-fish supper cigar. Damn that tropical testicle rot, just damn it to Hell and back. If only he'd worn wool next to the skin as the guide books had all advised!

He stumbled out of his reverie and remembered his official duties. 'Ambassador, if it meets with your approval ...'

'Oh, please – just call me "Eek", we can forget the formalities can't we, for the moment?' said the Ambassador, yet another of his brains tugging out the neckline of Her Majesty's frock a little while swooping in with yet another eye-nose stalk, and raising his ear-brows suggestively. Fortunately, the anti-overfamiliarity circuits built into the royal bra and panties deployed and a little localised blue lightning crackled, rather discouragingly. The Ambassador's exploratory stalks stiffened with involuntary muscle-cramps and decided unilaterally to withdraw and to explain to Central Brains & Overall Operations at some later date just why they had withdrawn.

'Well, er ... Mr Eek, if it meets with your approval I wonder if you would care to address The House of Commons tomorrow - we can formally welcome you to Earth, that sort of thing. Bit of a parade from the Horse Guards – on Horse Guards' Parade on horseback as a matter of fact! We should also make arrangements for the rest of your party. Scientisters to meet and greet, a little publicity, some photo opportunities, possibly a walk-about if you'd like, that sort of PR malarkey.'

'Absolutely, Prime Minister Brownaughs, that all sounds quite splendid.'

'Oh, please – call me Gordon; everyone else always does whether I want them to or not.' The P.M. looked a little regretful but took a deep breath and got himself over it. In truth he would have preferred "Clan Chieftain Brownaughs" or "Emperor Brownaughs" but still, you can't often have everything (except at a state banquet where it was positively expected and there was always a large car to take you home via a route without any bilious speed-bumps or antiperistalsis-inducing potholes).

'Splendid, Prime Minister Gorgon. Maybe my little green people could...'

'...arrange things with my green little people. Top notch idea!'

Ambassador and P.M. both waved discreetly to their little people who had been lurking separately in the nearby greenery, mostly scratching their own sweetbreads as they waited or occasionally, mostly in the case of the aliens, nibbling on aphids. Well, I say that both "waved", and indeed the Ambassador did, but the Prime Minister – as was his wont – more sort of, well... twinkled his fingers in the manner of a Liberace tribute act trying to attract the attentions of a Sommelier.

A number of the Secret Policemen were especially grateful for the long arms of the law as they stood, also mostly quite lost in thought. Unfamiliar territory for Secret Policemen, you see; thought. Not called out there very often.

No-one had much idea what the Secret Policewomen – or women in general - were grateful for since Mrs T-Rex of the

Cretaceous Godalming and environs has not been researched very much by the scientific community and has not been referenced at all during the telling of this story - until now that is. However, now that she has been brought into the intellectual fray, so to speak, we should briefly digress in order to speculate wildly just for the sake of non-avian Cretaceous gender completeness. Extrapolating from pure hearsay and circumstantial happenstance, like any good copper with itchy Policeman's Bits and an unsolved "crime" should, we find one theory that falls down the station stairs, Your Honour, better than all of the rest put together.

Consider if you will that the short arms of the female Surrey T-Rex might actually have been very handy indeed for hiding T-Rex lady-nipples while they were running or jogging in any serious hurry-up situation. Thus their primary purpose would have been the preservation of the nipular modesty of T-Regina dinosaurs while in screaming girlie flight from spiders, their poorly parked cars or tempting but calorie-laden fast-food. Not that it has been seriously suggested that T-Regina could achieve girlie flight, screaming or otherwise. Flight's a damned difficult thing.

Obviously the clinching self-evident, pre-mentioned evidence is that their arms were far too short for any serious gliding and we're surprised that the defence even brought it up - the leverage would have been all wrong. Plus, there would have been some serious safety concerns. How would they have got along with the early designs of parachutes when they couldn't reach behind their backs for the secondary chute-release? One touch of cumulonimbus turbulence, a dodgy fold or two in the parachute factory and they'd be goners.

'Pull the emergency rip-cord on the back-up silk, Lucy! Pull the rip-cord! Oh – Eek! Don't look. Marjorie, don't look! It's all too, too horrible to watch, I shall never be able look through these binoculars again! I think she landed in the High Street somewhere near Marcosaurs & Sparcosaurs!'

Maybe that's why the dinosaurs died out? Persistent sky-diving while still equipped with anatomy quite unsuited to the pulling of emergency or secondary rip-cords combined, fatally, with poor quality-control in the primary parachute packing area. Lousy origami combined with an overweening love of recreational free-fall? Given the number of accidents that still happen even after sixty million years of experience and development of the sport you've got to wonder – those early sky-diving days can't have been pretty.

Anyway. Most dinosaurs are known to have been sensitive about their nipples even if all T-Rex remains found so far have been face down, legs and arms akimbo, jaw in the screaming position and showing signs of tangled suspension lines in the surrounding rock formations.

Still. Who knows? Who cares? There's a reason, however obscure it may be, that Nature didn't give the T-Rex wings so let's just let sleeping dogs fly and get back to the aliens who landed under more controlled means.

'More tea, Eek?' Ambassador Eek-eek-wibble-squeak-growl-roar-fart mooted that he would much prefer – if there was time – to try his hands at a game of croquet instead please, Association rules of course. Prince Philip almost began an inter-species "embarrassment" by shouting 'Splendid!' and slapping Eek on what he had presumed to be his back. Eek, aware that Philip may not have had time yet to read all of the Concise Illustrated History, and certainly not the sections on mating rituals, diplomatically ignored Philip's signal invitation to "please fertilise the preserved eggs of my late grandmother", and just selected a mallet from those offered by Her Majesty's Personal Trainer, Sebastian.

Some of the alien entourage decided on a few rounds of cricket instead of croquet, and a match between the Wibble-squeak-growl-fart-roar-eek-roar first-ever First Elevens and the one hundred and twenty-seventh Buckingham Palace-Whitehall-Westminster Irregulars was arranged. Cook, as is her wont, gleefully officiated as scorer. The P.M., citing rustiness in both sports and an old but unspecified non-testicle related war-wound, served as chief wristwatch and pullover keeper. He was swiftly buried under a pile of discarded clothing and could almost imagine himself to be in The House on Prime Minister's Question Day. Her Majesty, naturally, opened for the Irregulars and did so very nicely with a century and her own pads. One then flipped One's bat end to end and spun it vertically on the palm of One's hand as One walked back to One's pavilion to One's applause from One's subjects standing in One's outfield in One's shade from One's Sun under One's trees.

Civilised extra-planetary inter-species first contact was thus fully initiated with croquet bats and cricket mallets but without recourse to firearms, nucular [SIC] weapons or the F.B.I., the C.S.I., the Chicago I.R.A. and Miami Vice or even the National Association of Acronyms Properly Indicated As Such by Full Stops.

Gifts had been exchanged (avoiding the cliches of aerodynamic Uranium and homosexual postgraduates; lessons having been previously learned), and hands and hand-analogues had been shaken, gently, in white gloves. Tea had been poured. Toast, scones, crumpets and biscuits had been nibbled and polite conversation had been engaged in without a single shot being fired or so much as a friendly fart being lit, let alone any LPG explosions.

Teams of humans and of aliens who all ended in a reasonably mutual "ology" or "ism" of some sort were busy swapping anecdotes and samples and fresh, moist datum. Grey chaps in even darker-grey bowler hats were busy making sure that the bottom-feeding tabloids didn't refer to the alien guests as "invaders" or "Martians" and the world, le Monde, el Mundo, was regularly tuning in to the wireless in the hope of more detail being released by the E.B.C. [The English Broadcasting Corporation.] The Six O'Sundial televisual news led with the optimistic note delivered in properly estuarial tones of the official confirmation that Elvis was indeed never coming back and that, furthermore, Sir Clifford Richard was likely to be disappearing soon too.

Dog-walkers on Horsell Common skirted lightly around the parked alien entourage support-craft, mostly successful in their attempts to avoid the vulgarity of actually noticing anything out of the ordinary. Naturally only the Mother-ship had been parked in a hover over Buckingham Palace, all of the smaller vessels had been more discreetly directed to overnight facilities on the Common where toilets, showers, a site shop, power-points, mains water and suchlike had been made available.

As the Japanese so correctly say; like nakedness, aliens are often seen but rarely noticed.

All in all it turned out to have been a splendid day.

The morning following first contact, The Morning after the Day Before, so to speak, when the world was no longer standing quite so still, a large alien boiler-stoker wearing a new E.H.S. [English Home Stores] dressing gown and three pairs of slippers from the Markus & Spencerus ,clomped down the ramp from his alien craft. He'd been sent to collect the two bottles of red-top, six strawberry Ski yoghurts and a thick-sliced white Mother's Pride that the Milkman had left there at dawn, rattling across the heath in an eclectic milk-float. A paper-boy (of the new disposable kind, made from recycled copies of The Dandy, The Beano and, occasionally for those destined to be artistic, Jackie) cycled up with the morning newspapers, some nice comics and a Wireless Times magazine, all of which the stoker tucked under a coal-dusted tentacle as he stretched, yawned and looked at the new day through alien eyes.

A little summer night-time ground mist was clearing quickly leaving just dew-damp grass and the distant sound of sparrows encouraging their chicks to get up and get ready for school. Red squirrels in wristbands, headbands, amateur rock bands and knee-length shorts were hanging upside down from oak and chestnut tree branches, doing stomach curls. Hedgehogs were waxing off their School Crossing Patrol lollipops and rabbits, all careful to not be seen by humans or aliens, were getting an early start on giving their lawns the once-over with miniature mowers and shears.

Various very relaxed Pressure Groups were setting out their folding seats, placards and tartan flasks of tea for another day's hard protesting outside their respective embassies in England, demanding the freedom to protest outside their respective embassies in England, a freedom that they explained that they needed in order to be able to protest about the lack of freedom in their own, abandoned countries where the word "embassy" was usually synonymous with the phrase "pile of smoking rubble".

Most of the protest placards and warm-up chants seemed to indicate that the very nature of imperialist English politics and of Anglo-Saxon post-Empire society in general was absolutely to blame anyway for their having to be in England to wave placards and chant about things they would otherwise be slightly killed for protesting about in the various non Anglo-Saxon ex-Empire republics, states or fiefdoms that they loved so much and would return to if only bastard England would take responsibility to do more to make it safer for them to do so, using gunboat diplomacy if necessary. Or something. Whatever the message was, it was usually presented in a font laced with irony.

The Day Shift truncheon, whistle and little notebook inspection parades in Police Station yards everywhere from Mablethorpe to Hove practiced formation formal direction-giving, old-lady assisting, corrective clip around the ear application and minor-offence blind eye turning. Chief Constables in every county settled down in modest, dusty offices and reached for well-thumbed volumes on the practise of pragmatic institutional honesty, accountability, integrity and the control of the uniformed ego. Do please excuse me for a moment while I check in with reality. Thank you.

Primary, Junior and Secondary School kitchens (as opposed to peculiar, risible and very foreign "kindergarten", "lower" and ersatz "faux-college" and "academy" kitchens) echoed to the sound of diesel-powered industrial gravy-stirrers, pneumatic potato mashers, chocolate concrete mixers and custard skin recycling centrifuges.

Hospitals slopped, steamily mopped and positively ran corridors-awash with the heady scent of barely diluted Domestos, with concentrated old-fashioned Ward Sister sweat and with experienced, local, sensible, intelligent, basically-educated and oops-I-actually-just-gave-a-professional-shit permanent not agency Nursing Staff who were all secure enough in their jobs to know that they would still be there the next day (on a fresh shift after sleep as opposed to still working the same one).

Her Majesty's Coast Guard checked that the coast was all still present, correct and safe, from Beachy Head to the sands of Southport, from Holy Island to Morecambe Bay, from Happisburgh to Land's literal and quite unnerving End.

From inside the alien craft came the clatter of crockery and the inviting aroma of tea, scrambled eggs, properly made toast and thick-cut lime marmalade.

As he clomped back up the ramp Stoker First Class Eek-eek-wibble-growl-growl-teehee-fart almost tripped over the ship's cat and snapped at it, not entirely un-seriously, with his extendable second jaw, before putting on his new tortoise-shell framed varifocal N.H.S. optics to read the headlines.

The tabloids were on top form. Hollywooden President shot at as Hollywooden Air Force One II returns. Hollywooden Senate proclaims that since Space is Hollywooden, aliens are Hollywooden property too. Westboro Baptists say Alien's Hollywooden snub is God's punishment for letting Bastard Gays into Nice God-Fearing Family Outer-Space. Russia bombs all of its Independent ex-USSR neighbours for peace. Putin's face voted least threatening of last two Russian Presidents. China continues to build another environment-improving coal-fired power station every minute. OPEC increases price of oil to help rest of world through recession. India vows to tackle population growth when it becomes necessary. African leaders meet in George Cinque Hotel in Paris to discuss hunger. French Farmers not sure if they're on strike or not and, if they are, what it's all about but burn a few of les moutons alive on les camions anyway just in le case. Standard stuff.

The Times headline said simply that the aliens finally knew now that they were not alone in the universe. Editorial content centred on how much of a relief it must be for them.

The Guardian ran a feature written by a putative "Professor" from something called a "Reading University" on an "M4 corridor" in Berk Shire theorising about the possible effects on the structure of alien society of making contact with intelligent terrestrial life. The professor concluded – as far as anyone could tell from his rather slap-dash paper – that with extensive Human support the aliens might come out of it alright.

The Hollywood Washington Post, the Hollywood Boston Globe and the Hollywood Chicago Tribune all ran some quite nice cartoons along with the shrill Hollywood Homeland Insecurity, Hollywood Central Integillence Agency, Feral Bureau of Instigation, Fearless Emergency Management Agency and Sheriff's Department advice that Hollywooden citizens should stockpile beans, grits, ammunition and Holy Bibbles. Travel, they said, should only be undertaken if absolutely fabulously necessary, and only then in either offensively armoured Army-led convoys or in massive civilian-vehicle stampedes in which latter case velocities should be kept below fifty-five miles an hour to avoid unnecessary mass carnage, driver-passenger stress or vehicles spontaneously bursting into flame. The editorial undertone was that serious first contact would only take place once there had been a few explosions and a few aliens had been cornered in corn crops grown by baseball players.

Punch ran an issue lampooning the lamentable lack of bunting supplies in the Home Counties and its deleterious effect upon street parties welcoming the aliens. Apparently no-one could find the stuff that had been used on V.D. Day. It had probably been boxed up and tucked into a forgotten corner of the loft at Downing Street.

'Plus ca change, plus c'est la meme chose' was all that the alien said as he scanned the headlines and disappeared back inside, scratching his hairy backside. 'Always with the first-contact bunting. There's never enough bunting. We should start bringing our own already. Oy. Bunting schmunting.' He dropped the newspapers off in the Common Room and then clomped away to get a shower while there was still some hot water and less chance of dropping the soap in the presence of C-Shift.

In Buckingham Palace Hice a cleaner in a worn-looking but cheery yellow pinafore was dusting an expensive-looking glass paperweight, the one with the eerie Dark Matter bobbing around inside it. When she peered deeply into the bauble it was rather like looking into the moment of creation all over again and reminded her of the headache she always got from pondering quantum chromodynamics or a really, really good Bakewell Tart recipe. Once again she accidentally on purpose popped the little alien gift into a desk drawer next to a box full of spare glass eyes. She moved on to the next room with a fresh duster, a hop and a mischievous mini-skip.

Over on Horse Guards Parade sawdust was being scattered so that the horses wouldn't slip during the procession. Horses were being buffed and brushed to the texture of velcro so that Horse Guards wouldn't slip and fall off their horses into the sawdust. Horses and Horse Guards were being reminded to visit the lavatory so that the sawdust and horses both would stay clean and dry during the parade, just in case either slipped off the other into one or other or into both. Bearskin hats were being released from kennel cages, fed, watered, and persuaded to jump up onto Guardsmen's heads.

The English Channel was doing a splendid job, covered as it was by a light to middling fog and isolating the Continent completely. According to our ambassadors overseas, foreigners were clamouring at the continental ports, waiting for information about the aliens and, maybe, even a glimpse of something horrible and unnatural, something not quite properly of this planet or their own species.

To the delight and incredible good luck of the more sober and mentally able of the foreigners who were able to appreciate a State Visit slash Audience-with, the Lord Sir Rear-Admiral Doctor Professor the Most Reverend the Honourable Mr Blair, X.P.M., D.S.O., O.B.E., G.C.S.E. etcetera had been at the The Hague Overseas Aid Department, arranging at-cost-plus-a-reasonable-percentage-for-God succour for those souls tragically trapped on the wrong side of the North Sea. He and Cherry Amoure had, no doubt through the direct actions of Bastard Satan and his bitch-cow, Miss Atheist, been doing missionary work converting continentals when news of the alien landing came through. Both of these true-saints-in-the-rough were as fatigued as les poodles petite after another long night handing out Mulligatawny soup, stale rolls and hymn sheets (translated into a simple pictogram form for the hard-of-worshiping).

However, fatty gooed and diary-disadvantaged as he was, Blair's conduite d'automobile pour mon Dieu and his les reactions de un simple sinner for the non-Mexican Jesus were still exemplary – even on the wrong side of the road and on inferior foreign tarmac. He slammed both of his Dutch Jesus-Loves-Me-This-I-Know-Because-She-Told-Me-So-Wooden-Clogs onto the brake pedal of his le G-Wiz L-ion electric car so hard that his polyester-mix socks slipped down, his glow-in-the-dark crucifix got tangled up in the steering wheel and his fresh travelling-dhoti rode right up unto the crack of his Arsenal Villa are still doing awfully well this year, don't you think?

Several boxes of Holy Bibbles in their sealed cellophane wrapping, left over from the previous day's Christianity-on-eco-wheels run would of sliddened right off the rear parcel-shelf had there been any lebensraum or English grammar to slide into in the misbegotten Benelux miasma where wanton begetting begat the entirely the wrong and sinful kind of begotten so beloved of the Bibble. It was barely Greenwich Sparrowfart (about seven-thirty a.m., real time, God knows what it might be there on the Continent in "metric" time) so, fortunately, he was still the only moving car on the road in Western Europe and there was no need for lots of hooting and cigarette-chewing, hair-disturbing, fist-waving, histrionics from Renaults and Fiats and Ladas stuffed to the gunnels with farm produce for the market, coquettish she-goats along for the ride and worn-out little great-great-great-grandmothers dressed head to foot in matt black and mourning.

Blair got out, leaving the car door open, to peer at the spectacle of the desperate crowd through his "Top Gun" sun-spectacles and while pulling his socks up and his unbleached Fair Trade organic cotton sub-continental style loincloth a little way down (just enough to attract the female voters but not the evil homosecksuals). He dipped into a "While in Rome, Abroad" genuflection: Shades; anti-radiation airport codpiece; travel-purse full of Mickey Mouse money and watch it – you could take someone's eye out with that airport customs wand, Garçon!

'What on earth do you think it might be, Cherrekinnypoopoos?' he said, his butch tones reverberating around the quayside and bringing to mind the commanding voice of Demis Roussos before his big Greek testicles dropped.

'Honestly Darlinginnywinnykins? I think it's a load of godless, indolent, garlic-chewing, over-emotional, over-demonstrative, untrustworthy and hairy, chanting, placard-waving foreign types just crying out for a little backbone, a stiff upper lip and some proper decorum, picketing a ferry terminal instead of getting on with their jobs and waiting for news from the correct sources – id est, England.'

'I think you may be right, Mother of my blessed trouser-seedlings, I think you just may be right.' he said, rolling up the sleeves of his organic hemp Nehru jacket. 'Bring me a box of assorted Holy Bibbles, my second-best pith helmet and my Service revolver would you please, Cherrewibblywobbles – I'm going in. God knows, someone has to sort this damned mess out and it doesn't look like any of the locals are going to do it sometime soon.'

Cherrydarlingwarling, dutiful to the last, even tore the cellophane on the Holy Bibbles to facilitate easy distribution and then tested his Revolver-for-God by firing a couple of warning shots into the air over the heads of the mob. She adjusted the sights a little before tucking the ten inches of cold, hard steel down where the sun rarely shone on Tony, and then adjusted his jacket to cover it. Tony patted his bottom to make sure that the holy safety catch was on, flexed his neck and strode forth to bring order to the screaming heathen crowd.

'I say! I say! You there! Yes – you ...'

Civilisation, like it or not, aliens notwithstanding, was on its way, again.

ABOUT THE AUTHOR

Ian Hutson was born in nineteen-sixty in Cleethorpes, England. His father was a deep-sea trawlerman turned Cold War electronic warfare expert turned Naval historian. His mother was pragmatically whatever was required whenever it was required, from socialite and lady to factory worker and croft-keeper. In times of fiscal inadequacy she made a mean, football-sized dumpling.

Almost immediately after H minor was born the whole family moved to Hong Kong, just in time for the worst typhoon, cholera epidemic and drought of the century. Initially H minor spoke only Cantonese and a little pidgin English. He learned to read and write aged nine on the Isle of Lewis in the Outer Hebrides of Scotland, helped keep two pet sheep and was a spoiled little brat. The family then moved to *inside* a family friend's open-to-the-public zoo in Norfolk, living in a shack for a year between the monkey house and the bear pit.

H minor studied for a BA in Operational Research Systems Analysis and an MA in Industrial Relations, wandered into the Civil Service to ask to use the lavatory and was offered tea and a job for ten years. He has since worked for a number of very ugly international corporations, left them all under an acrimonious cloud and now lives in a hedgerow in Lincolnshire as a penniless vegan peacenik atheist hippie.

Other works and more information may be found at

www.dieselelectricelephant.co.uk

CPSIA information can be obtained at www.ICGtesting.com
Printed in the USA
LVOW01s1112170315
430885LV00016BA/198/P
9 781493 532872